Nowhere But Up

Bobbi White

Paddleboard Press

Nowhere but Up

This is a work of fiction. Names, characters, places, and incidents are either a product of the author's imagination or are used fictitiously. Any resemblance to actual persons, living or dead, events, or locals is entirely coincidental.

Published by Paddleboard Press

Copyright © 2022 Bobbi White. All rights reserved.

No part of this book may be reproduced in any form or by any electronic or mechanical means, including information storage and retrieval systems, without written permission from the author, except for the use of brief quotations in a book review.

Editor: Genie Porter
Formatter: Rachel Bostwick
Cover Design: L1graphics

ISBN: 979-8-9861797-0-4 (paperback)
ISBN: 979-8-9861797-1-1 (ebook)

To David

My always and forever

To Stephanie —
A wonderful person
and a fabulous critique
partner!
You are a gem!
Your friend,
Bobbi

"It's pink," Drew said, examining his drink. "How do you mess up a gin and tonic?"

Holly threw hers back and smacked her lips. "So, what's different about this show?"

Jo shrugged. "No idea. Remy just said to be here. It's the first show of his tour, but as far as I know, the routine's the same."

"Ooh. Maybe he's going to propose to you on stage," Holly said.

Drew gave her a side-eye. "Don't be ridiculous, they've only been seeing each other a few months."

"*Six.*" Jo bit her top lip and wondered if she'd misread their relationship. "He did tell me he loved me."

Drew adjusted the cuff of his perfectly tailored shirt. "While having sex, which doesn't count." Both Holly and Jo made sounds of agreement. "Plus, he doesn't need to marry you."

Jo narrowed her eyes. "What's that supposed to mean?"

Drew pressed his lips together and glanced away.

"I think he means Remy's a bit...*user-y,*" Holly said.

Drew nodded. "A relative nobody until you came along."

Jo waved off their comments. "I helped him grow his brand, so what? It's what I *do.*"

Technically, that was true. Jo's trend forecasting consultancy, *The Prophetic Aesthetic*, charged clients a great deal for her services. But it was her various social media outlets, with over a million combined subscribers, that made her an influencer—and Remy the latest beneficiary.

Drew rolled his eyes. "Please, he'd still be delivering pizzas if you hadn't wanted to fuck him. And don't tell me he didn't know who you were. I was *there*. I saw his audition."

"Gotta give him props for using the pizza box as a puppet." Holly laughed, giving him an elbow. "See what I did there?"

"Clever. Maybe Jo can get you a gig on the comedy circuit too."

Jo threw her soggy olive at him. "Stop being a dick, Drew."

"I'm just looking out for you, baby girl."

1

I didn't give you the finger; you earned it.
- Bill Murray

Philadelphia

Drew held the phone up and the three friends squeezed together outside *The Laughing Stock Comedy Club.* "Say comedy!"

Blinded by the flash, Josette Singer waited for her vision to clear before scrutinizing the photo. "You didn't get the whole marquee!"

Holly leaned over and burst out laughing. "MY COCKBURNS. That's hilarious."

"I can't post that, Drew. Take another."

"We're at a comedy club, Jobo. It's funny. Where's your sense of humor?"

It wasn't her sense of humor she worried about, but she nodded anyway. "You're right. Remy won't mind." *Hopefully.* Jo added the caption, '*REMY COCKBURN'S debut at the Laughing Stock!,*' and posted it.

They walked into the venue and sat in the VIP area. A server appeared, took their drink orders, and arrived twenty minutes later with three unidentifiable cocktails.

Before taking a sip, Jo fished out an unappealing gray olive and dropped it on her napkin.

"By implying no one could like me for me?" Jo said, his words having hit a sore spot.

Drew put his elbows on the table and leaned in. "When a man comes along and asks you for nothing? I'll shut my face."

"I offered to help. Besides, if I waited for someone who didn't know who I was—especially in this city—I'd never date."

The Singer family was part of Philadelphia society. You couldn't open a local paper or magazine without seeing one of their names splashed across the pages.

"And Remy *is* funny," Jo said. "I didn't write his jokes, I simply gave him exposure."

Holly nodded. "She's right. He's got good schtick."

Drew pursed his lips, further defining his high cheekbones. "I do enjoy the puppets."

The lights dimmed, and the announcer came out to warm up the crowd. Ten minutes later, Remy walked on stage, and Jo grinned like a proud mamma. The talent was his, but the packaging? That was all Jo. With a little help from Drew—a professional stylist—she'd tweaked his unshaven, man-bun-wearing bohemian look into one of a refined hipster.

And the audience loved his self-deprecating nature. He left the rude, offensive, and vulgar humor to his puppets. People never attached these sentiments to his personal beliefs, but Jo knew you couldn't separate the wheat from the chaff entirely.

Tonight, Remy's routine began the same way as always, with jokes and audience interaction. A third of the way through the set, he brought out the dummies. Nonna Mona, the Italian grandmother, followed by Barf, the street-wise dog. When Poncho came out wearing a suit instead of his usual Mexican garb, Jo knew Remy had changed things up.

"Got a hot date, do you?"

"Si, I hooked a live one, my friend."

"No kidding? Where'd you meet her?"

"At the club. She was dancing with José."

"Oh, someone you know?"

"Everyone knows José."

"Okay, so what happened?"

"I went over and said 'I am Poncho,' then grabbed José and knocked him back."

"You threw José to the floor?"

"Why would I throw good tequila on the floor? No man, I drank it. You don't listen so good."

The crowd burst into laughter, and Remy waited for it to die down before continuing.

"So, when's your big date?"

Poncho looked at his watch. "Now."

"You brought her to The Laughing Stock?"

"Si, she wanted to go somewhere fancy."

Remy scanned the crowd. "Shall we bring her out?"

Jo froze in horror as he pulled Miss Money Honey from his trunk.

"Holy shit balls," Holly said. "He made you into a dummy!"

Drew shook his head. "Ooh, that's gonna cost you, funny man."

There was no mistaking the long dark curls, bright green eyes, and red-soled shoes. Two round orbs popped out of an evening gown, and a tiara listed to the side. One hand held a martini glass, which the puppet threw around with abandon while trying to hump Remy's leg.

Miss Money Honey was a farcical exaggeration of who Jo was—or more precisely, who Remy perceived her to be—a drunk, over-sexed, entitled party girl.

And the audience loved it.

Heat crawled up Jo's spine and settled into her throat. She imagined being a fire-breathing dragon incinerating the stage with her flames.

When the set was over, the audience gave Remy a standing ovation.

Jo stood along with everyone else, but didn't clap. Instead, she walked to the stage with only one thing on her mind—revenge. No one humiliated a Singer and got away with it. She ruled Philly, dammit! And she would prove it to this little man. Behind her, Holly and Drew shouted their approval.

Remy lost his smile when he noticed her climbing the steps, but quickly recovered and addressed the audience. "Ladies and gentlemen, Josette Singer!"

Game on, dick face. Let's see how well you improvise.

He wrapped her in a hug. "They loved you." Misunderstanding her laughter for acceptance, he grinned and whispered in her ear, "Imitation *is* the greatest form of flattery."

Jo broke free and grabbed the mic. "Everyone having a good time?" The audience hooted and clapped. "I have a little surprise of my own." She pivoted slightly and winked at Remy. "An impression I've been working on. Would you like to see it?"

The crowd cheered and Remy had no choice but to play along.

"I haven't perfected it yet, but here it goes." She held up her hand, making a show of folding her fingers, one by one, leaving only the pinky. "It's more of a likeness, really." She tilted her head as her eyes traveled down Remy's body to his crotch. Glancing up, she saw him grimace.

"I think I've captured it pretty well, don't you think?" Jo examined her little finger with a critical eye, letting it wilt slightly. "There, that's more like it!"

Nervous laughter echoed from the crowd, and one woman shouted, "I'll fuck his pencil dick if you don't want it!" spurring more laughter.

So much for female solidarity.

Jo reached around and grabbed the doll by its throat. "I'll take this, *fuck you* very much."

She strode off the stage, threw back her drink, and grabbed her purse.

The crowd went wild as the three friends strode out with their middle fingers raised.

2

*The only thing that separates us from animals
is our ability to accessorize.*
- *Steel Magnolias*

Three months later

Jo held the phone away from her ear as Drew's shriek echoed down Broad Street. A passerby looked over with concern. She pointed to the screen and smiled at the stranger. "It's okay—happy scream."

When Drew's voice quieted, she put the phone back to her ear. "So, now that we're officially *in*, I'm thinking, Marie Antoinette."

"Too literal, Jobo. We need to think outside the box."

"Who did you have in mind?"

"Carmen Miranda."

"The Chiquita Banana lady? Drew, the theme is *Queens of the Silver Screen*, how—" Jo spotted a pair of bright orange sneakers as she turned onto Walnut Street. "I'll have to call you back."

She tossed the phone into her Birkin and quickened her step. Her unfortunate choice of footwear—a pair of Stella McCartney stilettos—seemed to attract more cracks than a plumber's bottom, which made closing the distance impossible.

Jo stood along with everyone else, but didn't clap. Instead, she walked to the stage with only one thing on her mind—revenge. No one humiliated a Singer and got away with it. She ruled Philly, dammit! And she would prove it to this little man. Behind her, Holly and Drew shouted their approval.

Remy lost his smile when he noticed her climbing the steps, but quickly recovered and addressed the audience. "Ladies and gentlemen, Josette Singer!"

Game on, dick face. Let's see how well you improvise.

He wrapped her in a hug. "They loved you." Misunderstanding her laughter for acceptance, he grinned and whispered in her ear, "Imitation *is* the greatest form of flattery."

Jo broke free and grabbed the mic. "Everyone having a good time?" The audience hooted and clapped. "I have a little surprise of my own." She pivoted slightly and winked at Remy. "An impression I've been working on. Would you like to see it?"

The crowd cheered and Remy had no choice but to play along.

"I haven't perfected it yet, but here it goes." She held up her hand, making a show of folding her fingers, one by one, leaving only the pinky. "It's more of a likeness, really." She tilted her head as her eyes traveled down Remy's body to his crotch. Glancing up, she saw him grimace.

"I think I've captured it pretty well, don't you think?" Jo examined her little finger with a critical eye, letting it wilt slightly. "There, that's more like it!"

Nervous laughter echoed from the crowd, and one woman shouted, "I'll fuck his pencil dick if you don't want it!" spurring more laughter.

So much for female solidarity.

Jo reached around and grabbed the doll by its throat. "I'll take this, *fuck you* very much."

She strode off the stage, threw back her drink, and grabbed her purse.

The crowd went wild as the three friends strode out with their middle fingers raised.

2

*The only thing that separates us from animals
is our ability to accessorize.*

- Steel Magnolias

Three months later

Jo held the phone away from her ear as Drew's shriek echoed down Broad Street. A passerby looked over with concern. She pointed to the screen and smiled at the stranger. "It's okay—happy scream."

When Drew's voice quieted, she put the phone back to her ear. "So, now that we're officially *in*, I'm thinking, Marie Antoinette."

"Too literal, Jobo. We need to think outside the box."

"Who did you have in mind?"

"Carmen Miranda."

"The Chiquita Banana lady? Drew, the theme is *Queens of the Silver Screen*, how—" Jo spotted a pair of bright orange sneakers as she turned onto Walnut Street. "I'll have to call you back."

She tossed the phone into her Birkin and quickened her step. Her unfortunate choice of footwear—a pair of Stella McCartney stilettos—seemed to attract more cracks than a plumber's bottom, which made closing the distance impossible.

By the next block, she was even farther away from the teen. Afraid she'd lose him in the sea of pedestrians swarming up from the subway, she fished her phone back out and snapped a few shots from behind.

As she took mental notes—plaid shirt, sleeveless hoodie, cropped joggers—the light turned red.

Jo pushed her way through the crowd and with a bright smile, tapped the kid on the shoulder. "Hey, would you mind if—"

Before she could finish the sentence, he shoved her backward, sending her phone careening into the busy intersection.

"What the hell, dude?"

The youth's eyes darted between her and the phone before taking off across the street.

"I just wanted a photo for my blog, you asshole!"

Deciding not to tango with oncoming traffic, Jo waited for the light to change. She stared at the bedazzled case lying in a puddle of filth and wondered why things always landed face down.

Wiping moisture and sediment from the cracked screen, she stepped back onto the sidewalk, where a little old woman stood shaking her head.

"Such salty language coming from such a pretty mouth." A smile softened the rebuke and added lovely crinkles to the woman's cheeks.

Jo grinned and lifted her shoulders. What could she say? Being born and raised in Philly gave her a colorful vocabulary.

The woman shuffled forward, clutching a baby blue purse in front of her with both hands. "You may take a picture of me, if you'd like."

Jo didn't have the heart to say a photo of an octogenarian wouldn't quite vibe with the article she was writing on Philadelphia streetwear for her lifestyle and fashion blog. Instead, she held up her damaged phone. "I'm not sure I can."

"Ah, well. Timing is everything, I suppose." She made a slow, three-point turn to leave.

"Wait!" Wanting to capture the life that lined the woman's face, Jo pulled the Canon Power Shot from her bag. She snapped a few frames, zoomed in, then lowered the camera. "Do you want me to send you the pictures?"

"No, thank you, my dear. I know what I look like." The woman lifted a few fingers from her ancient purse and wiggled them in a wave before ambling across the intersection.

Jo laughed and dropped the camera into her bag, her eyes still on the slight figure.

Once on the other side, the woman seemed unsure in which direction to go. She held out a weathered hand to a passerby, but instead of stopping, the man nearly knocked her down.

Leaping into action, Jo dodged the honking hunks of steel in a real-life game of Frogger and slipped a protective arm around the woman. "Hi. Remember me?"

A glint of recognition lit her rheumy eyes. "Of course. You're one of Charlie's girl, aren't you?"

Jo shook her head, keeping her tone light. "No. Sorry. We just met a few minutes ago—but I have one of those faces."

"Oh, yes. Now I remember."

But Jo could tell she didn't. "Are you lost?"

"Well," the woman said, glancing around. "I might have gotten a little turned around."

Jo gave her delicate shoulder a little squeeze. "It happens to me all the time. Where are you going?"

The woman opened her mouth then closed it, shaking her head. "I'm not sure, dear."

Jo pointed to the purse on her arm. "Maybe there's a clue in there?"

Fifteen minutes later, after a tearful reunion with her daughter, the woman reached up and patted Jo's cheek. "You were always Charlie's favorite."

Jo glanced at her watch as she hurried to her previous destination. Shit! She'd passed fashionably late, entered ill-mannered, and rude was just around the corner.

Every Tuesday she walked from her condo in Washington Square to her parents' place in Rittenhouse, where she would sit through an evening of non sequiturs. As the only child of two only children, the conversation was guaranteed to devolve into the musings of three self-absorbed people.

Why couldn't Jo's family be more like Holly's? A home full of love and laughter, where hugs and kisses were doled out like beads at Mardi Gras. She enjoyed the chaos of a large family, the disorderliness, and informality of things. But all that happiness came at a price—no privacy, no place to hide, no opinion of your own. If you were a Rabinowitz, you drank the Kool-Aid.

The Singer method of child-rearing involved much less parenting. Jo had a voice as soon as she could speak. A choice in all things. According to her therapist, this hands-off approach fostered a sense of self-importance and neuroses—something Jo spent a lot of time obsessing over.

The early November wind had picked up, finding its way under her satin bomber jacket, but it made little difference to Jo. She dressed according to fashion, not weather. Yanking the hem down, she ignored the loss of sensation in her fingertips and strutted her impeccably dressed frozen ass four more blocks to her parents' brownstone.

"*Tu es en retard*, Josette!" Élaine Singer scolded upon her daughter's arrival.

"*Je sais, Maman. J'ai fini tard, désolée.*"

"In English, please," a voice called out.

Jo found her father in the formal living room reading the paper. She entered through the large arched doorway and kissed the top of Gil Singer's balding head, the mass of curls having long ago drifted into tufts around his ears. "What's wrong with French?"

"I like to practice my English. Your mother rarely indulges me."

"Your ancestors settled here almost two-hundred years ago. Maybe you should work on your Yiddish instead."

He placed the *New York Times* under his arm and stood. "Only if you work on your tardiness."

"Why? I'm an expert at it already!"

He gave her a little push toward the dining room. "Let's go, funny girl."

With elegance and grace, her mother backed out of the swinging kitchen doors and set a pot on the table. Like adagio on demi-pointe, the former prima ballerina turned and took a seat at the table.

"Smells delicious. I'm starved." Jo lifted the lid, her smile fading. "*Maman*, there's meat in this stew."

Her mother patted the chignon at the nape of her neck. "*Evidemment! C'est un bœuf bourguignon.*"

"You know I don't eat meat," Jo deadpanned.

Élaine leaned in. "Josette, when will you stop this obsession with vegetables?"

"I'm a vegetarian. So, I'm guessing never?"

Her mother threw up her hands. "*T'es française! C'est contre-nature!*"

"*Half* French, and there are a lot of vegetarians in France." Jo wasn't sure about this, but figured there must be a few at least.

"Pah! *C'est ridicule*! I made a nice chicken salad if you don't want to eat the meat." She waved a hand toward the kitchen and poured herself a glass of wine.

"Chicken *is* meat." Jo sat down, added some cheese and homemade cornichons to her plate of bread, and held out her hand. "Please pass the Bordeaux."

"At least you still drink the wine."

"No worries, *Maman*. I'd sooner eat meat than give up alcohol."

Élaine Marie Roullaud was the heir to Château de Roullaud, her family's estate and winery in France. She refused to take any profit from the business since she had little to do with running it and no need for more money.

Jo, however, collected a monthly stipend from both her mother's estate and the Singer Foundation, which she most assuredly did *not* turn down. It was an ongoing argument between her and her parents, who preferred to live simply, despite their wealth. Their frugality had the opposite effect on Jo, who spent lavishly, had no concept of moderation, and lived life to the fullest.

The only stipulation her father could impose on the iron-clad trust was that she remain gainfully employed, which wasn't a problem for Jo. Being idle gave her hives.

"I spoke with your young friend today," her father said.

Jo's brow knitted. "Who?"

"The one you sent my way?" A prominent civil rights attorney, her father worked closely with the LGBTQ community.

"I didn't send anyone, but I bet Drew did."

Jo was just ten when she met Drew outside her mother's dance studio. He stood—sometimes for hours—and watched the dancers through the large picture window. Despite his obvious neglect, Jo thought he was the most beautiful boy she'd ever seen. His flawless skin was neither dark nor light, and his eyes were like a cat's, both lazy and alert, the honey brown shot through with specks of gold.

One day, after months of observation, he walked in and asked to audition for a scholarship. Élaine, moved by his courage, had agreed. When she asked about music, Drew told her he didn't practice to any, so he would do without. He hadn't changed his clothes or warmed up; he simply danced.

His performance, although raw and unpolished, brought forth emotions so palpable it left everyone in the studio speechless. Jo fell in love with him that day.

Unfortunately, he could never love her in the same way.

"How is Antwon?" her mother asked. "He hasn't been by for some time."

Drew had legally changed his name years ago. "*Andrew* is fine. Busy. Flying all over the world, dressing famous people. Being seen."

Gil tore off a piece of bread and dipped it in his stew. "Well, tell him his friend has a strong case for gender discrimination."

"Will do. Oh!" She paused, waiting for their undivided attention. "I met someone."

Their reaction showed less enthusiasm than she had hoped, but given her track record, understandable.

Jo held up her palm. "I know what you're thinking, but you'd be wrong this time."

Her father wiped his mouth on a linen napkin. "You said the same thing about the puppeteer. Which reminds me, the deposition is next Tuesday."

The scene at the comedy club had exploded on social media, making Remy even more famous. It increased her following as well, but not in a good way. When he sued her for custody of the puppet, she counter-sued, placing a gag order on him and his routine—which only fed the flames. Unfortunately, most people sided with the humble, charming comedian. And she couldn't blame them—she'd done a hell of a job creating him. *When will I ever learn?*

Her mother sat back, holding aloft her glass of wine. "Josette, you are far too free with your money and your....*ton minou*."

Jo rolled her eyes at the reference to her vagina. "How delightfully anti-feminist. If only I had a penis." Her mother worked for women's rights, but was still a product of her time.

Ignoring her, Élaine continued, "And before the comedian, that boy with all the markings." She waved her hand across her body.

"Tattoos," Gil supplied.

"His band just released a hit record!"

"Thanks to your connections," her father pointed out at the same time her mother said, "Thanks to your money."

Jo threw down her napkin. "You're taking all the joy out of my news."

The two shrugged in unison and sat quietly.

"He's a doctor." Jo sulked, the wind having left her sails.

"Vraiment?"

"Yes, *really*."

Gil raised a dubious brow. "You're dating a physician?"

"No, Dr. Doolittle."

"Where did you meet this doctor?" her mother asked with skepticism.

"At a little coffee shop down the street from Jefferson Hospital. I stood behind him in line. He wore scrubs and smelled exquisite. Do you remember me telling you about the small boutique chain that hired me?"

Crickets.

"Well, they want to brand their own fragrance, so I asked him who he was wearing. He said Clive Christian. *Clive Christian!*"

"Are we supposed to know who that is?" her father asked.

"Of course not. The point is, if he's that discerning about cologne, he must have a great sense of style." And Jo *adored* a man with style.

A knowing look passed between her parents.

Jo heaved a heavy sigh. "Eric wasn't gay. He just liked to borrow my clothes." Of course, her parents would remember a boy she dated in high school but not something she said five minutes ago.

Her father reached over and patted her hand. "Gay, straight, male, female. If you're happy, we're happy." He sat back and poured the last of the Bordeaux into his glass. "Although a steady job would be a nice change of pace."

Her mother glanced at her plate. "I do hope he eats meat."

"I'll be sure to ask him." Jo reached over and grabbed a second bottle of wine.

3

True friends don't judge each other, they judge other people together.
- Emilie Saint-Genis

"Two tall trees—a birch and a beech—are growing in the woods..."

Jo smiled at the sound of Drew's voice. He gave her a light peck on the cheek before taking a seat next to her. Every Thursday, Jo met Drew and Holly for drinks at Dirty Gertie's, and every week, Drew started the night off with a joke.

"Don't continue! Holly isn't here yet."

"Then she'll miss the joke." He put one elegant arm into the air and signaled for a drink before continuing.

"A small tree begins to grow between them, and the beech says to the birch, 'Is that a son of a beech or a son of a birch?'"

"The birch says he can't tell, but just then, a woodpecker lands on the sapling. The birch says, 'Woodpecker, you're a tree expert. Can you tell if the sapling is a son of a beech or a son of a birch?'"

Drew stopped to take a sip of Jo's cocktail and scan the room. He often did this—pause for effect—and Jo twirled a finger, signaling him to continue.

Appearing only slightly put out, he resumed. "The woodpecker takes a taste of the small tree and replies, 'It's neither a son of a beech nor a son of a birch. It is, however, the best piece of ash I have ever poked my pecker into.'"

Jo laughed despite herself. "Nothing like a good penis joke."

Rick, the bartender, came over and placed a napkin in front of Drew. "What can I get you, handsome?"

"A Tanqueray and tonic, please." Drew turned his attention to Jo. "So, how was your date with Dr. Dumpling?"

"Don't call him that. His name is Dr. Masayori Honig—or Masi will do." She chewed on a thumbnail, her mind now on the issue at hand. "Dinner was fine, but he declined my offer for dessert."

"Baby girl, not every man has your libido. Maybe he had an early shift."

"We've been dating a month!" Jo didn't know how to handle a man that didn't make sex a priority. Maybe she was losing her edge—she was nearly thirty.

Drew's drink arrived, and he lifted it to his full lips. "You can't compare this new man to your roster of losers."

"They weren't *all* losers."

"Name one."

Her mind drew a blank. "At least they wanted to have sex. I thought dating someone less—"

"Like you?"

Jo's eyes narrowed. "I was going to say *free-spirited,* would be a good thing. But he's really dedicated to his work and kinda uptight."

"Then why are you still dating him?"

"Because he's beautiful and smart and interesting." Jo tried to find words to explain how he made her feel. "And he makes me want to be less—"

"Like you?"

Jo bonked him on the head. "*Wild.*"

"Same thing. Sounds boring. But at least he's not dating you for your money or connections."

"Definitely not. He thinks TikTok is a watch store, has no social media accounts, and texts full words without acronyms."

Drew grabbed her phone and scrolled through their messages. "You forgot to mention he uses punctuation. Ooh!" His eyes widened. "He's taking you to *Zahav* Saturday night. What're you going to wear?"

Drew and Jo could talk fashion for hours. "That amazing chartreuse, off the shoulder dre—"

"Oh, honey, no."

"What? Why?"

"That color's all wrong on you."

"But you told me to buy it!"

"Because I wanted to *borrow* it."

Jo was about to unleash on him when a plethora of puff and personality enveloped her.

"Hey, guys. Sorry, I'm late." Holly wedged her vertically challenged, full-figured frame in between them. Even standing, her head only reached their shoulders. "It's colder than a penguin's pecker out there." She shook off her coat and hung it on the back of Drew's stool. The only thing puffier was her wild auburn hair.

"Here you go, my little Holly berry. Take mine." Drew slid off his seat and offered her a hand.

She pulled herself onto the stool. "Thanks! Hey, Drewzy, get Rick's attention for me. He likes you. I'll have a Grey Goose martini. Have him muddle some cucumber, and maybe some mint? Oh, and a lime twist."

Drew hailed Rick over. "Another G&T, please." Rick took Drew's glass and walked away.

"Hey, I didn't order my drink!" Holly waved a useless hand in Rick's direction before slapping Drew's shoulder. "You can be such a bitch."

"All part of my charm."

"Pfft." She turned to Jo. "How was your date?"

Jo finished her martini. "Platonic."

"Huh?"

Drew leaned over and whispered loudly, "She's feeling a bit *thirsty*."

Holly's brow went up. "He turned you down? The last time that happened—"

"Exactly!" Jo threw an arm into the air.

Drew flicked his straw in her direction. "Honey, you were the only one who thought that man was straight."

Holly nodded solemnly. "I get it. Once bitten, twice shy."

"Ooh, I love a good song reference. Bon Jovi?" Like the wind, Drew changed directions.

"I'm thinking White Snake." Jo was happy to move on.

"No." Holly pursed her lips. "It's the group with the blonde bandana singer. The one that had the show."

Jo snapped her fingers. "Bret Michaels."

"Yes." Holly clapped. "*His* band."

"So, all bets are in. Let's see..." Drew Googled 'Once Bitten, Twice Shy,' and frowned. "Great White? Who the fuck are they?"

Absorbed in their eighty's song retrospective, they didn't hear the shushing throughout the bar until someone shouted, "Yo, dickheads at the end. Shut the fuck up!"

Their laughter trickled away as they turned their attention to the large TV behind the bar.

"... *Three American soldiers captured in Afghanistan's Nangarhar Province. We go live now to our senior war correspondent for the latest developments. Roland, what can you tell us?"*

"Thanks, Mike. A helicopter from the Army's elite one-twenty Airborne division went down in the Mohmand Valley in the southern Nangarhar Province. Sources at the Pentagon tell us that the covert mission was one of support and rescue and that the helicopter was taken down by a surface-to-air missile. We're told that of the twelve aboard, two died in the crash and three more during the conflict on the

ground. Of the seven survivors, four were rescued when a second helicopter landed safely."

"And the captured soldiers?"

Jo held her breath, her eyes glued to the TV.

"Sources close to the battle say the pilot, warrant officer Jackson 'JT' Taylor, returned fire while shielding medic sergeant Samantha Powell and weapons sergeant Kevin DePaul, who had been wounded. The three were seized from behind and used as shields for the retreating militants."

"Do we know which organization was responsible for the attack?"

"Unconfirmed sources say they're believed to be local insurgents with ties to the Taliban."

The bartender turned the volume down, and the bar buzzed with talk of the captured soldiers.

"I didn't know we were still there," Drew said.

"Holy shit." Jo said, as a picture of the smiling medic appeared. "She looks so young. Why would a sweet girl like that volunteer to go to war? Didn't she have any other options?"

"Guess she thought it was better than riding the pole." Drew glanced at the screen and did a double-take. "*Ooh*, I'd sign up to be bunk buddies with *that* one," he said, fanning himself.

Jo made a face at the inappropriate statement before her eyes landed on the pilot, Jackson Taylor. "Oh. *Wow*."

Drew nodded, his eyes wide. "Brad Pitt and Thor."

Holly shook her head. "You can't use movie characters in baby melds."

He tapped his lips. "It's a Hemsworth, just can't remember which one."

Jo kept her eyes on the handsome soldier. "Chris. I met him once. Nice guy. I'm going with Channing Tatum and Charlie Hunnam."

"Ooh, good blend. Holl?"

"I'll take Jo's Hunnam and your Hemsworth for the win." She swung her arms in a cabbage patch dance move.

Jo huffed out a humorless laugh. "We're sick, you know that, right? Those soldiers risked their lives—are possibly being tortured as we speak—and we're objectifying them." Her eyes drifted back to the photos of the three soldiers and prayed she was wrong.

It began innocently enough. The casual stalking. The social *not*working.

Jo sat at her desk and read the lead story of the kidnappings on her news feed. There was nothing new since the prior night.

She Googled 'captured soldiers.'

Who am I kidding?

She backspaced and entered a name, setting in motion a deep creep into Jackson 'JT' Taylor's life.

It always surprised Jo, the amount of information one could find on any subject or person—all with total anonymity. Her business depended on research, and she was very good at it. Although she rarely used her talents to delve into someone's personal history.

The voyeuristic and intrusive nature, the *thrill* of finding any small piece of data, was like panning for gold. The more she sifted through the pilot's life, the more fascinated and determined she became. No one was *that* perfect.

Jo wondered if she was trying to uncover some deep, dark secret to feel better about her own shortcomings, or—like a child on Christmas morning—she just wanted to believe in Santa Claus.

4

If you're going through hell, just keep going.
- Winston Churchill

JT walked with his arms outstretched. His palms caressed the airy spikes of winter wheat as the midday sun lent warmth to the wind, which carried the sweet smell of alfalfa from the southern field.

He ran as excitement coursed through his veins.

The stalks disappeared, and his feet moved over the field's green turf, the bright rays morphing into stadium lights as he reached for the ball. Fans cheered, kicking his adrenaline into high gear. He beat back players as he ran through their defense, turning upfield. The roar of the crowd became deafening as he weaved through more defenders.

JT stumbled and fell to his knees when a shock wave reverberated through his skull. The mortar impact muffled the cries of those hit. He crawled on his forearms, looking for cover, when he spotted a wounded soldier on his back holding a blood-soaked leg.

Getting to his feet, he ran through the incoming fire, grabbed the man's jacket, and pulled him through a haze of exploding debris until he found a wall to hide behind.

He doubled over, trying to catch his breath, but with every inhale he drew in liquid fire.

Someone pulled a rope taut around his neck, jerking him back, allowing his lungs to fill with air. He watched the water pool on the ground with detached fascination, knowing it was a momentary reprieve. His body tensed with anticipation as another assault plunged him back down...

JT woke with a start on the hard dirt floor. Pain seared through his shoulder as he rolled onto his back.

He'd made it through another night.

He breathed in the fetid air as dust motes danced in the dim light and watched the sun rise through the dung brick walls and woven branches of the roof. The angle indicated it was about noon.

He inhaled, halting short of a full breath, when he felt a sharp pain from a cracked rib. Afraid he would puncture a lung, he remained still—until his abdominal muscles spasmed, forcing him to his side where he vomited. Racked with pain, he lay motionless in his own filth and wondered if DePaul and Powell had gone through a similar fate.

He tried to shut it down, to stop replaying every mistake he'd made that led them to this mess—the would've-should've-could'ves. He needed to focus on survival, on finding the others.

On escape.

5

Hold on, I've gotta overthink about it.
- Unknown

2:22 AM. She Googled it. Multiple two's meant acceptance and forgiveness, a divine sign that a new cycle of experience and growth was underway. *Cool.* She texted Drew.

	I forgive and accept you
It's fucking 3 AM	
	Don't you want to know why?
Stop texting me	
	I'm going through a spiritual awakening
I'm blocking you	

Jo tossed the phone to the side and tried to go back to sleep, but her night worries kicked in, and she fixated on why she hadn't had sex with the gorgeous half Japanese, half Norwegian doctor yet. She sailed past the most obvious reasons and went straight to circus clowns and foot fetishes.

She punched her pillow, but competing anxieties kept her awake. Her new suspicion—that Masi might be selling black-market body parts—warred with thoughts of her attraction to Drew-alikes: tall, slim, androgenous men.

Although...

She fumbled for her phone and opened the folder labeled STAN. At least she owned her stalker-fan identity. Well, privately, anyway.

She clicked on a video of Jackson Taylor being interviewed twelve years prior by a local news station in Kentucky. The All-American boy had been awarded a full-ride to college on a football scholarship and had a bright future ahead of him. Jo's heart sank as she watched—knowing how it all would end.

She closed the link and tapped on a photo she'd uncovered on Facebook. Jackson didn't have an account, but plenty of people who knew him did—a few with open profiles.

She shook her head and chuckled. *Silly rabbits.*

In the photo, Jackson smiled down at a petite blonde whose back was to the camera. The look on his face made Jo's chest ache.

She clutched the phone to her chest and fell asleep trying to picture Masi looking at her that way.

Four hours later, Jo dragged her ass out of bed and headed to the gym. Unable to stop the night's ruminations, she scrolled through her contacts and tapped on a number. A sleepy voice answered—apparently, Dr. Loeb wasn't an early bird—and scheduled a therapy session for later that day.

After the gym, she headed to her office for back-to-back meetings and an afternoon presentation with a new client. Her passion was fashion, and she made a lot of money with her blog and YouTube channel, but they didn't constitute a real job—at least to those managing her trust fund—so Jo started *The Prophetic Aesthetic* trend forecasting consultancy. Since forecasting was more of a science than an art, and predicting markets spanned every industry, her clients were diverse. Even so, her three o'clock pitch *was* with a designer—of caskets.

Hours later, when she finally had a moment to breathe, she pulled her long legs onto the chair and closed her eyes, mulling over her therapy session from earlier.

Dr. Leob believed her infatuation with Jackson Taylor stemmed from a desire to connect emotionally to someone without the possibility of rejection. But then again, Jo could tell the therapist she hated Spam and somehow the woman would link the gelatinous 'meat' to her commitment issues.

Masi's ringtone snapped her back, and she swiped to answer. "Hey, I was just thinking of you."

A hospital page went off in the background.

"Hello, love. I'm not going to make it tonight. The flu is going around, and we're already short two, so I'll be pulling a double."

As an ER doctor, this happened a lot. Masi had little say in whether he went home at the end of his shift. If they were short, he couldn't leave.

Jo swiveled around and peered out the window, wishing she could cloak her voice in indifference. "So, I guess that means you'll be spending more time with your ex."

Masi sighed into the phone. "Yes, she's here."

Jo tapped her nails on the desk and recited the ABCs of jealousy. *Acknowledge, Be mindful, Challenge negative thoughts.* "What time do you think you'll get off?" She tried to make her voice light, but it came off as desperate. *Shit.*

"I'll be knackered after doing a double, Josette," Masi said, his cultured accent tinged with annoyance.

"Right, of course. Sorry."

He sighed. "Look, I have to go. I'll call you in a couple of days, all right?"

"Sure. Fine. We'll—"

He'd already hung up.

That night, Jo dreamed of lying under a beautiful old tree, with dappled sun shining through the leaves as a warm summer breeze blew. Birds chirped and bees buzzed. No, wait. Not *bees*. Just one large, annoying bumble bee she tried to shoo away. It became aggressive and loud, and she swatted it with all her might.

"Fuck!" Jo smacked her hand against the nightstand, grabbed the vibrating phone, and fell back on her pillow. "What the hell, Drew?" She checked the screen. "It's 3 AM!"

"Imagine that."

"You are such an asshole."

"Takes one to know one, honey. How was your date?"

She heard loud noises in the background. "Where are you?"

"Private party. So, did he chopstick your rice? Did you feed him your sushi?"

"Fuck off. I'm going back to sleep."

But she didn't—or couldn't. Instead, her mind drifted to Jackson Taylor. She opened her STAN file and wondered how hard it would be to get a copy of someone's high school yearbook from over a decade ago.

Turned out, pretty easy.

6

Everybody wants to go to heaven; but nobody wants to die.
- Albert King

They were moving locations.

The sun had barely crested the horizon when JT was pulled out of his cell. His wrists were bound behind his back, and cuffs were placed around his ankles. The butt of an AK-47 prodded him toward a truck idling some fifty feet away.

JT spotted Powell first. She wore a *hijab* over her shorn head. It'd been almost a month since they'd arrived, and had forced her to kneel, shaving her scalp with a knife. Blood had run into her eyes and over her face as they dragged her, still on her knees, into one of the mud houses that lined the street.

He let out a sigh of relief when she met his gaze. She appeared strong; they hadn't broken her.

When they hoisted him into the bed of the truck, his lip hit a metal flange. Blood flowed freely from the wound as he righted himself. JT turned, catching Powell's frown as he wiped his mouth on his dirty shirt. He gave a slight shake of his head. Weakness of any kind could mean death.

Her expression hardened, and she turned away.

DePaul sat opposite, in terrible shape. His eyes were glazed over with fever, and his leg, which had taken a bullet, oozed.

Since their capture, JT had tried to memorize everything, from his tiny, dank cell to the guards, and all the sights and sounds around him. Anything to aid in escape. Several tours of duty had given him some basic understanding of Arabic and Pashto—enough to understand the militants believed U.S. forces had a bead on their location, and that they would be heading into the Hindu Kush mountains. From experience, JT knew they could only travel so far up the mountain before having to continue on foot—something he doubted DePaul would be able to do.

They stopped about midday when another truck came from the opposite direction and pulled them over.

It was a desolate location, surrounded by tall, snow-covered mountains. Nothing grew here. No trees among the craggy peaks. No vegetation rooted in the arid soil. No sign of life at all.

Their captors got out, and after a brief discussion with the other men, hauled JT, DePaul, and Powell from the bed and drove off, leaving them behind.

Shackled and silent, they stood watching their new jailers unload video equipment from the back of their vehicle.

Powell's eyes widened. "What are they doing?"

"Proving we're still alive," DePaul said.

JT hoped he was right, because the alternative was unthinkable.

After a heated debate among its members, the group forced the three of them off the road. They shuffled a few yards into the moonscape earth before being forced to kneel some six feet apart.

The leader motioned for the video to start and after the camera panned the hostages, he began an impassioned speech. From what JT could decipher, the U.S. had not met their demands. For almost an hour, the militant aired his grievances until at last, his intentions toward them became clear.

JT's heart sank to the ground when one of the men approached, carrying black hoods.

DePaul was the first in line. He lowered his head in defeat as the fabric fell around his shoulders. Next came Powell. With one last shuddering breath, she disappeared under the hood, her soft prayers caught in the wind. They took their final steps toward JT.

As the material slid over his face, he closed his eyes and made his peace with God.

7

You can't have everything, where would you put it?
- Steven Wright

Jo entered the dance studio an hour before anyone arrived. She loved being alone—there was an energy, a vibration, that disappeared when surrounded by the sights and sounds of other dancers.

And the *smell*. She pulled in a deep breath and held it. It was nuanced, like a fine wine, with layers of moisture and sweat dominating the co-mingling of odors. The human toil that went into perfecting the art of dance—passion and pain, jealousy, and joy—had a particular aroma that couldn't be replicated anywhere else.

Jo ran her hand over the barre before bending and stretching, breathing in wood and rosin. Her thoughts drifted to the boutique chain and their desire for a signature fragrance. She'd spent months researching the field, analyzing markets, studying consumers' buying behavior, developing online surveys, and conducting focus groups. What her client ultimately decided, she never knew; she was merely the compiler of data points.

She bent into a plié, her mind drifting to a perfume for dancers. It would be unappreciated by the masses, but maybe a candle...

"Jesus!" Lost in her musings, she hadn't heard Drew until he was beside her. "You're like a fucking ninja!"

"Daydreaming about Dumpling, I suppose."

"Stop calling him that. It's racist."

"Not if you're a minority, Josette," he said, beginning a rond de jambe sequence.

"Um, yes, *Andrew*, it is. If you were Japanese, I'd give you a pass."

Drew rolled his eyes. "Please. That man screams white privilege. I'm poor, Black, *and* gay."

Jo huffed out a laugh. "You're far from poor."

"Honey, I will always be Antwon, that skinny boy lookin' for food in a dumpster." His tone was light, but she knew how much pain hid beneath the words.

She couldn't know what it was like growing up in poverty and neglect, especially as a minority, but Drew used it reflexively as a justification for bad behavior—and she often enabled it.

They stretched and moved to their own silent music before the kids trickled in. Every Sunday and two weeks during the summer, Jo, Drew, and a handful of others volunteered to teach dance to disadvantaged youth from the inner city, which the Singer Foundation funded.

When Jo joined the board at twenty-six, she'd been excited to use her knowledge of fashion and design to help raise money. The Fashion Bash & Ball, held every February, was Jo's inspiration. Designers from around the world donated items for auction and took part in the annual avant-garde challenge—which was always the highlight of the evening. This year's theme, *Queens of the Silver Screen*, was Drew's idea and incorporated drag queens instead of models.

After they finished teaching the class, the two friends grabbed their bags and headed out.

"Jobo, you need to add more sequins to my headpiece. It's so dull. I look more like Harriet Tubman than Carmen Miranda."

"Yes, because Harriet Tubman wore fruit attached to her headscarf."

"Well, she had to store food somewhere while working that underground railroad."

Jo pulled on her jacket. "If I put any more onto the headpiece, you won't be able to hold it up."

"No pain, no gain. I want to *win*."

"Less is more sometimes."

"Not according to every drag queen alive, honey."

He made a good point. She smacked her lips together. "Fine, more sequins it is."

Jo had a degree in fashion, but she wasn't a designer any more than Drew was a drag queen. He wanted to model in this year's show, so they entered as an honorary team representing the foundation.

Jo received a text as they walked out of the studio and put out an arm to stop Drew. "The foundation wants to add a new recipient this year."

"Isn't it a little late for that?"

Jo continued to read. "Oh, shit. Do you remember the story of the captured Americans?" When he nodded, she continued. "Well, the group responsible just posted a video. It shows them beheading one of the soldiers." A knot formed in her stomach. "The board wants to honor the fallen soldier's family at this year's ball."

"Which one did they kill?"

Jo glanced up from her phone. "Does it matter?" *Yes. Yes, it does.*

Drew shrugged, and the two continued to walk to the intersection where they would part ways. "Is it wrong for me to want the good-looking one to survive?"

Jo raised an incredulous brow. "Yes." *I'm such a hypocrite.* It'd been over a month since she first fixated on Jackson Taylor. He was a fantasy. Someone she knew intimately, yet not at all.

Drew stopped at the light and turned. "It wasn't that sweet girl, was it?"

She shook her head. "No, they referenced a 'he,' and before you ask, no, I didn't see the video. My stomach isn't much stronger than yours."

"Tell that to the bottle of tequila you finished off last night."

Jo flipped him the bird and crossed the street. She needed to see that video. To dislodge the lump in her throat. To know it wasn't Jackson.

She opened her apartment door, threw her keys on the table, and sat with her coat and boots still on. With a shaky hand, she tapped on the link and held her breath. It didn't open to the video, but to a news site. Navigating around the click-bait, she scanned the article for Jackson's name.

Yes!

Her arms opened wide, and she fell back on the sofa with a loud exhale.

It wasn't him.

Her smile faltered when she thought of the soldier who *had* died and the people who wished it wasn't him.

With subdued joy, she shrugged off her coat and reached for her phone, which buzzed with an incoming text.

> *Short dinner break at 6. Join me for rubbish cafeteria food?*

Jo had a million things to do.

> *I'll be in scrubs. You can't miss me.*

Her only night in, and it was No Shower Sunday.

> *I've missed you.*

There it was, Jo's kryptonite. How pathetic that she gave those three words so much power. Yet she craved them all the same.

Dinner with Masi would cost her three hours of much needed down time—two if she didn't wash her hair. *Or,* she could forgo the time she'd designated for her cyber crush.

Jo pinned up her hair and stepped into the shower.

What am I doing? He's a total stranger!

One she would have mourned.

Knowing her one-sided obsession had to end, she let the mass of waves tumble down her back and massaged the fragrant liquid into her hair.

8

Oh, bother.
- Winnie the Pooh

The holiday season was well underway, and Jo's calendar was full of events, concerts, openings, and parties. But the one she most looked forward to was Holly's surprise thirtieth birthday party.

"So, we finally get to meet the elusive Dr. Du—"

"Don't say it, Drew."

"I was going to say *delicious*."

Jo shut her computer and rubbed her eyes. "I'm exhausted." At least her busy schedule kept her from relapsing. She hadn't opened her STAN file in over a week.

"Come here, puddin' pop." Drew patted the cushion beside him.

She stumbled to her couch and sprawled out. He tried to run his fingers through her thick mass of waves. "Fuck, Jo. When's the last time you did anything with your hair?"

"Yesterday morning." She yawned.

"Lord, girl. You need to get your priorities straight!" He got up, and Jo curled into the warmth of his vacated seat. He came back with a brush and a hair repair mask. "Sit at my feet—where you belong."

Too tired to think of a witty retort, she sat between his legs and leaned her head against his thigh as he detangled her curls.

"Did you see the write-up from the gallery opening last week in *Philly Mag*? They mentioned you."

"Did they? I don't remember causing a scene." She barely remembered the event.

"They compared you to a young Sophia Loren."

"Mmm, I wore that vintage Dior." Jo fell into a trance as he massaged the mask into her scalp.

"It *was* gorge." He contemplated her. "You have similar facial features."

"Big noses."

He smacked her with the brush. "Same sultry eyes and mouth."

"Wild hair that needs constant taming." She yawned, letting her lids fall shut.

Jo woke to sunlight and the smell of coffee on her living room floor. She stood, stretched the ache out of her back, and ambled toward the kitchen.

Drew leaned against the counter, drinking from a steaming mug. "Morning, glory."

"Hey." Jo rolled her shoulders. "Thanks for leaving me on the floor."

"I thought about waking you, but you only have one bed and I sleep alone."

"There's a pull-out sofa in my office." She pushed him aside with her hip and poured herself a cup of coffee.

"I'm not sleeping in the same room as your Chucky doll."

"Miss Money Honey wouldn't stab you—although she might throw a Louboutin."

"You need to give your mini-me back to your ex."

"No can do. Ongoing custody battle." She would spend every last cent making sure Remy never mocked her again.

8

Oh, bother.
- Winnie the Pooh

The holiday season was well underway, and Jo's calendar was full of events, concerts, openings, and parties. But the one she most looked forward to was Holly's surprise thirtieth birthday party.

"So, we finally get to meet the elusive Dr. Du—"

"Don't say it, Drew."

"I was going to say *delicious*."

Jo shut her computer and rubbed her eyes. "I'm exhausted." At least her busy schedule kept her from relapsing. She hadn't opened her STAN file in over a week.

"Come here, puddin' pop." Drew patted the cushion beside him.

She stumbled to her couch and sprawled out. He tried to run his fingers through her thick mass of waves. "Fuck, Jo. When's the last time you did anything with your hair?"

"Yesterday morning." She yawned.

"Lord, girl. You need to get your priorities straight!" He got up, and Jo curled into the warmth of his vacated seat. He came back with a brush and a hair repair mask. "Sit at my feet—where you belong."

Too tired to think of a witty retort, she sat between his legs and leaned her head against his thigh as he detangled her curls.

"Did you see the write-up from the gallery opening last week in *Philly Mag*? They mentioned you."

"Did they? I don't remember causing a scene." She barely remembered the event.

"They compared you to a young Sophia Loren."

"Mmm, I wore that vintage Dior." Jo fell into a trance as he massaged the mask into her scalp.

"It *was* gorge." He contemplated her. "You have similar facial features."

"Big noses."

He smacked her with the brush. "Same sultry eyes and mouth."

"Wild hair that needs constant taming." She yawned, letting her lids fall shut.

Jo woke to sunlight and the smell of coffee on her living room floor. She stood, stretched the ache out of her back, and ambled toward the kitchen.

Drew leaned against the counter, drinking from a steaming mug. "Morning, glory."

"Hey." Jo rolled her shoulders. "Thanks for leaving me on the floor."

"I thought about waking you, but you only have one bed and I sleep alone."

"There's a pull-out sofa in my office." She pushed him aside with her hip and poured herself a cup of coffee.

"I'm not sleeping in the same room as your Chucky doll."

"Miss Money Honey wouldn't stab you—although she might throw a Louboutin."

"You need to give your mini-me back to your ex."

"No can do. Ongoing custody battle." She would spend every last cent making sure Remy never mocked her again.

"Can't you just..." He opened the roll-out trash can with his foot and tilted his head. "I'll take it with me. Toss it in the dumpster."

"I can't kill my doppelgänger, Drew. Bad juju." And she kinda liked having her around.

He gave her a dubious look and placed his mug in the sink. "I'm gonna run, but I'll see you tonight." He grabbed his coat and air-kissed her cheeks.

Jo leaned against the door, tamping down her anxiety. Tonight would be the first time she introduced Masi to her friends, and she wasn't sure she was ready. He'd only seen her shiny bits, the ones that put her in the best light—the Jo she *aspired* to be. The real, raw, and unfiltered Jo needed to stay hidden a little longer, because that bell couldn't be unrung.

Jo woke the next morning in a familiar bed—just not her own.

Oh, god. What did I do?

Too-bright sunlight streamed through the window, causing her to pull the cover over her head.

Holly came in and sat beside her.

Keeping her head hidden, she asked, "How bad was it?" When no reply came, she pulled the comforter down.

A mixture of emotions—anger among them—warred on Holly's face, which didn't bode well.

Holly was, well, jolly. It took a lot to change her positive demeanor. She was the ultimate optimist, the shining light in everyone's dark day, the one you turned to for support, no matter what.

Bravo, Jo. You eclipsed Holly's sun.

"I'm guessing bad, then." Jo sat up, her head pounding.

Holly handed her some pills and a glass of water.

"Did I puke?" Jo's stomach revolted, but she held it down with steely determination. "Punch someone in the face?"

Holly pursed her lips and turned away.

"Was it your uncle? The one at the barbeque last July?" Jo was convinced she'd seen him on *Cold Case Files*.

"You didn't punch or puke on anyone, Jo."

"That's a relief." She stared at the Pepto pink cover, noting her nakedness underneath. "Any chance you know why I'm naked and sleeping in your childhood bedroom?"

Holly stood, crossed her arms, and trudged to the end of the bed. "No idea. My mom called me this morning and told me to get your disrespectful, drunk ass out of her house."

Jo fell back onto the frilly pink pillow. "Okay, so worse than the time I accused your uncle of being a pedophile."

Holly took out her phone and walked to the door. "I'm getting you a car. Be thankful your boyfriend left the party early."

Jo had a lot of 'splainin' to do. If only she remembered the whys and wherefores. She scrambled around, collecting her articles of clothing. She was minus a shoe but found her purse. With an axe in her head and an unsteady gait, Jo slipped quietly out of the house to wait for her ride.

As she sat on the Rabinowitz's front step, she had a flashback of Masi leaving—of throwing back a shot or two. Of Holly, looking surprised. No, not surprised...*Oh, boy*. She needed to talk to Drew.

When her ride appeared, she hobbled over, got in, and leaned her head back. *Nope, terrible idea.* She flung the door open as it left the curb and threw up. *Great, there go the meds.*

Once home, Jo walked straight to her bedroom and peeled off her dress. Having no energy to shower, she grabbed a T-shirt that read, SURELY NOT EVERYONE WAS KUNG-FU FIGHTING, collapsed onto her bed, and slept like the dead. Hours later, she made a PB&J and popped a couple more pain pills. Flopping on the sofa, she closed her eyes and forced herself to recall the events from the previous night.

She'd been discussing the signature cocktail with the bartender when Masi walked in. He was wearing a dark blue-gray suit, which she recognized from Tom Ford's fall collection, having featured it in her article, *How to Dress Your Man*. If ever there was a sign they belonged together.

A loud knock startled her. Jo rubbed her temples and padded over to the door. Drew lifted his eyes to the messy bun on top of her head before pushing past her. "You don't deserve that hair."

"Hello to you, too." She closed the door and walked back to the sofa.

Drew remained standing. "Girl, you have really fucked up this time."

"I'm sure you're dying to tell me how." She spread her arms wide. "Have at it."

He put his hands on his hips. "You're a selfish bitch, you know that?"

"Apparently." But Jo didn't know why. She never did. Her good intentions had a way of getting lost in translation. Fortunately, Drew was fluent in Drunk Jo.

"You remember the song we did for Holly?"

Jo rubbed her forehead. "Of course. We wrote new lyrics to *A Holly Jolly Christmas*."

"Yes. Yes, we did." Drew nodded in agreement. "Only you didn't sing them the way we wrote them."

Jo closed her eyes and tried to remember the song's lyrics.

Have a Jolly Birthday, Holly
It's the best time of the year
A Jew was born on Christmas day
So have a pint of beer!
Have a Jolly Birthday, Holly
And enjoy your birthday feast
Say hello to friends you know
And ones you'd like to meet
Oh, how the years have flown
I can't believe it's nigh
Your 20s have come and gone

Kiss your youth goodbye!
Have a Jolly Birthday, Holly
And in case you didn't hear
Oh, by golly, our friend Holly's
turning thirty this year!

"I never liked nigh. We should have come up with a better word."

"Oh, honey. You did. You changed the whole damn thing!" Drew threw a hand in the air.

"I did?" Jo quirked her head as if listening to some inner dialogue. "Right. I couldn't remember the lyrics, so I improvised." Jo pinched the bridge of her nose as parts of the evening came back to her. "I was trying to be funny."

"How'd that work out for you?"

"I remembered nigh."

"Yes, you did, but you rhymed it with thighs, and I don't believe the word you used was complimentary."

"Zaftig. It's Yiddish for pleasingly plump. My grandfather used to say it about my grandmother. It's a *compliment*."

He looked on with skepticism, but his voice lost its edge. "Jobo, you embarrassed her in front of all those people."

There was no use trying to defend herself. "Drew, I was trashed. I'm sure everyone thought I was a total twat and Holly a saint for having to deal with me."

He let out a sigh, along with most of his anger. "Jo, you need to get your shit together." He sat on the edge of the sofa. "We both know I could take a trip around the world with my emotional baggage. But I keep it local." He tapped his chest.

Their eyes locked, and for the briefest of moments, Jo glimpsed pain he rarely revealed.

He tipped her chin up. "You need to learn to bleed less publicly."

After Drew left, she called Holly and invited her for dinner. To sweeten the deal, she offered to make crêpes for dessert. Jo had learned the basics of French cuisine from her mother. Loving carbs more than life, she enjoyed baking, especially desserts.

Holly arrived as Jo slid the asparagus and gruyère tart into the oven. When she walked in, Jo hugged her until she reluctantly hugged back. Jo wasn't a big hugger. Like Drew, she preferred air kisses with minimum contact. Holly, on the other hand, hugged for an unbearable amount of time. The 'Holly hug' took time getting used to. It was her thing, and Jo wouldn't change it for the world. She held on until Holly pulled back with a hint of a smile on her lips. All was right in the world again.

"I'm still mad at you, Jo."

Okay, maybe not back to one hundred percent, but I haven't served my crêpes yet.

Holly was her emotional weathervane, pointing her in the right direction whenever things got stormy.

"Holl, I'm so sorry. I would never do anything to hurt you."

"Not on purpose, but you have no filter, especially when you drink."

"This...is a problem." Jo bit at her top lip, wishing she could zip it shut. "But in my defense, Masi left, and I was upset—"

"Jo. Stop." Holly took off her coat and hung it in the closet. "Something always sets you off."

Jo hated this. The *after*. Drew was right. She needed to control her emotions. "I should have written the lyrics on my hand—"

Holly pivoted. "Jo, I'm not mad at you for fucking up the song."

"You're not?"

"No. Actually, I felt sorry for you."

A direct hit. Jo plopped down in a chair. "I'd rather you be mad at me."

Holly gave her a sad smile. "Do you remember our eighth-grade talent show? Where you convinced the school to let Drew be your dance partner? You were crazy in love with him back then."

"Hard to forget." Jo leaned back and closed her eyes. *Go on, Holl. Get your kicks in.*

"You caught him kissing Zach Friedman behind a rack of costumes."

Jo's head rolled to the side. "Are we really going there?"

"You refused to talk to him, and then you went on stage—"

A punch to her solar plexus.

"You'd forgotten the routine," Holly finished softly.

Well done, you. Jo took a steadying breath as shame engulfed her. "Well, at least I didn't wet my pants this time."

"You were twelve."

"Thirteen. Is there a point to this?" Jo snapped.

"It's just...the look on your face last night. Even after you sang those ridiculous words, I couldn't help but—"

"Wish I'd soiled myself?"

Holly squeezed her shoulder. "*Root* for you."

Oh, for Christ's sake.

9

You're braver than you believe, stronger than you seem
and smarter than you think.
- Christopher Robin

Winter had settled over the Hindu Kush, but JT barely noticed it anymore. Thirty-five days had passed since the beheading of DePaul, and they'd been on the move ever since.

They traveled by foot, by mule, and sometimes by vehicle, always moving, always one step ahead of rescue. Numerous high passages transected the jagged barren mountain range, forming a strategic network of places to stop. Their captors knew the terrain—every hidden pathway, every cave, every village safehouse where they could find sanctuary.

Powell had become more and more distant, keeping to herself and rarely making eye contact. He remembered when he first met her. She seemed out of place in both the desert and in the Army. She was unassuming—slight and pale, but full of optimism, always quick with a joke or a word of encouragement. Everyone loved her. He'd been wrong to judge her character by her outward appearance and demeanor. She was stronger than most men he knew.

The sky was gloomy gray when they stopped for the day in a small village of flat-roofed mud huts hidden between two ridges. Dust and grit from the thin alpine air blew less severely here. It seemed a place well known to the men, who were warmly received by the few inhabitants that came out to greet them.

They sat with their captors and hosts in a long ramshackle building and ate mutton stew with hunks of stale bread and tea. It was the first real meal they'd had since capture, and JT suppressed a moan when he bit into the naan drenched in the flavorful juice.

A rare glimpse of sun shone through the open doorway, and JT's eye caught on an object that refracted the light's rays. It lay half-buried in rubble next to a communal latrine.

His mind raced with possibilities. He called out, asking to use the facilities while keeping his voice steady. They waved for him to go. He walked the short distance, hands unbound and without escort, tripping near the entrance. As he righted himself, he slipped the object inside his sleeve and entered the dank outhouse, knowing his odds of survival had just increased.

10

The secret to happiness is low expectations.
- Warren Buffett

New Year's Eve was Jo's favorite holiday. She loved everything about it, not just dressing in a glitzy outfit and watching fireworks from Penn's Landing. To Jo, ringing in the New Year was about untainted optimism. Which was why, when Masi texted and said he was on call that night, her mood plummeted. Usually, she didn't give up the ghost of new beginnings until New Year's Day, when she watched the Mummers strut down Broad Street while eating a carton of ice cream.

They still hadn't had sex yet, and Jo had a lot of pent-up energy—the kind one couldn't get rid of with friends. She weighed the odds of him getting called in and decided to take a chance. Tonight would be Masi's reckoning. She'd either start the new year single or satisfied.

Four hours later, Jo found herself in front of Masi's apartment building, adorned in a very sexy, very backless, silk sheath dress which was way too short for her long legs. It screamed *fuck me!* If she couldn't get laid wearing that, then she had no hope at all.

In the early hours of dawn on New Year's Day, Jo slipped the key to Drew's apartment into the lock. She tried opening the door, but something impeded her entry. She heard a grunt as she pushed against the solid steel and squeezed through the opening.

Once inside, she regarded the body blocking her passage. A quick sweep of the area found five more passed out in positions no sober person could sleep in. She stepped over and around them until she came to Drew's bedroom.

Holly lay sprawled at the foot of his bed wearing *Hello Kitty* underwear and a bra, with a blanket covering her head. Jo climbed over her and crawled up to Drew, who was on his back. His right arm and leg hung over the side with his foot touching the floor, giving Jo ample room to lie beside him without physical contact. Drew didn't like to be touched unless he initiated it, so she just laid there, listening to Holly snore.

"Jobo."

She must have fallen asleep because the sound of Drew's voice startled her. "Hmm?"

"Girl, I know you weren't here when I passed out. You know how I know that?"

Jo rubbed at her eyes, the makeup from the night before gluing her eyes shut. "Because you like to sleep alone?"

He raised himself on one elbow and loomed over her. "Exactly! So how is it you're sleeping next to me?"

"I wasn't? At least not when I got here. I waited for you to wake up, but I guess I fell asleep," she said sheepishly.

"But *I* was sleeping. Which is, in fact, the point."

She stretched beside him. "Comfy bed, I've never been in it before."

"And why, may I ask, are you in it now?" he said, emphasizing each word with a poke to her ribs.

"Well," she started, pushing his hand away. "I didn't get to wish you a Happy New Year."

Drew grabbed his phone off the nightstand. She watched as he perused his missed calls. "Nope, didn't receive anything from you. Wait...Let's check texts. Oh, look. Here's the video Holly and I sent you." He held out the phone and played back the recording of them, counting down to midnight, and wishing her a Happy New Year. "Funny, there isn't anything back from you."

Jo covered her face with her arm. "My phone died."

He turned to her and raised himself on one elbow. "And the good doctor didn't have one you could use?"

"Valid point." Jo raised a brow and smiled. "But in my defense, we were having sex, which didn't seem an appropriate time to ask."

Drew sprang from the bed and smacked Holly in the head. "Get up. You're gonna want to hear this."

A fiery red halo appeared at the foot of the bed, followed by two forearms and a pair of surprisingly bright eyes. "What'd I miss?"

"Nothing yet. Jo's about to fill us in on her trip to Chinatown."

Drew ducked as Jo flung a pillow at him. "Can you *not?*"

Holly crawled to the other side of her. "He's yanking your chain. Ignore him. But I need the deets. Preferably in great detail."

Jo dreaded telling them the truth. "It was...nice."

Drew signaled to Holly. "We may need Bloody Marys for this."

"I'm on it, but not a word until I get back!" Holly bound off the bed.

"She's pretty peppy, considering she passed out at the foot of your bed with only a face blanket."

"She's probably still drunk." Drew turned to examine her. "You, on the other hand, don't seem a bit hungover."

Jo's smile widened. She hadn't been sober on New Year's Eve in over a decade. "Proud of me?"

He raised a finely tweezed brow. "Actually, yes. But also, a little freaked out."

"I know. Me too."

Holly entered a few minutes later with three well-appointed cocktails.

Jo downed half the glass. "Looks like I may have to rescind my sobriety card. Nice job with the drinks, Holl."

"Bartender's still here. I think he hooked up with your ex, Drew. Found the two of them in the kitchen. Bribed him into making these bad boys."

Unphased, Drew took a sip. "Ooh, strong—just the way I like my men."

They settled back on the bed and waited for Jo to begin. The three always shared the intimate details of their first night with a new partner, and although nothing they said would leave this room, she hesitated. Whether it was because it took her and Masi so long to consummate their relationship or because it wasn't everything she'd hoped it would be, she wasn't sure. Ultimately, she relented, wanting their take on the evening.

"Like I said, it was nice, but perfunctory. Restrained. *Beige.*"

Drew made a stank face. "Did he at least get you off?"

"Yes. It was very sweet."

Holly let out a sharp laugh. "Perfunctory? Sweet? What the fuck?"

Jo felt a twinge of disloyalty to Masi. This was why she needed to seal the deal early in a relationship, because waiting until she had feelings muddied the waters. "I'm not saying it was bad, although there *was* this one thing."

Holly took Jo's hands in hers and squeezed. "Micropenis?"

She laughed. "No. He's no Dirk Diggler, but he's perfectly adequate. It's just, well…"

"Spit it out, Jobo. What's his kink?"

Jo's head snapped to Drew. "How'd you know he had one?"

"Why else would you be hesitating?" He covered his mouth with his hand. "Ooh! Did you get off on whatever he's into? Are you embarrassed because you liked it?"

"Jesus, Drew. No!"

"Jo, just tell us, or he'll come up with some more outrageous shit."

"Fine." Jo took a deep breath. "He likes to suckle."

Drew and Holly exchanged glances. "Like your tits?"

"Yes, like that. He seemed pretty into them at first, which, you know, was great, but after we finished, he snuggled up to them and," she motioned with her hands, "until he fell asleep."

"Holy shit balls, Jo!" Holly laughed so hard she fell off the bed.

Drew shook his head as Holly ran to the bathroom with one hand between her legs. "As spectacular as your girls are, that shit's on another level."

Jo shrugged. "I kept thinking he was hoping for a second round."

"And fell asleep before his man parts woke up?"

"Something like that."

Holly scurried back into the room. "What'd I miss?"

"Jo's trying to rationalize her boyfriend's mammary fixation."

Holly nudged Jo over and sat beside her on the bed. She wrapped an arm around her head and brought it down to her shoulder. "Don't you listen to Drew. I think it's kinda sweet."

"Is that why you wet yourself a minute ago?"

Holly leaned toward Drew, pulling Jo's head in the opposite direction. "I'm being a supportive friend!"

"Ow!" Jo bellowed. She extricated Holly's fingers from her hair and pulled away. "Look, I like him, okay? I don't know why, but he intrigues me. He's confident and independent—even cold. Which, for some reason, turns me on. And my parents approve, which never happens." Jo hugged a pillow. "I just hope he doesn't have some deep-seated Oedipus Complex."

"And if he does?" Drew sauntered to the closet, wearing nothing but briefs. "You gonna continue to be his binky?"

Jo winced. "Maybe?"

Holly frowned, plucking a dollar bill from her cleavage. "So, how'd you leave it?"

Feeling guilty, Jo cringed and took a sip of her spicy drink. "I left before he woke up."

Holly glanced around before returning the bill to her bra. "Did you leave a note?"

"I was going to text him when I left, but my phone was dead."

"Maybe it's best to give it some time." Holly bent over and peered under the bed. "Where the hell are my clothes?"

Drew returned from the closet wearing a silk robe and lounged on a chaise by the window. "Strip poker. Look in the living room."

Holly gave him a quick thumbs up and went off in search of her things.

11

I'm going to stand outside, so if anybody asks about me,
I'm outstanding.

- Unknown

Jo arrived fashionably late for dinner. She shook off her hat, gloves, and coat, and headed toward the laughter coming from the dining room where her parents sat in rapt attention while Drew told a story.

Always the showman.

Jo could set herself on fire, and if Drew was there, she'd be lucky to get a glass of water to douse the flame. He had that kind of effect on people.

Her arrival caused a sudden lull in the room. "No need to stop on my account. Please, continue." She made a sweeping motion with her arm until her eyes landed on her prey. She pounced on the white Burgundy and took her usual seat. On the table, which was dressed in fine linen, sat bowls and plates of half-eaten food and crumbs from the crusty French bread she'd dropped off earlier in the day. She took a healthy sip from her glass. "Apparently, I wasn't missed."

"You can't expect us to wait until you show up, Josette. It could be *hours*," her mother said.

"I'm less than an hour late, *Maman*. From the looks of it, you began promptly at six."

"*Mais on a un invité ce soir, Josette!*" her mother exclaimed.

"Drew isn't a guest, he's family." She frowned at the remainder of a rib roast on the table. "Did you even cook anything I can eat?"

Drew piped up before her mother could utter a word. "Élaine made an eggplant dish *that is to die*." He passed the casserole to her and smiled. "How was your day, sunshine?"

Jo sighed and tried to let go of the jealousy she harbored for Drew and her parents' relationship. Of all the things, people, and causes she took a back seat to, she found this the hardest to reconcile—craving both her parents' attention and Drew's.

They'd taken him in more times than she could count over the years, but he always left before getting too comfortable—and before Jo's resentment became unbearable. Maybe he sensed it— her feeling like an outsider at her own birthday party. But it wouldn't have made a difference. There was always something or someone that needed her parents more than she did. It was a complicated mess of emotional baggage she'd tried to unpack for years.

"Fine. Busy." She inspected Drew. "Why are you wearing makeup?"

"Do I need a reason to beautify myself, Jobo?"

"If I had your face, I wouldn't need makeup."

Drew nodded in agreement. "You have a point. But one can always improve on perfection."

Jo smirked at the nonsensical comment and filled her plate. "Smells good."

Élaine shrugged off the compliment. "Only vegetables, but I do my best."

Gil's phone pinged, and Élaine grabbed it. "We don't answer calls at the dinner table."

"Technically, it's a notification, and since dinner is over, I don't see why I can't have a look."

Jo lifted a forkful of deliciousness. "Um. Still eating here."

"Everyone's head is in the technology! No one talks—always, tap, tap, tap!" Élaine mimed.

Nowhere But Up

As if on cue, Drew's cell beeped, and he gave it a guilty glance. "My news feed. Probably not important." He sent Jo a 'your mama's crazy' look before gathering up some dishes.

When he reached for Jo's, she slapped his hand. "Still eating!" He pocketed the phone before leaving the table. *Sly devil.*

A minute later, Drew appeared in the doorway. "You might want to reserve a couple more seats at the ball. They've rescued those two missing soldiers." He handed the phone to Jo.

Two American Soldiers Held Hostage for Months Rescued by Special Forces

JALALABAD, Afghanistan, Wednesday, January 7 — Last night, an American special ops team rescued Army Warrant Officer Jackson Taylor and Medic Sergeant Samantha Powell from a remote location in the Hindu Kush mountains where they were being held hostage. The body of a third soldier, weapons sergeant, Kevin DePaul, was also recovered. The three soldiers, whose helicopter went down last November, were held captive by a local insurgent group who demanded a prisoner exchange. The Pentagon had no comment on what went wrong, but on December 5th, a video of all three soldiers went live right before the execution of Sergeant DePaul. According to a statement by Brig. Gen. Carl Logan, Warrant Officer Taylor was able to signal their location, aiding in the rescue operation. "U.S. forces have conducted a successful rescue mission of two U.S. Army prisoners held captive in Afghanistan. They have been returned to a coalition-controlled area." No further statement was given.

Jo's heart took off like a racehorse. Jackson Taylor was alive! And the medic too, of course. She was equally happy both soldiers were safe.

And I will meet him. I mean, them.

Unless he declined their invitation to attend the ball. But what were the chances of that?

12

*Life is like riding a bicycle. To keep your balance,
you must keep moving.*
- Albert Einstein

JT couldn't remember ever feeling so tired.

After they'd been debriefed, he and Powell flew to Germany for physical and mental assessments. Ten days later—with Powell's sunny disposition returned—they headed home.

Before going their separate ways for the last leg of their journey, she'd said, "Don't be a stranger. If you ever need to talk, I'm just a phone or a flight away."

He'd repeated the sentiment, knowing full well he'd never take her up on the offer—and secretly hoped she wouldn't either. It wasn't that he didn't care for Powell, just that he wanted to forget the last few years had existed.

The commercial flight he was on was a hell of a lot nicer than the C-5 from earlier, but the little seat kicker behind him made him wish he'd stayed on the transport plane.

He was numb with exhaustion by the time he dropped his bag and hugged his mom, burying his nose in her familiar scent. He reluctantly let go and held out his hand to his dad, who pulled JT in for a tight hug. For the briefest of moments, the three enjoyed their reunion before flashbulbs went off and people gathered. Reporters shoved microphones at him, all talking over one another, while military security flanked and steered him toward an area set up for such occasions. An Army officer handled most inquiries, but the press wanted to hear from JT. Most of the questions were personal, how he *felt* about this or that. He recoiled when they called him a hero, and it took everything in him not to push back.

It all seemed surreal as if he were observing from the sidelines. It could have been five minutes or fifty by the time they let him go. He couldn't recall how he got outside, but when he spotted the old Ford truck in the lot, his anxiety lessened. It grounded him, that piece of normal, and he released a breath.

They drove in companionable silence to Fowler's Pond, the place he'd once called home.

He slept hard and woke the next morning to the smell of buttermilk biscuits. The familiar scent triggered memories of innocence and forgotten dreams. He hadn't been home in more than two years—before that, he couldn't recall. Unlike every tour, mission, and brother he'd lost since joining the Army ten years prior.

Charles Taylor sat at the kitchen table in the same spot he'd been in for JT's entire life. He had a plate of the same food, with a folded newspaper on his right and a cup of coffee on his left. Nothing had changed, and there was comfort in that.

He walked in and took a seat. "Mornin'."

His mother turned from the stove at the sound of his voice. "Good morning. How'd you sleep?"

"Good. Nice to be in a proper bed." JT studied her. Where his father had always appeared a little worn, his mother's usual radiance had dimmed. Lines creased her face, her mouth had taken on a permanent scowl, and she'd filled out around the middle, making her seem older than her fifty-four years.

She set down a plate for him filled to the brim with eggs, sausage, gravy, and biscuits.

JT dug in. "Thought I'd join you this morning. Make the rounds," he said, glancing at his father. He needed to be useful, to do something normal, to feel like a civilian again.

"That's a fine idea, don't you think, Charles?" Brenda wiped her hands on a dishtowel and sat with a cup of coffee.

His father kept his eyes on the paper. "The boy's gotta get back into the swing of things, I suppose."

It was hard to tell if his dad meant in a general sense, or that he needed to get re-acclimated to farm life. He'd told his parents he wouldn't be re-upping after this last tour, but that didn't mean he'd stay and work the farm.

They started out at the chicken run and house, and by midday, a pattern of disrepair became clear. When he asked about Harry, the farm manager, his father only said he'd left. JT didn't press the issue; he'd find out, eventually.

As he headed to the house for lunch, a high-pitched squeal sounded. Laura Leigh—better known as Lou Lou—jumped on his back, wrapping her legs around his body.

JT laughed and grabbed hold of his sister. "Hey, Cricket."

"You should have woken me when you got in last night!"

"What for? I'm not going anywhere."

His sister, no longer a girl but a young woman of twenty-one, made an unladylike sound and slid down his back. She came to the front, giving him the once over. "You don't look any different."

"Why would I?"

"I thought your head would be bigger, now you're a *hero* and all," she teased.

JT lost all sense of humor. "Don't call me that, Lou. I'm no hero."

She scrunched up her face. "Yeah, you are. You saved like a dozen soldiers. It's all over the news."

Of course, his family would get their information from other sources instead of asking him. It wasn't that they didn't care, it just wasn't their way. JT learned at an early age to hold his emotions close to the vest, to never expose his vulnerability or pain.

To Lou Lou, the takeaway was that he was the good guy, the hero. JT understood her need to pretend he wasn't damaged, that his time away hadn't changed him. Maybe if he pretended long enough, he'd believe it, too.

He continued to the back door, trying to ignore the invisible string that attached Lou Lou to him. He entered the kitchen and made his way to the fridge.

Lou Lou pushed him out of the way. "I'll make my famous grilled cheese with bacon. Grab a can of tomato soup out of the pantry, and I'll have lunch ready for us in no time."

He complied and accepted a glass of sweet tea, taking a seat at the table where he watched her cook.

The bacon in the pan sizzled and popped, making his heart race. He squeezed his eyes shut and breathed through his nose.

...He stepped over a small child cowering in a doorway. A pop, and then another. Faster, he ran down a narrow passage. Sounds of rapid fire, shouting, screaming. His back to the wall, he looked around the corner. Two women and a young boy lay slaughtered in a pool of blood. A baby cried; a woman wailed. An explosion. He crouched down, working his way through the rubble and over the small child's body...

"JT!"

His head snapped up and his throat clenched. He couldn't take in air. Dry lips refused to open as unseeing eyes tried to focus on the figure in front of him. He gritted his teeth and forced himself to swallow. When Lou Lou started toward him, he held up a hand. Closing his eyes, he concentrated on centering himself. *Breathe. Find a safe place.*

He pictured Lou Lou as a little girl, laughing. Her long blonde pigtail swinging in tempo with her gait as she walked alongside him.

He took another breath.

A different blonde ponytail appeared, this one blowing out the passenger window of his truck. Where a flawless face turned to him with a dimpled smile and leaned over to give him a kiss...

He swallowed and pulled more air into his lungs. The buzzing faded, and he opened his eyes.

Lou Lou sat beside him, searching his face. He pushed his palms into his eye sockets. "Sorry, I think I'm still jet-lagged."

She opened her mouth to speak but seemed to think better of it and placed her hand briefly on top of his before getting up to finish lunch.

It didn't matter if she believed him or not, JT was just grateful she let it go.

Ten calls already, and it wasn't even noon.

JT had hoped the calls would stop after a few weeks, but they hadn't. He let them all go to voicemail. Most were from reporters, a few from news stations, one from a TV producer, and one from a very persistent, Miss Josette Singer from Philadelphia, who wanted him to attend an event for DePaul. As much as he'd like to honor his friend, he had no wish to be scrutinized, picked apart, or questioned by anyone. He didn't even listen to the messages anymore before deleting them.

On his way to the barn, his phone buzzed for the eleventh time. *This has to stop.* He would change his number on Monday, but until then...He answered.

"Sergeant Taylor! Josette Singer from the Singer Foundation. Thank you for taking my call. It's an honor to finally speak with you."

JT didn't recall the sexy purr from her messages. "I'm not a sergeant, ma'am."

"Oh, right. Sorry. Would that be Officer Taylor then?"

He blew out a breath, trying not to sound irritated. "Is there something I can help you with?"

"Oh. Yes, of course. I'll be brief. The foundation will be honoring Sergeant DePaul at our upcoming charity ball in a few weeks. Unfortunately, his wife's doctor advised against travel this late in her pregnancy, which leaves us in a bind, as we don't have anyone to accept on his behalf. We'd love for you to do the honor of taking her place. The accommodations will be first-class with all expenses paid by the foundation."

JT didn't know DePaul's wife but remembered how happy he was to be a father, even carrying the ultrasound pictures with him everywhere he went.

After a brief lull, she piped up. "Officer Taylor?"

"JT's fine, ma'am."

"Miss."

"Pardon?"

"It's miss, not ma'am. That would be my mother." She chuckled.

He rubbed his eyes. "How 'bout you call me JT, and I'll call you Josie?"

"It's Josette, or Jo. Either is fine."

"Now that we got that out of the way. I'm going to have to decline your generous offer."

She stayed quiet for a moment. "I see. Can I ask why?"

He should have ended the conversation, but he liked her voice. It was soothing. He rested against a fence post and decided on the truth. "Not much into crowds."

"I see."

"Do you, now?" He didn't know why he kept talking. "I find that unlikely."

"Oh. I apologize, I don't presume to know, I mean—"

"I'm just bustin' on you, Josie." He smiled into the phone, hoping she could hear his teasing tone.

Her voice warmed. "You have a sense of humor. I wouldn't have guessed that."

JT wondered at the peculiar response. "On rare occasions."

"Mr.—*Jackson*," she corrected, "It would mean the world to Jenny DePaul if you could take her place."

"As I've said—"

"You don't like crowds." She sighed. "I seem to have an issue with them, as well."

"How's that?" He realized he'd become Chatty Cathy.

"Oh, well. It's not that I *dislike* crowds. It's just, I'm often unable to control my level of happiness while in one."

He laughed, very curious to know what Miss Singer looked like *happy*—or at all—and he could. He'd just have to search for her online. "I'd like to see that," he voiced aloud, surprising himself.

"Then say yes."

He rubbed a hand behind his neck. "I'll think on it. Best I can do." He heard her release a breath and damn if it didn't do something to his insides.

"Thank you, Jackson."

"You're welcome, Josie."

He hung up and stared at his phone. Why didn't he just say no?

Lou Lou brought JT a glass of tea and stood beside him, twisting a lock of hair around her finger.

"What's up, Lou?"

She tilted her head in a way he knew too well. She wanted something. "There's a great band playing tomorrow night at Bourbon Blue. Will you take me?"

He leaned his chair back on two legs, and hooked his thumbs on the sides, like he'd done since he was a kid. "You're twenty-one now, no need for me to go."

She blew a wayward strand out of her eyes. "That's not the point, and you know it. I want to show you off."

Her selfishness irritated him. "Don't wanna go, Lou."

"I kinda told everyone you'd be there."

"Not my problem."

The smell of burning cheese hit them, and she ran to the stove. "Dammit! I burnt one side." Lou Lou flipped the sandwiches onto plates and added a couple of pickles and a handful of chips. "Here." She dropped a plate in front of him.

He righted his chair. She'd served him the same lunch every day since he'd been home, minus the bacon. The gesture tugged at his heart. "Don't forget the soup."

She glared at him before grabbing two mugs. By the time she took a seat, her anger had subsided, and he sensed her change in tack when she turned sweet. "You know, I heard Addison and Tommy are getting a divorce."

JT stopped mid-bite at the mention of his ex-girlfriend. He put the sandwich down and took a sip of tea. "That so?"

"Yup, and I know for a fact she's gonna be there tomorrow night."

Emotions, both dark and welcomed, sprang forth, surprising him. He'd been shut down for so long, especially where Addy was concerned, that the feelings were foreign.

"Tell you what. Get one of the Hewitt brothers out to help me fix the thresher on the combine, and I'll think about it."

JT knew it was a mistake as soon as they entered the packed bar. He stood shoulder to shoulder with people who pushed and jostled around, making him hyper-focused and anxious. There were too many variables, too many unknowns. He tried to remember what the shrink told him to do when he became agitated. He concentrated on his breathing—long deep breaths in, slow release. After a few minutes, the prickly sensation diminished, but the thought of hours of this had him riled up all over again.

Lou Lou pointed to a group of people clustered by the stage. "I think I see some friends over there."

"You go on then, I'll just stay here." He'd found a spot with his back against a wall and wasn't about to give it up.

"I want you to *meet* them. You haven't gone out since you got home. Just come with me." She tried to pull him along.

He wasn't budging—not on this. "Lou, you go and bring them here if you want, but I'm staying put." He took a swig of his beer and motioned for her to go.

She scowled, turned on her heel, and left. JT's mind wandered to the real reason he was here—to see Addy. He should have thought it through, figured out a better way to run into her than at a crowded bar. Hell, Lou Lou might have made the entire thing up just to—

"I thought that was you, JT."

His heart thumped in his chest at the sight of her. She hadn't changed a bit, still pretty as a spring flower. "Hey, Addy. How's it goin?"

One side of her mouth turned up. "I've been better." Her pale blue eyes widened. "Oh. What a stupid thing to say. After all you've been through, I'm complaining about my petty problems." She leaned closer, her hand on his biceps. "How are *you*?"

He glanced down at where she touched him, not sure if he wanted to grab hold of it or push it away. "I'm doin' fine."

Her fingers moved to his forearm, and she gave a little squeeze. "I just wanna say what you did was so brave, and we're all so proud of you."

JT stiffened. *Fuck*. He didn't want to hear that, especially from her. He cleared his throat and looked away. "Thanks."

She swayed to the side to catch his eye. "Did I say something wrong?"

"No, it's fine." But it wasn't. Every time someone mentioned being proud of him, he got an ache deep in his chest and an overwhelming urge to bury himself deep inside a woman. Someone soft he could hold on to, who would make him forget about the soldiers who weren't coming home because of his mistakes. Especially DePaul.

They stood for a while in silence, neither of them knowing how to span the gap of the five years since he'd first seen her with Tommy. It'd been a stab to the heart that had twisted into rage when she married him two years later. JT wanted to hold on to that anger, but time had dulled the blade, and he caught a glimpse of the girl he'd once loved.

He couldn't remember the events that led to their break-up, only that time and distance played a part. Their future had been collateral damage to his freedom. He needed out of this small town—to be something other than a farmer. When his football career was cut short, he found another way not to return—the Army.

They talked about old times and old friends, sharing stories and memories one or the other had forgotten. History was a strong aphrodisiac, and he sensed her interest, but he wouldn't start something he couldn't finish. And he had no idea how long he planned on staying.

JT woke with a start, throwing his legs off the side of the bed, and scanned for signs of trouble, only to find his phone vibrating from an incoming call. He grabbed it. The time, 1:15 AM, illuminated the screen. He recognized the number, and curiosity got the best of him. He brought it to his ear and heard a female voice and the jingling of keys. *A pocket call.* Normally he would've hung up, but he didn't. Instead, he laid back and listened.

The sound of a door opening. Some rustling of clothes. Running water, the squeak of a bed. A female groan that went straight to his dick. *Damn.* She couldn't be, could she? He adjusted himself as he listened to her solo performance.

She must have noticed her phone, for a string of invectives preceded her sultry voice. "Hello?"

Voyeuristic guilt almost made him hang up. *Almost*. After a brief pause, he said, "Little late for a booty call, Josie." He could have sworn he heard her smile.

"It's a good thing I'm feeling happy, Mr. Taylor, or I'd be mortified."

Not wanting to let her go, he said, "Must have been a hell of a crowd tonight."

She sighed. "Can't overcome what you don't face."

He didn't know if it was the hour, her voice, or her being a relative stranger that made him say, "Facing your demons is easy. Not letting them control you is what's hard."

"A hero *and* a philosopher."

JT lost his smile. "Goodnight, Miss Singer."

"Wait! Please. Come to the ball. Samantha Powell is attending, and she specifically asked if you would be there." She paused, her voice suddenly sounding sober. "They were under your command, Mr. Taylor—Jackson. Don't you think you owe it to them?"

She'd hit her mark, and it stung. He *did* owe it to them. "Send me the information. I'll be there."

He hung up before she could finish thanking him.

13

I generally avoid temptation unless I can't resist it.

- Mae West

Drew and Jo rushed into The New Market Street Hotel the afternoon of the ball.

"I don't know why you insisted on bringing the tux. The shop would've delivered it to his room," Jo said, pushing the baggage trolley into the elevator. "We're already behind schedule."

Drew hit the button for the twelfth floor. "And miss the opportunity to see that fine man in his tighty whities? I don't think so. You go on ahead."

For some reason, the thought irked her. "Don't do anything to make Jackson Taylor change his mind. I barely got him to attend."

He gave her a side-eye. "How'd you do it, anyway? You never said."

Telling Drew she butt-dialed Jackson while putting on an enthusiastic performance with BOB—her battery-operated boyfriend—was about as likely as her telling him she was a cyber stalker. So, not very.

"I appealed to his sense of honor." She poked him in the chest. "So, no flirting."

Drew feigned offense. "Jo, I'm a professional. But if he finds me irresistible..." He smiled coyly.

Jo threw up her hands.

"You know I love a challenge. The brass ring, Jobo. The unattainable. The unicorn. He's out there, and one day I'll find him."

"Fine, go after your pot of gold, but if Sergeant Powell picks a dress you don't like, I won't be held responsible."

The elevator dinged, and she got out, pulling the trolley behind her.

She found the medic's room and knocked.

A fresh-faced girl answered the door.

Jo held out her hand. "Sergeant Powell? I'm Josette—"

The girl grabbed the outstretched arm and pulled her inside. Jo reached behind and snagged the cart.

"I'm so glad to meet you. I'm Samantha. Well, of course you know that. I'm just so excited to be here, and to meet Drew Johnson!" She took a breath and peeked behind Jo. "Oh, I thought he would be here with you. He is coming, right?"

Okay, then. Jo smiled kindly—at least she hoped it appeared that way. "He went to deliver Mr. Taylor's tux. He should be here any minute." She whipped out her phone and texted Drew. *Get your ass to room 1213 pronto.* "In the meantime, why don't we look at what he's selected for you and try some on?"

The light in her eyes faded. "Oh, okay. Sure. I guess."

Jo knew it wasn't personal, but *yeesh*. "I do have a degree in fashion, Samantha. Can I call you Samantha?" When she nodded, Jo continued. "And I run a popular blog and YouTube channel, *The Prophetic Aesthetic*. Have you heard of it?" Sam shook her head. "Well, it's all about being fashion-forward—"

Samantha waved it away. "I'm sure it's great, but I don't pay attention to trends. I just need to look good tonight. I've seen Drew on the Diane Frank show, where he takes normal women and makes them look beautiful. I need him to do that to me."

Jo wondered if Samantha's need to look good had anything to do with Jackson Taylor.

"Yes, well, Drew *is* the best." Jo looked around, wondering if she was being pranked. Could this be the same girl who suffered at the hands of the Taliban? Although, Jo supposed if anyone needed to forget the past, it would be Samantha Powell.

Sam misinterpreted Jo's expression. "I'm sorry, I'm sure you're good, too."

Jo laughed. "Look, you were promised Drew Johnson, and you got me, so I take no offense." She spotted the welcome basket. "Why don't we open some champagne and have a peek at a few dresses while we wait? Maybe we can narrow it down."

Drew had better work his magic quickly. They were on a tight schedule. A local station had an exclusive interview with the two soldiers before the ball, followed by the reception and cocktail hour with photographers and media from around the country. The foundation had snagged the first public appearance by both surviving soldiers for this charity event—thanks to Jo's persistence. Knowing what made people tick, what motivated them, was her specialty. For Samantha, being styled by Drew. For Jackson, his sense of duty and honor.

Jo relaxed into the cushions and examined the medic. The picture and stats Samantha had given them didn't do her justice. For one, her hair—although short—was the most brilliant shade of copper Jo had ever seen. Like a shiny new penny. She had a smattering of freckles on flawless skin, a smallish nose, and light brown eyes framed by almost invisible lashes and brows. Without makeup, she was the girl next door, but in a couple of hours, she would be a goddess.

Jo crashed into something, a table perhaps. She wasn't sure. All she knew was she couldn't get *in* or *out* of her dress. The zipper had gotten tangled in her hair, and the more she flailed about, the worse it became. *Okay, calm down. Drew should be back soon.* She breathed deeply and relaxed as much as she could—considering she had a sequined mesh gown stuck to her head. *How do I get myself into these predicaments?*

Since they were running behind, she'd dressed in Samantha's room. It seemed like the best solution since her clothes were still on the baggage cart and hair and makeup hadn't yet left. The gown, however, turned out to be an unfortunate choice.

She heard the door open and began her blind man's walk into the front room.

"Thank God you're back! Get this off me!" She turned around to where she hoped Drew could see the issue. "The zipper's stuck in my hair—and before you say it—I know I don't deserve it."

She waited. "Drew?"

JT tapped on the door as it rested against the jam and pushed it open.

A set of impossibly long legs in stilettos walked towards him, striking him speechless. The woman was talking, but he couldn't make out the words since fabric encircled her entire head. He was about to tell her so when she turned, displaying her backside. He stifled a groan when his eyes landed on the bit of red lace caught between her perfect ass cheeks. Never again would he question why women wore them. He adjusted the semi in his pants and tried to get command of his senses. One thing was for sure—this woman was not Powell.

She called out a name, and he suddenly recognized the voice. *I'll be damned.*

He moved forward until he was inches away from her. "Here, let me help." When she didn't speak or pull away, he slid his hands slowly up her back. Her skin was smooth as silk and smelled of some exotic place he hoped one day to visit.

He found a mass of soft dark curls and ran his hand down the length until he located where the dress had gotten caught. He tried to be gentle, taking his time removing the entanglement.

When she relaxed into his body, he stepped a little closer. Sweeping her hair over one shoulder, he caressed her neck with the back of his hand, his fingers gliding over her soft skin before retreating. He heard a hitch in her breath as she responded to his touch, making him think of their last phone call. He coughed, trying to stifle a groan.

When he could no longer hide the fact he'd freed the zipper, he stepped back. "That should do it."

Josie raised her arms and pulled the dress over her head before turning towards him. When she did, the first thing that struck him was her beauty. It was the kind of face that held your interest. Nothing about it was perfect, yet it all made sense together. Her eyes were large and pale green with specks of gold. They sat too far apart on either side of her aquiline nose, which had a slight bump along the ridge. She had high cheekbones and her mouth. *Good lord.*

It widened into a seductive smile. "Hi," she exhaled.

"Hey," he greeted. Neither of them said anything for a moment, each taking the other in. She had used her dress to cover her breasts, but he saw enough to make him want to readjust a second time.

She let out a small laugh. "Thanks for helping a girl out."

Her voice sounded like sex. "My pleasure."

Her smile widened. "You're Jackson Taylor."

"Yes, ma'am."

"I believe we're past formalities, don't you? Call me Jo." She held out her hand, and he took it between his two larger ones.

"Nice to meet you, Jo."

They stood smiling at each other until she broke the spell.

"If you're looking for Samantha, she already left."

"Appears so," he teased, wishing he had something witty to say.

She glanced around, biting her top lip. "I'd offer you a drink, but I'm running behind and…" She made a sweeping gesture with one arm. "Well, I'm naked."

JT laughed. He had the urge to pick her up and carry her into the bedroom. It would be a hell of a lot more enjoyable than what was waiting for him downstairs. But of course, he didn't.

"I'll leave you to it, then." He headed to the door, turning for one last glimpse of her bare backside as she walked away, her dress draped over one arm.

JT added loud laughter and small talk to his ever-growing list of dislikes. After the interview, he and Powell had to endure an endless round of introductions and photos. He didn't much care for the role of circus monkey. It made him want to jump out of his skin.

"Mr. Taylor!" A middle-aged woman bellowed and quickly approached.

He searched for an escape but found none.

She held out her hand ten feet before reaching his side. "Gail Rogers, producer of *HomeTown Heroes*. So glad to finally meet you!" She gave him a brisk shake and smiled with large, unnaturally white teeth. "You're a hard man to get a hold of."

"Not that hard, it seems." He smiled politely, hoping she would say what she needed and leave.

"I'll cut to the chase. *HomeTown Heroes* has no equal—in opportunity or exposure—we take the utmost care to tell our heroes' stories while helping them achieve their dreams. Our last hero—"

"Ma'am, I don't mean to cut you off, but I'm not interested."

The exuberant smile faltered, then reappeared. "Have you seen our show, Mr. Taylor?"

"I'm afraid I haven't had the pleasure."

"Being one of our heroes is like winning the lottery. We change lives, help communities. Think about what we can do for you and your family. Let us honor and reward your service to our country." Like a magician, she pulled a card from places unknown and handed it to him.

"I'd love the opportunity to get to know you. This is my direct number." She placed a hand on his forearm and gave it a gentle squeeze before walking off as energetically as she'd come, with one arm raised in a wave as she retreated.

"There you are!" Powell appeared by his side. "Who was that?"

"No one." He pasted on a smile. "You look happy. Having a good time?"

"I am! Aren't you?"

No. No, I am not. "I've had worse."

"Well, I'm a little star-struck, to be honest. I had my picture taken with Audra Helms! She's even more beautiful in person."

"I'm sure you outshined her." He wasn't blowing smoke. Powell looked real pretty tonight.

"Thank you." She blushed. "Drew and Jo are miracle workers."

JT had mixed feelings when it came to those two. They both made him feel uncomfortable, but for very different reasons. "They're something, all right."

Powell linked her arm in his. "Everyone's clearing out. Why don't we head into the ballroom?"

They passed a long hall where she stopped. "I'm going to powder my nose; you go on ahead."

JT entered the lavishly decorated room where a runway separated two sides. He located their table near the front and picked up the catalog on his seat. He flipped through page after page of items up for auction. The suggested bid prices made him laugh. *Rich people.* He threw it on the table and ventured off to find the bar.

14

There comes a time in every woman's life when the only thing that helps is a glass of champagne.

- Bette Davis

Jo found Drew in the large open room where the queens and their designers were making last-minute adjustments before the runway show.

"Where have you been?" he asked. "I need you to do a better job attaching my headpiece. It keeps going sideways! It's way too heavy. I've already got a crick in my neck."

"I warned you. Did you use the double-sided tape?" The gold lamé turban was no match for the enormous array of fruit, which included a life-size pineapple—all bedazzled with a shocking amount of glitz.

"Of course I did. Maybe we should glue it?"

"You'll regret that. I can add some type of strap to tie underneath."

"And ruin the silhouette? No, thank you. We'll just have to make it work." Drew gave her the once over. "What happened to you?"

"Thought you'd never ask." She went to work on the headpiece, shifting the bananas to the left. "I had a dress mishap."

"Looks like it ran into your hair."

"The zipper got caught in it." She did a shimmy, drawing her hands down the formfitting dress. "As you can see, there's not a lot of wiggle room." She picked up some wire. "Anyway, you'd disappeared, and as I tried to free myself, I heard the door open. I stumbled into the living room—thinking it was you—and a pair of very capable hands helped me out." She raised one brow. "Any guess who?"

"Just tell me, bitch!"

"Jackson Taylor."

Drew's hand flew to his mouth. "You lucky little hunty! Did he see your goods?"

"Considering I was wearing my dress as a headscarf, yeah, he got an eyeful. He came up behind me and placed his hands on my hips. I was pretty sure it was him at that point, but I said nothing—I was kinda turned on, to be honest—he then slid his hands up my back to my shoulders, and when he wrapped one around my hair, I thought, if he pulls it, I'm gonna have a mini orgasm." The memory sent a shiver through her.

"Shut the fuck up."

"I think there's something wrong with me. My body has a mind of its own. I actually leaned into him, and I gotta say, he wasn't unaffected by the contact either." She remembered his attempt at hiding his reaction and smiled.

"He popped a chub?"

"He did indeed. Unfortunately, he got my zipper unstuck and stepped away. But you want to know the craziest part? I didn't want him to see me struggle to get the skin tight dress back on, so I pulled it over my head and held it to my chest."

"Jo, I both hate and love you at this moment. I'll be casting myself in that little fantasy tonight—playing you, of course."

"Can't say I blame you. Might be on my rotation as well." There was no *might* about it. A pang of guilt hit her—she should be fantasizing about Masi.

Drew cocked a brow as if reading her mind. "So, the good doctor isn't enough for you?"

Jo changed the subject. "Did you see the strapless Valentino up for auction?"

"The red silk one? I did and it's divine. It'll set you back at least ten large."

She shrugged. It was the perfect color and size, and she had every intention of bidding on it. "What about you? See anything you like?"

"Why buy when I can borrow?"

"Because it's for charity?"

"Hmm, I suppose I could bid on that yellow Alexander McQueen scarf. I do love a pop of color."

Jo finished securing the headpiece with some more pins and a prayer. "That should do it. What do you think?"

Drew stood and turned toward the mirror. "Josette Singer, I take back every nasty thing I ever said about you as a designer. I am magnificent!"

Vivien Leigh sailed past in an over-the-top *Gone with the Wind* costume, which took the curtain creation to a whole new level.

"You are, but Scarlett might have you by a hair. Did you see that green velvet? And the silk cording with tassels could have come from the halls of Versailles," Jo said in awe. "She's a definite contender. Do you recognize her?"

Drew glanced away from his reflection. "I'm a gender bender, Jobo, not a regular queen. We don't all know each other."

A queen dressed as Marilyn slowed and gave Drew the once over. "Aren't you a little extra? But let's see how you turn it on the runway." She threw her feather boa over her shoulder and walked on.

"Nice shade."

"We're all catty bitches, Jo. It's part of our charm."

Jo grabbed her clutch. "Well, my work here is done. I'll see you on the runway. I'm going to find Masi and get a drink."

Drew continued to vamp before the mirror. "Sashay away, darling."

Jo spotted Masi talking to an attractive woman as she entered the reception area. When he noticed her, he smiled and held out his hand. She went to stand by his side.

"Claudia, this is Josette Singer. Jo, this is Dr. Claudia Vanheusen."

It hadn't escaped Jo's notice that Masi hadn't called her his girlfriend. "Pleasure to meet you." Jo extended her hand, squeezing the woman's hand harder than necessary when she realized who she was.

"Likewise," Claudia said, unsmiling.

Jo turned to Masi, trying to regain her composure. "I have to get back soon. Want to grab a drink? I could show you to our table." She slid closer, hoping for a show of solidarity.

Masi grimaced. "I, or rather, the hospital, bought two tables. I thought it might be best if I sat with my colleagues."

Claudia smirked.

"Oh, I see. Well, at least we have time for a drink," she said, trying to hide her disappointment.

A barrel-chested man in his fifties walked toward them, his tuxedo jacket straining against the lone button tasked with keeping it together. "There you are, Dr. Honig!" He nodded toward Claudia. "Dr. Vanheusen." He smiled at Jo. "And who might this lovely lady be?" His voice matched his stature, and his eyes held a glint of warmth.

She held out her hand. "Josette Singer."

"Ah, yes. Your family name precedes you. I'm Dr. Barry Warner."

"It's a pleasure to meet you, Dr. Warner."

"Please, call me Barry. Would you mind if I take Masayori away for a moment? Hospital business, I'm afraid."

Like pushing a pull door, sometimes you just had to let go. "Of course."

Masi leaned in and gave her a kiss. "Right. I'll see you later, then?"

She nodded, and the two men walked off, already deep in conversation.

"It won't last, you know," Claudia said.

Here we go. Jo sighed.

"You seem so sure of yourself." The woman's smile didn't reach her eyes. "You're a beauty, no doubt. But he'll come back to me. He always does." She paused and gave a slight shrug. "He occasionally gets restless, and I let him scratch his itch. But make no mistake, you're nothing but a temporary distraction."

Jo grabbed a glass of champagne from a passing server and took a sip before replying. "And here I thought all the drama queens were in the back. Enjoy the show."

She walked off, hoping to appear less affected than she felt.

JT found the cocktail area outside the ballroom and ordered a shot of bourbon and a beer. It was a sad excuse for a bar, just some makeshift roll cart stuck in the corner of a massive marble room lacking any kind of warmth. He knocked back the whiskey and grabbed the long neck, thinking he should get back when he spotted Josie walking straight towards him. Well, maybe not toward him so much as the bar.

He'd like to say he noticed her face first, but that would be a lie. The scrap of fabric that had been around her head now clung to every curve of her body. He wondered what kind of material could be so insignificant and yet sparkle so damn much. She looked like nothing he had ever seen.

She walked right up to the bar and ordered a vodka martini, neat. The spark he'd found so attractive earlier had disappeared, replaced by, well, he didn't quite know. She stood a few feet away, her focus never wavering from her glass. He wished he could look away, but something about her held him captive. Maybe the dichotomy, the drastic change in her demeanor from earlier. When the person between them left, he decided to find out. "Evening, Josie."

She took a sip of her drink before turning, a half-smile on her lips. "Ah, Mr. Taylor. I hope you're enjoying your evening?"

JT closed the gap. "Well, I could say the polite thing, but I was taught never to lie."

She raised an eyebrow and leaned against the bar, studying him. "That's a refreshing answer. Not much of a city person, then?"

"Not much into pretense would be more accurate."

She barked out a laugh. "You're quick to judge. I'm not sure if you meant that as a personal insult or a general one. I assume you don't have an issue with charitable causes?"

JT took a swig of his beer, trying to figure out why he wanted to provoke instead of flirt with her. "No, ma'am. Just don't think spending a lot of money on lavish parties makes much sense when the goal is to raise money."

She set her glass down and squeezed the edge of the bar. "I doubt you have the slightest notion of what's involved in fundraising for a charity, or what it takes to get people to *show up*, let alone donate to causes in desperate need."

JT leaned into her. "What I see, Josie, is a lot of rich folks using a party as an excuse to spend ridiculous amounts of cash on stuff they don't need so they can say it's for charity and write it off on their taxes."

Jo finished her martini and stepped away from the bar. "Tell that to the underprivileged kids who benefit or the cancer research we fund. Better yet, *JT*, tell that to Sergeant DePaul's widow, whose child will receive a full ride to college."

JT watched her retreating form and smiled. His mother would've called that an ol' fashioned set down. He didn't know what brought about the change in her, but he enjoyed sparring almost as much as he enjoyed flirting with her.

He made his way back to the table where Powell was talking to a vivacious redhead, whose laughter sliced through him like a rusty blade. Seated to her left was a distinguished-looking older couple. As he approached, the man stood.

"You must be Jackson Taylor." He held out his hand. "I'm Gil Singer, and this is my wife, Élaine. We're honored you could join us this evening."

He shook their hands. "Pleasure's all mine, sir."

"Thank you for your service, Mr. Taylor. We hope your stay in Philadelphia has been an enjoyable one?" the woman said with a French accent.

He smiled, thinking about his answer to Josie's very similar question. "Yes, ma'am. Thank you for asking."

Powell snagged his attention. "Holly was just telling me about the runway show. Apparently, it's all drag queens!"

The woman to Powell's left leaned forward and stuck out a hand. "Holly Rabinowitz. Welcome home, Mr. Taylor."

"Thank you. Please, call me JT."

JT sat and politely answered questions but didn't add to the conversation. He preferred listening, especially to Holly, who held his interest with her animated storytelling.

About a half-hour later, he heard Josie's voice. "Show's about to start!"

A genuine smile lit up her face as she slipped into the seat next to her mother. Turning her attention to JT and Powell, she said, "Sorry to have been gone so long, but I had to help the designers and models backstage. The show's a little unconventional this year, but it should be a lot of fun."

Élaine placed her hand on her daughter's arm. *"C'est vrai. Où est Masi?"*

Josie picked up her wine glass, her smile faltering. "He's sitting with his colleagues."

JT absently wondered if this Massy guy was her boyfriend.

The lights dimmed, and the show began. Since men dressed as women held little appeal, JT mumbled an excuse and slipped back out to the lounge. He took a side trip to the bathroom, called home, checked his email, and grabbed a beer. By the time he returned, the show was over. *Perfect timing.*

"You missed the whole thing!" Powell exclaimed as he took a seat.

"My apologies, Powell. Not really my thing."

"Well, I thought it was spectacular! Jo went backstage to help Drew 'untuck,' whatever that means."

JT choked on his beer.

"Not literally, of course. She's helping him out of his costume," Holly said.

He grinned. "I'm almost sorry I missed it."

Powell leaned in. "The costumes were outrageous, and I swear you couldn't tell most of them were men. Did you know Jo designed Drew's costume? It didn't win, unfortunately. Cleopatra did—which *was* beautiful—but Drew looked the most like a woman. He could definitely pass as one. Don't you think, Holly?" Powell said, taking a breath.

"Oh, yes, and he often does—dress as a woman, that is—just not in a drag sort of way. It's his way of not conforming to gender roles. You know, non-binary."

JT wasn't sure if he did, but Powell nodded as if she understood, so he didn't ask.

Both Drew and Josie arrived shortly before dinner. He watched as Drew helped her slide into her seat. She appeared to be very *happy*. And although everyone around pretended not to notice, he sensed they were on high alert.

"You both did an excellent job tonight," Gil said.

Josie nodded, looking down at her phone.

Drew spoke up. "Yes, we did. But you can't compete with a Makovsky creation. The woman's a genius." He pulled Jo's phone away and placed it face down. "What do you think, Jobo?"

"We couldn't have won, anyway; it was just for fun." She waved her hand dismissively and poured a glass of wine from the bottle on the table.

"Because they're here on behalf of the foundation," Gil said, addressing both JT and Powell.

"I thought your dress was gorgeous. Way more colorful than Cleopatra's."

Drew nodded at Powell's assessment. "And my headpiece was an absolute work of art." He side-eyed Jo, who appeared to be looking at someone in the distance. "I gave you a compliment, bitch."

Jo turned her head without disengaging her eyes. "What? Oh, yes. Cleopatra was stunning. Makovsky's the best."

Drew peered past her. "Holly, honey?"

"The chicken's left the coop," she responded.

"Let's hope it doesn't shit all over the barn," Drew said with an eye roll.

JT watched with fascination as they discussed Josie as if she wasn't there, which made him a tad uncomfortable.

The tension eventually lifted, and conversation flowed nicely during supper, which JT wished covered more of his plate. He noticed Gil talking to a server who tried to add a second bottle of wine to the table.

"Josette, eat something, *s'il te plaît.*" Élaine encouraged her daughter.

She glanced at her plate. "The meat is touching the vegetables."

JT didn't see the problem.

A short while later, the showcased items were brought on stage and the bidding began. The third item was a red dress, and Josie raised her paddle.

"Five thousand! Do I hear fifty-five hundred?" the auctioneer called out.

Time and again, Jo held up her paddle. It was down to her and another woman who sat at the table Jo had been watching. The bid was up to twelve thousand.

"*Arrête ça, Josette! Tout de suite!*"

JT knew enough French to know Élaine wanted her daughter to stop bidding.

"Non! Elle ne peut pas l'avoir, Maman!"
She can't have it.

JT had a feeling this was about more than just a dress.

Drew grabbed Jo's arm and yanked down. She tried to pull free, but he held firm. Their eyes locked in a private battle until Jo dropped the paddle and turned away.

"Sold! For twelve thousand dollars!" The gavel landed, and there was soft applause before the auctioneer brought forward the next item for bid.

"I hate you right now," Jo said.

Drew appeared nonplussed. "Yes, well. Rinse and repeat, honey."

JT drained the last of his beer and stood. As entertaining as this was, he wanted the night to be over. He had his own issues to deal with. "Powell, you wanna get a drink?"

She was up in a flash. "Sure."

Josie swung around and raised an eyebrow at Sam. "Powell? He calls you Powell?"

"Jobo," Drew warned.

Jo leaned toward Drew. "We turned her from a pretty penny into a copper goddess and he didn't even notice," she whispered loudly.

She reached out and grabbed Powell's hand. "You are a copper goddess!" She turned her focus on JT. "And you..." Her demeanor changed from scolding to sultry as her gaze roamed over his body. "...are a golden god."

The corner of JT's mouth lifted in amusement.

Drew snapped his fingers in front of her face. "Jobo, focus."

She glanced at Drew and then back to JT. "Right." She slapped the table. "You two,"—she crossed and uncrossed her arms, motioning to both him and Powell—, "are like Tarzan and GI Jane." Her eyes locked on him. "And it's obvious she wants you. So, you know, sure thing." Her arms deflated, and she turned to Drew. "I'm gonna regret this later, aren't I?"

"Yes, pussycat, you will."

JT ran a hand down his face. He didn't know whether to feel sorry for her, or for Powell, whose face had turned beet red.

Gil and Élaine stood. "Josette, why don't you help us get ready for the endowment portion of the night, hmm?" Gil held out his hand for his daughter while Élaine pursed her lips.

Holly lifted her paddle to fan herself, leaning closer to Powell. "Hell of a night, right?"

"Sold! For twenty-two hundred dollars!" The auctioneer said, pointing his gavel at Holly.

She dropped the fan. "Oh, for fuck's sake! What'd I buy?"

JT followed Powell to the bar and ordered their drinks. He knew he ought to say something. He just didn't know what. Luckily, she broke the ice.

"I should be mad at Jo for embarrassing me, but I'm not. If she didn't say anything, I'm not sure I would have." She took a healthy sip of wine.

"Powell—" he began.

She lifted a hand. "Call me Samantha, or Sam. Anything but Powell. I'm not a soldier anymore."

He took a swig of beer and cleared his throat. He made a quick mental calculation and realized he couldn't cross that line. "Sam, I think the world of you, you know that. But what we shared, what you went through…"

Her face hardened. "I'm not some weak woman, JT."

He was making a mess of things. "No, you're not. You're a very strong, attractive woman, but I'm not the right person for you."

She nodded and glanced away. "My therapist thinks I'm hung up on you because of what we went through together, because you saved me. I don't know, maybe he's right."

"I'm sure he is." JT put an arm around her. "If you ever need anything, anything at all—" he began.

"You'll do what? Fly out to Arizona and *not* sleep with me?" She scoffed. "I think I've made a big enough fool out of myself already."

"You haven't—"

"Let's get back. We don't want to miss the reason you're here in the first place.

The endowment ceremony marked the end of the evening, and JT accepted the fake check without incident. He stood for a few more pictures and introductions, then walked off the stage where Powell—*Sam*—was waiting for him.

"I thought what you said about DePaul was really nice, JT."

He hadn't planned on saying anything, but it seemed wrong not to. "He was a good soldier. Someone's son, soon-to-be a father. He deserved recognition."

She put her arm around his waist and gave him a side hug. "You're a good man."

"Didn't do anything special, Sam. Want me to walk you up?"

"Sure. My feet are killing me."

They walked out of the ballroom and into a shit storm.

15

When you see someone putting on their Big Boots,
you can be pretty sure an Adventure is going to happen.
- Winnie the Pooh

Masi hadn't replied to any of her texts, so Jo went in search of him as soon as she escaped her parents' clutches.

She checked the ballroom first, then the reception area. Next, she headed to the lobby where she caught sight of Masi's ex—*the dress stealing bitch*. Her legs had a mind of their own as they propelled her forward.

"You could never carry off that dress."

Claudia turned and raised a brow. "Is that so?"

"You just want what's mine."

"I *have* what's yours."

Jo gasped and moved toward her.

She felt hands grab her from behind as Drew swung her around. "Josette, darling. There you are." He smiled at the people watching the exchange—one of them a reporter. "Why don't we go see what's keeping Holly, hmm?"

"I was having a conversation!"

He tilted his head. "Were you, though?"

"Yes, Drew, I was. Now, if you would just let me…" She looked over her shoulder at Claudia, who was now talking with someone else. "Dammit, Drew! She got the last word."

"Let's hope so."

They spotted Holly a couple yards away, examining an article of clothing.

"Look what I got for my twenty-two hundred bucks." She held up a black leather mini dress with various openings crisscrossed with leather straps. "It's a size 2. I believe I saw something similar at the BDSM store off Samson Street."

"I know that store." Drew grabbed the hanger and examined the label. "I'll give you two for it."

"Two thousand?" Holly asked hopefully.

"Two hundred."

"Just take it. You can buy me drinks at Dirty Gertie's on Thursday." She grabbed Jo's arm. "Come on, I've gotta drain the line."

"What a pleasant euphemism. I'll wait here." Drew waved them away.

They walked into the bathroom where Jo checked each stall before choosing the handicapped one.

"You always do that," Holly said from the one beside it.

"Do what?"

"Check every available stall and then pick the handicapped one."

"Because it's usually the cleanest, with the most TP, and a disposable seat cover. A bonus if there's a baby changing table to put my purse on. Those are the best."

"Do you park in handicapped spots too?"

"What? No! That would be illegal."

They stopped talking when they heard voices from the front anteroom.

"I wonder why she stopped bidding?" a nameless voice asked.

"Who knows? Maybe her parents still hold the purse strings. They *are* Jewish, after all." Claudia chuckled. "Either way, I got a rise out of her, so it was worth it."

Anger and humiliation rose like a dormant volcano inside Jo.

"Do you think Masi is serious about her?" the unknown woman asked.

"I wondered until I saw her tonight. She's a little too..."
"Bold?"
"Déclassé would be a better word for it." Claudia's voice dripped with condescension. "Did you see her searching Masi out every chance she got? He doesn't like Velcro women, and she's *drunk*. He's been avoiding her like the plague."

Jo had enough. She reached for the TP, hearing the door next to her open.

"You might want to check the stalls next time," Holly said to the women.

"Excuse me?" Claudia said.

"My advice? Walk away now."

Jo swallowed the rising bile in her throat and stepped out. She wouldn't let them shame her. She entered the vanity area and washed her hands. "I hope you choke on your jealousy, knowing I'll be the one in Masi's bed tonight."

Claudia laughed, nonplussed. "Don't be too sure."

Amid protest, Holly pushed the two women out the door, blocking Jo's attempt to follow. "Let me through, Holly. I won't let her get the last word again!"

"Jo, let it go. She's baiting you."

Jo stepped back and closed her eyes. She took a deep breath, feigning calmness. "You're right." Another deep breath and a fake smile. "I'm fine, really."

Holly lowered her raised hands. "You sure?"

"Absolutely."

Holly regarded her skeptically but opened the door. Within seconds, Jo had pushed her way past and bee-lined toward the coat check where Claudia stood waiting.

"Oh, boy," Holly said, before calling out for Drew.

Jo confronted Claudia, who handed the attendant her ticket. "Masi doesn't want you, yet you wait around like a bitch in heat."

Drew rushed to her side. "Jobo," he said in warning as he scanned the room.

Claudia took her coat, put money in the tip jar, and turned to Jo with blatant disregard. "At least my pedigree is impeccable."

Jo's eyes narrowed. "You racist cunt."

Drew grabbed hold of Jo's arm as she entered the woman's personal space.

"And *you*," Claudia spoke through clenched teeth, her lips curled in an unnatural smile, "are nothing but a drunk, foul-mouthed *Jew*."

Drew's grip loosened at hearing the insult, and Jo pulled free. Her arm whipped forward, landing a solid crack to Claudia's nose.

"What did you just call me?" Jo shouted before she realized what she'd done.

Blood erupted from Claudia's nose, her wails of pain echoing in the cavernous space as Drew and Holly pulled Jo toward the elevators.

Samantha and Jackson waited by the doors as a small crowd gathered, some with phones pointed their way.

"Fuck, fuck, fuck!" Drew said under his breath as he jabbed at the elevator buttons. When the doors opened, he shoved her inside and turned to Holly. "Take her phone and make sure she stays in her room. I'll try to defuse the situation."

A stunned Holly entered the elevator, along with the two soldiers.

Jackson blocked the entry as a man tried to push his way in. "Back up buddy, before I back you up." The man stepped aside, and the doors closed. He turned to Jo. "What floor?"

Still in disbelief, Jo gazed up at him. "Did you hear what she called me?"

"Jo, honey. What floor are you on? Do you have a key?" Holly said, rooting through the clutch Drew had thrown her way. "The key doesn't have a number on it. Jo, what floor are you on?"

Jo wondered why everyone was making such a big deal out of finding her room. "Twelve. No wait, that's not right. I don't remember, never made it there. I got ready in Sam's room." She didn't feel very well.

"Just go to mine. Tenth floor." Holly leaned against the railing. "This is bad, Jo."

"How could Masi have gone out with that antisemitic bitch?"

"Are you serious right now?" Holly threw up her hands. "That *bitch* could sue you! There were witnesses. Cameras. Reporters. You'll be all over the news. It will go national. Jesus, Jo."

"I didn't hit her on purpose," she said, imitating a bobblehead.

"Only because Drew held you back! One way or another, she was going down, and you know it. We just have to hope it looked like an accident and someone besides us heard what she said. I barely heard it, and I was standing right next to you!"

The soldiers stood with their hands behind their backs, legs slightly spread, blocking the doors. They were calm but alert. Sam stepped forward. "I'll say I heard it."

Jo smiled down at her. "My little copper goddess, coming to my rescue." She tried to reach out, but her arms were too heavy. She blinked a few times to clear the spots in front of her eyes. "I feel a little funny..."

"Jo? Jo!" Sam's voice was the last thing she heard before everything went black.

JT had fantasized about holding Josie in his arms a few hours ago—before she got drunk, smacked a woman in the face, and passed out—but this wasn't what he had in mind.

Holly hurried down the hall, searching for her room key. "I know it's in here somewhere." She dropped Jo's purse and rummaged through her own. "Got it!" She opened the door and the four of them entered. JT placed Josie on the bed and moved out of the way so Sam could have a look. He didn't understand what the fuss was about.

"Take a pillow and elevate her feet," Sam ordered.

He pulled off Jo's heels, grabbed a pillow, and elevated them. "She's drunk is all. She'll be fine in the morning."

Sam gave him a cursory glance. "Who's the medic here? She didn't pass out from too much alcohol." Without looking up, she asked Holly, "Has this happened before?"

Holly paced back and forth, tapping furiously on her phone. "You mean faint? No. She wasn't even that drunk. *Comparatively speaking.*"

JT scrubbed at his face. "Faint, pass out. What's the difference?"

Sam pinched the skin on Jo's wrist. "I think she's dehydrated. Did anyone see her drink anything besides alcohol tonight?"

Holly checked her phone again. "No, and she didn't eat much either."

"Drop in blood sugar, dehydration, stress. Any of those can cause a person to faint, but most wake within thirty seconds. She's still out. It might have been a seizure. We need to call an ambulance."

After the EMTs pumped Jo full of fluids, she regained consciousness. They assured everyone she was out of danger but needed to go to the hospital for an evaluation.

To avoid the press, Drew had arranged for them to go through the underground parking and service elevators. After Holly and Jo left in the ambulance, JT and Sam headed to a local bar.

Sam downed half her drink as soon as it arrived. "That was the most excitement I've had since being home."

"You did great, Sam." JT knocked back his bourbon.

"I've missed it. The rush you get in a life-or-death situation." They sat in companionable silence until Sam spoke again. "Do you ever feel judged, JT?"

He regarded her. "What do you mean?"

"By civilians. Your family, friends." She shrugged. "People expect me to be sad or angry. *Depressed*. To...oh, I don't know, to be stuck in that hell." She polished off the wine and signaled for another. "They think I'm in denial, that I can't be happy after what I've been through. They just don't understand."

JT wasn't sure he understood either, but he'd be damned if he told her that. "I think everyone has their own way of dealing."

She leaned an elbow on the bar. "I'm happy because I survived. I'm grateful for the chance to be a better person. We watched our friends die, JT, and we *lived*. We owe it to them to make every day count, so we can look at ourselves in the mirror and know we're worthy of this gift."

He swallowed the lump in his throat. He wasn't worthy. People died because of his decisions, and being called a hero made it unbearable. "But what if I'm not, Sam? How do I live with that?"

She shook her head. "You need to stop blaming yourself for crashing that bird."

"I got too close; I should have maneuvered—"

She lifted a hand. "Stop. Just stop. I don't want to hear you second guess your decision. You took a chance, and it didn't pay off. But there were no good options once they got a bead on us. We were going down regardless." She softened her tone. "JT, you didn't just save DePaul and me that day, you held the line while others were rescued, and what happened to DePaul..." She took a deep breath and released it before continuing. "Well, you can't be blamed for that."

Sam swiped at her eyes, then straightened. "I'm alive today because you figured out a way to get us rescued. *You* did that, and you need to give that as much importance as your guilt."

JT nodded, even though he knew he wouldn't be able to. Crashing that helicopter was like burning down a building and rescuing only one person inside. That made him the opposite of a hero.

They said their goodbyes in the wee hours of the morning, and JT managed a few hours of shut-eye before heading to the airport.

As he leaned back in his first-class seat, he wondered how Josie was feeling. She had reached out and covered his hand with hers as he walked beside the stretcher and said, 'Seems I wasn't able to control my happiness very well, was I?'

He'd only had time to give her hand a quick squeeze before they lifted her into the ambulance. He should've told her not to waste time on a guy that didn't recognize her worth. Truth was, he envied the man for inciting such passion in her. Jo's rawness and honesty fascinated him and made him want to peel away the layers and find out where her demons hid. He had a crazy notion he might be willing to reveal some of his own as well. He'd like that—to find a kindred spirit, to unburden his soul.

Closing his eyes, he switched gears and drifted off to the memory of her walking away from him with nothing but a slip of red between her cheeks.

16

Things are never so bad that they can't get worse.
- Humphrey Bogart

Jo stretched like a cat in the noonday sun and opened her eyes. Light streamed through the window and bounced off the white walls surrounding her. An avocado-colored chair sat in the corner, and an IV drip hung from her arm. *Ah, that's why I feel so good!*

Her mood took a turn for the worse when she spotted the displeasure on her parents' faces and remembered why she was there.

"*Tu me fais honte, Josette,*" Élaine stated, her lips forming a straight line.

You're an embarrassment.

"Yes, I'm sure that's true." Jo lifted her hand to rub her eyes but was stopped short by the IV pulling at her skin. She looked down at her wrist and noticed her grandmother's bracelet was missing. Before she could question it, her father stepped forward.

"It's not just our family you disgraced, but the foundation. It's our heritage and reputation—"

She pushed herself up. "I was standing up *for* our heritage! That bitch questioned my *pedigree*, called me a foul-mouthed Jew!"

"You rise above, Josette, not sink below," her mother added unhelpfully.

She fell back. "I'll write a press release, explain what happened and take full responsibility. I'll even apologize to that woman."

"It's too late for that. The board has called for your resignation."

Her face grew hot with anger, but she reined it in. "I've raised more money than anyone else on the board. Pushing me out will hurt the foundation more than a slight altercation with an antisemite. Dad, we can spin this to our advantage."

"Jo, it's decided," her father started. "You have no choice. The morality clause states—"

"I don't care what it states. You're the chair. You can get them—"

"No more, Josette!"

Jo ignored her mother; she would get no sympathy there. "Why don't you have my back? You know how much it means to me to be part of the foundation."

"Gil, tell her the rest."

Gil sighed and pulled at his ear, his eyes not meeting hers. "The morality clause is also tied to your inheritance. Not all of it. You'll continue to receive a monthly stipend from the Roullaud estate, but the bulk will be suspended." He walked to the sink, taking his time to unwrap the plastic from a paper cup, and filled it. "You're also being sued." He took a drink.

Jo laughed from sheer incredulity. "That bitch is suing me?"

"She could have you arrested!" Élaine interjected.

Jo's head whipped around to her mother. "I'll be sure to write her a thank you note."

"*Mon Dieu*, Josette. You could go to prison!"

Gil placed his hand on Élaine's arm to quiet her. "Dr. Vanheusen is not asking for incarceration or financial compensation." Gil threw the cup in the trash before taking a seat next to Jo on the bed. "She wants you evaluated by the courts, and if warranted, sent to a facility for several weeks, followed by community service." He patted her hand. "If all goes well, we can put this behind us, and after a sufficient amount of time has passed, we'll work on getting you reinstated to the board."

Claudia had found the perfect way to humiliate her. Jo closed her eyes and took a few cleansing breaths to clear her head. "You want to sweep this under the rug instead of fighting it in court?"

Gil stood. "Going to court would mean further exposure and media coverage. My advice is to have the evaluation. It's up to the courts to determine if you need further treatment. They may very well dismiss the case as frivolous. But if we refuse her offer, she *will* have you arrested."

That bitch left me no choice. "All right. I'll do it. I'll have the evaluation." Jo didn't think they would have her committed, but if they did...

"Drew told me about a new rehab one of his clients just came back from. It's one hundred percent holistic. Lots of meditation and yoga, some reiki. I think he said it was plant-based." She continued to think aloud. "And I suppose I *have* been drinking too much. Of course, I'll have to increase my volunteer work when I get back—"

"*Non, non, non,* Josette! You do not understand! She thinks you are *deranged!*"

"She what?" Jo yelled back.

Gil shot his wife a look before focusing on Jo. "The facility is for mental health, not addiction. Think of it as a way to re-evaluate your priorities."

"Oh, you've got to be joking!" Jo got out of the bed, the need to escape overwhelming. "I've seen *One Flew Over the Cuckoo's Nest*. Fuck that shit!"

Élaine backed out of her way. "Where are you going?"

"Home. I'm all better now, see?" She held up the hand with the IV. "Lots of fluids." She yanked out the tube. *Holy shit, that hurt!*

"Give her this, Gil." Élaine shoved a pamphlet at him.

Jo grabbed it instead and threw it to the floor. "Nope. Not gonna happen."

"Jo," her father tried to reason, "if you don't do as stipulated, you'll go to jail. I can get you out on bail, but like I said, going to trial..." He shook his head. "It might take a year or more to clear your name, and in the end, you still might have to serve time."

Jo rummaged through her Hermes overnight bag. Drew must have packed it because her outfit was accessorized. "Yeah, well, it still sounds better than a stint at the Looney Tunes Saloon." She pulled out a pair of jeans and a butter soft sweater that she hugged close to her chest. Only Drew would know she needed the comfort of cashmere.

"You have until tomorrow to decide. Talk to Drew. He also recommended the facility in the pamphlet." Gil went over and kissed his daughter on the head. "Please think about it."

Her parents said their goodbyes and left.

When Jo emerged from a long, much needed shower, Masi stood in the doorway.

She shook off the sense of dread and smiled. "Masi, I'm so glad you came."

He rubbed his forehead. "Your texts seemed rather urgent. How are you feeling?"

"I'm good. A little dehydrated, low blood sugar." She waved it off.

"Yes. I read your chart." He looked around. "Look, love. I'm just going to be blunt. I don't think it's going to work out between us."

Jo plunked down in the drab green chair, accepting the inevitable. "I see. You won't even let me explain? I guess your ex was right. You were only using me to scratch an itch."

"Is that what she said?" Masi shook his head. "I can see how that might have escalated things, but I wish you would've come to me." He pulled at his face. "Well, in any case, she was wrong. Yes, Claudia and I have a history, and we occasionally get back together, but it has nothing to do with us. The truth is, I'm very fond of you. But in the long run, I just don't think we'd be compatible."

"Really? Why is that?"

Masi entered the room and sat at the corner of the bed opposite her. "Have you ever been to a circus? Sorry, bad example—to an amusement park?"

Jo nodded, stupefied.

"It's bigger than life, a place full of thrill rides and carnival games."

She didn't like where this was going.

"But by the end of the day, you're exhausted and have a bellyache from eating too much cotton candy."

Her jaw fell open, spilling her self-worth onto the floor. "Oh, wow. I don't even...I make you sick?"

Masi held up a hand. "Terrible analogy. Let me restate."

Jo sprung up from the chair. "No, no. No need." She gathered her belongings. "I suppose I should be grateful you didn't compare me to a zoo."

"Josette, please. I meant it as a compliment. Let me explain."

"Sorry." Jo pushed past him. "Park's closed."

Jo didn't go home but to the dance studio. After rummaging through her locker, she found a pair of boy shorts and a T-shirt that read, EAT FRUIT, NOT FRIENDS. She tucked her slippers away, deciding to go barefoot. Today was not about discipline and technique. It was about release.

She checked the schedule for an opening and recognized Drew's name scribbled next to one of the rooms. Heading down the hallway, she opened the door and stood just inside as Drew danced to Jeff Buckley's version of "Hallelujah." The poetry and grace of his movements synced with the song's somber celebration of death.

And it undid her.

When the song ended, he came over and swiped the tears from her face before queuing up another song. Drew moved aside and let her dance. She didn't recognize the song, but it was exactly what she needed. Dark and nasty, full of rage and angst, fitting her mood. He allowed her the freedom to express her pain, then joined her. They often danced together, but not like this. It was unrehearsed, unchoreographed. They began a push and pull, a coming together and a falling apart. They danced in sync and in disharmony. It was magic. Cathartic. As the last notes faded, they fell together in a heap on the floor, their backs to one another, breaths labored. After a few minutes, Drew broke the silence.

"Talked to your parents, did you?"

"Yeah. Thanks for the heads-up."

"Element of surprise. You would've bolted otherwise."

"Whose side are you on?"

Drew swung around to face her. "Yours, always yours." He reached out and clasped her hands. "You listen to me, Jobo. I've never loved another person as much as I love you. But you are a hot mess right now, and that's coming from someone who's no stranger to pushing boundaries."

Tears rose to the surface, and she bent her head. *How did everything go so wrong?*

"You're right," she finally said.

They sat quietly for a while, locked in an intimacy they rarely shared. Drew released first and stood. He walked to the barre at the end of the room and turned, grasping hold of the wood on either side.

"I'm moving to LA," he announced.

Jo blinked, her eyes wide. *No, no, no, no, no.* "You're moving? When? And why are you telling me this *now*?"

"I just found out. They offered me a weekly fashion spot on *The Buzz*. I leave next week."

Jo pinched her nose, trying to halt the burning sensation that signaled more tears. *Don't leave, don't leave, don't leave. I need you.*

Drew crossed his arms, looking down. "Not everything is about you."

In one angry movement, she was up. "Fuck you, Drew!" She grabbed her bag and left, half hoping he would follow her, but knowing he wouldn't.

Pull yourself together, Jo. She swiped at the tears blurring her vision and called for a cab.

Entering her condo, she noticed all the clothes, shoes, and other paraphernalia littering the space. An overwhelming sense of relief hit her when she spied her charm bracelet on the counter, triggering memories.

"Josette, my angel. We must go," her Mami said as they left the beach for the short walk home. "We can visit the elephant again tomorrow."

Jo loved Lucy, the 65-foot-tall elephant who lived on the beach in Margate, New Jersey, where she spent her summers as a child. She would enter its left foot and climb the spiral staircase into the belly of the beast and look out its glass eyes to the Atlantic Ocean beyond. Taking the side stairs, she would climb onto Lucy's back, stand in the ornate howdah, and pretend they were best friends traveling the world together.

The only thing she loved more than Lucy was her Mami, who traveled every year from France to stay with her for the summer. Her Grand-Mère's delicate hand would clasp hers as they walked, her golden charm bracelet tinkling softly. Mami had bought it at the Porte de Clignancourt flea market in Paris. It wasn't of any real value; she had said. But to Jo, it was more precious than all the diamonds in her mother's jewelry box. It had classical glass intaglios set in open bezel frames made by Bohemian glassmakers more than one hundred years ago. No two charms were alike. She would hold them up to the sun, each refracting the light differently. Interspersed on the chain were three fleurs-de-lis, raised in relief on golden shields. She would rub the smooth petals every night as her Mami read to her in French. The summer after she turned twelve, her Mami came for the last time. Before she left, she gave Jo the bracelet.

"Ma belle petite-fille. Pense à moi quand tu le portes et je serai toujours à tes côtés."

(My beautiful granddaughter. Think of me when you wear it, and I will be by your side always.)

Jo noticed a new charm hanging from the chain. It was a replica of Lucy the elephant, with the howdah on her back. "Won't you miss it, Mami?"

"Non, mon chou."

(No, sweetheart.)

Jo brought the bracelet to her chest and slid to the floor, rubbing the different stones and charms between her fingers like she had so many times as a child.

Surrounded by discarded wealth, Jo held onto the only thing in the room of any true value.

17

*True heroism is not the urge to surpass all others at whatever cost,
but the urge to serve others at whatever cost.*

- Arthur Ashe

"Hello, Mr. Taylor, it's Gail Rogers, producer of HomeTown Heroes. I wanted to apologize for showing up unexpectedly at your house yesterday. I know you said you weren't interested in being part of our show, but if you could give me ten minutes of your time, I think you'll see—"

JT deleted the message and tossed the phone on the seat next to him. She was persistent, he'd give her that. But he wasn't desperate enough to accept that kind of help. He parked the truck outside the bank and went in.

Hank Sloane came out of his office to greet him. "Welcome home, JT. It's good to see you. Come on in."

An old photo of Hank with his father and grandfather hung on the wall. The bank slogan, *For all your savings and loans, trust your money to Sloane's*, featured prominently at the bottom. JT liked the new motto better: *Bank with Hank*. It was short and sweet. He wondered whether Robert Sloane Sr. named his son Hank to rhyme with the word bank.

They talked for a while about football—a topic everyone seemed to think JT still wished to reminisce about—the Army, and the changes to the town. Finally, there was a lull in conversation.

"So, what can I do for you today?" Hank asked as he sat back in his chair.

JT handed him the notice of default he'd found in his dad's office. "I'd like to know what it would take to pay this off."

Hank scratched his chin uncomfortably. "Well, now JT, I can't tell you that, as you aren't the one in default."

JT pulled on his face. "So, you're telling me I can't make the back payments?"

"No, I'm saying without permission from your dad, I can't *discuss* it." Hank hesitated as if he wanted to say more.

"What *can* you discuss?" JT prodded.

Hank tapped on the desk blotter, considering the question. "Well, son, I suppose you'll find out sooner than not, since it's no secret around here. Your dad has debts all over town. Most businesses have cut off his credit—some won't even sell him supplies until he's out of arrears."

JT knew things were bad when he found the foreclosure notice, but not this bad. "Without credit, the farm can't operate."

Hank lowered his gaze. "Not for long, no."

Fowler's Pond had been in his mother's family for generations, and the thought of losing it hit him hard. JT stood and held out his hand. "I appreciate the heads up."

Hank walked him to the door. "You might want to talk to Addison Jennings. She approached your dad a while back about someone wanting to buy the farm. Heard they offered a fair price. You can reach her at The Jericho Agency."

Why hadn't she told him? JT had seen Addy around a few times since he'd been back, and she never mentioned it. They even walked together from Hawley's Deli to the park. Hell, she could have called him any time she wanted.

"I'll talk to my dad first, but thanks for the information."

He sat in his truck and tried to make sense of it all. Shock turned to anger when JT recalled his father's insistence that everything was fine. If only he'd confided in JT, they might've been able to save the farm, or at least hold the creditors at bay until they could come up with a solution.

He slammed the truck into gear and headed home. The talk with his dad was long overdue.

There was an unfamiliar car parked in the drive, but JT recognized the owner's voice before he made it through the back door. The conversation halted when he entered, but he had a fair idea of what Addy and his dad were discussing.

His father stood, addressing Addy. "Why don't we continue this another time? I gotta get back to it. Thanks for coming out." He shook her hand and nodded to JT before walking out.

Addy gathered her papers without glancing over.

Normally his heart would beat faster at the sight of her, but right now his feelings took a back seat. "You here about selling the farm?"

She turned and the pained look on her face was confirmation enough.

He nodded. "I just came from the bank. We can't save it, can we?"

"This is a discussion you need to have with your dad, JT."

"Yeah, I've been hearing that a lot lately." He leaned against the counter and folded his arms. "Tell me something, Addy. Is it a good offer?"

Addy's brow shot up. "You heard about Tommy's interest?"

Tommy's? No, he hadn't heard about that.

The Beuchards were as rich as it got in their small town, probably richer than anyone within a thousand miles, and the thought of selling the farm to him chapped JT's hide. "I heard something to that effect. Guess that's why you didn't tell me. You think I'd try to stop it?"

Addy shook her head. "No—Maybe. I don't know. I'd hoped it wouldn't come to this. I tried—"

"You think my folks should take the offer?"

She let out a deep breath. "It'd be enough to pay off the debt and leave your folks with a little something extra."

"A little something extra? Like, enough to retire on? Enough to buy another farm? Or enough for a trailer down by the river?" With each question, his voice got louder.

And hers grew softer, just like it used to whenever he got upset. "I'm not the enemy, JT."

The look on her face reminded him of the first time he saw her with Tommy, and his jaw clenched. "I don't need your pity."

Addy stood and moved toward him. "Oh, JT. It's not pity." She put her hand to his cheek.

He tried not to let it affect him, but it'd been a long time, and he leaned into her touch. When she stepped closer, he wrapped an arm around her waist and pulled her to him. It felt natural, like coming home, and his resolve from weeks ago waned. "Is this what you want, Addy?" he whispered, brushing his mouth against her forehead.

Addy lowered her gaze and stepped back. "We...I can't."

JT felt the rebuke. "You still in love with him, then?"

Addy sighed. "No, but it's complicated."

"Got it." JT nodded and moved away from the counter.

Addy reached out to him. "No, you don't."

"Then tell me."

She pulled her lips in a tight line.

JT was tired of people not trusting him with the truth. An unbidden image of Josie entered his head. Now there was someone who told you straight up what they were thinking—whether you liked it or not.

"I'll walk you out." He opened the door, and Addy sailed past.

JT found his father in the horse paddock, fixing a couple of pieces of rotted wood. JT hauled himself onto the fence and waited for his dad to finish.

After the last rail was in place, his father walked by, signaling JT to follow. "Let's go grab a beer." He hung up his tools, removed his gloves, and grabbed the keys to the truck.

They sat in silence as they drove the fifteen minutes to Levi's bar.

The bar belonged to JT's older half-brother—a child born from his father's romance with the daughter of a migrant farm worker while he was still in high school. By the time Charles' parents found out about the relationship, Silvia was pregnant. She left at the end of the season, and it took years before Charles could arrange for her to return with Levi. By then, Charles had married his mom and moved to Fowler's Pond.

Levi and Silvia lived close enough for Charles to visit, but his brother never came to the farm. It was the only subject he ever heard his parents argue about, and no matter how many times JT had asked to visit his brother, he wasn't allowed. Of course, that all changed when he was old enough to drive...

JT licked his dry lips and smoothed down his hair. As he jumped down from the truck, the front door to the house swung open and a smiling woman with long dark hair came onto the porch. When she realized it wasn't Charles in the familiar truck, her face fell. JT approached cautiously, raising a hand in greeting, and introduced himself.

"I know who you are," Silvia said.

As JT stepped closer, he was surprised by how beautiful—and thin—she was.

A man appeared in the doorway behind her. "What do you want?"

JT told them he came to meet his brother.

The woman walked back into the house, leaving the man, who leaned against the door frame and said, "You're lookin' at him."

After that day, JT refused to pretend his brother didn't exist. Levi had regarded him with reserved amusement when he came around but never turned him away—even when he had company. JT wouldn't call their relationship close, but they were family.

Charles parked in the gravel lot, and the two walked into the bar.

"Evenin', Charles. JT," Levi said from behind the bar and put a couple of coasters down in front of them. "What can I get y'all?"

"Shot and a beer for me." JT didn't need to say what the shot would be. Everyone knew Levi made the best bourbon around.

"I'll have a diet cola, if you don't mind." Charles didn't drink but went to the bar a couple times a week to see his son.

"Sure thing." Levi left, but Charles' gaze remained on his eldest son, a look of regret in his eyes. After a tick, he glanced JT's way. "I can't save the farm, but I'm guessing Addy told you that."

JT shook his head. "It wasn't her. I found the default notice. How long has it been?"

"Long enough."

"I have some money saved—"

Levi came back, placed their order down, and walked away.

Charles turned to his youngest son. "You never once showed an interest in farming. Why try to save it if you don't want to run it?"

His dad had a point. He never considered farming. "Because of you, Mom, and Lou Lou, I guess. It belongs in our family."

Charles looked away and picked up his soda. "Yeah, well, nothing's forever."

"What kinda bullshit is that? Why won't you fight for it?"

His dad slammed the glass down. "I've been fighting for it, dammit! Every day I wake up before dawn and work past sunset, just to keep things afloat."

JT took a sip of beer and let the dust settle. "How did it get this bad?"

His dad shrugged, his anger dissipating. "Lots of reasons. I made some bad choices, had a poor season or two. It only takes a couple of years for the ball to start rolling and, well, it came to where I couldn't cover expenses. I took out a loan, which helped for a while, but I should've leased the land instead of trying to make it work." He paused, shaking his head. "Farming ain't what it used to be. Barely enough to sustain a family, even with subsidies."

JT let it sink in. They were going to lose Fowler's Pond. "Addy said Tommy wants to buy it."

Charles nodded. "Corporate farming is profitable. The Beuchards own all the cattle farms around here. The farms they don't own grow corn and soybeans to feed the animals that they cram into sheds by the thousands. That's what farming is nowadays, JT, and there ain't nothing good about it."

He'd heard it for years, big corporations taking over, making it impossible for small farms to compete. "I heard they cut off your credit in town. Was that Tommy's doing? Is he forcing you to sell?"

"Now, I don't know about that. The Beuchards didn't rack up the debt, I did. Businesses need to get paid." Charles rubbed the stubble on his chin, deep in thought. "When your mom and me married, we didn't change how things were done. We had horses and cattle, raised hogs from farrow to finish. Grew corn, beans, hay, and oats. Times changed, but we didn't, and now we're gonna lose it all."

For the first time in his life, JT felt small. He hadn't been there to help shoulder the burden his father carried alone. But he was here now, and he wouldn't give up until he exhausted all possibilities.

He thought of the message he deleted that morning, and the one last week, and the one before that. He would have literally bet the farm against this outcome.

"What if I had a way of potentially saving the farm? Would you consider it?"

Charles regarded his son. "You don't have enough money, son."

"No, I'm guessing I don't, but what if there's another way? *HomeTown Heroes* wants to do a feature on me. What if they can stop the foreclosure or even save the farm?"

Charles raised his brow. "That's a tall order, JT. What would they get out of it?"

"Ratings, I suppose. All I know is they've been after me since I got home."

Being on the show would dredge up the past and open his life to public scrutiny—two things at the top of his 'when hell freezes over' list.

Charles rubbed the rim of his glass with a calloused thumb. "You're not one to talk about yourself, but that's what you'll have to do. These Hollywood types don't care about our farm. They want to exploit you, and that don't sit well with me, son."

JT agreed, but it made little difference. "What kind of man would I be if I let the farm go when I could save it? Let them have their slice of me, Dad. It's a small enough price to pay."

His father straightened. "I guess I wouldn't be much of one either if I didn't let you try."

JT smiled and clapped his father on the shoulder, feeling just a little bit taller. "I'll give the producer a call in the morning, then."

18

You're only given a little spark of madness. You mustn't lose it.
- Robin Williams

It'd been fifteen days since Jo stood before a judge and pleaded guilty to a misdemeanor battery charge. It had also been the most humiliating experience of her life.

A court-appointed psychiatrist had diagnosed her with Intermittent Explosive Disorder, or IED for short. The sentence—six weeks at a mental health facility, thirty hours of community service, and a $1,000 fine—made her want to punch Claudia all over again.

The next day Jo boarded a plane and headed to *Harmony House*, a treatment facility in the hills above LA. Its tag line, *Holistic Health and Healing*, did nothing to relieve her stress—no matter how epic the alliteration. To be fair, the estate seemed more like a small luxury hotel than the quackery she'd envisioned. There were no white walls, padded cells, or Nurse Ratcheds to be found. Only the soft hues of nature, the aroma of essential oils, and the white noise of flowing water.

Jo sat in a circle with other privileged "guests" and waited for the doctor to start the day's group session.

Alex Fielding began by tapping the stack of papers on his crossed legs. "So, who would like to begin today?"

Jo wondered why the doctor always brought papers to these group sessions. He never checked them or jotted anything down.

Her mind continued to wander until she heard her name called. "Pardon?"

"I thought we might start with you, Jo."

She glanced around at the others in the circle. "I'm good. No issues at the moment. Carry on." She sat back and waited for someone to jump in, but they all stared at her. "What?"

"Jo," Dr. Fielding began, "for treatment to be effective, we need to be honest with ourselves and others."

"Absolutely agree." This time, when she scanned the room, no one met her gaze. "What am I missing?"

Dr. Fielding leaned forward. "Why don't you share with us how you dealt with your setback at breakfast this morning?"

"Um, I had a setback at breakfast?" She laughed uncomfortably.

"Does anyone want to help Jo with her recollection of this morning's events?"

Timid Tori raised her hand. "Jo, I, um…I think you use humor to, you know, uh, hide be-behind, and, and I think you can be mean, you know, sometimes, um, without knowing it." Tori looked over to Dr. Fielding. "I…I might have been wrong. Maybe Jo doesn't hate me, but you know, I still felt hurt by what she said. S-sorry."

"Tori, you don't need to say you're sorry. Emotions heal when they're heard and validated. Jo? Can you respond to Tori's concerns?"

Jo nodded. She may not know *why*, but she knew *what* the correct response was. "I'm very sorry, Tori, if I hurt your feelings." Her eyes snapped to Pervy Mike, who coughed the word 'liar.' Ignoring him, she continued, "I don't always know how my words will affect others."

"But why did you tell Mike I wanted to ga-get him kicked out for non-compliance?"

Mike barked out a laugh.

Jo finally understood what all the hoopla was about. "Oh," she drew out. "You mean the comment about you *shtupping* him?" She tried to wave it off. "It was a joke. No one thinks you would really want to—above all, Mike." She looked around at all the serious faces and sighed.

Dr. Fielding addressed her. "There needs to be a level of trust within the group. Information shared should never be used against one another or as a joke." He motioned to the group at large. "Mike is dealing with sexual addiction and Tori has social anxiety complicated by low self-esteem. Can you see how your comments could be harmful?"

"To Mike? No. But, I shouldn't have teased Tori." She turned and smiled at the shy girl.

"Bu....but why did you? I thought we were friends."

"We are. I wanted to make you laugh. Everyone treats you like this delicate little snowflake, and I think you're made of tougher stuff."

"I didn't realize you had a degree in psychotherapy, Ms. Singer," the doctor said, the one side of his mouth ticking up.

Jo threw up her hands. "You got me there, doc."

He spoke to the group. "Does anyone else have a comment?"

Klepto Kara raised her hand. "I agree with Jo. Tori needs to develop thicker skin."

Dr. Fielding brought his palms together. "Remember, our goal here is to share feelings and experiences, not advice. We want to be open and honest but not pass judgment."

Naomi pursed her overly plump lips. "I'm siding with Tori," she said, her face void of all natural expression. "Jo's a bully."

Jo stared at Botox Barbie. "Wow, did you even listen? Just two seconds ago, he said not to pass judgment."

"Okay, let's move on." Dr. Fielding turned to Jo. "We'll dig further into your motivation during our one-on-one."

Jo thought—for the first time ever—that she needed a day off from thinking about herself. Self-reflection was exhausting.

On her way to reiki, Jo ran into Deuce Deming, Hollywood's rising action star. She loved his latest movie, *Backbone Alley*. There was a distinct possibility she fangirled when they first met—followed by awkward silence. Turns out, Deuce wasn't a great conversationalist. Since then, Jo had mastered the art of the one-sided chit chat.

"Hey Deuce, missed you at group this morning."

He stared down at her, his dark, hooded eyes showing little emotion on his handsome face. "Had a call."

"Cool. Cool." Jo, at five-ten, felt dainty in his presence. Some women liked to feel dominated. Not her. She preferred men of equal stature, not too big, not too small. Like Goldilocks, she liked them *just right*. An image of Jackson Taylor popped into her head. Okay, perhaps a little man-handling wasn't out of the question. Not that she'd see him again, which was a shame, really…

She looked up when she realized Deuce was talking. "Sorry?"

Deuce tilted his head. "I said, watch out for Naomi. She doesn't like you."

Jo laughed. "What's she going to do? Have me sent to a mental—oh, wait. Someone already did that."

The right corner of his mouth lifted ever so slightly. "See you around." He turned to the side so he could pass without making physical contact.

"Later!" she called, waving to the retreating wall of muscle.

After her appointment, she headed to the pool, where she spotted Kara swimming laps. Jo didn't want to disturb her, so she reclined on one of the lounge chairs and thought about all the puffy coats back in chilly Philly.

"Hey," Kara said.

Jo shielded her eyes as droplets of water hit her skin. "Hey, Kara. Nice form."

"Thanks. Sorry if you had to wait."

"No worries, the sun feels good, and I don't have to be anywhere until later this afternoon."

Kara grabbed a towel and wrapped it around her toned body. "I want you to know, I'm not a klepto."

"Oh, I didn't—"

"I overheard Mike telling you I was, but I'm not. It's my OCD. I'm much better than I used to be, but when I'm stressed—" She glanced away as if recalling a memory. "I don't like things to be out of balance. I notice color and texture and vibration, you know?"

Strangely enough, she kinda did. Jo nodded, her curiosity piqued.

Kara sat across from her. "I have a stressful job. Long hours, days where I don't stop. When I need a release, I put things in order. Mostly I *rearrange*, but if something doesn't fit, I take it and place it where it should be. Unfortunately, if I remove an item from the premises, it's considered stealing."

"That's probably the coolest disorder ever. Way more interesting than being a klepto. Gotta say, I'm a little jelly." She stood and pulled off her cover-up—too much sharing made her skin itch.

Kara smiled. "Thanks for listening."

"Anytime." Jo walked to the side of the pool and dove in. When she surfaced, Kara had left. She swam a few more laps, then set out for her room to change before her one-on-one with Dr. Fielding.

The session marked the end of her two-week evaluation. If everything went well, she'd get her phone and laptop back. She missed Holly's sunny disposition, but more importantly, she needed to thank Drew for setting her up in the Shangri-La of mental health facilities. If it weren't for him, who knows where she would have ended up?

She walked down the stone steps to the caretaker's cottage. The door was ajar, which signaled the doctor was in and ready for his next client.

"Knock, knock." She peeked through the opening.

"Ah, Jo, welcome. Come in and close the door."

She entered the mid-century modern room and sat in the Eames-style lounge chair opposite Dr. Fielding, who bore an uncanny likeness to her father.

He looked up from the file he was examining. "How was your reiki session?"

"I can honestly say it's one of my favorite therapeutic modalities."

"Has it given you any insight into today's earlier conversation?"

"Well," she drew out, trying to think of something insightful to say. "I wasn't motivated by anger, so I'm gonna put that in the win column." She gave him a cheeky smile.

Dr. Fielding—immune to her charm—steepled his fingers and set them to his lips. "That's because you've been misdiagnosed. You don't have an anger disorder."

"Hallelujah!" Jo sprang to her feet, throwing her hands into the air. She'd been vindicated. *I wonder if I can sue for malicious persecution?* "So, when can I leave?"

Dr. Fielding waved her down. "You're still under our care for another four weeks. But you won't be treated for anger. Instead, we'll focus on the cause—your lack of empathy."

Jo's face fell. "I'll take back my original diagnosis." She recalled him saying something similar to Naomi last week in group. "You think I'm like Botox Barbie?"

He pinched the bridge of his nose, his glasses lifting. "I'm not passing judgment here, Jo, and I'm not comparing you to anyone. Naomi—as you well know—has body dysmorphia. Can you see how labeling her could be perceived as insensitive?"

"Yes, but she's a bitch, so..."

Dr. Fielding sighed. "Hostile language is self-defeating and often used as an attention-seeking device. You're reactive and defensive, which allows your ego to drive your actions and decisions instead of empathy."

Jo pressed her lips together to stop herself from making it worse.

"You use humor as a shield and a way to deflect. You're uncomfortable with vulnerability—in yourself and in others—and consider it a sign of weakness." He jotted something down on a piece of paper, then glanced up. "We'll need to work on your indifference and sense of entitlement, along with your social skills."

The fuck? That was a bridge too far. "My social skills have been honed since birth. I run a profitable business and have over a million followers on social media. Not to mention the fundraising I do for my family's foundation. I've conversed with heads of state, speak three languages, and have traveled the world. I'm *the very definition* of social."

Dr. Fielding held up a palm. "You are indeed a very accomplished woman and an expert within large social gatherings. You're good in a crowd because you're not required to interact on a personal level. You move among, you *blend*, yet remain detached. Having meaningful dialogue exposes your emotions, brings on anxiety, and causes you to lash out. Your intimate relationships fail because they lack depth. Once you release control—*express* rather than *suppress*—you'll form stronger connections."

Commitment issues. Jo heard Dr. Loeb in her head and had a moment of clarity. It only took two therapists, a guru, a handful of psychics, an astrologer, and a court-appointed shrink to get her to see it.

"The first step in healing is acknowledgement. Once you shift your thought pattern from your needs and desires to those around you, you will find it easier to open up and create meaningful bonds. We will push you out of your comfort zone, challenge you, show you that being vulnerable isn't a four-letter word."

He pulled a key from his pocket and strode to the cabinet, returning with a vape pen and cannabis cartridge. "I think this could be beneficial. Studies have shown promising results with the use of medical marijuana. In your case, it will help with anxiety, inhibit ego, and heighten the awareness of others. It's not mandatory, but I recommend you give it a try."

Reaching behind him, he picked up a folder and handed it to her with the rest of the items. "Here's a comprehensive treatment plan for the next four weeks. We'll monitor your progress and tailor accordingly."

Jo examined the paraphernalia. Alcohol had always been her drug of choice, but any port in the storm.

She walked out without a witty retort or the last word. It wasn't much, but it was a start.

19

*I walk around like everything's fine, but
inside my shoe, my sock is sliding off.*
-Unknown

JT peered over the porch railing at the black SUV coming up the drive. It parked in front of the equipment barn at the same time his father came out of it. Charles wiped his hands on a rag before greeting Gail Rogers, the producer of *HomeTown Heroes*.

A young man about JT's age exited holding a fancy-looking camera and started taking pictures of the house. Gail stumbled back on the gravel drive, trying to avoid a barn cat like it had mange, and followed Charles to the porch where JT stood waiting.

"Mr. Taylor!" The producer extended her hand well before she made it up the steps, reminding him of the first time they met in Philadelphia.

"Ms. Rogers." JT leaned over and shook it, not wanting to leave her hanging. She didn't let go until she stood next to him.

"So glad to see you again," she said, beaming. The woman acted as though the first time they'd met—and the second—were pleasurable events. She glanced behind her. "This is Vaughn Bergen. He'll be the field producer for this segment."

"Pleasure." JT nodded to the man, who put two fingers to his temple in a salute before continuing to take photos.

Upon entering the house, the producers looked around like they'd never seen the inside of one before.

Vaughn hesitated, lifting his camera in JT's direction. "Okay if I take some interior shots?"

JT motioned toward his father. "Not for me to say."

"Take as many as you like," Charles said, walking into the front living room, where Gail examined a wall of photographs.

"You have a lovely family." She pointed to a picture of Lou Lou in her cheerleading uniform. "Is this your daughter?" she asked Charles, who nodded in response. "She's a very pretty girl." She moved to a painting of the original homestead which hung over the fireplace. "Was this the original house?"

Charles stood next to her. "Oh, yeah. Still is. Fowler's Pond—that's the name of our farm—has been in my wife's family for generations. You're standing in the new house, although it's gotta be seventy years old by now. The original farmstead, built in 1884, is located close to the road, on the south side of the property. You probably passed it on your way. Harry Talbot—he used to be the manager here—lived there with his wife. Left about a year and a half ago." He shook his head. "Hard to believe we might be leaving, too."

"We'll do all we can to stop that from happening." Gail gave him a sympathetic smile. "It's going to feel very intrusive with us here, but it won't be constant. After the initial filming, where we get to know you and your family, your town, etcetera, we'll only be here for follow-up interviews and check-ins. We stagger multiple shows at a time. That way, we can see the progression in our heroes' lives over six to twelve months."

Months. JT tried to shake off the sick feeling in his stomach.

They continued to tour the house, with Vaughn taking shot after shot, and Gail asking questions. The subtle scrutiny felt like a violation to JT, who knew it would only get worse.

When they'd seen enough, they headed out to the rest of the farm.

Vaughn wandered off when Charles or JT stopped to explain how something worked or what it was for. The man spent an inordinate amount of time taking photos of things of little significance—the silos, an old rusty tractor, their farm truck.

"We raise cattle, chickens, and other livestock. Grow various crops," Charles said as they entered the milking barn. "I guess you can say we do it all."

Gail took notes while Vaughn snapped photos of the bunkhouse, equipment building, and two barns. By the time they got to the stables, Vaughn had disappeared.

"I hope you don't mind if he goes off on his own. Vaughn's more interested in the cinematic aspects than the dirty details." She laughed, holding her notebook aloft.

"Not at all." Charles turned to his son. "Doc Marshall is coming to look at Nello's hind leg. Why don't you go on without me?"

Gail and JT left the barn and walked the short distance to the original farmhouse. The white clapboard building, with its chipped paint and lopsided porch, had an air of neglect. Weeds had taken over a once well-tended garden, and a porch swing hung askew.

"No one has lived here since the Talbots. Watch your step." JT pointed to a rotting board.

The pungent smell of abandonment struck them as they entered. Cobwebs and dust lay on every surface, and a haze clung to the windows. There were odd pieces of furniture here and there and a tea kettle on the kitchen stove.

"We could clean it up a bit if you need some place to work," he offered.

Gail smiled politely. "Thank you, that's very kind, but I've rented out the Iron Bridge Inn, and they have a lovely solarium, which will do well."

Lovely. The woman sure liked that word. They walked back to the main house, where Lou Lou and his mother greeted them.

"Ma, Lou Lou, this is Ms. Rogers from Los Angeles. Ms. Rogers, this is my mother, Brenda Taylor, and my sister, Laura Leigh."

"Nice to meet you both, and please, call me Gail."

"Would y'all like to stay for supper?" his mother asked.

"Oh, no. We couldn't impose."

"No imposition. I got some Burgoo cooking on the stove."

"Sounds lovely."

It occurred to JT when the woman said lovely, she meant something entirely different.

When Vaughn and Charles returned, they sat down for supper. Gail didn't say lovely once, so JT figured she liked the stew.

His eyes narrowed as he watched Vaughn interact with his sister. JT recognized a player when he saw one.

"Ma," Lou Lou said, turning toward their mother. "Vaughn needs an assistant and said I could have the job. Isn't that great?"

JT glanced over at Gail, who sent daggers in Vaughn's direction. She cleared her throat. "I'm not sure that's—"

Vaughn waved a dismissive hand. "She'll be finished with her undergrad in a month, and last summer, she interned as an assistant. That's all the qualifications my last PA had when I hired him."

"Will interned on a film set." Gail turned to Lou Lou. "Where did you do your internship, Lou Lou?"

JT's sister straightened in her chair. "Glenford Veterinary Hospital. It's a busy practice with two doctors. They offered me a job, but it doesn't start until the end of the summer, and Vaughn said you should be done before that."

"It would help the budget, too, Gail, hiring locals," Vaughn suggested.

"I see. Well." Gail's lips tried and failed at a smile. "It's your decision."

Lou Lou shrieked and bounced in her seat.

JT noticed the smug look on the cameraman's face and realized Vaughn thought a country girl like Lou would be easy pickings. Boy, did he have that wrong.

20

Your comfort zone is a beautiful place, but nothing ever grows there.

- John Assaraf

Jo exploded up from a lunge and shifted her weight to her left foot. She pulled her right knee toward her chest and twisted, snapping her leg forward to kick the punching bag.

"Whoa. Remind me never to piss you off," Kara said, walking into the gym.

Jo turned, using her forearm to wipe the sweat from her brow. "Seems counterintuitive, doesn't it?" She smiled and grabbed her bottle. "Treating anger issues with aggression." She took a swig, enjoying the cool, lemon-infused water.

The two had become close since their conversation at the pool. Jo appreciated Kara's blunt honesty and self-deprecating nature and found her quirks...quirky.

"Oh, I don't know. Gives you a healthy outlet for all that rage." Kara squealed, as Jo circled around her, throwing fake punches. "Why are you still being treated for anger, anyway? I thought the doc changed your diagnosis."

Jo collapsed on the mats and started unwrapping the tape on her hands. "Anger is considered an underlying condition, and honestly, I prefer the physical modalities over the therapeutic ones." She cracked her neck from side to side. "You know, I don't think I ever used the word modality before coming here." She looked at her Apple Watch. "I have a deep tissue massage in thirty, followed by chakra balancing. Tell me this place ain't the bomb."

Kara laughed and sank into a cross-legged position in front of her. "I got your text. So, what can I do for you?"

Jo had been mulling over an idea ever since Kara told her what she did for a living. "It's more about what I can do for *you*." She gave Kara her most engaging smile.

Kara shook her head. "Oh, I know that look. You used it on Deuce the other day when you wanted to sneak out for gelato." She tapped her knees. Five taps on one, five on the other, then ten on both.

"It rarely fails me," Jo said, her smile waning. Asking Kara for a favor made her uncomfortable. She preferred to be on the other side of things, the grantor of wishes. This position made her feel vulnerable. *Just what the doctor ordered.* "You mentioned the other day you often hire trend forecasters. I want to offer my services."

Kara's eyes widened in surprise. "You're asking me for a job?"

"It appears that I am."

"I'm a lowly production manager for a TV show. Don't you know famous people you can hit up?"

Jo's back straightened. "I do, but none that require my services."

Kara nodded. "I see your point. Have you ever worked in the TV or film industry?"

"No, but forecasting is a methodology, a science. It can be tailored to any industry."

Kara remained silent. Thoughtful.

Jo would rather eat a dead cow than grovel, but she needed a job. It wasn't just the punch; it was the sentence. Once word got out that she had to do time in a mental health facility, no one would return her calls.

The opposite had been true for her social media presence, which had blown up—but not in a good way. Bullies loved to kick someone who was down, forcing Jo to shut off the comments on her social media platforms.

She shook off the negative thoughts and focused on what Kara was saying.

"...We have regulars we use for the show, but I can talk to the producer—we're always looking for new talent." When Jo's smile brightened, Kara held up a palm. "But I want something in return."

Jo understood reciprocity. It took her out of the needy category and into the needed—her comfort zone. "Name it."

Kara's chin tilted slightly down, her eyes on Jo. "Okay, here's the deal. I have someone at each location to...lend me their support. You would be that person."

Jo's brow knitted. "Support you how?"

"Keep an eye on me. Watch for signs of restlessness, erratic behavior."

"You want me to be on location? I thought I could work remotely."

It was Kara's turn to look confused. "Have you seen *HomeTown Heroes*, Jo? You would be an integral part of the show. Like, be *on it*. Mostly in the beginning, to explain what the farm needs to be profitable, and then later, to check in on the progress."

"Oh. I...hmm. That does complicate matters." Jo had hoped to lie low for a while.

"You've got a great look. You're already in the media, and being controversial? That's ratings gold. The more I think about it, the more I realize you'd be a great asset."

Jo had no desire to be in the spotlight again, but it would get her out of her old environment and create new challenges—two of Dr. Fielding's requirements. Still, she needed more information before she committed. "Exactly what would be expected of me, and for how long?"

Kara picked up Jo's discarded tape and started rewinding it. "Filming runs for six months to a year, but not continuously. We stagger concurrent heroes, checking their progress over time to see their evolution. If you're hired, your job will fall mostly in pre-production, and deal strictly with the one episode, or rather one hero. You'll be on location for the initial filming, and then we'll call you back for follow-up interviews to report on the impact your recommendations have made. If you do well, we'll hire you for future segments. Cushy job really."

Jo had no problem with that. "So, who's the hero, and what will I be forecasting?"

"We're featuring a war hero whose family farm is in foreclosure. Gail—she's the executive producer—will go into greater detail, but in short, you'll be forecasting the future of small farms. Big corporate domination makes it impossible for them to be competitive. Gail's convinced we can save this guy's farm. The plight of the American farmer is very hot right now."

Something niggled in the back of Jo's brain. "Where is this farm?"

"Kentucky. We start filming next month, but pre-production starts in a week. You can work remotely until you're sprung. No one here cares as long as you show up for group and your one-on-ones." Kara jumped up in one fluid motion.

All Jo heard was Kentucky. "Kar, is the hero you're profiling Jackson Taylor?"

Surprise showed on Kara's face. "Yeah, I guess you've seen him on the news. It's not every day we get to feature someone so prominent."

Jo got to her feet, grinning. "Oh, I've seen him—in the flesh. He attended the fundraiser in Philadelphia." *And was my pervy obsession for months.*

"The one that...?"

"Yes, the incident that got me sent here."

Kara handed Jo the neatly rolled tape. "Crazy coincidence."

Jo laughed. "Is it? Do you know the difference between fate and destiny?"

Kara shook her head.

"Fate is what you are given, destiny is what you make of it."

"So you're fated to take the job?"

"And destined to make the most of it."

Kara started for the door, her fingertips tapping against her thighs in some unknown code. "I'll set up a video call with Gail for later today." She stopped abruptly and pivoted, almost running into Jo. "You are good at what you do, right?"

"The best." Jo smiled and pushed her out the door.

Jo's deep tissue massage was not relaxing, and restoring a harmonious flow of energy to her chakras was an epic fail. She blamed it on all the ideas knocking around in her head. Every new project started like an explosion in her mind, going off in all directions. Eventually, it would settle down, and the left side of her brain would take control by prioritizing and making lists. Creativity would elbow its way back in after hundreds of hours of research, and the Yin and Yang of forecasting would develop. Her mentor called her a pit bull—once she latched onto a project, she didn't let go until someone smacked her in the head and offered her a treat.

She ran into Deuce Deming on her way to her room. "Whoa, big fella." She patted his arm and stepped aside.

Deuce gave her his signature half-smile. It was more of a smize, really. "Sup, beautiful."

Huh. He'd never called her that before. "Oh, not much." As usual, she couldn't pass him in the tight corridor. "Just heading back to flesh out some ideas I have."

"Yeah, for what?"

"Are we...did you just ask me a question?"

He seemed surprised himself. "Yeah. I guess I did."

"I'm getting to you, aren't I?" She wagged a finger and smiled. "If you're not careful, we'll be having an actual conversation soon."

He chuckled and moved to the side. "I'll be out on the veranda if you want to join me."

Jo stuck out her bottom lip. *Was he flirting?* She was still watching his retreating backside when she opened the door to her room.

"AAHH!" A loud pop had her clasping her chest. She fell back against the door as an onslaught of rainbow-colored confetti rained down upon her.

"Surprise!" Drew and Holly said in unison.

Tears welled in her eyes as she stared wide-eyed at the laughing duo.

"For fuck's sake. Come and give us a hug," Drew said.

She couldn't help it. The flood gates opened, and she cried for the first time since the night she lost everything.

"Holy shit, Drew. They broke her. They broke Jo." Holly hurried over and pulled her into the room. After closing the door, Holly led her to the bed, where she tried to press Jo's head onto her ample bosom.

"Holl, you're going to break her neck. Here," he said, handing Holly a tissue. "Clean up that mess." Drew rested his hands on his knees and peered into Jo's eyes. "I think you're right. She won't stop crying."

Jo sprung up and wrapped her body around Drew.

"Girl, have you lost your ever-lovin' mind? I just talked to you yesterday."

She climbed down and wiped her nose on his sleeve. "I know! But you're both *here*." Jo's face squished up, ready for another round.

Drew peered over at Holly. "Think they zapped her brain?"

Jo waved it off and blew her nose. "I'm fine, just give me a minute."

Holly began reading from the pamphlet she found in the room. *"We offer multiple therapeutic modalities in an intimate and inclusive milieu, giving clients the time and care they need to focus on sustainable wellness."* She snickered. "I'd cry too if I had to eat that bullshit for six weeks."

Jo shook her head. "It's my medication. It makes me emotional." She knew it was more than that but held off sharing.

Holly's head popped up from the literature. "What they got you on? Zoloft? Clozapine? A little Valium, some Xanax?"

"Fuck, Holl. I'm a little left of center, not off the reservation. They gave me a weed pen."

"Ooh, pharmaceutical grade. Nice."

Surprisingly, it was.

They took a walk around the estate, stopping here and there for Jo to make introductions. When they ascended the steps to the veranda, she noticed the broad shoulders of Deuce Deming standing at the far corner with his back to them. As they cleared the top step, Drew threw his arm in front of her, stopping their progress. "Is that—"

"Deuce Deming? Yeah."

"Shut up!" Holly peeked around Jo's shoulder, her eyes widening as she took in the man's physique.

"Jobo, honey, I'm gonna need to call in my chips," Drew said.

"Huh?"

"I want you to get me an exclusive interview with Deuce for *The Buzz*. No one has seen him for weeks. He went MIA on the set of his latest project."

Jo's brow knitted in confusion. "You do a weekly fashion spot. He's worn the same sweatpants for a week."

Drew pursed his lips. "I worry about you, I really do. I told you last week they're looking to replace the co-host for the daily *What's the Buzz* segment." He pushed her forward. "Now go in there and help me get it."

21

I never said it would be easy, I only said it would be worth it.

- Mae West

JT couldn't breathe. He threw open the back door, jumped over the porch rail, and stormed to the barn, where he saddled Clive. The horse was responsive and had enough stamina to outlast his need to fly. He abandoned the trails and dirt paths and headed out into the fallow fields.

The day had started off with a series of contracts for him to sign, followed by an inundation of questions. It astonished him, the breadth and depth of information the show had gathered. They had a whole binder filled with it, some things he didn't remember doing, with photos he'd never seen, and quotes from people he'd never met. It took everything in him to stay rooted to the chair. It felt like an assault. How would he survive the next few months?

JT pushed the horse hard. The wind was dry and crisp and carried the promise of spring. The trees had already begun to leaf out and the earth to soften. He eventually slowed to a trot, and his body relaxed into the saddle. The escape was a brief reprieve, and the feeling of freedom only an illusion. But it calmed him.

He circled onto a path and gave Clive the reins as he headed back to the barn. As he drew closer, his eyes rested on the neglected house beyond. An idea grabbed hold, and after he took care of Clive, he walked the short distance to the old homestead and had a look around. He was glad the show didn't take him up on his offer to use it. He made mental notes of what he would need to fix it and walked to the house in a much better mood than when he left.

"Hey, Cricket."

Lou Lou appeared deep in thought as she sat at the kitchen table, tapping away on the new laptop the show had given her. She popped her head up and smiled. "Hey yourself. Where'd you go off to?"

"Took Clive out. I needed some fresh air."

His sister's face softened. She went to him and wrapped her arms around his waist. "I keep forgetting how hard this is for you. All these strange people coming and going." She brought her head back. "Wanna go to Levi's? I could use a break and a beer."

"Sure. Let me shower the stink off first."

They pulled into the crowded parking lot, and JT had to circle around before finding a spot on the grass. "Seems kinda busy for a Tuesday night."

"Does it?"

Warning bells went off. "Lou, why are we here?"

She turned in her seat to face him. "Vaughn and the crew like to come here."

His head fell back on the seat rest, and he closed his eyes. "Why am I not surprised? You've been following him around like a bloodhound on a scent. Don't you see him enough during the day?"

"No, actually. I rarely do! He's always off scouting shots or something. We mostly communicate through emails."

"Be careful, Cricket, he's not here for long. Don't get too attached."

Lou Lou ignored him and hopped down from the truck. "Oh, look." She pointed to a car in the lot. "That's Addison's car." She smiled brightly. "You can thank me now."

"Not on your life. Let's go." JT pulled her along, ignoring the flutter in his chest.

They walked into the crowded space and scanned for empty seats. His eyes landed on a high-top halfway down the room. Even though her back was to him, he knew it was Addy who sat across from Tommy. A knot formed in his gut, and he looked away, guiding his sister to some vacant stools at the far end of the bar. He wasn't big on sitting, so he stood next to his sister and waved Arlene over.

"Hey, JT. Lou Lou. What can I get you?"

"I'll have a shot and whatever you have on tap," JT said.

"I'll have the same, minus the shot, please, Arlene."

"You got it." A minute later, she placed the beverages down and wiped the bar. "I gotta say, JT, you doin' the show has brought in a lot of business."

"Yeah, I noticed."

"They don't pay much attention to the day of the week—not that I'm complaining. I like to stay busy."

When Arlene sauntered off to serve another customer, JT let his eyes wander. They stopped on his brother, who was talking to a couple of women at the other end of the bar. When one of them pulled him down to whisper in his ear, Levi reared back with laughter, causing the locals to take notice. It wasn't every day someone got him to smile, let alone laugh. The man could be harder than year-old taffy.

As if sensing JT's stare, the woman in question turned in his direction. Her face lit up with recognition but not surprise.

"Who's that over there with Levi?" Lou Lou asked.

JT didn't turn when he answered. "That, is Miss Josette Singer." He watched as she slid from the stool and made her way over. *Damn, but she's pretty.* Something about her turned him sideways, and the closer she got, the more twisted he became.

"Hello, Jackson."

"Josie."

She stood close enough he could smell her exotic scent.

"Seems I'm the only one surprised to see you here. Although I'm at a loss as to why you'd be in my town. Outside of an occasional wedding, we don't do many formal affairs."

She *tsked, tsked.* "There you go, making assumptions again." Her smile let him know she'd taken no offense to his teasing.

He laughed, not caring why she was there, just happy she was. He'd forgotten the pull she had over him. "Let me buy you a drink." He raised a hand to call Arlene over when she stopped him.

"Nothing for me, thanks."

He gave her a quizzical look, which morphed into a knowing one, and nodded.

She laughed softly. "No, it's not because of what happened in Philadelphia. Although that is why I'm here—in a roundabout way."

"I don't follow."

"I'm surprised you haven't guessed since I'm sitting with the only group of people not from around here." She waited for him to catch on. When he didn't, she continued. "*HomeTown Heroes* hired me. I'm here to advise on the fate of Fowler's Pond."

JT snorted in disbelief. "You're joking."

She raised her chin and held his gaze. "No, I'm not."

He rubbed at his face. "I mean no disrespect, Josie, but how can someone like you possibly know what's best for a small-town farm in Kentucky?"

She nodded. "Hmm, I see your point. I'd be skeptical too. However." She gave him a wry smile. "*And I mean no disrespect.* Fowler's Pond is a business. One that's been outdated and underutilized for years. They've hired me to turn it into a profitable enterprise, which is something *someone like me* is very good at."

Tired of being ignored, Lou Lou leaned over and extended her hand. "I'm Laura Leigh. JT's sister."

Jo reached over for the shake. "Jo."

"I recognize your name. I work for Vaughn."

"Ah, yes. Vaughn," Jo said, with a smile and an eye roll.

Lou Lou didn't find humor in the gesture. "I'm not sure you should be disrespecting your boss."

Jo puckered her full lips in contemplation. "He's not my boss, but if he *were*," she paused for emphasis, "I'd most likely file a sexual harassment suit against him."

Lou Lou's eyes narrowed. "I don't believe you. He told me about you and how you got your job. That you were in a—"

"Lou," JT said in warning. "I see Kasie over there. Why don't you go over and say hi?"

"Ask her, JT. See if she tells you the truth. Vaughn said—"

Jo let out a heavy sigh. "Listen, Laurel—"

"*Laura Leigh*," she snapped back.

"Whatever. You've obviously made your mind up about me, so I won't bother trying to change it. As for Jackson." She glanced over and winked. "I'm happy to tell him anything he wants to know."

Lou Lou grabbed JT's arm. "Don't say I didn't warn you." She glanced at Jo, giving her the stink eye before walking off.

"Charming girl."

JT took a swig of beer. "Wanna tell me what that was all about?"

Jo opened her mouth, then clamped it shut as her eyes followed Lou Lou's retreating form. "Hold on, I'm fighting my baser instincts here…" She let the sentence trail as she tapped her fingers on the bar. After a moment, she swiveled around wide-eyed. "You know what? The doc was right."

"Not following again."

"It's not important." She waved it away. "Okay, look, your sister is young and naïve. And Vaughn? He's a real meat stick. So, you might want to keep an eye on them."

He nodded. "Yeah, I figured. But don't let Lou's appearance fool you. The girl is wily and smart as a whip. She can handle herself." He turned and leaned against the bar, facing her fully. "She's sure got it out for you, though."

Jo shrugged.

"So, how *did* you get the job?"

One side of Jo's lips twitched up. "Funny story. You remember the woman I hit at the fundraiser?"

JT nodded.

"She decided it wasn't humiliating enough to have me arrested, so she asked the courts to evaluate me for mental illness." She held up her hand. "It gets better. I was diagnosed with an anger disorder and sentenced to six weeks at a treatment facility."

"Damn." He coughed out a laugh.

"Yeah, well, the joke's on her. I enjoyed it."

JT burst out laughing. "You're pulling my leg, right?"

"Nope, I stayed at the Ritz of mental health, very posh. And on the crazy scale, I weighed in *slightly* below the guy who believed his cat was the reincarnation of Princess Diana. Perfectly manageable. Anyway, long story short, I met someone who worked for the show, and she needed a trend forecaster, so here I am."

JT couldn't stop grinning. "Small world." He sure liked her kind of crazy. She made him laugh, and she was refreshingly honest.

"Isn't it though?" She gave him a dazzling smile.

His mind took a side step as he caught the scent of cotton candy mixed with freshly baled hay. Addy appeared next to him, smelling the same as she had since high school.

"Hi, JT."

He pulled his eyes away from Jo. "Hey, Addy. This is Miss Josette Singer. The show hired her to help save Fowler's Pond."

"Oh, that's fantastic." Addy beamed up at him before turning her attention to Jo. "It's such a wonderful place; we'd sure hate to lose it."

Jo raised a brow. "Are you related to the family?"

Addy laughed. "Oh, no, I'm not. I...well, JT and I dated for a while, but I just meant the town. We would collectively feel the loss."

Jo nodded, her smile fading. "I should go." She turned to JT. "I was hoping to come by the farm tomorrow. See the place before I make my final recommendation."

"Sure." JT couldn't take his eyes off her as she walked back to the other end of the bar. He noticed Levi doing the same. It was apparent to anyone with a set of eyes that Levi was interested in Jo—and it bothered him.

"She's very...tall," Addy said, following JT's gaze. "Lou Lou said she was a viper, and I should come over and save you." She put a hand on his arm and squeezed playfully.

JT glanced at her hold on him, unsure what to make of it. "I noticed Tommy left. For a separated couple, you two sure see a lot of each other."

Addy withdrew her hand. "We still have a few things to work out."

JT huffed. "You're either with him, or you're not, Addy. Simple as that."

She chewed on the inside of her cheek—something he used to find endearing. "It's not that simple." She looked up at him, her eyes moist. "I wish I could tell you, but I can't. Not yet."

There was a time when her tears made him want to give her the world. Now they just made him frustrated and angry. "You don't owe me an explanation, Addy. We're not together, and whatever you're playing at, all these mixed messages you're sending, they gotta stop." Without waiting for a reply, he tossed some money on the bar and went to find Lou Lou.

Levi's bar was the nightly hang-out for the crew. It was within walking distance of the inn, served food and alcohol and was the only place in town that stayed open past eight. Jo and Kara had spent the last few days chatting up Levi, who was friendly and fun to flirt with—no doubt something the handsome bar owner was used to.

"How'd it go?" Kara asked after Jo returned.

Jo kept the smile pasted on her face as she sat back on her stool. "Peachy."

"Then why are you back here with me? I would have locked that shit down. He's hot. Like six-ways-to-Sunday, do-me-on-the-floor hot. I'm getting overheated just looking at him." Kara took a sip of her margarita and placed the glass on a napkin.

"Seems like I've got a bit of competition." Jo slammed back her club soda and lime.

Kara stretched her neck to look behind Jo's shoulder. "The Smurfette? Don't see it."

"She's his high school sweetheart."

"Oh...The one he's still in love with."

"*Allegedly*, yes. The old me would have accepted the challenge. The new me?" Jo shrugged and watched with interest as Jackson walked away from Addison. "Not so much."

"I don't know, looks like easy pickings."

Levi came over and laid a dry napkin in front of Kara before addressing Jo. "Would you like something else?"

Jo wagged her eyebrows. "What do you have in mind?"

He laughed. "If you're not careful, I'll tell you."

"Color me intrigued." She swirled the ice around in her glass.

Levi leaned over, close enough she could see the specks of gold in his brown eyes. "Do you really want to know what I want, Jo?"

His voice was so sexy she almost forgot she was acting. "Damn, you're good. Almost as good as me."

He pushed off the bar and chuckled. "There *is* something I'd like to discuss with you. Stick around?"

Jo raised a questioning brow, but nodded.

He tapped on the counter. "You won't be sorry." He grinned and walked backward a couple of steps before turning to help another patron.

"What was that about?" Kara asked.

Jo chewed on a piece of ice. "I have no idea."

22

This smells like potential.
-Ted Lasso

Jo turned in a circle, every inch of her room covered in clothing and footwear.

Kara chuckled. "You've got it bad."

Jo continued to peruse her options. "I do this for all my clients."

"*I'm* your client, and you're wearing a T-shirt that says, SOMETIMES I WET MY PLANTS, and a pair of boxer shorts."

Jo put her hands on her hips and turned to Kara, who was rearranging her outfits. "What are you doing? I just put those together."

"Well, they're wrong. You can't put wellies together with these jeans and that shirt. And those chocolate suede boots would look much better with the classic white button-down. And this," she held up a silk crepe de chine blouse, "has no business trying to fit in with the rest of the Midwest chic—or whatever you call this—collection."

"It's plaid," Jo countered.

"It's silk."

She fell back on the bed, her arms splayed above her head. "Fine. You pick it."

Kara chose a white tailored oxford shirt and a pair of camel-colored fitted pants. She added Burberry riding boots and a

Balenciaga houndstooth blazer, which she laid on top. "That's your outfit."

Jo didn't even look over. "What am I doing, Kara?"

"Dressing for a man?"

She turned to face her. "Where's my resolve? Have I learned nothing from therapy?"

"Sure, you have. You've got all the tools necessary to create meaningful relationships. This just isn't the time to implement any of it. We're on *location*. Think of Jackson as your last hurrah, your final performance, your swan song."

"I don't know, Kar. I'm trying to break patterns, not repeat them." Jo reached over and rubbed a silk sleeve.

"You're not going to fall off the wagon of self-actualization. Use what you've been taught, practice mindfulness, and listen to your gut."

"You make a compelling argument." Jo stood and picked up the clothing Kara had laid out. "Just do me a favor. If you see me sliding down the slippery slope of self-sabotage, stop me before it ends in my humiliation."

She walked into the bathroom, knowing the odds were not in her favor.

Jo drove up the long gravel drive, mesmerized by the iconic scene. Norman Rockwell would have painted the hell out of it. White farmhouse, red barn, silver and blue silos, livestock in the pasture beyond. It was such a slice of Americana it made her chest hurt.

She parked the car and approached the house. The screen door squeaked as Jackson came onto the porch, greeting her in bare feet, a pair of old jeans, and a fitted white T-shirt.

As she got closer, the smell of soap triggered visions of him in the shower—with her wrapped around him. *Oh, good Lord. I'll be humping his leg by noon.*

"Mornin', Josie." He gave her a lazy smile.

She tried to focus. "Good morning. I hope I'm not too early. You didn't mention a time."

"You ran off before I had a chance. But no, it's not too early." He held the door open for her, and she might have accidentally brushed up against him on purpose when she passed.

She found the interior charming, if a little worn. It was a functional space, but looking around, she realized it was also a place full of memories, and, she suspected, love. She absently rubbed at her chest.

"Josie Singer, these are my parents, Brenda and Charles Taylor."

Jo had thought the nickname was a way to rile her, but apparently not. She smiled warmly at the middle-aged couple. "So very nice to meet you."

"Would you like some coffee, Josie?" Brenda asked. "I made a fresh pot and there's a butter cake cooling in the pan."

"Thank you, that sounds delicious." Jo never turned down an invitation for baked goods.

As she'd hoped, the cake was divine. But her true purpose for the little coffee klatch was to get a feel for what they were like. According to Levi, her proposal for re-inventing the farm would not go over well with the Taylors. When she'd questioned him, he wouldn't elaborate. Instead, he pitched an idea of his own. His enthusiasm was so contagious she agreed to look into it, even though the show had already signed off on her recommendation.

The Taylors were warm and friendly and seemed open to new ideas, making her wonder why Levi thought they wouldn't like her suggestions. It was a solid plan which would show a profit within a year. She said her goodbyes to Brenda and Charles with more optimism than when she'd arrived.

"Ready for your tour?" Jackson asked, leading her out the back door.

"I am." She didn't need to view the property; the production company had already done the preliminary survey. But it was a perfect excuse to spend more time with Jackson.

As they walked, he peppered his commentary with anecdotes from his childhood, and Jo found herself becoming dangerously smitten by the tales of his wholesome upbringing.

"I think you'll like this next part," Jackson said as he led her to a barn.

From the smell of things, she highly doubted it.

"It's a little late in the lambing season, but we've got a ewe that was in labor this morning." He grabbed her arm so she would miss a pile of...something. "Watch your step."

They walked to the far corner where a man stood. "Hey, Ray. How's she doing?"

"Oh, fine. Shouldn't be long now."

They stood and watched the ewe get up and pace, then lie back down.

"Oh! She just pushed it halfway out." Jo watched the contractions start again, and when the ewe rose, the lamb slid out.

She grabbed onto the post and leaned closer. Jackson put his arm out to stop her, pressing against her breasts and sending a jolt of electricity through her.

"Your scent," he breathed in, his nose pushing against her hair, "could confuse the mother. You don't want to get any closer."

Holy crap. The periodic table didn't have this much chemistry.

They left the barn and passed the new lambs huddled against their mothers in the field. "That was amazing. Thank you."

Jackson glanced her way. "My pleasure." He took her hand and ducked under a low branch. They walked down a dirt path that led to another corralled area where horses grazed.

"So, what do you think?"

That your eyes are the color of ripe blueberries. "Sorry, think about what?"

"I asked if you'd like to tack up. Go for a ride."

"Oh. Well, I..."

"You'll get less dirty on a horse than you will on the quad."

"Are they my only choices?"

Jackson's low-throated laughter set off another spark of attraction. "If you want to see the other seventy-five percent of the farm, they are. I'd take the truck, but there are some places it can't go."

Jo looked over his shoulder at the mud-encrusted ATV. "I don't mind getting a little dirty." *Not entirely true*, but it was still preferable to the alternative.

He grabbed two helmets and walked over to the bike. "You ever been on one of these?"

"I've been on a motorcycle." *While parked for a photoshoot.*

"Then you'll be fine. Just hold on tight and follow my lead. Ready?"

Nope. "Yup."

JT handed her a helmet and showed her where to put her feet and hands. They started slowly, but after a few bumps, she let go of the handles and grabbed onto him; her fists clenching the shirt on either side of his broad back. She wanted to enjoy the way his muscles reacted to every movement of the bike, but fear kept her lust at bay.

It wasn't long before they stopped along a rise overlooking the farm.

"Sorry about your shirt." She tried to smooth out the twisted cotton.

JT took off his helmet and smiled. "You sure you've been on a motorcycle? I barely got out of first gear."

Jo rolled her eyes in response. She hopped off, placed her helmet on the seat, and turned, taking in the scenery. There was a low metal building to her left—the patina rusted in a way high-end stores replicated—an overgrown pasture and woods beyond. Completing the circle, her eyes traveled to where the land sloped into a myriad of purposeful patches, some cordoned off with livestock, others delineated by the crops they contained. A large body of water sat to the right, and beyond, a small white building that reminded her of an old-fashioned schoolhouse. It was idyllic.

Jackson's voice pulled her back. "Maybe you can find some use for it."

"Hmm?"

"The fallow field. We haven't grown anything up here for years." He walked toward the building, signaling for her to follow. "I want to show you something." He leaned down and pulled on the handle of a large bay door. Inside was a small plane. "It's a fixed-wing Cessna used for crop dusting—least it used to be. It's how I became interested in flying."

She followed him in. "You must miss it."

He ran a hand along one wing. "Sometimes." He reached inside the plane and pulled out a dark green canvas duffel. "But not very often. Not yet, anyway."

They walked to the edge of the woods. "I thought you might like to see one of my favorite places on the farm." He grinned and grabbed her hand, pulling her along a well-worn path through tall evergreens.

They came to a small clearing that sloped down to a wide creek. JT took an Army blanket out of the bag and laid it on the ground. "Didn't want you to get your clothes dirty." He winked and made his way to the water's edge, where he skipped a couple of stones.

Jo leaned back, stretching her long legs out in front of her. "It's beautiful here. I can see why you love it."

She wasn't looking at the scenery at all, but his broad back. How the muscles moved when he threw the stones, his jeans straining around his powerful thighs as he crouched down to gather more. He exuded power and masculinity, something she normally wasn't attracted to. Then again, the muscle-bound men in the city were a different breed. All vanity and show. Jackson seemed, if not unaware, then unaffected by the beauty of his body.

He shook the pebbles in his hand, sending one off after another, and spoke without turning. "I should never have left. I spent most of my life trying to get away, never realizing or caring how much I was needed here." He skipped a few more. "Now it might be too late."

Jo halted like Pavlov's dog—newly conditioned to weigh her words before speaking. "There's nothing wrong with wanting to be your own person. To find what makes you happy. That's not selfish, it's self-preservation."

Jackson turned and held her gaze, brushing his hands against his jeans. "You know what true self-preservation is, Josie? It's being able to control your emotions."

Jo's eyes widened in recognition of a kindred soul. She pulled her legs up and leaned forward, curious to hear more.

"The Army teaches you how to turn fear into something else—anger, excitement. Loyalty to a common cause. It's different for every soldier." He kept his tone light and conversational, but Jo felt the weight of his words. "When your brain and body kick into survival mode, you need a way to channel your fear. For some, it means turning inward and becoming hyper-focused. For others, just plain hyped and ready to fight. And the ones that have no control?" He shrugged and glanced away. "They shit themselves."

"That's...Wow. Which one are you?" The words spilled out before she could catch herself.

"None. All—at one time or another." Jackson cleared his throat. "Your body prepares for damage the second you engage. There's no rational thought, only survival. You do what you've been trained to do. Some even enjoy it, the euphoria after a mission. They crave it like an addiction. The top brass loves those guys." He made a sound between a laugh and a cough. "I honestly don't know why I'm telling you all this."

Jo didn't either, but he fascinated the hell out of her. "Sometimes it's easier to talk to a stranger."

"Is that what we are? Strangers?" Jackson gave her a lopsided grin.

"I hope not." Glad to be flirting again, Jo rose, walked to the rocky edge, and grabbed a handful of stones. "So, how does this work?" She tossed one into the flowing water. It landed with a resounding *plunk*.

JT laughed and came to stand beside her. "Not like that." He turned her hand over and examined the contents. "You start with a flat stone." He took two. "You can dump the rest."

She did, and he handed her the two he'd kept.

"It's all in the flick of the wrist. The trick is to skim the surface at an angle. The horizontal velocity determines if it sinks or skips." He crouched low and tossed one in.

Jo wasn't sure how many times it skipped since her eyes were on him.

"Now give it a try."

Jo made a wide arc with her arm. The stone flew off to the right.

"You've got no spin. Here." He reached over and wrapped his fingers around her hand. She lost focus when his thumb caressed the soft skin of her wrist. He turned her palm inward and, with a quick snap, sent the stone careening across the water.

Jo let out a whoop and smiled up at him. He brought a hand to her cheek, letting his fingers trail down her neck and leaned in. She smiled knowingly...as he passed her lips on the way to pick up a rock.

Dammit!

Jo tried to hide her disappointment as Jackson stood, rubbing a smooth pebble in a contemplative manner.

"Something special about that one?"

He glanced up. "Nah, not really." He slipped it in his pocket.

"Why'd you keep it then?"

"It's a worry stone."

Jo tilted her head and waited for him to explain.

He pulled it back out. "There's an indent in the middle. You rub it when you're feeling anxious. Or to relax, I guess." He held it out for her examination.

She took it, moving her thumb across the hollow. After several passes, she understood the appeal.

"Keep it," he offered. "I've got plenty."

"Thanks." Her thumb fit perfectly in the warm groove.

He held out his hand for her, and they made their way back to the blanket.

"So, why *did* you want to leave here?" she asked as they sat down.

"Don't really know. I was bored, restless. Just wanted out." He leaned back on his elbows, legs crossed in front of him. "When I lost my football scholarship, I panicked. Thought I'd be stuck here forever. If it wasn't for the Army..." He let the words drift as he fell onto his back. "Now I'm thinking I might've been better off had I never left."

Jo's newfound empathy skills were working overtime. *Listen, be engaged, ask questions.* "What would your life have been like had you stayed?"

Jackson folded his arms behind his head. "Probably would've worked the farm, gotten married, had a couple kids by now."

"Sounds boring." *Dammit, Jo. Redeem. Redeem!* "But very nice."

Jackson barked out a laugh. "How about you? Have you ever thought about leaving the city?"

"You mean permanently? No. But I travel all the time and if I get restless, I go to the Jersey shore. The ocean is just an hour from the city." She turned the charm bracelet around to where Lucy dangled. "As a kid, I'd climb this big elephant monument and imagine all sorts of adventures."

He grabbed a bottle of water from the bag. "And now?"

She watched him drink, his Adam's apple moving up and down as he swallowed. Her eyes fell to the hollow at the base of his throat. She'd like to put her mouth there...

"Josie?"

"Hmm?"

He laughed. "What are your hopes and dreams now?" He handed her the bottle.

"Now? As in, this moment?" *Wishing my mouth was where this bottle had been.*

He shrugged. "Now, tomorrow. Next year."

She decided to be honest. "I don't have dreams anymore. I have wants."

He gave her a curious look. "What is it you want, then?"

Jo turned her body toward his and lowered herself to one elbow. "To help save Fowler's Pond, to be reinstated to the board of my family's nonprofit, to see the Temples of Siem Reap," and before she could stop the words from tumbling out, "And to kiss you."

Jackson licked his bottom lip and lowered his eyes to her mouth. Jo didn't wait for him to make the first move this time. She brushed her lips softly against his and hoped she hadn't misread the signals. Thankfully, he cupped the back of her head and deepened the kiss, lowering her onto the blanket.

Jo had experienced more first kisses than she'd ever admit, but none came close to the achingly slow and intense one she shared with Jackson. It felt monumental in a way it shouldn't have.

When he tried to withdraw, her lips followed. He smiled down at her, running a thumb, and then his tongue, across her bottom lip before moving his mouth to her cheek, her eyes, her brow. He did it with such reverence and focus, she knew she'd remember his kisses long after all others had been forgotten.

They stayed that way, in innocent exploration, tiptoeing around desire, until the leash on their passion became strained.

Her hand moved down his chest to his hard abs and tugged at the hem of his shirt, wanting to feel the skin beneath.

Jackson sucked in a quick breath at the feel of her fingers, then began an exploration of his own. A low throaty groan escaped when he unbuttoned her shirt, pushing it aside to reveal her lace bra, and lowered his mouth to the mound of flesh above the delicate material.

Jo was so lost in his touch, she barely registered the hard squeeze of her hip before he pulled back and sprung to his feet. She watched him pace and adjust the bulge in his jeans.

Clearing his throat, he glanced her way. "I'm sorry. I haven't been with a woman in a while, and I'm afraid it's clouding my judgment."

Feeling foolish, she stood, buttoned her shirt, and brushed off her pants. "We should go." She turned to leave, but before she took a step, Jackson reached for her.

"Wait. I'm sorry. That came out wrong."

"It's fine. I understand."

"I'm not sure you do. I didn't want to take advantage of you, is all."

"No need to explain." Jo shook off his hand, and the weight of rejection as the Ghost of Therapy Past walked beside her.

"Jo, why do you think you are so free with your body, but not your emotions?"

"Sex makes me feel powerful. I get off on the way men look at me, want me. Emotions are complications. They get in the way."

"Of what, exactly?"

"Look, I was trying to be respectful." Jackson moved to the front of her, walking backwards. "I'm not a mind reader, Josie. Tell me what you're thinking."

"It's okay, really. I'm fine." She smiled and patted his arm, wanting to just move on. This whole thing was a bad idea. She needed time to think, to get Dr. Fielding out of her head.

"Your pattern of short-term, superficial relationships stems from an inability to connect on an intimate level. You sabotage relationships, ending them before becoming emotionally involved..."

Jackson moved to her side. "I'm sure you're used to men wanting you, and I'm not gonna lie and say I'm any different. But that's not all I'm after. I *like* you. I like talking to you. I've been drawn to you since that first phone call, before I knew how beautiful you were."

He had it wrong. She wanted him to stop being so *goddamn nice*. It was fucking with her no-attachment vibe. This was not the time or place to test her emotional depths. This was a temporary situation. She needed to snap out of it, deep-six the mental mind fuck, and get him on the same page.

She turned to him with her hands on her hips. "I like you, too. But trying to protect my honor has the opposite effect on me—it makes me feel cheap. I like sex, Jackson. I have a high sex drive, and I don't need the trappings of a relationship to enjoy it. You feeling guilty tells me you *do*—or at least you expect a woman to." An image of the beautiful copper goddess popped into her head. "What happened between you and Samantha back in Philadelphia?"

"You mean physically? Nothing."

"Was that your decision or hers?"

His brow furrowed in confusion. "Mine."

He turned that beautiful girl down.

His need to attach sex to something more spelled a whole lot of trouble for Jo 2.0. He was like a Matador waving a red cape. Jo recognized the danger, but like the bull, she would charge forward regardless, even knowing his sword might pierce her newfound heart.

They didn't talk again until the ATV was parked in its original spot near the utility barn.

Jackson took off his helmet and ran a hand through his short blonde hair, pinning her with a stare. "I can do temporary, Josie, if that's what you want. But I'd like it to be more than sex."

His words had a way of sneaking under her skin—a warning for her to be careful. But she knew she wouldn't heed it. "What did you have in mind?"

He shrugged. "Companionship, friendship. Just because there's a time limit doesn't mean it can't be real."

She bit at her top lip. She wanted him. *Badly*. But his wishes came dangerously close to a relationship. She nodded anyway, unable to get the feel of his kiss off her lips.

JT woke in a pool of sweat, his heart racing. He grabbed a stone off the nightstand and practiced his breathing. After a couple minutes, the symptoms dissipated, and he no longer bore the weight of dread. He put the pebble back with the rest and picked up his phone. 1:42 AM.

His thoughts wandered to Josie and that ridiculous agreement. He'd only suggested it for fear she wouldn't agree to date him. Either you connected with someone or you didn't. You couldn't tame your feelings like a horse, put a bit in its mouth, and tell it where to go. He only hoped they were heading in the right direction.

23

When nothing is going right, go left.
- Unknown

"Hemp," Jo began. She stood before a room full of TV producers, cast and crew, members of the Taylor family, and community leaders to pitch an idea that had already been decided on—all for the benefit of the cameras. The Taylors—whose lives would be affected—weren't told ahead of time, so the cameras could capture their reaction.

After a few raised eyebrows and whispers, she continued, "Hemp is the future of farming. It's one of the most lucrative crops in the U.S. today, and Kentucky ranks among the top states in the nation for cultivation."

"You want to grow marijuana on my land?" Charles said, a sharp edge to his voice.

Jo should've expected that. Levi *had* warned her. "Mr. Taylor, industrial hemp has less than .3 percent THC and is completely legal in Kentucky."

"I won't grow drugs."

Jackson laid a hand on his father's arm. "Dad, let her finish."

Jo's eyes softened, and she nodded her thanks before resuming. "Industrial hemp has many applications. From food and feed, to fuel and building materials. It produces high-quality oil and protein products, plus we get the bonus of textiles and bio-plastics. It's already used in animal agriculture around the world." Jo addressed Charles directly. "I assume you use baler twine on your farm?" When he nodded, she continued, "Plastic baling twine kills wildlife. It pollutes their habitat and produces tons of waste in local landfills. Hemp-derived twine is completely biodegradable and won't harm the environment." Jo clicked on the next slide. "Not only is it better for our ecosystem, it's up to four times more profitable than soybeans and corn and offers unlimited growth potential." Jo hesitated, knowing this next bit would be even less appealing to the Taylors.

"There is another very lucrative way to harvest hemp, and that's in the extraction of its oil. CBD oil has many health benefits—"

Charles leaped to his feet. "I've heard enough. If this is all you have to offer, I'm not interested."

Gail stood and held out a hand. "Mr. Taylor, if you would please just hear her out—"

Amidst the heated debate, Levi entered wearing a suit and carrying a box. Jo blessed his timing and tried to regain control of the room. "I think you all know Levi. He approached me several days ago and asked to present an idea for a partnership. I've done some preliminary research and believe his proposal has merit."

She stepped aside and let Levi take center stage. She should have forewarned Gail. The scowl on the producer's face confirmed the surprise wasn't a pleasant one.

"I want to thank Miss Singer for the opportunity to present my idea to help turn Fowler's Pond into a profitable enterprise." He pulled out four bottles and lined them up on the conference table. Each one had a Fowler's Pond label. "Now, you all know I make my own bourbon, and it sells pretty well locally, but I don't have the means to scale up production. Miss Singer has been working with me to create a plan to partner with the farm, using their crops and land to make bourbon and other spirits on a larger scale..."

Levi held the interest of those in the room, most notably Charles, who nodded encouragingly, asked questions, and clapped at the conclusion. But the one person Levi needed to impress looked anything but. Jo sensed Gail's displeasure from the moment he walked into the room. Jo had miscalculated and feared the cost might be her job.

The production staff had turned the inn's sunroom into a makeshift office. It was here that Jo was summoned. She took a deep breath and opened the French doors to her execution.

"Ah, Jo. There you are." Gail waved her in.

Jo took a seat and waited for her ass whooping.

Gail peered up from the rim of her glasses. "Didn't go as we hoped, did it?"

Jo sighed. "No, it didn't."

"Changing crops is inexpensive. We've got advertisers, product placements, environmental group involvement, experts in the field…Tangentially, we have a slew of avenues we can go down to make money for the show and for the Taylors." She raised her brows. "You know what we have now, Jo?"

"It certainly changes our—"

Gail slapped a hand on the desk. "We got bupkis! That's what we have. We'd need to start from scratch. It would set us back weeks and blow our budget. *HomeTown Heroes* is about Jackson and his family farm, not about townies looking to profit from free advertisement."

"I think if we—"

"We didn't plan for it. It wasn't in your proposal." She flipped through the stack of papers in front of her. "Anywhere in here mention the production of alcohol?"

"No, but it's—"

Gail held up her hand. "My questions are rhetorical. We've already spent too much on the original concept. Which means…"

Jo stayed quiet, uncertain if she should speak.

The producer leaned in. "You're going to change their minds. Get them to agree to the original plan, or there won't be a show, and they *will* lose the farm."

"What did they say?" Levi asked as Jo entered the bar.

She pulled out a stool and motioned for him to pour from the bottle on the counter. "I'd like to try your famous bourbon first."

He smiled and poured two fingers into a tumbler. "*Fowler's Pond's* famous bourbon."

Jo raised the glass and downed half the fiery liquid before raising her eyes to Levi's hopeful ones. "We hit a little snag."

He nodded and capped the bottle. "What went wrong?"

Jo tossed back the rest of the whiskey. "I misjudged the show's ability to switch gears." She reached out a hand to get his attention. "Levi, I forecast trends. I have no knowledge of actual implementation and have zero experience in the film and TV industry. They've already invested weeks developing the hemp concept, and as a crop, it's an easy transition with little output of capital. They've lined up experts related to hemp agriculture, product placements, eco groups—the whole nine yards. It would take twice that amount of time to retrofit a building for a distillery, and at least double the cash outlay. It might be feasible after the farm turns a profit, but now? They're not going for it. I'm sorry."

"But what else do they have? Charles won't go along with your idea, and he seemed real enthusiastic about mine. I've done my research. The potential is there."

"It's not just about the business model, it's a show about Jackson and his family. Unless you're family, it doesn't fit within the parameters of the show."

He leaned against the back bar and pulled on his short, dark beard. "What if I was?"

Jo motioned for another shot. "Was what?"

"Part of the family."

Jo laughed. "Planning on marrying Laura Leigh?"

"God, no! I'm Charles' son."

Jo's eyes grew wide. "Get the fuck out."

He shrugged. "Not a secret around here, Jo."

"I bet the producers don't know that. This could change things, Levi." Jo hopped off the stool. "I'll be back." She turned at the door. "You realize you'll be part of the show, right?"

"Yeah, I figured. But I doubt they'll focus too much on me. I'm not the hero."

One hour and thirty-seven minutes.

That's how long it took for Jo to be rejected for the second time. To be dismissed, to pack a bag, and head to the airport.

They didn't fire her. *Not yet, anyway.* She had a week to persuade the Taylors of the enormous benefit of hemp agriculture *or* come up with an alternate plan that wouldn't cost more time or money. *Easy peasy.*

Not wanting to disappoint Levi again, and knowing it would be an uphill battle to convince Charles to change his mind, she flew to Philadelphia. Wealth was a great equalizer, and she had a plan that would make everyone happy—she hoped.

The trip took longer than expected, almost a week, but she accomplished what she set out to do. When she got back, she headed straight to Levi's to celebrate.

24

Be so good they can't ignore you.
- Steve Martin

JT parked the bike in the gravel lot across from Levi's and enjoyed the low rumble of the 158-horsepower v-twin beauty before turning off the engine. The producers had presented it to him that morning. It was one of the perks of product placement, and all he had to do was ride it for the show.

He spotted Addy as he climbed off the bike, and she waited for him to catch up.

"Nice ride. You here to see *The Walleyes*?"

The band was a local favorite, which meant standing room only. "Nah, just stopping by to congratulate Levi." JT wished they'd picked another day to celebrate the partnership of *Fowler's Pond Distillery Company*.

"I heard he's gonna be part of the show."

"Word certainly gets around."

Addy linked her arm in his. "It's a small town, JT. Everyone's excited about it. Mrs. Hillerby told me they asked her to do catering for the crew while they're in town."

They were about to enter when she stopped him. "Can we talk later? I don't mean tonight, but maybe tomorrow, by the old oak tree."

That tree was full of memories and firsts—first kisses and words of love. Where he and Addy lost their virginity to one another. It wasn't a place for a casual conversation. "Why there, Addy? Why now?"

She stared at the ground. "I've made a decision, and I wanted to let you know—to explain why I've been acting the way I have for the last few months. I thought, well," she pinned him with her pale blue eyes, "I thought it would be a fitting spot."

While half of JT wanted to go, the other half realized it was too late. His heart no longer jumped at the sight of her, and he suspected it was because of Josie. Since they weren't filming tomorrow, he agreed. "Yeah, I'll be there."

She squeezed his arm. "Great! I'll pack lunch and meet you at noon."

They pushed their way through the crowd blocking the entrance, and JT found a spot to stand near the restrooms. "Why don't you wait here and I'll grab us a couple of beers?"

Addy clung to him. "I'll go with you."

JT had to tamp down his fight-or-flight reflex as they made their way to the bar.

He spotted Josie waving around a martini glass as she talked with her co-workers. He'd never seen her dressed so casually in a pair of faded jeans and T-shirt. Her hair was in a messy bun at her neck, with loose tendrils framing a face void of makeup. She looked young and fresh and beautiful, and he couldn't keep his eyes off her.

She must have sensed his stare, for she pivoted and leaned against the bar. Her shirt read "Fowler's Pond Distillery" and fit her like a glove. The vibrant smile on her lips died as she watched them approach.

"Hey, Josie. You remember Addy?"

She nodded. "Yup."

JT had the feeling Jo thought he and Addy were together. "Can I get you anything to drink?"

Jo held up her glass. "Got one, thanks."

"Just water, please. I have to meet with clients in the morning." Addy smiled up at him. "Thank you, JT."

Josie snorted as he elbowed his way to the front of the bar. When he returned, he handed Addy her water and motioned to Jo's martini. "I thought you didn't drink on the job."

"It's Friday. Plus, I no longer work for the show, so..." Jo raised her glass and took a sip.

"They fired you?"

"Not exactly."

"Then what exactly?" He moved closer. "I haven't seen you all week. Where have you been?"

"JT," Addy said, putting a hand on his arm.

He stepped back, taking a deep breath. "Sorry. It's none of my business."

"No, I should have told you. I tried calling—"

"I changed my number."

"Oh..." Jo drew out, nodding. "I flew home to Philly. Just got in this afternoon."

JT's frustration turned to concern. "Is everything okay?"

"Yes, fine. Holly says hello, by the way."

Addy eyed them curiously. "So, the two of you already knew each other?"

He pulled his eyes away from Jo. "We met at a fundraiser in Philadelphia. I was there to honor Kevin DePaul."

"I heard about—Oh!" Addy's eyes widened, and she turned to Jo. "I know who you are. You're that socialite, the one who—"

"Guilty as charged." Jo chuckled. "Actually, I was never convicted."

"I can't believe I didn't put it together sooner."

"Put what together?" Jo asked.

"Well, Lou Lou—"

"Don't listen to Lou," JT said, cutting her off. "She's got a squirrel up her skirt when it comes to Josie."

The band began to warm up, and people pushed their way onto the already crowded dance floor.

"Hey, Jo. You're up!" Levi called from behind the bar.

Without turning, Jo raised an arm and gave him a thumbs up. She finished her drink and handed the glass to JT. "I lost a bet, and now it's show time." She pulled herself onto the bar as the band played Joe Cocker's 'You Can Leave Your Hat On.'

It wasn't the first time someone danced on the bar, and people moved their drinks out of the way in anticipation. A few men cheered when she kicked her shoes off. With bare feet, she worked her way down the bar, embracing the song like a second skin. Stopping near the end, she turned to the crowd, and in one fluid motion, slid her hands down her inner thighs and pushed her knees apart, sinking into a crouch. The crowd went wild when she reached out and grabbed someone's cap, putting it on as everyone sang the chorus.

JT couldn't take his eyes off her body as she eased back up. She danced with a sensuality that made men throw money at her. When a guy reached for her, JT hauled him back by the collar. Another jumped onto the bar, only to find himself flat on the floor seconds later. The song ended to cheers and catcalls, and Jo took a bow. JT used the opportunity to grab her by the waist and swing her around. He held her close as she slid down his body to the floor.

"Well, hello there." She smiled, her eyes traveling between their bodies. "I see you liked my dance." Her smile disappeared when she spotted something over his shoulder. "Uh, Jacks, your girlfriend doesn't look too happy."

"Who?" He turned reflexively.

"Addison. She just walked out the door. You might want to go after her."

"Jo, Addy and I aren't together. We haven't been for years."

Jo took a step back and accepted a drink from someone who complimented her dancing. She thanked them and clinked her glass to theirs before turning to him, her smile fading once again.

"I wish you wouldn't do that," he said.

"Do what?"

"Stop smiling every time you look at me."

She sighed. "Can we move to a quieter spot? I can't hear myself think."

JT grabbed her hand and led her down a hall to Levi's office. He reached for a key above the doorframe and unlocked it.

"Um, I'm pretty sure that's breaking and entering, and since I already have a record..."

"We're just entering, not sure that constitutes a crime." He replaced the key and opened the door. "And don't worry, Levi won't mind."

He *would* mind, but the bar was so busy JT doubted his brother would notice.

He closed the door as soon as she walked through and pulled her to him. "I missed you," he said, kissing the top of her head.

She pulled away, taking a step back. "Why were you with Addison tonight?"

He shook his head. "I wasn't. We walked in together, is all."

"Does she know that?"

JT rubbed his neck. "Yeah, of course."

"Do you still love her?"

"Christ, Jo. I don't want to talk about Addy."

Jo's head fell forward. "So, that's a yes."

"No, it's not. But I'm not gonna lie either. I was in love with her most of my life and I can't just shut that off." He cupped her face in his hands. "I thought about you all week. Even checked at the inn." He ran a thumb over her full bottom lip before placing a gentle kiss there. A playful smile pulled at the corners of his mouth as he brushed a stray curl from her face. "You sure dance like you know your way around a pole, Josie."

Jo laughed and punched him in the arm. "I've had years of formal training."

"I bet." He leaned down and nipped at her lip, smiling into her mouth.

Jo wanted to sink into the kiss, but she couldn't. Not yet. She'd thought a lot about him while she was gone, and when she saw him walk into the bar, her stomach flipped like a world class gymnast—until she saw Addison by his side.

Seeing them together dredged up feelings from her relationship with Masi, and she refused to be in that position again. Even for a short-term affair.

Jackson stepped back. "What's wrong?"

Her hands brushed over his pecs, itching to explore, but pulled back to avoid distraction. "I want to be with you. I *really* do. But before we go any further, you need to figure out if *this*"—she motioned between them,—"is what you really want." He blinked in confusion, and she tugged on his shirt. "I have a life in Philadelphia, Jackson. That's not to say we can't enjoy one another while I'm here, but I won't share you." She shrugged and put her hands on the desk behind her, needing to put distance between them. "Is a fling with me worth ruining a chance with Addison?" She took a deep breath and waited.

Jackson pulled at his lower lip. "I can't flip a switch and turn off my feelings for you, Josie, any more than I can predict the future or forget my past." He closed the gap again and rested his hands on her hips. "But I can promise you one thing. You'll have no competition while we're together."

She let out the breath she'd been holding and grinned. When he pressed closer, she sat back on the desk and wrapped her legs around him. He lifted her up and walked to the couch, where he turned and fell back. She straddled him and ran her hands over his chest. "You are one fine looking man, Jackson Taylor."

"I'm more than just a pretty face," he said with mock indignation.

She raised a brow, looking at the bulge in his jeans. "Who said anything about your face?"

He threw back his head and laughed. The sight of his joy, of his muscular neck, twisted her insides. She licked the column of his throat, eliciting a moan, before moving to his ear.

Jackson pulled her in for a long kiss, his hands stroking down her body and under her shirt, caressing the skin beneath.

It was Jo's turn to vocalize her pleasure when he unhooked her bra, kneading the soft flesh of her breasts. His thumbs brushed over her taut peaks and she pressed into him, rocking back and forth on his impressive hard-on—until he stopped and tilted his head back.

He brought one hand to his eyes, pinching the bridge of his nose, while the other rested firmly on her thigh. "Gotta give me a minute, or I'm gonna embarrass myself."

But Jo didn't want to—she wanted to see him go off. She slapped Dr. Fielding's warning into next Tuesday and brought his hands back to her chest.

Jackson chuckled, shaking his head. "All right. Come here, sugar." He hooked his thumbs under the hem of her shirt and lifted it above her breasts. Catching her under the arms, he pulled her towards him.

The sensation of his mouth and tongue on her breast went straight to her core. "Yes, Jacks. *That*. Don't stop." Jo wrapped her arms around his head and held him to her. He latched onto a nipple, making the ache in her groin unbearable. She needed pressure. She needed release.

"*Jacks.*"

She felt the cold air on her wet flesh as he let go.

"Take your hair down for me, Jo," he said in a strained whisper.

Her eyes moved to the door as she lifted her hands to her hair.

Jackson followed her gaze. "I locked it."

She smiled and removed the pins, shaking out the mass of curls.

"Damn, if you don't do it for me." He wrapped a hand around the dark length and pulled her head back. With the other, he stroked her exposed neck and breasts. His touch became less gentle as he pushed up, rubbing his erection against her. Their breathing became labored as they moved against each other, both reaching for their climax. His fingers pinched her nipples, sending her over the edge. She jerked back and forth until he grabbed her waist and pressed down, using the friction to bring himself to completion.

Her head fell to his shoulder, and they slowly regained their senses.

"Well, that was unexpected." She huffed out a laugh.

"Christ, I feel like a teenager dry humping in my truck." He leaned his head against the couch and brushed back her long silky waves. "You sure got a lot of hair, Josie."

"Too much. Some days I fantasize about chopping it all off."

"I hope you don't." He swept the long mass over her shoulder. "The first time I met you—when I saw you in that hotel room." He made a sound deep in his throat, twisting a curl around his finger. "I fantasized about wrapping it around my...body." One side of his mouth twitched up. "Still do."

The thought had her biting her lip. "You might just be my ideal man." She gave him a quick peck before climbing off. "But I think we tempted fate enough for one night." She hooked her bra, pulled down her shirt, and bent to find her hair pins.

Jackson stooped to help. "Night's still young," he said, flashing her a smile.

As much as I would like to... "How about tomorrow night?"

"Sure." He leaned in for a kiss, then stood. "I'll pick you up at six?"

She hopped up, twisting her hair into a knot. "Can't wait."

Jackson glanced down at the sticky moisture on his jeans and shirt. "Uh, I think I'm gonna head out the back." He pulled her in for one last kiss. "Tomorrow."

25

You can't have your Kate and Edith too.
- Statler Brothers

"You look rather perky this morning," Kara said, sliding into the chair across from Jo in the inn's dining room. "Did you tell him?"

Jo popped a piece of fruit into her mouth. "About investing in the distillery? Nope, not sure I'm going to."

"Uh, bad idea. You don't want him finding out from someone else."

"Last night wasn't the right time. We were dealing with other issues."

"You mean hot sex? Please tell me you did the nasty."

"Not exactly. Not with Dr. Fielding in my head."

"Ew."

"He's like a psychological ninja, Kara. A stealth emotional manipulator who appears out of nowhere in my subconscious. I won't label it brainwashing, but it was a definite quick rinse."

Kara shook her head. "Dude, to live a minute in your brain." She reached over and grabbed a strawberry from Jo's plate.

"Hey! Get your own."

"Jackson basically marked his territory last night. Throwing those guys to the ground and then pulling you off the bar and into his arms." Kara sighed. "I would have dropped to my knees on that dirty floor and given him a proper thank you."

"Oh, don't worry, I showed him my gratitude." Jo grabbed her coffee and sat back. "But I want him to like me, Kar, not just want to fuck me. Which is one peanut short of a Snickers, since that's exactly what I told him I wanted."

"Jo, all men rate a woman's fuckability factor first, before they invest the time in getting to know them. It's like, in their genetic code or something."

Jo raised a brow. "I'm sure these studies have been peer-reviewed." She placed her cup down. "Dr. Fielding said I wield my sexuality like a sword, cutting out the intimacy and setting boundaries before I allow myself to get too close. This would be a terrible time for me to rethink that strategy."

"Then don't. Put your emotional growth on the back burner and enjoy what Jackson has to offer, or I will."

"Touch him and die."

Kara laughed. "Something tells me he wouldn't accept. Besides, I'm holding out for my perfect match. Speaking of things that *match*, I'm gonna need your help this afternoon."

Jo's phone lit up as soon as she got back to her room. She'd missed two calls and five texts from Drew. He picked up on the first ring.

"Where have you been? I've been calling for *days*."

Jo glanced at her watch. "It's been less than an hour."

"I'm in no mood to argue. You need to come to LA; I've booked you a flight for this afternoon."

Used to Drew's dramatics, she remained calm. "Um, not going to happen. I have a date tonight."

"Jobo, this is important."

"So is my date. But humor me. Why do you need me? Can't Holly fly out?"

"It's not that kind of disaster. I need you to be a *beard*."

That's a new one. "I'm pretty sure everyone knows you're gay."

"Not me! Deuce Deming. He needs a date for an awards show."

"Yeah, well, he's already given you an interview, and I'm sure he can find his own dates, so…"

"Jobo, listen to me."

"I'm all ears."

"I found my unicorn."

I'll be damned. Jo sat on the bed. "You're telling me Deuce is your unicorn?"

"Yes! Now listen, someone spotted us together. I don't think they got a photo, but I can't be sure. And since you've already dated him—"

"Holy shit. And no, I haven't."

"It was in all the rags."

"We snuck out for gelato." *And that bitch Naomi followed and took pictures.*

"The tabs dubbed you, 'Deuce's Darling.'"

"For a hot second."

"It has to be you. Everyone knows we're besties, and if a pic does surface, we'll spin it that I was hanging with him because of you. Oh, and I'll be covering the event for *The Buzz*, so we can add some back story." Drew paused. "I need you, Jobo."

Jo sighed. "If he's the one, you'll eventually get called out."

"On our terms, Jo, not like this."

"Fine. Send me the flight info."

"Already sent. I'll have a car waiting and a crew to make you Deuce-worthy."

She hung up and started to pack. *Dammit!* She'd have to postpone her date. She needed to lock Jacks down before Addison snared him in her web. The old Jo would have enjoyed the challenge, but the new Jo wanted someone to choose her without having to fight for it.

Jo hurried after Kara, who rushed down Main Street with a mysterious bulge in her jacket. "What are we doing again?" She checked her watch—less than two hours before she had to leave for the airport.

"Making things right, Jo."

"Yeah, but it's not illegal, is it? Because I have a record..."

"You just have to be my point man."

"Being called that is kinda disturbing, as it implies—"

"Here we are. Now just stand out here and feed the birds or something. I'll be back in a jiff."

Jo scanned the area. "You want a Jew to stand in front of a church and look natural?"

"This isn't the Third Reich; you'll be fine. If someone *does* ask, tell them you're thinking of converting."

"And if someone wants to enter the church?"

"Stall them."

Jo wandered over to a bench and sat diagonal to the building. She had a good view of both the church and the park on the corner. She saw Addison step out of a sandwich shop and head in her direction.

"Hello, Josette. Beautiful day, isn't it?" she said with a sugary smile.

"Um, sure." Jo wondered if all small-town people crossed the street to greet a familiar face.

"I was just on my way to meet JT for a picnic lunch."

Jo raised a brow. *No competition, my ass.*

"I'd ask you to join us, but I only have enough for two."

"Yeah," Jo drew out. "Not a big fan of shade wrapped in southern charm. If you have something to say, say it."

Addison's smile vanished. "I have no idea what he sees in you."

"Something he doesn't see in you, obviously."

Addison gasped. "You are not a nice person."

"And you coming over here is what? A public service announcement?"

"Yes, and here it is: JT and I have loved each other for a long time, and will continue to love each other long after you're gone. He's only interested in you because he thinks he can't have me. We'll see who he chooses after today."

If I had a nickel.

Jo spotted Kara out of the corner of her eye. "Well, thanks for the warning—I mean chat." She stood and walked toward the church. "Enjoy your picnic."

26

When the past comes knocking, don't answer.
It has nothing new to tell you.
- Unknown

The tree looked the same. Nothing had changed, yet everything had. JT watched Addy in the distance as she set out the food. When she caught sight of him, she jumped up and brushed off her jeans.

"Looks like quite a spread, Addy. Thanks."

She beamed up at him, reminding him of the girl he once loved.

"You're welcome. I got your favorite sandwich from Hawley's."

"That was real thoughtful." JT sat on the quilt, trying to remember what his favorite sandwich used to be. He took a few bites and noticed she hadn't touched her food. "Aren't you going to eat?"

"No, not yet. I'm too nervous."

He put down the sandwich. "So, we're having this conversation now, I guess."

"Oh, no. You can eat. I'll wait."

"Not gonna happen. Go on, then." He felt a twinge of annoyance as he sat back.

Addy wiped her palms against her thighs. "I left Tommy."

"Yeah, I know."

"No, I mean, I really left him. For good."

"Okay...?"

"This isn't coming out right. Remember when I told you it was complicated?" When he nodded, she continued. "Well, here's the truth: I stayed with him because of you, because of your family."

"Sorry, I don't follow."

"Tommy owns the mortgage on your farm, JT, or more specifically, The Beuchard Holding Company does." She stood and paced. "For years, I've been giving them leads to properties that are about to be foreclosed on. There's nothing illegal about it, and I told myself since they offered fair market value, it was better than taking a chance on foreclosure." She stopped and faced him. "But when Fowler's Pond came on the list, I didn't tell him. I couldn't. Instead, I called Hank and asked him to either hold the loan or sell to someone else. Of course, Tommy eventually found out and was furious."

"Why? Farms are a dime a dozen around here."

"Because it was *yours*. He's always been jealous of you. Of us." She sat next to him. "Our marriage was already in trouble. The more I pulled away, the more he blamed you, and the more determined he was to own the farm. He talked to your father first, but he refused to sell. He then threatened to pull his business from Sloane's if they didn't sell him the note. Hank finally caved a couple months ago."

I'm the reason my family's going to lose the farm.

His head was spinning. "This was after I went to the bank? When you tried to get my dad to sell to Tommy?"

"Yes, I was hoping he'd agree to Tommy's deal. I knew if he didn't, they'd call in the loan and your family would get nothing."

"But he hasn't."

"No, he offered me a deal instead. If I stayed, he'd hold off on the foreclosure."

"Addy, that's insane."

"The divorce papers were already signed. All I had to do was file the paperwork. But I didn't. *I couldn't.* Tommy had finally found a way to keep us apart."

JT was at a loss for words. He took one of her small hands and rubbed his thumb against the soft skin. "I can't believe you stayed with him for me—for my family." He shook his head. "I don't know how to react to that kind of sacrifice."

Addy laid back, bringing his hand to her chest, and stared at the sky. "I remember the first time we made love here. I think it was the happiest day of my life. July fifteenth. You left for college the next month, and I was heartbroken." She turned to him. "You know what I thought, what I *felt*, when you got hurt and lost your scholarship? Joy. I thought you would come home to me and we'd start our life together."

He let go of her hand. "You know that I wanted—"

"Yes, I remember. To finish college, to get a good job, to leave this town. To be better than your father."

"I never said that."

"Yes, you did."

"I thought we were on the same page," JT said, letting her suck him into the past.

"I went along with it, but I never understood it. You had me, your family, friends, the farm—a *life* here. But it was never enough."

He let out a frustrated sigh. "Ad—"

"Let me finish." She sat up, her arms around her knees. "You need to know all of it. I supported you when you joined the Army to pay for college. I thought, surely after you graduated, we'd get married and then go wherever you were stationed. But that didn't happen. So, I waited some more." She picked at the crumbs on the blanket. "When you came home for Christmas your second year in, you said you had something important to tell me. I thought you were going to propose."

"Please stop, Addy. I know how this ends."

"I'm not sure you do." She took a calming breath. "Do you have any idea what a punch in the gut it was to be told you were enlisting for another four years so you could fly? When I expected a proposal? *Jesus*, JT. I'd already waited six years, and you wanted me to wait six more."

JT rubbed at his eyes. "I remember how upset you were."

"Upset? I was destroyed!"

Perhaps he deserved her anger ten years ago, but now? She'd made her own choices in life. "You seemed to bounce back quick enough."

"Ahh," she said, shaking her finger at him. "That's where you're wrong. Where you have always been wrong. I didn't date Tommy to get over you or get back at you. I did it hoping you would choose *me*. I threw a Hail Mary pass, hoping you would fight for me. For *us*."

JT knew they should have had this talk years ago. They both needed the closure. "I was a dumb, selfish kid. I never thought you would leave me. And you never—" *Told me how you felt.* He knew saying that wouldn't change a thing. He wiped a tear from her cheek and softened his voice. "I came home when I could, called you every chance I got, but coming home and seeing you with Tommy?" He shook his head. "I didn't deserve that. And you *married* him, Addy."

She nodded and swiped at her face. "You're right, I'm not blameless. But we have a chance to be together now. We can get back what we lost. I *know* we can." She reached out and entwined their fingers together.

It was almost too easy to slide back into her life, to pull at the threads of memories and feelings that made up their past. Part of him wanted to heal the hurt he'd caused, to *be* healed. To be the man she wanted him to be.

He just wasn't sure he could—or that he ever was.

Addy continued, "When I found out about the show, I thought I could hang on a little longer, until the farm was safe, but I'm losing you, JT. I can feel it. The way you gawked at that woman last night..." She closed her eyes and shook her head as if to clear the memory. "Please tell me I'm not too late."

JT couldn't say it. He needed time to process, and he refused to make promises he couldn't keep. "I don't know what I'm feeling right now. I thought when I first got back, when I found out you and Tommy had split..." He loosened her hold. "I wish you'd told me sooner."

Her back straightened. "I'm just asking you to give us a chance. I think I deserve that much."

JT arrived at the inn and watched Josie bound down the front steps with her usual energy. She was radiant and full of life, and he couldn't help but smile at her infectious joy.

"Hey! I was coming to find you. Crazy thing," she said with a grin, "I don't have your new number. So, before we get sidetracked..." She pulled out her phone and handed it to him. "How about you punch in your digits?"

JT took the phone and entered his number.

"So, listen, about tonight—" she started at the same time he said, "Jo, I need to talk to you."

Jo mouthed a silent 'ah' as a mask of indifference transformed her face. The lack of emotion reminded JT of how she looked all those months ago when he watched her walk into the ballroom bar.

She took her phone back and tossed it into her bag. "Don't bother. I ran into Addison earlier today. She told me you two were having a *picnic*. I can guess the rest. Funny you didn't mention it last night when you had your tongue down my throat."

He deserved the hit. "I was going to tell you tonight."

"On the date you were just about to cancel?"

JT ran a hand over his head and waited for a group of people to pass by. "Can we go somewhere and talk?"

She pasted on a smile. "Sorry, I don't have time. Turns out, I had to cancel anyway. I'm flying to LA."

JT wanted to ask her why she was going and when she'd return, but he didn't have the right. "We'll talk when you get back?"

She gave him a dry smile. "You bet." She turned on her heel and re-entered the inn.

JT spent most of the day working on the old house. He needed physical labor to block out the dichotomy of feelings that bombarded him. Addy was comfort, she was love. She was the past and possibly his future. Jo, well... She was beauty and excitement, and when he thought of her, he felt more alive than he had in a very long time.

Addy was the safe choice, Jo the wild card.

It was dark by the time he walked into the house. He found Lou Lou sitting on the couch, eating popcorn, and watching TV.

"Hey Cricket, how about a movie?"

"Not tonight, *The Indies* are on. You can watch it with me if you want."

He scooped up a handful of popcorn and sat on the armrest. "Not really my thing." He was thinking about calling a couple of friends and hitting a bar when Lou grabbed his arm.

"Oh. My. God. JT, look who's on the red carpet."

"Huh?" he said, cleaning the spilled popcorn.

"Josette Singer! She just got out of a limo with Deuce Deming." She punched him in the arm. "And here I thought she was interested in you. Ha!" She threw some popcorn into the air. "She *is* gorgeous. I'm gonna have to suck up to her now." She drew in an excited breath. "I bet she can get Deuce to appear on *HomeTown Heroes* now that they're official."

The words hit him like a punch to the gut. "Official?"

"They were spotted together months ago, and now he's brought her to a public event. He's never done that. He's like a recluse or something." She pushed him off the couch. "Now shut up so I can listen to Drew's interview."

"...rumors are true? Are we talking exclusive?"

He watched Deming tighten his arm around Jo, pulling her to his side. She gazed adoringly at him, her hand on his chest, waiting for him to answer. JT had a hard time focusing, and his urge to hit something increased exponentially as Deming leaned in for a kiss. "Yeah, she's the only girl for me."

"What the *fuck*?" JT sprung up from the couch.

"Shhh!"

He needed fresh air. Grabbing his helmet, JT headed out the back door. "I'm going out," he shouted to no one in particular and slammed the door behind him.

27

If Monday had a face, I would punch it.
- Unknown

"Whoops!" Jo stumbled up Drew's stairs in her jewel and satin Manolo Blahnik's.

"Easy does it, babe."

"Thank you, Druece." Jo smiled and patted his cheek. "You're *great* guy. A great, big, guy."

The three of them made it to the second-floor landing, where Jo grabbed Drew's jacket. "He's real *lepercon*."

"Oh my god, are you having a seizure?" Drew tried to pry her fingers off his lapel.

"Pfft, noo, it's wink, it's a... *I'm winking*." Her mouth opened wide as she tried to squeeze just one eye shut. "Cause he's your lepercon."

"Well, you look like you're having a stroke." Drew turned to Deuce. "Let's drop and hop."

"We can't just leave. *Look* at her."

"What the—" Jo twirled in circles, the hem of her dress caught on the heel of her shoe.

"Darling, I've done this a time or two. She'll be fine. Just..." He made a shooing motion with his hands, "push her onto the bed."

Instead, Deuce lifted her into his arms and placed her gently down.

Jo fell into a cocoon of softness. "This-is-nice."

"Maybe we should turn her on her side."

"Probably," Drew said as he pushed Deuce out the door.

"Drew," Jo said in a rough whisper, her mouth thick with dried saliva.

"Hmm?"

"I need you to shoot me."

"That's Jean Luc's job. We leave in an hour for the photo shoot."

Jo groaned and peeled one bleary eye open. "No."

"I booked you an IV. The hangover special. Should be here any minute."

"Get off my bed."

"Honey, you're in *my* bed."

"I think I might be sick."

Drew sprung up. "Get up." He grabbed the sheet and yanked hard, sending her sprawling to the floor.

"Ow! What the actual fuck, Drew?"

"Bitch, these are high-end sheets."

Jo pulled herself up. "I hate you right now."

"Rinse and repeat, honey." He walked to the bathroom and came out with a trash can. "I have no time for your pity party. Here."

Jo stood on shaky legs and grabbed it, heading into the bathroom. "Leave."

"I'll need you downstairs in ten."

He ducked as the hairbrush she threw sailed past his head.

After her infusion, Jo walked among the living again. She stepped outside to the waiting limo, where Drew handed garment bags over to the driver. Once loaded, they headed to Deuce's villa for the shoot.

Drew eyed her wet hair and blotchy face. "You should demand a refund from Harmony House. You're still a hot mess."

"Don't start with me. I'm not in the mood."

"Hometown boy upset you broke your date?"

Jo closed her eyes and took a deep breath.

"You're not gonna hurl, are you?"

"Just need a little compassion here, Drew."

He turned in his seat, bringing one leg up so he could face her. "What happened?"

"He chose someone else." She shrugged and rolled her head to the side. "What's wrong with me? And don't spout a bunch of bullshit."

Drew pursed his lips, as if giving it some thought. After a beat, he said, "You're *unique*, and most men don't know what to do with you. You're not just a pretty face, Jobo, you're a guy's wet dream. You're smarter, stronger, richer, funnier, and more ambitious than anyone I know. But you're intimidating as hell. You have no filter, curse like a sailor, drink like a fish, and are brutally honest. That's enough to shrivel any set of testicles." He vamped over his right shoulder. "I think you're perfect."

Jo laughed. "Yeah, the gays just love me."

"Oh, *no* honey, we want to *be* you."

Jo pulled into the inn's parking lot well after midnight, exhausted. She hauled her bags up the steps to the front door, only to find it locked. She cursed under her breath and texted Kara, who appeared moments later in a satin teddy.

"Well, if it isn't Deuce's Darling," she said, opening the inn's front door.

Jo pushed past with an eye roll. "Can we do this in the morning?"

"Just tell me one thing. Does Jackson know?"

Jo ignored the question, eyeing the sexy lingerie. "Did I interrupt something?"

Kara looked down and shrugged. "I like how it feels against my skin." She took one of Jo's bags. "So, this thing with Deuce—"

"Thought we weren't doing this until morning?"

"It just doesn't make sense," Kara continued, following her up the steps.

"What doesn't, Kar?" Jo entered her room and set her bag down.

"You with Deuce."

"Yeah, and why's that?" She took off her coat and dropped it on the bed.

"Well, for one, you haven't mentioned him since leaving the nut hut. And, two, he's gay."

Jo's head snapped around. "How'd you know that?"

"I didn't."

"Great." She threw up her arms. "I just outed him."

Kara shook her head. "Boy, did he choose the wrong girl—should've picked an actress. You're gonna be terrible under media scrutiny."

"Believe me, it wasn't my idea. Just helping a friend."

"You mean Drew Johnson."

Jo's eyes widened. "Christ, what are you, psychic?"

"You suck at this. I was *fishing*."

Jo fell back on the bed. "I'm going to ruin his career."

She woke early the next morning and went for a run. About a mile in, she spotted Levi loading boxes into his truck. "Hey, Levi."

"Jo," he greeted, slamming the back gate.

"I was hoping to come by later today to talk about the partnership. Did you get the contract the lawyers sent over?"

He leaned against the truck and folded his arms. "Yeah. Weren't we supposed to do that yesterday?"

"Sorry. Last-minute change of plans. I meant to text but got sidetracked."

"Yeah, I figured as much when I saw you on TV."

"Huh, didn't take you for an awards show type of guy." She flipped the cap off her water bottle, taking a long pull.

"It was on the news, Jo. Everyone knows where you were."

"Really? I'm surprised *The Indies* made the local news."

"They didn't, at least not until somebody released video of JT pulling you from the bar Friday night. Let's just say they're not calling you Deuce's Darling anymore."

"The show released footage?" She needed to be more careful.

"No, it wasn't them. It's not high-quality either, probably taken with a phone. How have you not seen it yet? It's all over the internet."

"Oh, I'm sure my phone is blowing up. I just can't remember where I left it."

Jo told him she'd come by the bar later and jogged back to the inn where a half dozen paparazzi had lined up along the street. She got inside without answering a single question, thanks to Gail, who had called the cops to keep them off the property.

"Let's have a chat in my office." Gail extended her arm and led Jo to the back room. She took a seat behind the desk and motioned for Jo to sit across from her. "Before we begin, I just want to say, that publicity stunt you pulled in LA? Brilliant. It'll stir up a lot of interest for the show. Well done."

"Um, thanks?"

"There's no such thing as bad publicity."

"I'm gonna have to disagree with you on that." Jo couldn't think of one time where it worked in her favor.

"The public loves a redemption story. You'll find a way to spin it." Gail flipped through the papers on her desk. "So, let's talk about what happened in Philadelphia."

Finally, something she could smile about. "I've solved your budgetary problem. The production can proceed."

"True. I am curious though, why'd you do it?"

"I know it seems crazy—"

The innkeeper knocked and entered, carrying a tray. "I thought you might like some coffee and sticky buns. I baked them this morning." She placed the tray on the sideboard.

Jo's stomach wept with joy as she reached over to grab some gooey goodness.

The woman hesitated and turned to them before leaving. "I wanted to ask...have either of you seen the gold platter in the reception area? It has engravings from Matthew 6, from the King James Bible. I use it for the guest comment cards."

Jo choked on the pastry, remembering Kara's visit to the church. "Nope. Haven't seen it." She pounded on her chest.

The woman's eyes narrowed suspiciously. "If you do, please return it—no questions asked." She walked out with her eyes still on Jo.

"What was that about?" Gail asked.

Jo shook her head. "I have no idea." She poured herself a cup of coffee to wash down the lie and motioned to the tray. "Sticky bun?"

Gail waved her over, accepting the proffered treat. "So, tell me. Why'd you do it?"

"You mean invest in the distillery?" Jo sipped her coffee. "Mostly guilt."

"Go on, I can't wait to hear why."

"I never consulted the Taylors about what they wanted for the farm, treating it like any other business—with you as my client—when it should've been them. I explained to Levi that regardless of who his father was, the show didn't have the budget to change concepts, and we needed to win Charles over on the original proposal." Jo raised a hand when Gail began to speak. "I know. The Taylors are contractually obligated to go with what we decide. But do you really want to force them into something they adamantly oppose?"

Gail sat back with a dismissive flick of her wrist. "They would've come around. I read through your research. Hemp was, and still is, the most profitable option."

"But it's not always about money. Levi told me Charles would rather go bankrupt and be sued for breach of contract than grow drugs on his land."

Jo hesitated, knowing she had to reveal the rest. "Levi's mother is a drug addict, and Charles spent years and a lot of money trying to get her straight. It's one reason he's in debt." She leaned back. "The bottom line? He believes hemp is a drug, and nothing we say will convince him otherwise."

"But he's fine with making bourbon?" Gail rolled her eyes and flipped through the contract between the show and the newly formed company. "This is a good amount of start-up capital. I'm impressed."

"We'll need it once HTH airs." She gave the producer a brilliant smile. "It may have started as guilt, but I'm not stupid. The show will put the craft distillery on the map."

Gail grunted her approval. "Shame you couldn't stay on. You're a real asset. What are your plans now?"

Jo hadn't realized, until after the fact, that there was a conflict of interest clause in her contract. "I guess I'll head home, start my community service." *And look for another job.*

"You know," Gail tapped her chin, "*HomeTown Heroes* is a community-based show. It allows industry professionals to do their service with us, and since you're no longer getting paid, the COI wouldn't apply. You'd be able to continue working for us while adhering to the court order."

"Gail, you're a genius." Jo glanced at her watch. It was nine o'clock in LA; Drew would be awake soon, and she needed to talk to him. "I've gotta make a call." She stood. "Any chance you found a phone lying around this morning?"

Gail nodded as she tried to dislodge the chewy dough from the roof of her mouth. "The innkeeper found one on the front porch. Check at the front desk."

As expected, Drew had left a dozen calls and texts, some with social media links. Jo went directly to the video of her and Jackson. Levi was right, the quality wasn't good, but it showed JT pulling men from the bar and the two of them in an intimate embrace. She replayed it five times before calling Drew, who picked up immediately.

"Are you in the hospital?"

"No, why?"

"Because you haven't called, and we are in crisis mode! We need to get our stories straight before you say some damn, fool-ass thing—like the truth."

"Drew, I'm a relative nobody—"

"Honey, you attached yourself to a *somebody*. You know what that makes you?"

"Somebody's nobody?"

"A target! They're gonna eat you alive. If we don't spin this the right way, they will tag, bag and *bury* you," he said, nearing hysteria.

"Sounds ominous."

"You think this is a joke, Jobo?"

Jo settled into the oversized chair and looked out the window. A few reporters milled about with a couple more in cars. "What do you want me to do?"

"I sent you Deuce's statement. Read it, memorize it, and don't go off-script. You had a fight, you were trying to make him jealous, it worked, you're back together. Got it?"

"No."

"Then read it until you do."

"I mean, no. I'm not pretending to be his girlfriend. I want fewer paparazzi, not more."

The line went quiet. "I need you to do this for me, Jo. Just until I know there isn't any footage of me and Deuce out there. The industry isn't as woke as they'd have you believe. At least not in his audience demographic."

Jo sighed. She'd take a bullet for Drew, but that didn't mean she'd go down easily. "I want something in return—from Deuce. I'll even throw in another trip to LA." Jo heard shuffling and voices talking before Deuce got on the line.

"What can I do for you, Jo?"

"Deuce. How's my cuddle bunny today?" Jo could almost hear him smize.

"Wondering what my little Shnookums is up to."

"Oh, you know, *things*. Like saving a small American farm from big corporate greed. Imagine—and I'm just spit-balling here—if an actor who played an action hero helped an *actual* hero save his farm by becoming a spokesperson for..." She lowered her voice and mumbled, "bourbon."

"You *almost* had me."

"The bourbon, right?"

"Young kids look up to me, Jo. No alcohol. But I'll do a cameo for the show."

"You're possibly the best boyfriend I've ever had, Deuce."

"Back at you, babe."

Jo read the press statement on the steps of the inn, and after a few questions, was relieved to see them all leave. She promised Drew she'd keep an eye out for anyone lurking about, but when no one popped up from behind a bush, she drove to Levi's.

It was still early when she pulled into the empty parking lot. The bar hadn't opened yet, so she headed around back to Levi's vintage trailer. Her inner artist had squealed with delight the first time he'd shown her the retro beauty.

She knocked on the screen door. "Hello?"

Levi appeared, holding a shirt, his jeans unbuttoned. He smiled unabashedly as he pulled the cotton tee over his head and buttoned his pants. "Didn't hear you knock. Come on in."

Jo raised her eyes and cleared her throat, climbing the two steps into his home. "I hope it's okay I came here. The bar was closed."

"Yeah, of course. Have a seat. Can I get you something to drink?" he asked, as he ambled toward the small kitchen.

"Some water would be great, thanks." Jo watched him with curiosity. He was almost as tall as Jackson but much leaner. Dark where Jackson was light—and very much her type.

Levi smiled at her perusal. "Not used to seeing me out from behind the bar, I guess."

He had nice teeth. She smiled back. "Sorry, I didn't mean to stare. It's just, you look nothing like your brother."

"Half-brother, and yeah, I get that a lot." He looked over his shoulder at a disheveled blonde appearing from a back room. He didn't turn to greet her or offer her a beverage. The woman grabbed her shoes and purse, whispered something in his ear, and left.

"Nice to meet you, too." Jo said, chuckling as the front door swung shut. "She's a keeper."

Levi grinned into his mug but didn't comment. He grabbed a water bottle and joined her at the table. "I thought you were coming by later." He handed her the bottle but didn't release it right away. *"At the bar."*

"Oh, I gathered that," she said, her smile expanding as he let go. He slid in beside her and they sipped on their drinks in comfortable silence until Jo pulled out the legal documents.

"I'll have my lawyer call you this week, but you should retain your own council. The show's legal team is handling the Taylors. I'm sure they'd be happy to do the same for you."

He shrugged. "I trust you. Yours will be fine." He flipped through the contract, stopping to point out the paragraph that outlined the roles of each partner. "What does this mean?"

"I'm considered a limited partner, which means I won't be involved in running the day-to-day business, and I'll have no liability for debts beyond my investment."

"And the Taylors?"

"They'll lease the building to us, and we'll pay them for any crops grown and harvested. They'll also receive a percentage of net sales for the use of the farm's name."

"Do you think it'll get them out of debt?"

"If you're asking me if it'll be enough to save the farm, probably not. Even with you signing over your share of the profits, it'll take years." Jo sat back with her water. "Explain to me again why you're doing that?"

Levi looked over the rim of his mug and took a sip before answering. "Partly because of what I already told you—to pay Charles back for my mother's addiction. But also because he gave me the money to buy the bar."

Jo's brow shot up. "Did he? How'd he manage that?"

Levi's lips formed a straight line, causing the tuft of hair under his bottom lip to stick out. "He borrowed it—which I didn't know at the time—I'd just assumed..." He raked a hand through his hair. "He mortgaged the farm for me, Jo. When I told him I'd sell the bar, he refused. Said it was my inheritance."

Jo sat back against the vinyl bench. "Wow. Does anyone else know?"

"Just my mom," he said, pinning her with a stare. "I won't be the reason they lose the farm. One way or another, he'll take my money."

She reached over and placed a hand on top of his. "Levi, you aren't the only reason they're losing the farm. But if you like, we can go to the bank and show them our business plan, including the Taylor's projected revenue. You can use the bar as collateral."

He tilted his head and studied her. "Why are you bothering? To invest in the distillery, I mean. Don't get me wrong, I'm thankful. Just trying to figure out your motivation."

It was Jo's turn to hesitate. She picked up the stack of papers, tapped them together on the linoleum table, and slid them into the folder. "Before coming here, I sat on the board of my family's company—an accomplishment that meant a lot to me. But I never *owned* anything, not even my condo, which is held in a trust. But they can't take this away from me, not like they did my seat on the board."

Levi's brow shot up. "Your family fired you?"

"More like a suspension until I learn how to behave." Jo gave a slight shake of her head, her smile lacking any warmth. "They used a morality clause to remove me. My father didn't even speak on my behalf."

He drew a breath between his teeth. "That's cold."

Jo nodded. "I used to think so." Now, she wasn't so sure.

"So, what'd you do?"

Her lip twitched up. "I clocked a bitch."

Levi roared with laughter. "Seriously, what did you do?"

The door to the trailer opened, and Jackson walked in, saving her from having to explain.

Levi was still smiling when he greeted his brother. "Hey, JT. What brings you out so early?"

Jackson eyed the two as he tucked the helmet under one arm and ran a hand over his head. "Didn't realize you were entertaining."

"Well, I am, so can we talk later?"

"Yeah." He turned to Jo. "We need to talk."

Levi leaned back and draped his arm behind the banquet seat. "Jo's the one I'm entertaining, brother. You'll have to wait your turn."

Jackson moved to the kitchen and placed the helmet down. He put his hands behind him on the counter and crossed his booted feet. "Then I'll wait."

Jo watched the stand-off with fascination, her eyes pinging between the two.

Levi caved and stood with his gaze locked on Jo. "I'll be in my office if you need anything." He walked out without another word.

Jackson didn't wait for the door to swing shut. "Were you going to tell me about Deming?"

Jo got up from the bench. "You have no right, *none*, to act like I've done something wrong."

He pushed off the counter. "You flew to LA to be with another guy. I'd call that something."

"You went on a picnic with your ex-girlfriend and broke our date, after I *told* you I don't share. I'd say that trumps it."

"You planned on canceling before I did!"

Jo came forward, her hands balled into fists. "I owe you *nothing*!"

He pulled her roughly to him and kissed her. She wanted to push him away, to fight. Instead, she grabbed his shirt and kissed him back. He picked her up and sat her on the counter. She trailed hungry kisses down his neck, biting at the curve of his shoulder, her hands exploring every hard ridge and muscle of his chest. He yanked at her blouse, his touch setting off fireworks throughout her body. When he pressed against her, Jo lost control and ripped at his jeans.

He broke away. "Jesus, Jo, what are you doing to me?" He stepped back, rubbing his face. "I can't control myself around you."

Her head spun with confusion and anger. She hopped off the counter. "I'm a little tired of men wishing they weren't attracted to me. It's not a compliment."

"That's not what this is."

"Well, I'm a tad confused, then. Why'd you stop?"

Jackson pinched the space between his eyes. "Who's Deming to you?"

Of course. He thinks I'm with Deuce. She blew out a relieved breath. "Deuce is a friend. I was doing him a favor. He needed a date for an awards show. His..." Jo had to walk a fine line here, "significant other couldn't make it."

"So, there's nothing between you?"

"No. We're just friends. We met months ago at Harmony House."

He nodded, but the hairs on the back of Jo's neck stood up. There was more he wasn't saying.

"This isn't about Deuce, though, is it? You're still hung up on your ex."

Jackson looked down and pinched the bridge of his nose. *Not a good sign.*

Jo's mood took a nosedive. "Why?" She shook her head. "Why come here and kiss me, *question* me, when you still want to be with Addison?"

He lifted his head, his eyes boring into hers. "I want to be with you."

She turned away, gathering her things. "But you want to be with her, too."

"You're *leaving,* Josie. After you're done here." He moved in front of her. "Is there a chance we could have a future? Can you give me anything, any hope that this—" He waved a hand between them. "Can be more?"

Jo shook her head, her anxiety rising. "This wasn't supposed to be complicated. We were in this for the same reasons, weren't we?"

He stood silently, hands on his hips, eyes downcast.

"Jacks, I really like you. You *know* that." Unable to resist one last touch she lifted a hand, her fingers gliding through his silky hair. "But we hardly know each other." She swallowed the lump in her throat, thankful it was ending now instead of in six months. "You made the right choice."

His eyes searched hers, but he said nothing. Jo kissed his cheek and walked to the door. With her hand on the knob, she paused, waiting—*wanting*—him to refute her statement. But of course, he wouldn't.

She left without a backwards glance.

As she made her way to the car, Levi came out of the bar. "Jo? Jo!" He caught up with her. "You all right?"

"I'm fine." She pulled up her big girl panties and gave him a shaky smile.

"I got a call from the show. They're flying in a distillery expert. He gets to plug his book and workshops, and we get his help for free. We're meeting him at the farm tomorrow to see if we can retrofit the old barn on the southwest corner. That's why JT came by, to let me know the show will be filming it. We have to be there by ten."

Apathy engulfed her. "I have very little knowledge of the industry," *apart from consumption,* "and won't be involved in running the business. So, I think I'll pass."

Levi canted his head. "You're part of the show, Jo. Pretty sure they expect you to be there."

Her cheeks puffed out before letting the air seep slowly out. "Then I guess you'll see me in the morning." She quickly pivoted and walked away.

"Ten o'clock." he called out.

She lifted a hand in acknowledgment before climbing into her car. *I can do this; I will do this.* Putting the car in gear, she drove out of the lot.

28

She sort of fades into the background after a while.
You know, like a smoke alarm.
- David, Schitt's Creek

One month later

According to the expert, the abandoned utility barn made for a great distillery, and its location was perfect, with great visibility and easy access from the main road. For this, Jo was eternally grateful. She had no desire to run into Addison, who was now a permanent fixture at Fowler's Pond. The show had embraced the romance between her and Jackson like a death grip, and Jo had no stomach for it.

She pulled into the expanded parking area and marveled at the barn's transformation. The amount of work they'd accomplished in the ten days since she'd last seen it was impressive. Walking through the sliding double doors, she weaved her way around the hive of activity, carrying two coffees and a box of donuts.

"Hey," Levi said from behind.

"Ahh!" Jo jumped, splashing hot liquid down her shirt.

"Shit. I'm sorry. Here." He pulled out a rag and blotted the wet stain on her chest.

Hands full, she glanced around as he dabbed, looking for a place to put the donuts. Finding none, she shoved the box at him and grabbed the rag to stop him kneading her breasts. "It's fine, I've got some logo shirts in the car." She dropped the wet cloth on top of the box. "I called earlier; didn't know what kind of donuts you liked."

"Oh, yeah, sorry. Addison was here."

That got her attention. "What did she want?"

"To invite us to her housewarming on Saturday."

"Us? You mean, *you*," she said, pointing a finger at him.

He ran a hand over his short beard. "She specifically mentioned you."

Jo narrowed her eyes. "I find that hard to believe."

"In these parts, everyone gets invited. Even the enemy."

Jo picked up the rag and lobbed it at his head. "I'm busy that day."

He caught it and grinned. "No, you're not."

"But *she* doesn't know that!"

"*Yeah*, she does."

Her eyes widened. "Why do you hate me?"

He snorted and pulled her into a side hug. "You can't avoid them forever."

"Um, I believe I can."

"Come on, we'll go together. I'll even pretend to adore you. It'll drive JT crazy."

"No thanks, I already have a fake boyfriend." She opened the box of donuts in his hands. "I got you a cruller and a Boston cream."

He grabbed the jelly-filled. "I want this one."

"Figures." Jo took the cruller. "The show wants us at the farm this morning for some big reveal. I guess I should go back to the inn and change."

Levi shoved the rest of the donut in his mouth and reached for another. "Since they're filming, wear one of our T-shirts. It's free advertising and great for business, especially when you wear it."

She smirked. "A bit sexist, but thanks."

"Like how you stared at JT when he put one on? That sexist, too?"

Jo feigned shock. "I was checking to see if he needed a larger size." *And wishing I was the shirt.*

Levi took the coffee and tossed the box into a nearby bin. "Nothin' wrong with admiring the attributes of the opposite sex." He motioned for her to follow. "Come on, they're setting up the equipment in the back. The hammer mill and storage hopper went in yesterday and the stills should arrive this week." He stopped and pulled a business card out of his pocket. "I almost forgot. Gail's assistant—can't remember her name—dropped this off for you yesterday."

Jo took the card. "Sandy."

"Yeah, that's her. She couldn't reach you. Said to call Gail as soon as you can."

"Okay, give me a minute, and I'll meet you in the back." Jo's thumb smoothed over the embossed black lettering as she waited for Gail to answer.

"Hi, Jo."

"Hey, I got your message—along with a random business card."

"Addison Jennings came to see me."

The woman was like a bad rash. "Okay, I'll bite."

"She was very upset, told me Fowler's Pond was being foreclosed on. Handed me that card and said to call."

"That's not news." Jo examined the card. There was no title, no company logo. Just a name and a number. "Did you call?"

"Yeah, it's a real estate holding company. They're calling in the Taylors' loan."

That *was* news. "I thought the bank wouldn't do anything for six months to a year at the earliest."

"*They* wouldn't, but they sold the loan to the holding company."

"So, Addison came to warn you, or to ask for your help?"

"The second. But she doesn't understand how this works. We aren't a charity."

"But if the show has to shut down…"

"We have an iron-clad contract. The bank signed off on it. We have until we finish shooting, or the end of the year, whichever comes first."

Unfortunately, the distillery didn't have the same contract. "And you gave me the card because?"

"She asked me to."

"I see." *The girl has a set of cajones.*

"You're rich, she's desperate. That would be my guess."

Addison didn't know about Jo's investment in the distillery, so she had no reason to think Jo would help. "Why is she even involved? It's the Taylor' farm. Speaking of which, do you still want me to pitch that idea?" Jo had been out-of-town all week visiting profitable niche farms to back up research she'd done for the show.

"As far as we're concerned, nothing's changed. It'll be a shame if all our hard work doesn't benefit them, but there's a limit to what we can do. You might want to talk to Levi about the future location of the distillery."

Jo heard someone talking to Gail on the other end of the phone and the producer's muffled response.

"I have to go, Jo. We can discuss this after the brand marketing shoot. Don't be late."

Jo decided not to say anything to Levi. Why upset him unnecessarily? She'd look into it, call the holding company, and see if there was something she could do. After all, she had a stake in the outcome now.

JT gripped the edge of the sink and closed his eyes. They would be filming all day, and he needed to get his head straight. The entire day had been scheduled in fifteen-minute increments—everything was staged, but little was scripted. They gave advice and lead-ins as to what they were looking for. Some he went along with, others he didn't. Since news of Addy and him surfaced, they often included her. He'd balked at it, not wanting to put his private life on display, but it made little difference. Like Sisyphus, he pushed the boulder up the hill only to see it roll back down time and time again.

After dressing, he picked up the day's timeline and headed to breakfast, thankful they didn't start filming until later.

"Morning, Jackson," his mother greeted as she sat drinking coffee at the table.

"Mornin'. Where's Lou and Dad?"

"Lou left about fifteen minutes ago with Vaughn and your father right before you came in."

JT poured a cup of coffee and sat, reading over the itinerary. "Says we all have to be at the fallow field, but there's no other direction." He took a sip, looking over at his mother.

"Hmm, yes. I noticed that," she said with a faint smile.

His mother had a terrible poker face. "You know something I don't?"

She stood and put her cup in the sink. "Only what's on that piece of paper." Avoiding his stare, she walked toward the doorway. "I'm going to get my jacket. I'll meet you up there."

JT knew something was up, but let the boulder roll down the hill.

He took Clive out, thinking he'd go for a ride after the segment, and as he crested the hill, he saw family, friends, and crew standing about. His eyes locked on Josie, who stood off to the side and like always, the familiar ache was back. Memories of the last time they were here came flooding back. He'd taken her to his favorite spot, and they'd kissed…

"JT!"

He tore his gaze from Jo and focused on Addy, who stood with his family outside the old hangar. Dismounting, he waited for someone to mic him, then walked toward the building as the cameras rolled.

Kent Brock, the host, strolled up next to him. "Good morning, JT. I'm sure you're wondering what all this is about."

JT had a pretty good idea but stayed silent.

"We've got a little surprise for you." The host waved his arm and the hangar door opened to reveal a new plane.

Kent walked over to a smiling, middle-aged man who mopped sweat from his brow. "JT, this is Mr. Anderson from Argent Aircraft. The finest agricultural aviation company in the world."

JT held out his hand. "Nice to meet you, sir."

"Pleasure's all mine, Jackson. We at Argent Aircraft want to thank you for your heroic service and present you with the Thrust 220G, the most dramatic innovation in agricultural aviation. This new-generation aircraft is powered by the GE H80 turbine engine. It has a power output of 800 SHP, a lighter airframe, and delivers exceptional power for takeoff and climb. It also carries a maximum load weight with one of the best swath and spray patterns available anywhere. And like all Argent airplanes, it boasts superior handling and has incredible performance stability. You can trust Argent for all your aviation needs." The man finished his speech and stepped back looking proud as punch.

"Thank you, Mr. Anderson. I appreciate your generosity. Your airplanes are some of the best on the market. I look forward to taking her out; I'm sure she'll fly like a dream." JT patted the plane and made a show of admiring it.

All of what he said was true. The plane was a beauty. But he'd been fixing up the Cessna, and it was like finding out an old friend had died without saying goodbye.

Kent stood beside him. "We know how hard you've been working to get that old plane up and running, Jackson. But now, with the new Argent Thrust 220G, you'll be dusting crops in no time!"

A little piece of JT died every time he swallowed his pride and accepted another hand out from well-meaning and opportunistic advertisers alike. This wasn't him. The whole thing stunk, and it permeated every cell of his body—making him want to scrub his skin raw to take away the smell of selling out, of using his notoriety as a 'hero' for personal gain.

JT hated himself for it, but he couldn't surrender to gravity. He had to push that rock, accept his fate, and save his family's farm.

29

Simple it's not, I am afraid you will find,
for a mind-maker-upper to make up his mind.
- Dr. Seuss

Levi rested one booted foot on his coffee table and popped some nuts into his mouth. "How'd your meeting go yesterday? Charles like your fancy sheep idea?"

Jo slapped his foot down. "They're cashmere goats, and it's a very lucrative, under-serviced niche. Cashmere never goes out of style." She grabbed the bag of mixed nuts. "Of course, there are more profitable avenues I could've pursued, but I do as I'm told."

Kara came in and squeezed between the two. "You mind moving over a little? There are three cushions for a reason; we *each* get one." She peered into the bag. "Where's the rest of the snacks?"

"Sorry, didn't get to the store." Levi grabbed the bag back from Jo.

"I'm not putting my hand in that bag," Kara said.

Levi leaned past her to Jo. "Lucrative enough to save the farm?"

Jo shrugged. "Like I said before, no *one* thing is going to save it." She glanced at Kara. "We can order pizza."

"He owns a bar. They have food, and it's *literally* twenty feet away."

"It's my night off." Levi tossed a couple nuts in the air and put his boots back on the table.

Jo glared at his feet. "You're depreciating the value of a pristine vintage table, Levi."

"It ain't worth squat to me if I can't use it the way I want."

Kara began tapping her thigh. "I thought it was snack night. Nachos and wings, maybe even a veggie tray."

Jo knew it was a battle she couldn't win, so she got up. "Fine, I'll get food. Levi, you sticking with your nuts?"

"I'll eat whatever you put in front of me."

She walked around to the front of the bar—using the back would imply she came from Levi's trailer and she didn't need more gossip. Her pace slowed, and her heart quickened at the sight of Jacks' bike. She walked in and waved to Arlene, suppressing the urge to look around.

"Hey, Jo. You wanna add to the order?"

"Yeah, Levi call?"

"No, Kara. She's very specific in how she wants her food prepared."

Jo laughed. "Yes, she is. Would you mind asking Eddie to add a cup of vegetarian chili?"

"You got it." Arlene left, and Jo felt the pull of Jacks' stare from the other end of the bar.

When their eyes met, her lids fell—as if drunk on the sight of him. She allowed the moment of vulnerability. Stealing it. Savoring it. Knowing it wouldn't last. Pulling herself together, she lifted her shield and walked over. "Bad day?" she said, eyeing the beer and two empty shot glasses in front of him.

He grabbed the long neck and drained the bottle, his eyes never leaving hers. "I've had better."

Since their "break-up," Jo had avoided being alone with him. But they texted—often. It had started when he sent a picture of Vaughn smiling down at Lou Lou, holding a bag of fast food. The caption read 'Handing over his balls.' Jo had laughed out loud and responded that it couldn't have happened to a nicer guy.

She could often read his mood by the photos he sent. A picture of a cloud shaped like a bunny was a good day. Moss growing on a rock down by the creek was not.

They were different people in those texts. *Friends.*

As she stood in front of him, she pictured the abandoned corn crib, which sat alone at the edge of a field with wild roses climbing through its slats. They were bound in such a way that they held each other up. You couldn't remove one without destroying the other. Their friendship was like that, enhancing her *want* of him—and no matter how hard she tried, she couldn't separate the two.

Jo gave herself a mental slap and attempted actual conversation. "I like your shiny new plane. Although, to be honest, I found the whole thing kinda sad."

One side of his mouth lifted as he sat forward, a glint of amusement in his eyes. "Yeah? How so?'

"Well," she pulled out a stool and sat. "You were fixing up the old one, giving it new life and," she lifted her shoulders and laughed. "I felt bad for it."

Jacks tilted his head back and closed his eyes. "Shit, Jo."

Not the reaction she was hoping for.

He signaled to Arlene for another beer and regarded her. "You ever feel you're damned if you do, damned if you don't?"

Jo nodded in case it wasn't a rhetorical question.

"I've been selfish most of my life. Never realized how much until I came back." He gave her a meaningful look. "I'm trying to change, to be a better person. Do the right things."

"Well, that's just stupid." *No empathy points for you, Jo.*

Jacks didn't seem to notice. "You're right. If I change, I'm not happy. If I stay the same, I don't deserve to be. Like I said, damned cither way."

"I don't think wanting to be happy is selfish." When he looked at her like she was his lifeline, she continued, "A guru once told me—and I'm paraphrasing—if obstacles keep blocking your path, maybe you're going the wrong way."

His stare was so intense, she quickly added, "He also said Love is a Battlefield, which makes you wonder if all his wisdom came from eighties rock ballads."

His laugh twisted her insides.

They sat smiling at one another until Arlene came over with his beer and a glass of water. "Thought you might be thirsty, Jo. Seems like the only thing you drink anymore."

"Thanks, Arlene."

"No more Happy Jo?" Jacks asked.

"Oh, I wouldn't count her out entirely, but I'm learning to confront my feelings instead of using alcohol to numb them." She gave a half-suppressed laugh. "It's a slow process, I assure you."

Jacks smiled and gave her hand a squeeze. It was such an innocent gesture, she wondered if they *could* be friends...for all of 1.2 seconds before the mood shifted and a spark of attraction ignited. The look on his face told her he felt it, too. She yanked her hand away and stood, unable to be near him without being *with* him. "I better go."

"Jo! Your order's ready."

Bless Arlene's timing.

She'd almost escaped when Jacks called out, "Will I see you Saturday? At the housewarming?"

Jo gathered the food, giving herself a few seconds to invent a reason to say no. When that failed, she turned and gave him a weak smile. "You bet."

The phone buzzed with an incoming text, the light illuminating the dark room. Jo almost ignored it—only Drew texted in the middle of the night—but curiosity got the better of her and she pulled the phone off the nightstand.

I've never been to the beach

Bobbi White

She rolled to her back and stared at the cryptic message. Jacks wasn't texting animal clouds at two in the afternoon. It was 2:00 AM, and the words felt private, intimate. She chewed on her top lip, deciding how to reply.

Feeling restless?

Yes. Can you describe it to me

The ocean or the beach?

Both. What's it smell like

Briny. Seaweed and salt, wet sand, and sunscreen

The sounds?

Crashing waves and lapping surf. Gulls crying and children's laughter

Sights

Colorful umbrellas, sandcastles, and shells. Boats on the horizon

What's it feel like?

Sand feels like silk or sandpaper if you're burned. Waves slap cold at first, then lull you in a rocking motion when you pass the break

And the taste

Salt on your lips

She waited for the bubbles. When none appeared, she put the phone back on the table. A minute later, it lit up.

Thank you

There was a reason she never told anyone about the texting—she knew it was wrong. And no amount of pretending, of hiding behind silly memes and pictures of clouds, would make it right.

But tonight, they'd come close to crossing a line, and she needed to let him go.

3 0

Sounds to me like someone's trapped inside life's most complicated shape. A love triangle.
- *Ted Lasso*

"I'm impressed," Kara said.

"Hmm?" Jo responded, on her hands and knees inside the small closet.

"I only see one dress on your bed."

Jo's head appeared. "That's because I found the perfect thing to wear. Now if I could only find my other sandal."

Kara tapped her on the shoulder with a shoe. "This it?"

Jo backed out and grabbed the missing shoe. "Yes. Thank you."

"Cute dress, by the way." She looked at the label. "Is this…?"

"Off the rack? Yup. I bought it yesterday at the mall where I got a housewarming gift."

"Gift? I was just gonna bring booze."

Jo slipped on the flouncy boho mini dress. "What do you think?"

"I think you've got legs for days. Levi's gonna go nuts."

Jo rummaged through her jewelry case, picking a pair of large hoop earrings. "Levi?"

"Uh, yeah. He's been crushing on you big time."

"That's…No. You're wrong." *Was he?* Jo's brow furrowed as she pulled her hair into a messy side braid.

"Whatever. At least he doesn't have a girlfriend, and he's sexy as hell, so if you can't get what you want…"

Jo threw up her hands. "Now it's going to be weird. You just made it weird, Kara."

They descended the stairs to the inn's foyer, where Levi lounged against a wall.

His face brightened as he walked to the bottom of the steps. With a lazy smile, he looked her up and down. "*Damn*, you look fine."

Jo stopped mid-step. *Oh, shit.*

Kara passed her. "I'm sorry, I didn't realize I was wearing an invisibility cloak."

Levi glanced her way. "Sorry, Kar. You look nice, too."

"Gee, thanks."

They drove about fifteen minutes east, where suburban sprawl spread into the farmland. Addison lived in a charming older neighborhood within walking distance of the town. *The perfect place to start a family.* She pictured Addison and Jacks holding a baby. *Ouch.* She shook it off, reminding herself that she was a city girl—not a white-picket-fence girl.

Levi rapped on the screen door and called out. A shout from inside told them to come in. As they made their way to the back, Jo excused herself—she didn't have to go to the bathroom, she just wanted to scope out the house. It was bland with minimal art and decor. *Like Addison's personality.*

As she entered the bathroom, she heard Addison greet Levi and Kara. Jo should've gone with them. Now she'd have to make a solo entrance. She flushed the toilet, washed her hands with *Lavishly Lilac* soap, and dried them on a *Home Sweet Home* towel.

After dropping her gift on the kitchen table, she opened the slider to the back deck where people stood chatting with cocktails and plates of food. Catching sight of the wine and beer table, she made her way over.

"Hello, Josette."

Damn, I almost made it. "Hi, Addison. Lovely home."

"Thank you. I didn't think you would come—but I'm glad you did," she hastened to add. She leaned in and lowered her voice. "I was hoping we could talk later. About, you know."

Jo caught a whiff of Addison's perfume—it smelled like her bathroom. "Ah, yes, the reason I was invited."

Addison gawped. "I, why, no…"

Jo laid a hand on the woman's arm and forced a smile. "Don't worry, I understand you perfectly." She pointed to the table. "I'm going to get a drink and mingle. Let me know when you want to have that talk."

Jo poured a large glass of white and greeted Sandy and a young boom operator whose name she could never remember. When they walked off, Jo's eyes roamed farther afield until they landed on Jacks. He stood by the grill holding tongs and wearing an apron that read, DOES THIS MAKE MY WEINER LOOK BIG? She laughed and sauntered over. "It suits you."

He looked down and grinned. "I lost a bet to Levi."

"If Levi wants to bet you, it's because he's sure to win."

Jacks lost his smile. "You think so?"

"Haven't seen him lose, have you?"

He lowered the tongs and grabbed his beer. "I want to apologize for texting so late the other night."

Guilt engulfed her as she scanned for eavesdroppers. "Jacks, does Addison know about our texting?"

He shook his head, taking a swig of beer. "She wouldn't understand."

Jo sighed. "I'm not sure I do either. We have to stop."

His eyes flicked to the side. Seconds later, Addy appeared, holding an empty platter.

"I brought you something for the ribs." She reached around and put the plate down before snuggling into his side.

Jo watched as he absently rubbed her back.

I've taken masochism to a whole new level.

She turned to leave, but Addison piped up before she could make her getaway. "Would you like a tour of the house?"

Jo threw back her wine, not even trying to hide the three large gulps it took to complete the job. "Sure." She gave Jacks a tight-lipped smile and followed Addison. They entered the small kitchen and traveled down a hall to a back bedroom, where Addison closed the door.

"Did you call the holding company?"

"Right to it then." Jo frowned at her empty glass, wishing she'd gotten a refill for this conversation. "I did."

"So, Dan told you the Taylors have until the end of the month to pay off the debt."

Jo, wishing she were anywhere but here, leaned against a dresser. "Yes, and he also said they were upside down on the loan. They owe more than the farm is presently worth. I'm not even sure how they secured that much credit."

"Hank Sloane—he's an old friend of the Taylors—kept advancing them money."

Jo nodded and put her glass down on the dresser. "I'm not a bank or a holding company. What exactly do you want me to do?"

Addison clapped her hands together and brought them to her chest like a cheerleader before a routine. "I want you to make an investment in the farm. Buy the loan, hold it until they can refinance. With all the changes, it shouldn't be long before they're back on their feet."

Jo crossed her arms and walked over to the window, looking out over the manicured lawn. "What makes you think I have that kind of money?"

"It's public knowledge. Plus, I Googled your family's net worth."

"I see." Jo turned. "Well, here's the truth about *my* net worth. Most of it's in a trust. I can't touch it, and even if I went to the board and asked them to buy the loan, they wouldn't, because it's a poor investment." That might not be altogether true, but she didn't like Addison making assumptions.

Addison slouched on the bed, deflating like a party balloon. "That's it, then. I have nowhere else to go."

"Why is this your problem?"

"Because it's my fault if they lose the farm."

Jo raised a questioning brow.

"The Beuchards—that's my ex's family—they own the holding company. Tommy said he would take Fowler's Pond if I went back to JT. So, I stayed away, making excuses for why we couldn't be together. I thought the show would save the farm and stop Tommy from holding it over me. But then you came along, and I knew if I didn't tell JT the truth, I might lose him. So, that's why the Taylors will lose Fowler's Pond. Because I couldn't give JT up."

Jo wasn't sure what she expected, but it wasn't selflessness. "You didn't create the debt, Addison. If your ex didn't buy the loan, someone else would have. Chances are, they'd lose it either way."

Addison nodded and looked away. "I appreciate you hearing me out, considering our situation."

Jo wanted to laugh at her own stupidity. There was no situation. Addison and Jacks shared a history; were each other's first loves. She couldn't compete with that. Jo was a rookie playing in the big league of love. She needed more practice before taking a turn at bat. "I'll make a few calls. But I can't promise anything." She opened the door, the urge to cry shockingly close. "He's lucky to have you." She walked out of the room, wanting to continue straight out the front door.

"Hey. There you are." Levi appeared around the corner. "I found a few vegetarian options on the table and made you a plate."

Jo softened at his thoughtfulness, fighting the urge to give him a hug. "Thanks, Levi. You're the best." She accepted the plate. "I think I'm gonna need some wine to go with this."

Charles and Brenda Taylor found her after the second—or was it her third?—trip to the wine table. "Wanted to let you know the goats are settling in nicely. Already got a contract for their coats," Charles said.

"Laura Leigh has really taken to them," Brenda added. "She never wanted to get close to the lambs because we always sold them. But knowing the goats are here to stay, well, she's decided she wants to try her hand at farming, which means the world to us."

Jo's stomach churned. The Taylors' newfound hope would be crushed by the end of the month if someone didn't save Fowler's Pond.

"...So, you'll be here for the festival?"

Jo's skin began to itch. "Sorry?"

"It's at the fairgrounds, the biggest spring festival for miles. The town celebrates every spring to—"

"I'm sorry, I'm...I have to go, I just remembered..." Jo trailed off as she hurried toward the gate.

"Are you leaving?"

She stopped at the sound of Jacks' voice. His apron, as well as his smile, were gone.

"Yes, I need to get back."

He stepped closer. "I wanted to talk to you."

She glanced toward her escape. "I've already spoken to Addison. I'll see what I can do, but I can't make any promises."

He frowned. "You spoke to Addy about what?"

Jo had assumed they were on the same page. "Oh, well..."

"Ready to go?" Levi appeared at her side, saving the day.

"Yes."

"Kara said she'll get a ride back." He smiled at Jacks. "Great house. I'm sure the two of you will be very happy here."

"It's not my house," Jacks snapped.

"Either way, great party." He turned to Jo. "Wanna watch the new episode of King's Pawn tonight?"

"Are you two seeing each other?" Jacks asked, sounding both surprised and angry.

"No, but you might want to check why you'd care if we were." Levi opened the gate and glanced back at Jacks. "Later, brother."

Jo scurried out, having no desire to get in the middle of their pissing contest. "Thanks for the save."

Levi gave her shoulder a quick squeeze. "I'm surprised you lasted as long as you did. Especially after disappearing with Addison. What was that about?"

"She asked me to buy the mortgage to Fowler's Pond before her vindictive asshat of an ex forecloses on it." They got in the car and headed back to the inn.

"Tommy," Levi said. "The Beuchards own a lot of the farms around here. I heard he tried to buy it. Guess he doesn't need to now—unless you're considering it?" He glanced over.

"As I told Addison, most of my funds can't be touched. I get a monthly income and yearly dividends, but I'm not a big saver. What liquid assets I *did* have, I used to partner with the distillery. Any new investments would have to be approved, and there's a good chance the farm won't be."

"But you'll try?"

Jo looked out the window at the passing farmland. "Yeah, I will. If I don't, we'll have to move the distillery, and we've already invested a lot of time and money into the barn."

Levi nodded thoughtfully. "You know, I wondered why Addy didn't jump at the chance to be with JT months ago." He tapped on the steering wheel. "I bet it was to hold Tommy at bay." He glanced her way with a raised brow. "I'm guessing she changed her mind when JT turned sweet on you?"

Jo shrugged. "I don't think I was ever much of a threat."

"Oh, I wouldn't say that. Even today, *in his girlfriend's house*, he couldn't keep his eyes off you."

Jo didn't comment. They drove in silence until Levi reached over and placed his hand on top of hers. "You look gorgeous, by the way."

"Thanks." When he didn't move his hand, she dragged hers out from underneath.

They arrived at the inn where Levi parked in the lot instead of pulling up out front. He turned to face her, draping one arm over the steering wheel. "Jo, I like you. I think you know that."

Not until today. "Levi—"

He lifted a hand. "Just wanted to put it out there. I have no expectations. I know you're still hung up on JT."

Jo shook her head. "It doesn't matter. I'm not staying."

He sat back, scratching his beard. "If Tommy gets the farm, we can move the distillery to Philadelphia. I'm not tied here, Jo."

He'd move to Philly for me. "What about your mother?"

Levi leaned his head back against the seat and closed his eyes. "I can't live my life worrying about Silvia anymore. She's sick, and nothing I—or anyone else—do, will make a lick of difference if she doesn't want help. My leaving won't matter to her."

"I'm sure that's not true." Although Jo was pretty sure it was.

He shook it off. "If you asked me six months ago if I was content, I would've said *hell, yeah.*" His eyes searched hers. "Then you walked into my bar. You made me *feel*, Jo. And for the first time in my life, I wanted more than what I had."

Jo's chest swelled with affection. "I'm flattered, Levi, but I think you might be confusing gratitude with desire."

"Don't sell yourself short. Any man..." He faltered, momentarily glancing down, his long, thick lashes fanning out against his high cheekbones. "I've had lots of women, Jo. Running a bar, well, it's easy to meet them." He looked up, meeting her eyes. "I've just never wanted one outside my bed before."

Jo recognized the flutter of attraction. It wasn't the twisting ache she experienced with Jacks, but it was definitely something. And his words...they struck a chord. Most men wanted her *in* bed, not *out*. "That's possibly the nicest thing anyone has ever said to me."

He laughed, lightening the mood. "Hell, I wasn't even trying." He leaned forward and pulled on her braid. "JT's a damn fool." He turned and started the car. "No pressure. If you decide we're better off as friends and business partners, then that's what we'll be."

Jo leaned over and gave him a hug. "Thank you, Levi."

"Anytime, sugar."

She opened the door and got out, leaning in before closing it. "I'm flying home on Monday. I don't know how long I'll be gone. A week, maybe two."

"You don't answer to me, Jo. But I appreciate the heads up. Call me if you need anything."

She watched him pull out of the parking lot.

There were times in Jo's life when she would have killed for someone like Levi. Yet here she was.

She needed to get her head and heart on the same page.

JT collected paper plates, cups, and napkins, tossing them into a black contractor bag, while Addy went around with a recycling bin. They worked alongside one another until the backyard was in order.

When she smiled and tilted her head toward the house, he shook his. "I think I'm gonna head out."

She walked her fingers up his chest and hooked them around his neck. "Stay?"

He unlocked her arms. "I can't tonight, Addy."

She pouted. "Please? I promise you won't regret it." Her hand slid down to the front of his pants.

He pulled back, putting space between them.

Addy stomped her foot. "Jackson Howard Taylor! When a girl propositions you, it's rude to turn her down."

He sighed, his lids falling shut. *Damn, I'm tired.* When he opened his eyes, Addy was smiling again, thinking she'd gotten her way. "Addy, why haven't you asked me about Afghanistan?"

Her smile vanished. "I didn't think you wanted to talk about it."

"Aren't you curious?"

She bit her cheek, taking her time before answering. "I'd rather not know if it's going to upset you."

He nodded slowly, struck by the realization that the pieces would never fall back into place because they had never actually fit.

Leaning down, he kissed the top of her head. "I'll call you tomorrow."

He used his foot to shut the bedroom door, his hands busy texting Josie.

Tell me about the goats

> *I thought we agreed no more texts*

This is business. Why goats?

> *I was tasked with finding something that pulled your sister into the storyline and goats fit the narrative*

What narrative?

> *Cashmere is a luxury. Craft bourbon is a premium product - same market share/ advertisers*

And Lou?

> *She wanted air time. You were right not to worry. She gobbled Vaughn up like a midnight snack.*

JT smiled at Jo's assessment of his sister. Pulling off his boots, he sat back against the headboard, not ready to let her go yet.

*The shiny new plane landed me
some local contracts. Won't get
rich but will help pay bills*
                        Are you spraying pesticides?
I won't be spreading fairy dust

He had an incoming call. "Josie?"

"Pesticides and fertilizers contaminate soil and water, kill beneficial insects and birds, and pollute the environment."

"*Okay.*"

"*So,* you shouldn't use them."

"I'm hired to spray crops, not proselytize."

"But you can steer your clients towards a safer solution." Her voice rose with increasing agitation. "Soil ecosystems are destroyed by tilled and sprayed crops. If farmers focused on soil health, they could address the root cause and create a healthier environment."

JT was impressed with her knowledge. "Jo, I'm a pilot, not a salesman."

"Can't you at least tell them there's an alternative to chemicals?"

"They know it. Organic fertilizers aren't new. They're just too expensive."

"Well, if they used a no-till drill with cover crops and incorporated plant rotation, they wouldn't need so many chemicals."

JT understood her passion and agreed with everything she said—but where was the fun in that? "Change takes time, costs money. These people are trying to hold on the best they can."

Jo snorted. "It's widespread apathy."

JT admired her resolve. "Tell you what, I'll cut the upcharge on the organic as an incentive. Best I can do."

"No, please don't do that. Not for me, I—"

"Think of it as my way of being less apathetic."

Her throaty laughter hit him in the gut. "Mother Earth thanks you, and so do I."

"Happy to do my part."

"Good night, Jacks."

"Night, Josie." He tapped the phone against his heart and smiled—he was no longer going the wrong way.

31

Find out who you are and do it on purpose
- Dolly Parton

JT was trapped in a life he'd left over a decade ago, only this time he didn't have an easy way out. No university to escape to, no Army to fight for, and the key to freedom would come at a high price.

He was suffocating under the pressure of other people's expectations and their misguided assumptions of who he was. They fed off his accomplishments, eating up every morsel of truth and fiction without discernment. He was the golden boy; failure was not an option, and neither was desertion. Especially when the show—and their romanticized narrative—made it much harder to extricate himself from the life he wished to leave behind. They magnified his virtues and ignored his shortcomings, making him into some mythical hero. He understood they were in the business of creating a persona the audience would root for, but he still felt like a fraud. One misstep after another had led him down this path, and it was time he took back control of his life.

JT stood outside Addy's front door, knowing this first step would be the hardest. He hesitated before entering, wondering if he should knock. He had no right to her inner world any longer—or he wouldn't as soon as he told her the truth; that he loved her, just not in the way she wanted. JT closed his eyes and took a deep breath.

Start as you wish to proceed, his mother would say.
So, he knocked.

He found it didn't take long to crush someone. To take the 'what ifs' of a person's lifetime and destroy them. That's what he'd done to Addison Jenkins, to a relationship that spanned decades.

To love someone, yet not love them enough, that's what it boiled down to. He was no longer *in* love with Addy, and no matter how he wished it otherwise, he longed to be with someone else.

JT didn't know if he and Josie had a future, but he couldn't pretend he didn't want her. He was no longer satisfied with scraps—waiting like a hungry dog for a text, or a few shared words. He wanted all of her or nothing. There could be no in-between.

After leaving Addy's, he rode over to the hole-in-the-wall boxing club at the edge of town. He needed to hit something, to feel pain, to do penance.

Lowering the kickstand, he grabbed his gear. It was still early, and being a Sunday, the gym would most likely be empty, as most folks were either getting ready for church or sleeping off a hangover.

He changed and wrapped his hands, making his way into the deserted gym. The boxing ring was to the left, with some weights and equipment to the right. Passing the ring and ropes, JT headed to the bags on the other side of the raised platform and heard the snapping sound of someone hitting their mark.

He passed the speed bags and headed over to the row of heavies, stopping in his tracks when he spied the fluid motion of the person circling the last bag.

Jo danced around, throwing punches with a series of kicks and turns, which ended in a backflip off the bag. Her moves were more acrobatic than technical, and they mesmerized him.

He watched her spin with the poise of a ballet dancer, then seamlessly transition into a modern dance move, lost in whatever music played through her earbuds.

Jo must have sensed his presence, for she whirled around. Her skin glistened under the bright lights as sweat dripped off her body—her sports bra and shorts soaked with perspiration.

"Hey," she said with an out-of-breath smile, pulling the buds from her ears.

"Josie," was all he could manage as he grabbed mitts off the shelf, suppressing the all-consuming need for her. Pulling on the pads, he held them up, moving toward her. "Let's see what you've got."

She laughed and started throwing jabs in the air, unaware of the tension building inside him.

He advanced. "Hit me."

He wasn't smiling, and she took him more seriously, leveling jabs into his mitts. She was fast and remarkably accurate as he continued to advance.

"You hit like a girl. Throw your body into it."

That got her. She narrowed her eyes and lunged, becoming less precise, more powerful, pushing his hands back with her assault. He kept on the offense until he had her up against the cinderblock wall. She panted, her breath fast and erratic. When her arms finally gave out, JT yanked his gloves off and caged her in. He could feel her chest pound as he molded his body to hers.

Her eyes widened in surprise as he lowered his mouth to hers. It wasn't a soft kiss, and it wasn't nice. It was raw and filled with so much need he thought he would explode with the sheer want of her.

And she allowed him in. He deepened the kiss, savoring her sweetness until he sensed her reserve and pulled back. Cupping the side of her face, he placed his forehead to hers. "I want you so goddamn much, I *ache* with it." He felt her stiffen. "No. Don't do that. Don't close down on me." He tilted her head up so she would look at him. "I'm drowning, Josie, and part of me doesn't want to come up for air."

She relaxed, her expression softening, and wrapped her arms around him. And he lost it. Like a fucking baby, he cried.

Jo was out of her depth—and had no idea what to do next. It had taken only seconds to go from excitement to guilt to fear, as Jacks' behavior bordered on manic. But when he forced her to look at him, she witnessed a pain so deep it took her breath away. She wanted to soothe him, to heal wounds scraped raw by whatever demons he held inside. But she didn't know how. She was the last person he should trust with his vulnerability. All she could do was hold him and whisper that it was going to be okay.

Someone entered the gym, and like a shot, he was off her.

The two squared off, standing feet apart, staring at one another.

Had she been another woman, an *empathetic* person, she might have reacted differently. But she just raised one brow and said, "You good?"

JT laughed.

She'd made him *laugh*. Tears of absurdity and relief replaced tears of pain. He didn't know how she did it, how she turned his sorrow and grief into something light and of little consequence. She stared at him like he'd lost his mind, and maybe he had, but he knew one thing for sure. In that moment, Josette Singer was his savior.

He didn't tell her about ending things with Addy—it wasn't the right time, not after laying so much emotional baggage down. He wanted Jo to see him as a whole man, not some emotional cripple who didn't know his own mind. This was his second chance, and he wasn't going to blow it. He'd have to prove to her they belonged together.

There was one minor complication. Addy had asked him to pretend they were still a couple until filming ended, so she wouldn't be humiliated in front of millions of viewers. He couldn't say no, not after he broke her heart for the second time. He just hoped Jo would understand.

JT rode for hours after leaving the gym, with no clear destination, and by the time he turned onto the road leading home, his mood had improved. He spotted Levi's truck as he passed the renovated barn and decided to stop in. His brother had shown a lot of interest in Jo, and he wanted to put his cards on the table and have Levi do the same.

He parked the bike and walked into the two-story open space, feeling a twinge of envy as he took in the nearly completed tasting room. They had stripped the interior back to the original frame, highlighting its thick timbered beams. The walls were a soft white with limestone floors, and a steel staircase led to a second-floor loft. They'd added a wall of windows at one end, which suffused the space with light. A double-sided stone fireplace separated the massive area with high-top tables on one side, and leather chairs and sofas arranged into conversation areas on the other. Toward the back, they'd built a full-length bar, its shelves soon to be lined with Fowler's Pond bourbon, vodka, and gin.

Levi sauntered over. "To what do I owe the pleasure?"

"Hey. The place looks great. Meant to come by the other day."

"Guess you were too busy with your new toy."

JT regarded his brother. "It belongs to the farm. Whereas this," he spread his arms wide, "belongs to you."

Levi just shrugged and stood with his hands in his pockets.

"You got a minute to talk?"

Levi gave him a curious look but nodded. "Yeah, hold on." He walked into a back room and returned with a bottle of bourbon and two glasses with logos on them. He poured three fingers of whisky in each glass and handed one to JT. "I'm thinking whatever brought you here might require a drink."

They settled in the club chairs near the fireplace and enjoyed the first sips of the fiery liquid in silence.

JT dealt the first hand. "What's Jo to you, Levi?"

Levi cocked his head. "With all due respect, JT, that's none of your business."

"I broke things off with Addy," he said, pinning his brother with a stare. "So, I'm making it mine."

Levi laughed, raising his eyes to the ceiling. "And now you want me out of the way?"

"I'm just letting you know where I stand, is all."

Levi upped the ante. "Well, then, I'll do the same. Jo and I've gotten real close since becoming partners." Levi noted the surprise on JT's face and smirked. "What, she didn't tell you? The show refused to finance the distillery—said they didn't have the budget. Jo invested in the business so our father wouldn't have to grow hemp. Without her, this..." he surveyed the room, "wouldn't exist." He brought the glass to his lips with a look of smug satisfaction.

JT squeezed the bridge of his nose. *It'd been a hell of a day, and it just kept punching.* "So, you're using her?"

Levi laughed. "Using her? Hell, you don't know her at all, do you?" He rested his elbows on his knees. "I want her every bit as bad as you, and I'm not going to walk away because you want to stick your wick—"

JT snapped. He sprang out of his chair and hauled Levi out of his, overturning it. "I wouldn't finish that sentence if I were you."

Levi didn't fight back.

"It's ironic, don't you think? JT said, letting him go. "Coming from you, the guy known for *fuckin' and chuckin'*? Hell, you were already a legend when I entered high school." JT cocked his head. "Have you ever taken a girl out to dinner? Shown her something besides your naked backside?" JT snorted and shook his head. "Nah, I didn't think so." He grabbed the bottle and filled his glass.

Levi smoothed his shirt, then righted the chair. "That's what scares you, isn't it? That I want more from Jo, that I actually *like* her." He scoffed. "The great and powerful Jackson Taylor losing out to his Mexican half-brother. A real hit to the old pride, huh?"

JT knocked back the bourbon like water. "Is that what this is about? Jealousy? You want what's mine?"

"She ain't yours."

JT nodded. "You're right. She doesn't belong to me, you, or anyone else. But, make no mistake. I'm gonna do my best to get her back."

Levi picked up his glass and fell back into the chair. "She'll never be happy here, JT. You gonna desert the family again?" He raised a questioning brow, knowing the answer. "Me? I don't mind moving, only stayed this long because of Silvia, and she doesn't care if I'm here or not, as long as the bills get paid and the drugs continue to flow." He poured himself more whiskey.

JT felt the fight leave him. "I'm sorry for that, Levi. I really am."

"Don't feel sorry for me now, brother. I'm long past wanting to be accepted by you and yours."

JT knew it was a lie but kept the veil of pride intact. "Thanks for the bourbon," he said, placing the glass down. "Still the best around." He turned and staggered a bit, deciding it might be best to walk home. "I'll come back for the bike." He waved over his shoulder as the iron doors parted.

32

*I miss being surrounded by loose acquaintances who think
I'm funny, and smart, and charming.*
- Alexis, Schitt's Creek

It was good to be home. Jo had missed the sights and sounds of the city. Even the smells—which were not always pleasant—held thirty years of memories for her. A spring rain had given way to a cloudless sky, and she breathed in the acrid scent of dirt and concrete, but also of life. The city was *alive*. It had an energy and a vibration that filled her soul.

The trustees of her estate and the foundation had shown a lot of enthusiasm for Jo's plan to start her own nonprofit. She originally thought to ask them to buy the Taylors' loan as a favor to her, but after her conversation with Jacks, she realized she could help other small farms in the same position. There was no time to make a formal pitch, but luckily, she didn't have to. They'd wanted to diversify into the rural nonprofit arena, and this fit perfectly. Since she had their attention and momentum, she swung for the fences and asked to be reinstated to the board.

Best birthday gift ever.

She took a detour through Rittenhouse Square. The cherry blossoms were long gone, but the square was still redolent with the lush new growth of spring. Everything felt full of promise as Jo strolled through the streets to her destination.

"*Salut!*" Jo entered her parents' spacious foyer. "*Maman?*"

"Josette?" Élaine called from above. "*T'es en avance.*"

"I am?" Jo checked her watch. "I thought you said five-thirty?"

Élaine appeared on the second-floor landing. "*Oui, mais je ne t'attendais pas avant sept heures.*"

Jo raised her brow. "Seven? That seems a little drastic, don't you think?"

"Pfft." Élaine waved her hand. "I wanted you to be *on time*."

"Well, I'm here now, so…." Jo followed the soft padded sounds of her mother's bare feet as she made her descent.

Élaine greeted her daughter with outstretched arms. "*Joyeux anniversaire, ma chérie.*"

Jo stepped into her mother's embrace—a rare and awkward treat. "Thanks."

"You are thirty years old today." Having performed her maternal duty, Élaine motioned for her to follow down the long hall, past the front rooms, and through the French doors to a lovely brick patio.

The backyard was large for the city. A corner lot enclosed by a brick wall and two iron gates, one with an entrance to the side street and the other from the back alley. The patio stepped down onto a manicured lawn surrounded by lush landscaping, where two long tables were set up. Strings of lights hung between the trees, with lanterns scattered among the flower-filled vases on the tables.

"Oh, *Maman.*" Jo brought her hands to her chest. "*C'est magnifique!*"

Élaine shook her head. "I cannot take the credit. Holly and Antwon arranged for it all."

Jo reached out and clasped her mother's hand, knowing that wasn't true. "Thank you."

Élaine allowed the brief contact before pulling away. "I have done very little. It is but a small affair."

Warmth filled her as she followed her mother back into the house.

With over an hour to kill, Jo curled up in the library. Checking her messages, she went straight to the one from Jackson. Her thumb ran over the three simple words, *Happy birthday, Josie*. She'd thought a lot about their encounter at the gym and how she made him laugh with two insensitive words—and how he thanked her.

She wished he hadn't shared his pain. It had opened something soft and needy inside her, and she hated him just a little bit for it.

They stood under a canopy of lights as a server came by with a tray of champagne.

"Holly's coming with a *man*," Drew said, accepting a glass.

"A real one?" Jo joked, wide-eyed.

"You know that girl hasn't fed the kitty in *months*." He took a sip of the rosé champagne. "Ooh, lush."

Deuce appeared behind Jo. "Talking about me, I see." He placed a kiss on top of Jo's head.

Drew's eyes traveled the length of him. "You are definitely *lush*."

Deuce bent close to Jo's ear, but his eyes were on Drew. "I can't wait to get you alone."

"Okay. That's just…I don't need to be in the middle of this, do I?"

"Yes. Yes, you do." Drew glanced around conspicuously.

Jo flicked her wrist. "These are all our friends. What are you worried about?"

"Your mother insisted on having tonight catered."

"Ah, I see. Prying eyes. Well, then I guess you're the only one without a date tonight." Jo gave him a cheeky smile and put her arm halfway around Deuce's thick waist, hugging his side. "This is going to be so much fun!"

"Jobo."

Someone pushed on her shoulder. "Hmm?"

"Wake up."

Jo rolled away from the sound and into a wall. Or more precisely, a warm, breathing wall of muscle. A hand pulled her onto her back. She blinked, trying to focus on the looming figure above. "Holl?"

"Bitch, please."

"Drew?"

"Get your ass out of my spot."

Jo lifted onto her elbows and looked around at the familiar surroundings. "No can do, Drewzy. This is my bed." She smiled, still slightly inebriated. "And I believe this big fella," she gave Deuce a couple of pats on the back, "is *my* boyfriend." She waved Drew away. "So scoot." She fell back and closed her eyes. A bright light burned a hole straight through her frontal cortex. "Holy mother of Moses!" She sat up, putting the heel of her hands against her eye sockets.

Drew lowered the phone's flashlight. "Deuce wandered in here, and I can't move him, so *you* have to go."

"It's my birthday."

"*Was*, buttercup."

"Drew," she tried to reason, "it's a king-size bed. Just…" she scooched over, "Get in."

"Have you lost your ever-lovin' mind?"

Jo couldn't stop giggling. She didn't know why she found it so funny, but she did. "Come on, we'll share him. We'll do a reverse Oreo." She realized her mistake the moment she moved closer to the edge of the bed. "AAHH!" she yelped, as Drew dumped her unceremoniously onto the floor.

"Reverse Oreo, my ass." He stepped over her body and laid on the bed, wrapping his arms around the furnace that was Deuce.

"You're lucky I'm feeling generous." She snatched Drew's blanket and trudged to her office.

Her alter-ego, Miss Money Honey, leaned against a pillow on the made-up sofa bed. "I should've tossed you in the bin," she said with a soft chuckle. And it hit her; she didn't have negative thoughts attached to the doll anymore. *Progress.* Finding the box, she laid the puppet in its shrine and considered giving it back to Remy.

Nope, I'll never be that evolved.

Something was bound to upset the cosmic calm that had defined her trip. Things were so good, in fact, Jo started to panic. While she waited for the Roadrunner to drop an anvil on her head, she tried to enjoy her walk to *Oy Veg*, where she was meeting Holly for lunch. She ordered a Beetstrami on rye, then went outside to snag the last bistro table where she spied her friend's bright pink and green dress as it turned the corner.

Jo shielded her eyes. "Wait, let me get my sunglasses."

Holly put a hand to her chest. "It's Lilly Pulitzer!"

"I'm kidding. It's adorable." Jo lifted off the chair to give her friend a peck on the cheek. "I already ordered."

"The Reuben Hood or Beetstrami?"

"Beetstrami. Sauerkraut gives me gas."

"Oh, that's true, and I have a meeting at two. No need to subject my clients to that. I'll be right back."

Jo glanced at her phone, noticing a missed call from Levi. He hadn't left a message, so she decided to call him back after lunch.

Holly returned with a couple of sparkling waters. "We're swamped at work. Had to sneak out the back before anyone saw me leave, or I'd *still* be there."

"I thought tax season was over?"

Holly gave her a befuddled look. "I'm a corporate attorney, Jo. Not a CPA."

She laughed it off. "Of course. I knew that." *I've been a terrible friend.* "So, how's Ben?"

They spent the rest of the hour dissecting Holly's new relationship. And it was…refreshing. When it was time to leave, they hugged, and Jo didn't hate it. She even squeezed back.

"I love you, Holl." *Where did that come from?*

Holly's bemused look turned to one of concern. "Are you all right? You're not sick, are you? Is there something you need to tell me?"

Jo laughed it off, waving her hand around as she tried to stem the ridiculous tears pooling in her eyes. "Don't be silly. I'm fine. I just miss you."

Holly nodded and gave her another quick hug before hurrying back to her office.

Jo took her phone off mute. She hesitated, her finger poised over the send button. She wanted more time before calling Levi. More time to enjoy her blissful bubble. More time away from Jackson's physical and emotional draw. Being home, in the City of Brotherly Love, was good. Healthy. She'd come a long way since her time in LA, but she still feared she wouldn't be able to put a leash on her desire for him. The memory of their last encounter was so intense; she had a visceral reaction every time she recalled it. They had crossed a line, and she wouldn't let it happen again. Just punching in Levi's number made her break out in a sweat.

Strolling down Market Street, phone to her ear, Jo decided a week at the beach house might be just what she needed to clear her head before returning to Kentucky for the spring festival.

The black to her white, the yin to her yang, the opposite of happy. That's where Jo found herself the next day. On a plane heading back to Kentucky to attend Levi's mother's funeral.

Levi had insisted on picking her up at the airport. He stood with his hands in his pockets as she approached—a pair of dimples transforming his handsome face.

She let go of her suitcase and hugged him. "You shaved your beard." She ran a hand along his cheek. "It suits you."

His smile broadened.

Those dimples! "You shouldn't hide that face."

He huffed out a small laugh and took her bag. "You know, you didn't need to fly back early."

"Of course I'd come back." *Although I'd rather do the Hokey Pokey naked down Broad Street during rush hour than attend a funeral.*

Levi put the bag in the trunk. "Well, I appreciate it."

They drove in silence until they hit the highway. "It wasn't unexpected," he said, glancing her way. "Silvia never stayed clean for long. In a way, it's a relief—I know that sounds awful—but her pain...her demons, they're gone now." The muscles of his jaw clenched and unclenched and his voice grew softer. "Surprised it took so long, actually."

What must his childhood have been like? Jo's chest tightened. She slid her hand blindly into his and peered out the window, unable to think of anything meaningful to say. The warmth of his fingers closed around hers, and she gave a little squeeze.

He brought their joined hands to his lips and kissed her fingers, his warm breath gliding across her knuckles until he reluctantly lowered them to his lap.

Jo dropped her suitcase at the foot of the bed and headed to the bathroom, where a knock on her door turned her around.

A grinning Kara stood outside. "I've got news." She expanded her arms. "Big news."

"Can it wait until the morning? I just flew in."

"You'll want to hear this." Kara rolled up and down on the balls of her feet.

"Fine, come on in."

Kara closed the door and leaned against it.

Jo flopped into the chair by the window and took off her heels, rubbing the bunion on her right foot. "Go on, let's hear it."

"Jackson-broke-up-with-Addison," Kara said in a high-pitched rush.

Jo sat forward. "Say again?"

"He did it. He broke up with her."

"Huh." Jo stood, her heart pounding.

Kara's fingers tapped against both thighs. "That's it? That's all you're gonna say?"

"I'm processing." Jo unsnapped her bra and walked to the bathroom. Closing the door, she spiked an imaginary football. *He picked me!* A goofy grin greeted her in the mirror.

She moon-walked out the door, transitioned into a side glide, and turned toward Kara with a chest pop, throwing her hands into the air.

"Now, that's the Jo I know and love."

Jo laughed and grabbed her toiletry bag. "Does Gail know? They invested a lot of time into their romance."

Kara waved it away. "Yeah, it's fine. Jackson agreed to keep the storyline."

Even *that* news couldn't dampen Jo's excitement. She headed back to the bathroom, undressed, and brushed her teeth.

Kara stood by the door. "Happy belated, by the way. Great pics of your birthday celebration. I especially liked the ones of you and Deuce in bed."

Jo spit into the sink and swung the door open with her arm. "Say *what*?"

Kara backed up. "I thought you posted them. You know, to make it look like..."

Jo walked out wearing nothing but a thong and grabbed her phone, angrily punching in Drew's number. It went straight to voicemail. "Fuck!" She clicked over to Instagram.

Kara tried to hand her a robe. "You might want to..."

Jo ignored her and sat on the bed, scrolling through her social threads. "I can't believe he did this without asking me."

That was a lie, it was exactly something Drew would do, and part of her knew the old Jo would have laughed it off.

Kara leaned over her shoulder. "You look pretty hot, though, even in that old T-shirt."

Jo regarded her. "Really, Kar?"

"Sorry. You're right. It's majorly fucked up." She squinted. "What's on your nightstand?"

Jo glanced at the photo before flinging the phone to her side. "Gumby. My birthday gift from Drew."

"Oh, well sure. That makes sense."

"It would if you knew Drew." Jo fell back on the bed, vowing never to let Gumby drag Pokey along on any more adventures.

"Right. I think I'm just gonna..." Kara pointed toward the door, backing up.

Jo raised her arm in a half-hearted goodbye. "See you tomorrow."

33

If you wanna dance, you gotta pay the band.
- Rocky

Jo had a particular aversion to funerals, and she didn't need Dr. Fielding to tell her why.

"That weed pen's seen more hits than Jay-Z," Kara said, glancing over as they drove from the church to Levi's bar.

Jo put the pen back in her clutch. "I'm trying not to stand out."

Kara chuffed. "I'm pretty sure walking around stoned will guarantee it."

Jo's brain tried to catch up with her head as it swiveled toward her friend. "It calms my anxiety and makes me more empathetic, so I don't say stupid shit."

"*Weed* makes you say stupid shit."

Jo nodded. "Truth." She opened the window and stuck her head out.

"What are you doing?"

"Feeling the breeze."

"When are you going to come down? Because Levi needs you."

"*When are you going to land...*" Jo sang. Elton's words eerily similar to the situation she found herself in. Farms, fathers, holding on.

When they entered the parking lot, she pulled her head in and belted out the rest of the refrain.

"Interesting rendition."

Jo gave her a lopsided grin. "I'm a song *slayer* at Dirty Gerties on Karaoke night." Which was true—she murdered every song she sang.

Kara chuckled. "Let's go, songbird."

They entered to the sound of a Mariachi band warming up. A couple notes of a trumpet, a tuning of a guitar. It all seemed so lively.

Levi walked over wearing a light blue button-down, dark denims, and clean boots. He tilted his head toward the five-piece band. "It's what Silvia wanted."

"I think it's great." Jo grinned—immediately regretted it—and sealed her lips in a close-mouthed smile. She looked around, absently running a hand over her black Valentino dress, regretting that, too.

"You shaved your beard," Kara said, tapping a staccato against her thighs.

"Something else she always wanted," he said with a hint of a smile.

An older couple walked in, and he excused himself.

Jo raised an eyebrow and gestured toward Kara's drumming. "Always meant to ask, is that part of your OCD?"

Kara stopped momentarily and looked down at her hands. "The tapping? No, it's a technique to relieve stress and anxiety."

"Oh." *Good to know.*

Jo scanned the room for Jacks, hoping she wasn't being obvious. They hadn't spoken at the church, but she'd raised a hand in greeting when their eyes met. He'd been sitting with his family and Addison. Jo wondered if Kara had gotten it wrong, and they were still together. They certainly looked good together. Although, to be honest, Jacks could swallow Addison's petite frame in one gulp. One big gulp. *I haven't had a Big Gulp in years...*

"Hey, Josie."

She jumped. "Jacks! Hi."

"Can I get you something to drink?"

A shot would be great. "No, thanks. I have some water." Jo held up the seltzer Kara had brought her before walking away to take a call.

The band started, and he leaned in close. He smelled like man soap. Clean and dirty all at once. She'd like to get dirty with him and then clean him up with his man soap.

Please tell me I didn't say that aloud. "I'm sorry. Did I say something?"

Jacks gave her a lopsided grin. "I asked how long you're staying in town, but what I really wanted to know is if you're free this weekend."

"So, you and Addison?"

"Broke up, yeah." His warm breath tickled her ear. "Happened right before the boxing club. I was really messed up. I'm sorry you had to see me like that."

The revelation slapped her back. She was pretty sure the outcome of their encounter would have been slightly different had she known.

"So, can I take you out?" he asked.

"What?" She tried to think clearly, but her high made it impossible.

"I'm asking you on a date. Unless you've got other plans?"

Giggles erupted out of nowhere, followed by unchecked laughter. Without a doubt, this behavior was unacceptable at a wake. But she couldn't stop. And now she had to pee. "Excuse me, I've got to…" She waved a hand toward the restroom and clamped her mouth shut as tears pooled in her eyes.

Jo felt everyone's eyes upon her as she moved across the room. After giving herself a stern talking to and a moment to reflect on eyebrows—did they really serve a purpose?—she walked back out. Only a few looked her way—less than she'd imagined while peeing.

Jacks seemed both amused and concerned. "You high?"

She nodded, pressing her lips together to stop another round of giggles.

"I'm gonna take it from your reaction that you're free?"

She shook her head, then nodded, the confusion loosening the restraint on her laughter.

Jacks chuckled and cupped the back of her head, bringing her face to his shoulder. She wasn't sure how long she stayed planted to his shirt, but she never wanted to leave. She wrapped her arms around him and closed her eyes.

He lowered his head and whispered. "I've missed you, Josie."

She hugged him tighter. "Me too, Jacks."

Jacks and Kara left for a scheduled shoot shortly before the band switched to Latin dance music. If all funerals ended with a celebration like Silvia's, Jo might not need to medicate.

Levi twirled her into his arms. "Last song. Let's show them how it's done."

People moved out of their way as they swung around the room. He was light and playful, and she wondered—not for the first time—why her heart chose Jacks over his brother.

As the last notes played, the bar emptied. The few remaining stragglers huddled together telling stories, too drunk to make their way home.

It'd been a long day, but Jo didn't feel right leaving. She sat in her usual place with Levi behind the bar.

"I wanted to give you something before you left." He reached under the counter and brought out a wrapped package. "Happy birthday."

Jo's eyes widened at the thoughtful gesture. "You didn't need to get me anything." The wrapping was haphazard, but Jo suspected it wasn't from a lack of trying. She ripped at the paper.

"Kara said you liked funny T-shirts." He looked uncertain as Jo held it up.

The soft gray cotton had a picture of three goats in a boat with the words, WHATEVER FLOATS YOUR GOATS.

Jo held it to her chest. "I love it. Thank you." She wrapped an arm around his neck and leaned in for a hug. He moved his hands to her face and lowered his lips to hers. She should've stopped the kiss, but curiosity mixed with affection let it happen. It was technically flawless and achingly sweet. "Levi—"

"I know." He put his lips to her brow. "I just wanted one kiss, Jo." He pulled back. "Before JT stakes his claim."

Jo scoffed. "You make me sound like a possession."

"Yes, but a prized one," he joked.

"No one owns me, but I do think of myself as a prize," she said, wagging her eyebrows.

Levi laughed and threw a couple of nuts back. "You'll win the dance off, that's for sure. JT's a great clogger."

"You mean at the festival?" When he nodded, she continued. "I'm not even sure what clogging *is,* but it doesn't matter. We won't be partners."

"Why not?"

Jo rested her chin on her palm. "My faux beau is flying in to do a cameo for the show—which Gail conveniently scheduled for next weekend. She's milking it for all she can. Instead of a five-minute spot, she's got him for an entire day. Drew's coming too, for *The Buzz.* I just hope I can act like a loving girlfriend when all I want to do is strangle both of them."

"Why? What'd they do?" he asked.

Jo pulled out her phone. Finding the links, she handed it to Levi.

She watched him swipe through, his face growing angrier with each one. "Are you telling me they published these without your knowledge?"

"Not just published. Deuce wasn't there when I went to bed."

"You're shittin' me."

"At least I'm not naked."

Levi tapped on the TikTok link. The song "I'm Too Sexy For My Shirt" accompanied a compilation of photos on a loop. Mostly Deuce, in and out of shirts, but they had Jo in a sports bra, a bikini, and in bed with Deuce wearing a T-shirt. They also did a mock-up of her, ripping his shirt off. Shaking his head, Levi tossed the phone onto the bar. "What're you going to do about it?"

"What *can* I do? They're out there, even with Drew taking down the original post. I'm just glad they're relatively benign." Good thing no one found photos of her on the topless beaches of Ibiza.

"So you're giving them a pass?"

"No...Maybe?" She waved it off. "I have my reasons. Besides, I think Drew did it partly to teach me a lesson. Drink like a house on fire, you're gonna get hosed."

"That's just crazy—"

"Listen, this is between me and Drew. Yes, they went too far, but Drew and I are friends. *Best* friends."

"With friends like that..." He shook his head. "You better hope JT doesn't see them."

"Doubtful. The man has no social media presence, so unless someone *tells* him..." she said, raising a questioning brow. He answered with a shrug and a wink. Jo huffed out a laugh. "You mind your own business." She leaned over and kissed him on the cheek. "I'm gonna go. Get some sleep, and I'll talk to you tomorrow."

On her way back to the inn, Jo thought about Levi's reaction. She couldn't muster the same level of anger—had she been sober, none of it would have happened.

Thankfully, nothing stayed relevant in the media for very long. By tomorrow, it would all be forgotten.

34

When life closes a door, just open it again.
It's a door, that's how they work.
- Unknown

Jo held out her arms. "So, what do you think?"

Kara cocked her head and made a circular motion with one finger.

Jo rotated, the dress hugging every curve.

"I give it five."

"Out of ten?" Jo put her hands on her hips.

"Minutes. Before it lands on the floor."

"Ooh, that's good, right?"

"Depends on how hungry you are. Here." She rooted around in her bag, tossing Jo a bag of peanuts. "I took these from Levi's. The man has a serious love of nuts."

Jo caught them, laughing. "Thanks, I have a feeling dinner will be late." Her phone dinged with an incoming text. She snatched it off the bed. "It's from Jacks."

Dress casual

Her head snapped back. "I have to change." She texted back.

How casual?

No dresses

She looked over at Kara. "I guess we can cross 'five-star dining' off the list."

And no heels

Jo whipped off her stilettos and waved a hand down her body. "It took me an hour to decide on this. Now I've got ten minutes. Doesn't he realize Rome wasn't built in a day?"

Kara started rummaging around Jo's closet. She pulled out a pair of jeans and threw them at Jo. "We'll go edgy rock chick. Where's that black Versace belt with the studs?"

Twenty minutes later, Jo descended the staircase in a black tank, a butter-soft lambskin moto jacket, and a pair of Jimmy Choo biker boots.

Jacks let out a low whistle of appreciation.

Not bad for ten minutes. Her swagger disappeared when she caught sight of what he held in his hands. "We're going on the motorcycle?"

"Wouldn't want to waste the biker-babe vibe you got goin', and since you're an experienced rider…" he teased with a smile.

Jo rolled her eyes. "We both know I lied, and if it's anything like the tri-ped—"

"Quad. This will be much smoother. I promise."

She stopped on the last step. "Don't you have a car?"

He came forward and encircled her waist with his free arm, giving her a quick kiss before swinging her around. "Nope, it's my only mode of transportation, unless you count the old Ford."

She slid down his body, sending a jolt of desire through her. "Let's go with that, then." She patted his jacket and stepped back before she did something stupid, like reach for his man parts.

"Josie." He ran a thumb along her cheek. "I want to feel you wrapped around me on my bike."

Well, damn.

Jo held on with a death grip, her screams blending in with the roar of the engine as they pulled onto the road. It was both terrifying and thrilling, the blur of colors, the white noise, the *smells*. She was hyper-aware and hyper-alive, all her senses engaged, turning dread into excitement.

They rode for about thirty minutes before pulling into a large, paved area with low metal buildings lining the perimeter. Jacks parked outside the first building's entrance and lowered the kickstand. He tapped her leg, signaling for her to swing off.

He unstrapped her helmet and set it on the bike. "That wasn't so bad, was it?"

Jo beamed. "I loved it."

He leaned in, his blue eyes turning a soft denim in the sun. "Happy birthday, Josie."

"Thanks," she whispered into his kiss.

He stepped back with a disarming smile. "I know it was last week, but can we pretend it's today?"

"I believe you get a month to celebrate when turning thirty. It's a big transition year."

A man stepped out of the building and extended his hand to Jacks. "Taylor! Good to see you."

Jacks grasped the man's hand. "Reese, been awhile. How's the family?"

"Good, good. Twins just turned five. Handful for Tabby, since they don't start school until the fall."

"I still can't believe you have kids." Jacks shook his head. "Would've bet money you'd be running a bar somewhere with your toes in the sand." He laughed. "Did, in fact."

Reese chortled. "Yeah, life turns on a dime, doesn't it?" He lost some of his cheer. "Glad to have you back."

Jo watched the two men communicate through a bond forged long ago.

"You still flying for the One-Twenty?"

Jacks rubbed the back of his neck. "Nah, didn't re-up."

"Their loss." His eyes turned to Jo. "Hell of a pilot."

She smiled and stuck out her hand. "Hi, I'm Jo."

Reese gave her a wide, toothy grin. "Kyle Reese. Pleasure to meet you." He cocked his head in Jacks' direction. "I trained your boy here to fly. Best I ever trained."

Jo listened to them talk about old times until the technical jargon became impossible to follow, and her eyes trailed off to the planes dotting the landscape.

Tiny planes plus Jacks plus birthday equaled...*Oh, dear baby Jesus.*

"...The Tomahawk?" Jo heard Jacks ask.

"Yup, all ready to go. Did the pre-flight myself. She's right over there." He motioned to a small white plane with a red stripe, sitting about a hundred feet away on the tarmac.

Reese noticed her look of panic. "You're in excellent hands, Jo." He tipped his cap before sauntering away. "Enjoy your flight."

There'd be no romantic dinner. No moon-lit sonata or dancing under the stars.

Just *this*.

Jacks turned her toward the setting sun. "See that? In about fifteen minutes, it will hit the horizon. No better way to see it set than between the clouds."

Jo gave him a weak smile and dragged her feet toward the flying death trap.

Jacks easily maneuvered onto the wing and crouched, extending an arm for her. "I've got you."

She stepped onto the tire and raised her hands to his. He pulled her up in one fluid motion. "Jo. Look at me." He exuded a calm confidence that allowed her to take a breath.

She swallowed and focused on his face.

"You afraid of heights?"

"Well, that depends on your definition. I don't like roller coasters or Ferris wheels, but I'm fine on a 747."

Jacks pulled her close, putting his chin on her head. "I'm guessing this falls into the first category. We don't have to do this."

Man up. This was his gift to her, and she would soil her shorts before ruining it. "No, it's fine. Really. What doesn't kill you makes you stronger, right?" She tried to laugh it off, but it came out as a squeak.

He took a few steps along the wing with her in tow. "Stay on the wing grip so you don't slip." He turned sideways at the entrance to the cockpit. "Here. Grab the handle." He leaned forward and wrapped her fingers around it.

The wind whipped her hair into her face, making her panic.

"Shh. I got you." He brushed it back and gave her a quick kiss. "You're doing great. Now, hold on to the opening and slide your legs in."

Jo did as told and found herself inside the cramped quarters.

Jacks pivoted and thrust his large body into the seat next to hers before he strapped them both in.

Jo eyed the identical equipment in front of them. "Jacks, what am I supposed to do with this?" She waved a hand at the control stick and instrument panel.

"Babe, just relax and keep your feet clear of the rudder pedals."

She pulled her feet back as far as they would go. "Roger that."

Jacks laughed. "You're too damn cute."

Adorable. Jo focused on her breathing and awaited further instructions.

"Here, put these on." He handed her a headset and started the engine.

The smell of jet fuel hit her nostrils, and she started to sweat, her heart racing.

Calm the fuck down, Jo.

"We're green to go." Jo heard him say through her headset.

Jo focused on Jacks and his complete control of the plane. She gripped the handle on the door as they taxied.

At the runway's edge, Jacks turned toward her. "You ready?"

She nodded before squeezing her eyes shut, wanting to just get it over with.

"Okay, time to roll."

Within seconds, they were airborne. It wasn't like flying commercial, where it took an eternity to leave the ground. They were up and banking left before she had time to blink.

"Jo, darlin', open your eyes."

She peeled her lids back and viewed the panoramic scene. They flew over green fields and brown pastures, a quilt of squares and rectangles, surrounded by fences and dotted with buildings. She could see the freshly tilled land, the dark earth turned into neat little rows.

"Oh, it's...not so bad." She took a deep breath and let it out. *Nothing to be afraid of.*

The plane leveled off, and she relaxed as they flew above the beautiful countryside. She'd just begun to enjoy herself when suddenly, *WHOOSH!* Her stomach rose to her throat as they swooped down close to the ground. Jo could practically see the wheat's chaff from her window. There was mischief in Jacks' eyes as they soared up for another pass. This time, she laughed out loud.

"That was just mean!" she choked out.

Jacks glanced over, grinning. "I think the word you're looking for is exhilarating."

He was right. She'd never felt more alive.

The ride was remarkably smooth as they glided over a body of water, which rippled into frothy waves.

"Recognize it?"

Jo nodded. "Fowler's Pond."

Jacks yanked back hard at the end of a field, blurring the colors of earth and sky. It took a minute for Jo's throat to release the hold on her innards, but once the plane leveled off, so did her organs.

"Are you ready for your gift?"

Jo nodded, excitement replacing fear.

They flew above a carpet of clouds as the sun's sinking rays lit them from within, turning them into golden puffs. The bright orb took one final gasp before its descent, bathing the sky in hues of pink, orange, and indigo so intense Jo's heart ached with the beauty of it.

"I've never seen anything like it," she whispered, turning away from the kaleidoscope of colors. "Thank you."

He looked over briefly and winked. "My pleasure, Josie."

When the sky darkened, Jacks headed back. They held hands in the intimate silence, both lost in thoughts of things yet to come.

They landed like a feather falling to earth, soft as a whisper.

Jo relaxed and leaned into the curve, becoming one with Jacks and the bike. The temperature had dropped, and the wind blew cold, but she felt warm against his back—every muscle moving in sync with the machine. He was a part of it, and of the road, and Jo imagined, part of her.

They slowed and pulled into the drive that belonged to the old farmstead. Jacks lowered the stand and helped her off. He put their helmets on the bike and turned, scrubbing his scalp.

"You're a natural, Jo."

She could still feel the bike's vibration between her legs. "A couple more rides and you won't even know I'm there."

"I hope not." He pulled her to him. "I like the way you feel pressed up against me." He ran his thumb over her face and leaned down for a kiss. "Want to see the place?"

"Sure."

"Come on." He pulled her to the front of the house. "So, what do you think? I've been working on it for months." He squeezed her hand.

The newly painted white clapboard glowed in the remaining light, and the pretty blue door beckoned them onto a porch that no longer sagged with rotting boards.

"It's lovely."

Jacks chuckled. "I'm gonna take that as a compliment. Come on, I'll show you the inside." He drew her up the steps and into the house.

When he'd first shown it to her, it'd been old and sad, smelling of decay. The kind that stung the nose and made you want to run for the hills. What he'd done to the place, well...She could see herself living here.

Instead of several small rooms, Jacks had knocked out walls, expanding the space to include the kitchen and dining area. It wasn't a large house and by opening it up, he made it look spacious while still retaining its charm.

"Jacks, it's beautiful." She walked into the kitchen, her hand grazing the honed concrete countertops. "Did you have these made?"

He ran a thumb along the edge of his bottom lip. "Nah, did it myself. Nothing to it, really."

"Nothing?" She laughed. "I'd have to disagree." She loved the mixture of modern industrial and rustic ease. Her own kitchen, with its simple lines, modern glossy cabinetry, and monochromatic color scheme, seemed cold and uninviting in comparison.

Her eyes landed on a pitcher of fresh-cut wildflowers and a gift bag on the table. "Another surprise?" She walked over and breathed in the fragrant blooms. "Can I open it?" she asked, her hand reaching for the bag.

He shrugged, hands in his pockets. "Sure. It's nothing much."

She pulled out a bar of goat's milk soap and a jar of goat's milk and honey cream.

"We're still trying out different products. Those are Lou Lou's favorites."

Jo opened the lid and brought it to her nose. "Smells great." She placed the jar back in the bag and turned. "Thank you, Jacks. I love them."

"I've got some goat cheese too, if you'd like to try it," he said, giving her a slow smile. "Unless you'd rather see the rest of the house first?"

Butterflies took flight in her stomach. "The cheese can wait." She intertwined her fingers with his and followed him to the stairs. "Nothing more down here?"

He looked over his shoulder with a sexy grin. "Nothing of note, no."

They climbed the steps to the small second floor, which consisted of a full bath and a bedroom. Jacks opened the door and stood aside for her to enter, his hand resting on the knob. "I haven't slept in here yet. Just finished it this afternoon."

It was a masculine room with dark charcoal walls. The king-size bed had a leather headboard and luxurious bedding in pale gray. The only other furniture was a long wooden dresser and a nightstand. Jo walked to the bed and ran her hand across the soft cotton.

"Another thing Lou picked out," he said, walking into the room.

"She did a good job. It suits you," she said, her eyes focused on his mouth.

He reached for her, his fingers gliding across her face, hair, and neck. "I want you so damn bad, Josie." He began to kiss everywhere he touched.

Jo met his need with her own, running her hands beneath his shirt. His skin was soft and warm. She moved from his back to his hard abs, which tightened in response to her touch. She skimmed the space between his jeans and waist, her fingers working on the button.

He stopped her. "You sure you don't want something to eat? You gotta be hungry."

Jo loosened his hold and resumed her task. "I am, Jacks, so very hungry."

That was all the encouragement he needed. Their kiss deepened and he gently pushed the jacket off her shoulders. They undressed one another, neither wanting to break the contact, and laughed as they fell onto the bed, pants around their ankles.

Jacks took his time savoring every inch of her body. Jo tried to do the same, but he stopped her, his exploration a single-minded task.

"You are so fucking gorgeous. Every inch of you."

Jo was beyond thought as she indulged in his worship of her body. Forgetting all else, she allowed the gift of pleasure without reciprocation.

She went off like a rocket when his lips found her core, and again when he covered her body with his. Entering her, moving with her, coming with her.

He kissed her softly as he swept back the dampened hair from her face. "I'm sorry. I was so caught up, I didn't think to ask—"

Jo licked the salty column of his neck. "I'm on the pill."

He lifted his weight and moved to her side, his hand cupping her face as he leaned in for a kiss. "Thanks for trusting me."

"I believe that goes both ways. What if I wasn't protected?"

He smiled. "You would've stopped me."

"Hmm, good thing we didn't need to test that theory." She sucked one of his fingers into her mouth, swirling it around with her tongue, and felt a slight hardening at her hip. Smiling, her teeth pinned his finger.

"Babe, you're gonna need to give me a minute."

Jo pulled it out with a 'pop' and laughed. "I'll give you five."

They lay together, kissing and exploring, talking, and laughing until the heat flared again, and they came together with an urgency that surprised them both.

"Jesus, Jacks. If this keeps escalating, I'm going to spontaneously combust."

"Then we'll go down in flames together," he said, leaning back. "Why do you call me Jacks and not JT?"

"Hmm? Oh, I don't know. Why do you call me Josie?"

"Because it fits you, and it's mine," he said, nuzzling her neck.

"I guess that's why I call you Jacks." Jo drew her fingers through his soft hair, which had grown in, and played with a golden curl as he snuggled against her.

The sound of Jo's stomach roused them from sleep and she turned to face Jacks. "Ready for round two?"

He laughed and wrapped her in his arms. "I think we're going to need fuel. I'll get us some food." He pivoted, pinning her underneath, and gave her a quick, hard kiss before bouncing off the bed.

Jo rose onto her elbows, watching every move of his muscular body as he pulled on his jeans. The hands that had played her body like a Stradivarius now hid her greatest source of pleasure. She sighed and fell to the pillows. "Hurry back."

He walked in minutes later with a tray laden with fruit, cheese, crackers, and wine. They sat on the bed, eating, drinking, and talking until the sky glowed with the coming dawn.

And they made love. Over and over until they knew every inch of one another. When exhaustion could no longer be held at bay, they slept.

The sun was high in the sky when Jo opened her eyes again. She stretched her arms into the emptiness beside her. Hearing sounds from below, she threw the covers off and stood, the ache in her body a pleasant reminder of the night before.

She padded down the steps, pulling his shirt over her nose, breathing in his scent. She wanted to bottle it and take it with her wherever she went.

He smiled over his shoulder as he poured coffee into a mug. "I'm afraid I don't have a lot for breakfast. I usually eat at the main house." He turned and offered her the cup. "There's a little milk in the refrigerator, but I don't have any sugar."

Jo took a sip of the coffee. "No need, I can drink it black." She sat at the island and watched him make another cup for himself.

With mug in hand, he smiled and leaned back against the counter. "Good morning."

"It sure is." She grinned back.

"So," he started, setting his cup down. "I wanted to talk to you about the show, about me and Addy. I didn't want to ruin our night, but we need to talk about it."

Jo waved a hand dismissively. "It's fine, Jacks. I know you agreed to be together for the show."

He lowered his chin, his eyes locked on hers. "I'll be partnering with her for the games next weekend, too."

"Not a problem. Deuce is flying in for a cameo, and Gail convinced him to stay the weekend. I have to be his partner."

His eyes narrowed. "Explain to me again why you're pretending to be a couple?"

Jacks' phone vibrated with an incoming call.

Happy to have the distraction, Jo stood. "I'm going to take a quick shower."

He nodded and put the phone to his ear.

Jo brought the bag of soap and cream with her to the bathroom. After a hot shower, she donned his shirt again—having no intention of giving it back—and pulled on her jeans.

She skipped down the steps. "How about we go out to...eat." She stopped when she caught the look on his face. "What's wrong?"

Jacks swiped the screen on his phone, his lips in a tight line. "Were you going to tell me about these pictures?"

She entered the kitchen and sat on a stool. "No," she replied honestly.

Jacks scrubbed his face. "Why are they all over the internet, and why are you in Deming's bed?"

"*Technically*, he's in my bed." The look on his face made her realize she couldn't joke her way out of it. "Levi shouldn't have told you."

"Levi? What the hell does he have to do with this?"

Way to go, Jo. "Then how did you find out?"

Jacks ignored her question. "I'm gonna ask again, why are you sleeping with Deming?"

The only way to make him understand was to tell him about Deuce and Drew's relationship. "Okay, this goes no farther than this room." She tapped her ring against the concrete counter. "Deuce is Drew's partner." When he raised an eyebrow, she elaborated. "I'm a *beard,* a decoy. The two of them are in a relationship. They're trying to hide it."

Jacks ran the back of his hand along his jaw as he processed the information. "Still doesn't answer my question."

She didn't know how to extricate herself without throwing Drew under the bus. "I may have passed out."

"With Deuce next to you?"

Jo sighed. "Not that I recall."

He pressed his lips together and glanced away. "So, they staged it, and you're *okay* with that?"

"*No*. But—"

"They didn't ask your permission." He walked a few paces, then spun around. "They took advantage of you—they *used* you."

"That's enough, Jacks."

"What kind of person pimps out their friend?"

Jo's body stiffened. "Please tell me you didn't just call me a whore."

Jacks raked a hand through his hair. "Just so I've got this straight: You got drunk and passed out, Deuce got into *your* bed and manipulated you into different positions, Drew took pictures, then posted them. That about sum it up?"

"You make it sound—"

"Exactly like what it is. Hell." He threw his arms into the air. "Maybe you *enjoy* being seen half-naked by millions of people in bed with someone famous."

The insult felt like a slap—mostly because he wasn't entirely wrong.

"And maybe you're being an *asshole*." She pushed her stool back and stormed out of the kitchen and up the stairs. Shaking with anger and shame, she gathered her things and stomped back down to get her purse. She passed Jacks, who sat on the arm of the sofa. He stood and followed her into the kitchen.

"Look, I'm sorry. I may have overreacted, but I'm not okay with what they did."

A barrage of emotions pelted her, triggering her fight-or-flight response. She texted Kara for a ride. "Yeah, well, you don't get a say. *I* decide how to deal with what happens in my life. Not you."

Jacks swung her around to face him. "Then what are we doing here, Jo?"

She pulled her arm free. "I thought we were having a good time." *Self-sabotage. Nice.*

"A good time?" He barked out a laugh. "So, after last night, you still just want to be *fuck buddies*?"

"That's not what I meant." Jo crossed her arms, not knowing how to fix what she'd broken. *Why aren't you in my head, Dr. Fielding?*

Jacks' voice became measured. "How do you see me fitting into your life, Josie?"

She hesitated and looked away. "I honestly don't know."

He rubbed the back of his neck. "If you won't even try to see a future with me, then tell me now before you rip my heart out."

Her eyes fell shut. "Jacks—" Words, so many words stuck in her throat, but none came out. It was probably for the best—she'd just say the wrong thing anyway.

Jacks gave a curt nod. "I'll take you home."

Jo swallowed hard. *Don't you fucking cry.*

She canceled her text to Kara, dropped the phone into her purse, and followed him out the door.

35

Storms make trees take deeper roots.
- Dolly Parton

"What time is it?"

"Five minutes past the *last* time you asked," Kara said, drumming her fingers on the card table. "It's your turn."

Jo glanced down at her hand. "I don't know what I'm doing."

Kara threw her cards on the table. "Why don't you call him? It's been two days."

"And say what? Nothing's changed."

It wasn't Jacks she was angry with, but herself. He'd called her out, made her feel cheap. And she didn't like it. Because she *cared* what he thought of her.

"Then say that. Say *something*. Just stop moping around."

"He wants too much from me. More than Remy, the puppet master, and he had a doll made of my likeness."

"Okay, that's just...I don't even know where to start."

"And he'll never understand my relationship with Drew."

"I think—"

"I'm addicted to his scent. Like creepily so. Did I tell you I stole his shirt? That's creepy, right?"

"Well, I mean—"

"The sex was stratospheric. He's now the benchmark by which all others will be judged."

"Jo." Kara reached over and grabbed her hand. "Why don't we go to Levi's?"

"No. I've been avoiding him. He knows about my date with Jacks. He'll ask questions."

"We'll go somewhere else then. The crew's on location today. Gail said they were going to a local bar afterwards. Why don't I text her and get directions?"

"Jacks will be there."

"Yeah, that's kinda the point."

Jo sighed. "Okay."

It took them an hour and a half to drive to The Landing Strip, a bar outside the Army base where they'd been filming that day.

"He's going to know I came all this way to see him."

"You just realized that now?"

Jo felt like a contestant on *Naked and Afraid*. Exposed. "I didn't think this through." She scratched at her neck. "Maybe we should leave."

"What's wrong with you? You're the most confident person I know."

"This isn't about confidence, Kar. It's about *feelings*, more specifically, the sharing of them. Jacks wants me to do that."

"What a bastard."

Jo gave her a stink face. "You're not being helpful."

"Why? Because I won't feed into your neuroses?" She tapped on the steering wheel. "You've always been with men who live in self-absorbed bubbles right alongside yours. Jacks isn't like that; he wears his heart on his sleeve. You need to let him in and allow yourself to do the same."

"I'm not sure I can."

"Love ain't for the faint of heart. Go deep or go home."

"I live a thousand miles away, I'm a vegetarian, a liberal, and a Jew. I know nothing about farms or horses or country music—"

"All excuses, Jo. Fish or cut bait. Plenty of women with their lines in the water wanting to catch Jackson. Addison would shank a bitch and use her as chum for another chance to be with him."

Jo snorted. "You paint a vivid picture."

"It's a gift." Kara stopped tapping. "Let's go."

Closing her eyes, Jo took a deep breath. *Inhale, exhale.* Bringing her hands together, she began a mantra for inner peace.

"AAHHH!" Kara swung the car door open and pulled her out.

They walked into the aviation-inspired bar, where bits and pieces of aircraft littered the large, open area. A wing lined one wall as a makeshift counter, and at the end sat an ejection seat and what appeared to be landing gear. Epoxy-covered wooden tables encased all types of memorabilia: patches and photos, dog tags, and notes. The bar itself had names and pilot call signs carved into the surface. A dart board, popcorn machine, and a beat-up pool table lay at the far side of the room.

They headed toward boisterous chatter coming from the back room, and as Jo entered, a red-haired beauty turned in her direction.

"Jo!" Samantha Powell squealed, rising to give her a hug.

Jo didn't flinch, accepting the greeting in kind. "Hello, copper goddess. It's good to see you."

"You look great! I heard you were working for the show. What a crazy coincidence, and all thanks to that horrible woman who deserved worse than you gave her. I can't believe she sued you, but if she hadn't, you wouldn't be here, would you?"

Jo laughed and gave Sam a rough hug to shut her up. "Enough about me. What are you doing in Kentucky?"

Sam's smile faltered, and she tilted her head in confusion. "Um, I'm here for the ceremony. JT received his Silver Star today. Isn't that why you're here?"

Jo stood in stunned silence, her eyes darting between the faces of Charles, Brenda, and Laura Leigh Taylor. Her vision blurred when she noticed Levi sitting quietly beside his father.

"Of course, yes, that's right. Will you excuse me?" Jo heard Kara calling her name as she hurried off. She spotted a sign for the bathroom and made a beeline for it, her face on fire. She couldn't process all the feelings bombarding her.

Embarrassment. Anger. Hurt. She ticked off the emotions, shoving each down—until she ran smack into someone. "Sorry, excuse me." She tried to move around, but a voice stopped her cold.

"Josie?"

Her head snapped back, unable to clear her face in time. Without the mask to hide behind, she broke.

Jacks pulled her into a tight embrace.

Humiliation caught in her throat. She wedged her hands between them and pushed off. "Congratulations," she said, swiping angrily at her eyes.

"How did you find out?"

"That's what you're leading with?"

He pulled her down the hall and out a back door. A light illuminated a small area where they stood facing one another.

"I need to know why you're here, Jo."

"Well, it's not to watch you receive a once-in-a-lifetime honor since that's already happened."

He pinched the bridge of his nose. "What is it you want from me? Because I'm pretty confused right now."

She crossed her arms. "I've already told you. I don't know. But it's pretty fucking cruel to treat me like I mean nothing to you, that we mean nothing to each other. You're punishing me for being honest. Just because I can't promise you forever, it doesn't mean I don't care or I want to stop seeing you. *You* decided that."

"You're right." He noticed her shivering and took off his jacket. He placed it around her shoulders and pulled her in by the lapels. "I'm sorry. It's not that I didn't want you here—I didn't want *anyone*. If I could've declined the honor, I would have. I don't deserve it. I tried to tell them, but no one wants to hear the truth."

He let go and stepped back. "It was bad enough having my family here—and the cameras—but if I saw you sitting there..." He ran a hand through his hair. "I can't pretend around you. You're the only one I've opened up to, the only one who sees me for who I am."

Jo exhaled her anger and wrapped her arms around his waist, knowing she needed to let him see her too.

"Jo?" Sam opened the back door. "Oh. I..." A look of confusion turned to understanding. "I see now why you were so upset." She nodded slowly, and backed up, disappearing inside. Jo made to follow, but Jacks held her back.

"You can explain later. We need to finish this first." He slid his hands down her arms. "I don't need you to promise me forever. Just don't shut me out. Let me be a part of your life. To have a say in it—even if it's a small one."

"Okay," Jo whispered onto his lips, trying to convey in a kiss what she'd left unsaid.

"Balls!" Sam called from one side of the pool table.

Levi took the point gracefully. He sauntered over to her and leaned down to whisper something in her ear. Sam blushed and shooed him away.

The game of Crud—as Jo found out—required only the cue ball and a striped ball. No pool sticks. It was a fast-moving game where players alternated from each team trying to hit the moving striped ball with the cue ball. If you moved to the long end of the table while striking, you got 'balled', lost a point, and had to buy the referee a drink. Jo watched Levi happily head to the bar.

"Looks like Levi's moved on." Kara pounded a shot, her head wobbling as she leaned over and whispered loudly in Jo's ear. "S'alright, though." She tapped Jo's hand and burped. "She's cute. Lil bubbly for my taste, but..." She tried to shrug, but it was more of a slump. *"C'est la vie,* right Jo? You're French."

Jo raised her brow, her mouth slightly opened. How hadn't she noticed Kara had the hots for Levi? She really needed to work harder on her self-absorption issues.

"Oui, bien sûr, mon amie."

Kara tried to place her chin on her palm, but it kept falling off. "So cool. I wish I could speak French. Think he'd like me if I spoke French, Jo?"

"He's a fool if he doesn't like you just the way you are, Kar. You're the bee's knees."

Kara snorted, sending curious glances their way. "Thanks, Jo, and you're the cat's pajamas." She nearly fell off her chair laughing.

"Glad I could amuse you." Jo stood, suddenly feeling tired. "I'm going to say goodbye to Jacks, then I'll drive you home."

Jo's eyes collided with his across the pool table. Someone shouted and tried to move him to the end for his turn, but he didn't budge or take his eyes off her. Amid shouts from his buddies, Jacks moved away from the game and toward her.

"You leaving?" He grabbed her by the waist and placed a kiss on her forehead.

Jo relaxed into him. "Yes. In a surprising role reversal, I'm the sober one."

"How about I give Levi the bike and drive you both home?" He nuzzled her ear and whispered, "I need to taste you."

The words went straight to her happy place, and like a shot of espresso, she was no longer tired. "Let's go."

36

Too much of a good thing can be wonderful.

- Mae West

Jo sat in the inn's empty production office and closed her laptop. *So much for a quiet afternoon of research.* "Why does this have to be me, Kar? Can't you do it?"

"I'm not part of the cast, and Gail specifically asked for Deuce's leading lady."

"But I don't know how to ride a horse."

"You just have to sit on it. Someone will walk you out. Oh, and there's a costume—"

"Tell me again what happened to the festival's original Winter Queen?"

Kara mumbled something under her breath, looking away.

"Did you just say she fell off a horse?"

"Yes, unfortunate timing. Don't believe the rumors."

Jo didn't want to know. "Why not pick someone who actually lives here?"

Kara started tapping on the desk. "Bad omen. Has to be an outsider."

"What kind of queen *is* this?"

"One that demands a sacrifice to ensure good crops and healthy livestock. It's a superstition, like knocking on wood, or throwing salt over your shoulder."

"Or throwing someone off a horse."

"Already happened, so you should be good."

"How reassuring." Jo twirled the ring on her thumb, hoping for the same calming effect as Kara's tapping. "What does this queen do besides drink the blood of virgins?"

"She's not a vampire, Jo," Kara said, rolling her eyes. "You crown the May Queen, who most likely *is* a virgin, and you start a fire with a corn doll full of evil spirits."

"That's the sacrifice?"

"Do I look like the town historian?" Kara continued her rhythmic tapping. "Once you ingest the bad mojo, you're free to go."

"Ingest?" *Oh, hell no.* "You said I had to burn an effigy."

"There might be more to it, I don't know all the details."

Jo threw up her hands. "How do you know *any* of it?"

"Gail. She heard it from Sandy who heard it from Brenda who's a member of the hive."

Jo put her fingers to her temples. "Dare I ask?"

"That's what they call their quilting bee. Every year they make a quilt that goes to the winner of the games." She stopped tapping. "I really want that quilt."

"That's it. Nice and slow. Ease into it. Yeah, just like that."

"Jacks, I don't think—"

"You've gotta trust me, sugar." Jacks took hold of her leg and hitched her up a tad. "The side saddle takes a little getting used to, but you'll take to it just fine."

Jo swallowed her fear and allowed Jacks to walk the powerful beast along the fence. "Can't you find a smaller horse?"

"Myrtle *is* a small horse and sweeter than honey. Aren't you, girl?" Jacks ran his hand over the pony's neck. "I'd never put you on one you couldn't handle, Josie."

"My brain hears you, but my gut disagrees."

"How about I offer you an incentive?" The corner of his mouth twitched up as he glanced her way.

All kinds of lustful thoughts crossed her mind. But sweet ones, too. Romantic ones. "Does it involve a big stallion between my legs?" In the end, lust won out.

"Damn Jo, you just woke him up." Jacks laughed and adjusted himself.

They'd spent the last week together without a break, something she'd never done before with anyone. Alone time had always been a necessity for her. She became anxious and irritable if she couldn't escape the company of others. After two days, not only did she feel no need to be alone, she missed him when he was gone. On the third morning, she woke to an empty bed and went in search of him. He was in the mud room, doing her laundry. *Squish, squoosh, splat.* She was flat out in love with him.

He led the horse around the barn and started down the path to his house. "I've got a surprise for you. All you gotta do is stay on the horse until then."

"I like where this is going, Jacks. *I really do.* But it has to be a quick one. I promised Drew and Deuce I'd be there by five."

The two men had flown in from LA and wanted Jo to stay the weekend at their rented villa to keep up appearances.

"I still think you let them off too easy for what they did."

Jo shrugged, wanting to put the incident behind her. "They apologized."

He cocked a brow but didn't say anything until they got to the house. Sliding a hand under her long boho skirt, he caressed her leg. "Now, as a precaution—although the likelihood is very small—I want to show you what to do in an emergency."

She tensed. "What kind of emergency?"

"Well, let's just say Myrtle here gets spooked and either kicks up or runs away."

"Seriously?"

"It's not gonna happen, but you need to listen just in case."

Jo nodded and tried not to imagine either of those scenarios.

With his hand still under the thin cotton, he grabbed both thighs and pressed them together around the pommels. "I need you to clamp your legs around these and hold on to her mane. If you do, it'd be very difficult to fall or get bucked off. Now let me feel you grip 'em."

Jo did as he asked, but the constant presence of his hands distracted her. "Like this?" she said in a breathy whisper.

Jacks groaned, his forehead falling to her leg. After a few seconds, he gave her thigh a squeeze, and pushed back. "Now, unhook your right leg and take your left foot out of the stirrup."

Again, she did as he requested and slipped down into his arms. He held her face, sweeping his thumbs over her cheeks. "I've fallen hard for you, Josie. You're all I think about." He kissed her once on the lips, then pulled her to him, resting his chin on the top of her head.

Jo held him tight. "Me too, Jacks."

They stood for a while, next to the horse, with Jo's head pressed against his chest. The pulse of his heartbeat matched the rhythm of her own, and she imagined them as one singular being.

Jacks' scent caught on the breeze as he shooed a fly away, and her chest bloomed with warmth and want. It was a heavy feeling, an ache that was both pleasant and disturbing in its intensity.

She refused to think about tomorrow, or the next day, and allowed herself a moment of pure joy.

37

Gravity cannot be held responsible for people falling in love.
- Albert Einstein

Jo pulled up to the estate's entrance, punched in a code, and waited for the iron gates to swing open.

Two men stood in front of a sprawling ranch-style villa. One, dressed like a technicolor dream, waved his arms. The other, wearing all black, looked like he'd eaten something disagreeable.

"Jobo!" Drew's kaftan billowed in the breeze as he brought her in for a double air kiss. "Give your keys to Deuce, he'll get your bags."

"Here you go, Papa Bear." Jo threw her keys to Deuce.

"Wait until you see the grounds. *Divine.* I feel like I should be wearing a big hat and drinking a mint julep. If only I knew how to make one."

Jo hooked her arm in Drew's, and they sauntered out to the back patio. "No staff?"

"Oh, honey, no. We can't take that chance. I booked under an alias. No one followed you here, did they?"

"Um, no?" Jo scanned the rolling landscape dotted with large oaks and grazing horses. "It's very peaceful. I'm glad you came a day early."

"Deuce wanted to escape the paparazzi. *Blackthorne* has become one of the most anticipated films of the year."

"So, they'll be all over the place."

Drew smirked. "Not until tomorrow. Tonight, he's all mine."

They sat by the pool where Jo leaned back on a chaise, basking in the sun. "Speaking of, I'm to be the Winter Queen at tomorrow night's ceremony."

"About time they recognized your worth."

"It's not an honor, she's like the goddess of death."

"Even better, evil queens are the best kind. You'll rock that shit."

Deuce joined them, carrying a tray of drinks. "Looked up mint juleps. Got the mint in the herb garden, but no bitters or simple syrup."

Drew slid his sunglasses down, looking over the rim. "So, bourbon with a mint sprig."

"Yeah, Drew. Got a problem with that?"

Drew flashed him a thousand-watt smile. "I'm sure it's delicious."

Deuce took a seat, which moaned under his weight. "I got an itinerary from someone named Sandy about the games. You signed me up for hatchet throwing?"

"Thought that'd be a good one for you," she said.

Deuce shrugged. "What's the other one? The itinerary stated two individual competitions."

Jo took a sip of whiskey. "Don't know, it's random. They pick for you. I signed up for the pie-making contest. Not really a game, but who am I to argue? I'm making a southern buttermilk pie with a twist using goat's milk and bourbon, with a mixture of lavender, mint, and rosemary. It's my *homage* to the two new ventures at Fowler's Pond."

"So, *not* a buttermilk pie," Deuce said.

Jo gave a dismissive flick of her wrist. "Anyone can make an ordinary pie. I'm going to make an *extraordinary* one."

Drew turned to Deuce. "Jobo makes the most amazing desserts. Last summer we stopped for fresh Jersey peaches at a farm on our way to her house in Margate. I still get a tingle in my dingle when I think of that pie."

"Most of the credit goes to the peaches, but thanks." She regarded Deuce, weighing her options. "Any chance you know how to clog?"

Deuce sat stone-faced.

"No? How about dancing in general? Got any rhythm?"

That earned her a grin and an eyebrow wiggle.

"I'm not talking about the horizontal mambo."

He shrugged. "I can freestyle, do a little hip-hop."

"Not even close to clogging. It's sort of like tap and line dancing. We'll have to wing it." She pulled at her bottom lip. "There are two other team events. Plenty of ways to make up the loss."

"Look at my two alphas taking on a challenge." Drew swirled the mint around in his glass and cocked his head toward Jo. "Speaking of alphas, how's lover boy?"

"Fantastic, and looking forward to kicking your ass."

"Ooh, I might enjoy that."

Deuce laughed—which was like a sunny day in Ireland.

Jo watched the two and realized it wasn't about opposites attracting, but how one brought out the best in the other.

"So, what did I do to offend Captain America?"

"Does posting pictures without my consent ring a bell?"

Drew put a hand to his chest. "You looked gorgeous. I made sure of it."

"Not the point, Drew, and you know it."

"Why's he so mad, anyway? We already apologized to you."

They'd also sent gifts. Drew gave her a painting from their time in Paris together, when she was in design school and he was modeling. It was of a mangy dog lying at the feet of an old man, and had always haunted her with its beauty. And now it was hers. Deuce, for his part, donated ten thousand dollars to a charity of her choice.

"We'll make it right, won't we Drew?"

Drew averted his gaze. "Mm hmm. I'll think about it."

Hours later, Jo lay in bed and typed a message to Jacks.

> *What are you wearing?*

Just finished setting up the barrel racing for tomorrow, so nothing

> *Cheeky monkey. Wanna know what I'm wearing?*

Please NO

> *Since you asked so nicely ...a sheet*

Josie...

> *Everyone's in bed. I'll give you the combination and leave the back door unlocked.*

Jo bit her lip and waited for a response. It seemed like an eternity before he texted back.

Address

Jo did a horizontal happy dance and typed in the information. She'd lied about wearing a sheet; she was in her normal attire, T-shirt and underwear, which made her think she should hit up some booty boutiques. For the next half hour, she browsed online for things Jacks might enjoy, but nothing appealed to her. She liked how he crawled up her body, pushing the hem of her worn cotton tee up, kissing his way to her mouth, where he'd smile down and say in a rough whisper, "lift up, sugar," and she would raise her arms as he pulled it off and...

Jo bolted upright. *Oh, fuck.*

She'd told him to take the first door on the right, but didn't say which hallway—there were two, one on each side of the main living area.

A high-pitched scream and the sound of something crashing had her running down the hall.

Jacks stood outside a bedroom door with his hands up, squaring off with Deuce—who wore nothing but a smirk—and a laughing Drew in an aqua and pink kimono.

"Left! I forgot to say the hall on the *left*." Jo skidded to a stop and grinned up at a very confused Jacks.

He brought her to his side and kissed the top of her head—something that always gave her a sweet ache in her chest.

"Buddy, do you mind putting on some clothes?" Jacks turned Jo's face into his chest.

Deuce backed into the room, and Drew stepped forward. "Wanna drink?" He didn't wait for a reply before heading down the hall to the bar.

Jo and Jacks followed in his wake and sat in the expansive living room where Deuce joined them, fully clothed.

A minute later, Drew appeared with a bottle and four glasses. "Nothing says welcome like a shot of tequila."

"I'll get the limes." Deuce set off in search of fruit.

Drew poured a healthy shot into each glass and handed them out. When Deuce returned with lime slices, the ritual began as they passed the salt around.

Drew picked up the bottle for another round and addressed Jacks. "So, I hear you weren't a fan of my boudoir shots."

Jacks kept his eyes on Drew as he threw the tequila back. "No, I wasn't." He placed the glass down but didn't avert his eyes.

"Well, the lighting was superb, and Jo had this angelic look on her face."

"Drew," Deuce warned.

"But I suppose it was wrong of me not to consult her before posting."

"You took pictures of her half-naked without her consent."

"Oh, honey, is that what's bothering you? That ship sailed years ago. I've seen her naked more times than her gynecologist. I think the first time was when we skinny-dipped in the Atlantic. Way before her body blossomed into the cream dream it is today."

Jacks pinched the bridge of his nose. "Jo…"

She squeezed his thigh. "Drew, stop provoking him, or I'll punch you myself."

"Jo's right." Deuce took his second shot, put the lime wedge into his mouth, and pulled it out, stripped of pulp. "We were wrong for doing it, and we're sorry. Isn't that right, Drew?"

Drew sat back, contemplating Jacks as he swirled the liquid around in his glass. "What makes you entitled to my apology?"

Jo thought she might have to physically restrain Jacks, but he relaxed next to her.

"I'm not. Never asked for one. Just don't like seeing her being used."

Drew pursed his lips and narrowed his eyes, signaling trouble, but Jo could do nothing as the two squared off. "What is it you *do*, lover boy? For a living, I mean."

Oh, boy.

Jacks stayed calm. "At the moment, just trying to save my family's farm."

"Oh, I think Jo already did that for you."

Her pulse quickened, but Jacks seemed unfazed by the statement.

"You're right, without Jo's talent, we might've lost the farm."

Drew smirked. "Well, to be fair, it wasn't just her talent—"

"That's enough," Jo snapped, cutting him off.

She watched as the pieces clicked into place for Jacks.

His jaw tightened and he nodded slowly. "You're the one who bought the farm from Tommy?"

She glared at Drew before answering. "*Technically—*"

"It's a yes or no question."

She released her breath. "The *non-profit* bought the lien, not the farm."

Jacks rubbed his eyes. "That's what you were talking about at the barbeque, and why Addy wanted you there; she asked for your help."

"Yes."

Jacks gave a curt nod. "We'll talk about this later."

She patted his thigh. "Let's go to bed."

Drew continued undeterred. "So, what's next? You need a little cash? Some start-up capital like your brother Leroy? Perhaps you'd like Jo to introduce you to the *right people*?"

Jo stood. "His name is Levi, and you know it. Why are you being such a dick?" She grabbed Jacks' arm. "Let's go."

He brushed the back of her bare leg. "It's fine. He's feeling me out, is all. Trying to make sure I'm with you for the right reasons."

Drew smiled and raised an eyebrow. "That's right, I am." He waved Jo down. "Relax, Jobo. He passed the test." He poured a fresh shot for Jacks, and the two clicked glasses. "Congratulations, Captain America, you're the first man who has."

Jo rolled over as Jacks got out of bed, her eyes roaming the work of art that was his naked backside. "What time is it?"

"Six."

She reached for him. "Come back to bed."

"I've got things to do before heading to the fairground." He leaned over and brushed her hair back. "They're doing an interview with Addy and me before the festival. It's sort of the wrap up for the show. After today, they'll only be back for follow up segments." He sat down, caressing her arm. "I've gotta make it look like we're a couple. You okay with that?"

"No." A possessive hand wrapped around his neck, bringing him closer. "Yes. As long as she knows you're mine."

He moved over her, caging her in with his arms. "*I know.*" He trailed kisses down her neck and shoulder. "You've got me in your pocket, Josie." He slid lower, exploring her breasts.

Jo ran her hand through his hair. "*Jacks,*" she pleaded.

"Don't worry, I'll take care of you." His mouth moved lower.

She yanked him up. "No, I need you inside me."

He smiled and positioned himself above her. "You're a bossy little thing."

She arched a brow and pushed him over, straddling his waist. "So I've been told." Reaching down, she grabbed his arms and raised them above his head. "Don't move." She sat back, her hands on his thighs, and rocked her hips against him.

He watched with heavy lids, his breath quickening. When she moaned and arched her back, he lowered his hands to her ass and tapped lightly. "Lift up, sugar."

Jo leaned forward, her hair falling in waves around them as he placed himself at her entrance and pushed inside. She straightened her legs and lay on top, wanting every inch of their bodies to touch, and caressed his cheek with her own. The words 'I love you' slipped out in a whisper so soft she wasn't sure she'd said them aloud.

The intense look he gave her left no doubt she had.

He grabbed the sides of her face, bringing their mouths together in a passionate kiss. Raising his knees, he captured her hips between his powerful thighs and lifted, pushing himself deeper inside her. One hand wrapped around her shoulders, yanking her down as the other held her tight against him. The sweat between their bodies eased the friction and heated their skin as they crashed together with an intensity that left them both speechless in the aftermath.

The sex was emotionally charged. Unexpected and powerful. And the first time, Jo realized, she'd truly made love to a man.

She fell to his side and nestled close. He brought her hand to his mouth and kissed every finger before holding it to his chest.

"I love you too, Josie."

3 8

Let the games begin, and may the odds be ever in your favor.
- *The Hunger Games*

The starter pistol went off, and groups of three-legged couples hobbled down the field to the finish line. Deuce had to practically carry Jo as they weren't in sync and their feet kept getting tripped up.

As tri-ped after tri-ped passed, she realized most of those in the race had done this a time or two. At least they outpaced the eighty-year-old Mayor and his wife who came in dead last. Jacks and Addy—despite running like a well-oiled machine—were third.

When Jo crossed the finish line, Jacks gave her a wink and a smile.

Dammit! I should be the one tied to his leg.

Deuce said something she didn't catch—being preoccupied by Addison's hand running down Jacks' back as he bent to untie them. *That bitch.* Knowing they weren't together didn't stop her reaction to the overly familiar gesture.

"Ow!"

Drew pinched her arm from behind. "Stop giving that girl the stink eye. Someone will notice you looking at her man instead of your own."

"Jacks *is* my man."

"Not today, honey."

Nowhere But Up

She closed her eyes and turned away from Addison's laughter.

"Jobo, you need to put a leash on that green-eyed monster."

Nothing could hold that emotional demon back, but she pressed her lips together and nodded.

"Now go watch *your* man throw a hatchet." Drew used his fingers to push her forward.

Unsurprisingly, Deuce knew how to throw an axe and won his individual challenge without breaking a sweat.

They needed to hurry to the horse field if they wanted to watch Jacks compete, but Deuce stopped every time someone asked for a photo or autograph.

"Just wave or look the other way or we're going to miss the barrel racing."

"Don't see the problem, Jo. Go without me." He lifted his chin and smiled at someone over her shoulder.

Deuce was right. They were supposed to be a couple, not Siamese twins. As she turned to leave, he pulled her into an embrace and kissed her soundly. He then wheeled her around and smacked her ass.

"You can thank me later," he said before strolling away.

A stunned and somewhat confused Jo caught sight of Jacks' intense stare, and knew why Deuce had done it. *The man had just earned himself a pie.*

All kinds of dirty thoughts went through her mind as she and Jacks walked toward each other.

Until Addison and a film crew approached from the side.

Jacks noticed them too and stopped—closing his eyes briefly. He put his hands on his hips and lowered his head, licking at his bottom lip. Jo knew that look; he did it when he needed to gain control of himself. When he looked back up, he only had eyes for Addison.

Jo's mood went down like a B-52 bomber. She passed the scene with barely a glance and headed toward the bleachers.

When Addison entered the field minutes later, she took her place near the fence where the cameras could capture her cheering on her high school sweetheart.

The first rider came out and made a figure eight around two barrels but knocked the third one down. The second was quick but shouldered a barrel. Jacks was next. With speed and grace, he clover-leafed around all three and sprinted to the finish, making it look easy. She stayed to watch the rest but knew he'd won before the judges called it. She lingered a moment too long, catching Addison congratulating Jacks with a kiss before skipping off into the arena—no doubt to do something horsey.

When Jo walked past, Jacks didn't even glance her way, which only intensified the sick feeling in her stomach. She shook her head hard. *It's not real.*

Since her chosen event had required her to submit her pie early, Jo wandered around the fairground until her next individual challenge: archery. She had good upper body strength but had never picked up a bow. *How hard could it be?*

She found the open field where they'd set up big round targets with colorful rings. A few people milled about, looking over the bows. As she approached the rack, someone brushed against her.

"Hey," Jacks whispered.

Jo noticed the film crew but no media. The majority followed Deuce. The rest stayed within designated areas, far from the field. "Nice win." Her voice sounded colder than she'd intended.

"You mad at me?"

She shook her head. "No, it's just...I don't enjoy seeing you with Addison. It brings out the worst in me."

"That why you kissed Deming?" he said, his voice playful.

She pursed her lips. "He kissed *me*, but I should've known it wouldn't make you jealous."

Jacks laughed, "Oh, I'm plenty jealous. As a matter of fact," he lowered his eyes and checked out her ass. "I'm thinking I might have to fight off these shorts later."

"No need. I'll gladly cede their control over my backside to you."

He stilled. "You're gonna have to stand in front of me now." He shifted to stand behind her and surveyed the archery paraphernalia. "Pretend I'm explaining the finer points of archery."

Jo picked a bow. "This one any good?"

"Not for you." He placed it back and grabbed another, handing it to her. "You ever barebow before?"

Jo gave him an incredulous look. "Sure, millions of times. I carry a quiver of arrows on my back and shoot pigeons off skyscrapers."

He shook his head in amusement. "And *yet*, you know what a quiver is."

"Drinking game." When he raised a brow, she explained. "*Princess Diaries*. We had to drink every time tea, princess, or Anne Hathaway's dead dad was mentioned in the movie. We were drunk twenty minutes in."

"But you remembered what they called a bag of arrows?"

"It's a funny word, and when you're drinking, it's hilarious. Especially when doing word association. Quiver, quip, quad, quid...*queef*." Jo wiggled her eyebrows.

Jacks burst into laughter. "Yeah, I can see how that last one would stick." He handed her a bow. "Come on, we have a few minutes. I'll show you what to do."

"What about the cameraman?" She looked over her shoulder.

"They can edit it out later."

They moved to the target area at the end, and he held out his bow for her inspection. "A traditional bow is simple. You've got two basic wood limbs with a grip, and a string with a riser. There's no sight for you to line up your target, so, *barebow*."

Jacks turned her at a ninety-degree angle. "Stand with your feet shoulder-width apart." He placed his hands on her hips and squeezed lightly before adjusting her. "Hips square to the target. When you pull back, you want to place your thumb joint right under your cheekbone, here." He swept his thumb lightly across her face. "Take your three middle fingers and put them on the riser. One goes on top and two below the arrow, then pull back."

He watched her follow his direction. "You've got a death grip on the bow. Unlock and rotate your elbow or you're gonna get a nasty string burn." He stood behind and mimicked her stance, leaning close to her ear. "There's a break after the second partner challenge. Meet me behind the row of horse trailers."

Jo nodded, dizzy with anticipation and the feel of his body touching hers.

Jacks stepped away and notched an arrow for her. "Now draw back again." His fingers stroked down her spine. "Use your back and shoulder muscles, not your arms. Feel how they flex together."

If he didn't stop touching her, she was going to flex something very inappropriate.

He must have sensed his own lack of control because he dropped his hands. "When you release, your hand should continue straight back for the follow through." He checked her stance again. "Now let it soar."

She released the arrow and watched it arc into the air. "I did it! I hit the target." She danced a little jig before jumping into his arms.

"You're a natural." He pressed his lips to her hair before putting her down.

She noticed people staring and backed away, smiling. "Sorry, I got excited."

"You never have to apologize for lovin' on me, Josie."

Squeeze.

When the time came, she stepped to the shooting line and let them fly. All her arrows hit the target.

Jacks had three bulls-eyes but so did two other competitors. Jo wanted to stay and watch the tiebreaker but knew if she did, she'd miss Deuce competing for his second win.

She stood behind the rope, unable to find Deuce among the participants in the log rolling event.

"There you are!" Drew grabbed her hand and pulled her through the crowd of onlookers, weaving in and out of narrow stalls, to stand in front of a series of long tables.

Jo tilted her head in confusion. "I thought his challenge involved rolling heavy logs down a grassy path to victory."

"His publicist changed it."

"So, this is on purpose?" She surveyed the line of pie plates filled with whipped cream. "What exactly *is* the purpose?"

"You have to find the cherries, eat them, and spit the seeds into individual cups."

She noticed the plastic cups staggered randomly in front of the plates. "Okay, but why is Deuce doing it?"

Drew looked like a mother dealing with a petulant child who asked too many questions. "He needs to appeal to a wider demographic. Show his humorous, lighter side."

"His what? *Oh.*" She nodded in understanding. "Attract people who might be less homopho—"

"Yes, now shut up."

They watched Deuce smile and take his seat good-naturedly among the rest of the...women and children and waited for the starting bell.

Jo had to give him credit. He was funny and self-deprecating. Behind the line, paparazzi and cell phones captured him trying to blow cream out of the plate, only to have it whip up into his face. He tried to mimic the other participants' techniques, failing miserably to the crowds' riotous laughter. In the end, he pulled out a single cherry by the stem, wiggled his eyebrows, and tossed it into his mouth, expertly spitting the seed into the farthest cup.

Cheers erupted as he stood and moved around the table, heading straight to Jo. She squealed when he grabbed her by the waist and brought her in for a kiss.

Jo's eyes widened in shock as he deposited something between her lips. He put an arm around her shoulders as she retrieved the cherry stem tied in a knot.

When the crowd chanted, "Deuce! Deuce! Deuce!" she laughed along with them and wiped the cream from her face.

The judges disqualified him for using his hands, but he had won in every way that counted.

Ah, the power of PR.

"Are we going for the sympathy vote next?" Jo asked as they suited up for laser tag.

Deuce pulled on the tactical vest covered in sensors. "I can do funny, but I draw the line at being a pussy." He adjusted her vest, tightened it around her waist and checked the shoulder harnesses.

"Seems like you've done this before."

He smized. "Yeah, a time or two." He held out his hand. "Let me see your gun."

She handed it to him, and he checked it before handing it back. "I want you on defense. Stay hidden until I give you this signal." He made a hand gesture. "Then break into the open."

"You're using me as bait?"

"I'll take them out before they get to you. Find the nearest cover and keep down. If you get a clear shot, take it, but leave their flag unless it's an easy grab."

"Wow, you take this seriously, don't you?"

"I don't tap dance for a living."

"Yeah, but..." *You're an actor*, her facial expression said.

"I didn't always act, Jo."

"So, you used to kick real butt?"

His lip twitched. "Why? Someone need an ass whooping?"

"No, no. Just, *good* to know."

"I think Jackson can handle anything that comes your way." He gave her a serious look. "Unless he's the one that needs a beat down."

The game lasted almost forty-five minutes, with over fifty percent tagged within the first ten. Deuce didn't signal for her until the last minute when the playing field had dwindled to a few.

She ran out from behind a large boulder into a clearing with her eyes on a group of bushes in the distance. About halfway there, she sensed movement among the trees. She didn't stop running until someone materialized in front of her. Jo grinned at the smiling face. If she had to go down...

A beam of light came from behind and shot Jacks in the chest.

Deuce and Jo entered the makeshift interview area and stood off to the side, waiting to be called over to where Drew was interviewing Jacks and Addison for *The Buzz*.

Deuce leaned over and whispered in her ear. "I would've shot you."

Jo nodded. "No doubt."

"...And joining us now are the winners of the laser tag challenge, megastar Deuce Deming and his darling, Josette Singer!"

Pasting on smiles, they entered the circle of director chairs where Drew held court. Once seated, the host got down to business.

He turned to Deuce first. "As an action hero, do you think you had an unfair advantage in this challenge?"

"I've had training, but I'm no soldier, not like Jackson here. He's the real deal."

Drew turned to Jacks. "It looked like you had a clear shot at Deuce's leading lady. What stopped you from taking her out and winning the game?"

Jacks shrugged. "I don't shoot women."

Drew vamped. "And here I thought you were a *lady killer*." The line sank like a pair of concrete shoes.

Trying to recover, Drew turned once again to Deuce. "How about you? Any pangs of conscience when you shot sweet Addison?"

Deuce scratched his chin. "Nah, it's easy for me to shoot someone when I know they're gonna get up and walk away."

Drew nodded and pursed his lips. "That certainly puts a unique spin on it." He turned wide eyes to Jo, trying to salvage the interview. "Jo, both you and Addison lost your first individual challenges, but now go head-to-head in the pie-making contest. As your BFFL, I can attest to your culinary skills, but how do you think you'll stack up against the hometown girl?"

Biffle?

She arched a brow. "I think I've got a shot—I mean a chance," she corrected.

"Just as long as everyone walks away, honey." Drew laughed and turned to the camera. "Stay tuned for more live updates when our HomeTown hero cuts a rug in tonight's..." He glimpsed at his cue cards, "clogging competition."

Cut!

Drew fanned the cards and hopped down. "Well, that went over like a fart in church."

Jo and Jacks exchanged glances and headed off in different directions, only to meet minutes later behind the horse trailers.

"Thanks for not killing me," she said, hugging him.

"It was enough to know that I could've," he said, playfully tugging on her ponytail.

"That kinda takes the romance out of the gesture."

He kissed the top of her head. "Wanna sneak off to my place? We've got a couple hours before the ceremony."

Jo glanced at her watch and groaned. She was already late. "I can't, I have to help Levi set up for tonight." She gave him a quick kiss. "Wait until you see what the set designers came up with for the distillery." She lifted her fists to the sides of her head and made an explosion with her hands. "It'll blow your mind." She turned to leave, looking over her shoulder with a seductive smile. "And so will my costume."

"Costume?"

She walked away, laughing at the look on his face.

39

Losing isn't always the end,
sometimes it becomes the beginning.
- Joseph Duffy

After helping Levi stock the makeshift saloon at the fairgrounds, Jo hurried back to the inn to shower and change for her role as Winter Queen. She would meet Jacks at the barn and he'd walk her and Myrtle into the ceremonial circle where she'd crown the young May Queen.

Jo ran into Kara on her way out. "Hey, didn't see you today. Can't win the quilt if you don't play the games."

Kara seemed more anxious than usual. "Show's wrapping up, Jo. Lots to do. Lots to do."

Jo raised her brow, wondering if this was what Kara had warned her about back at Harmony House. "You okay?"

"Yeah, yeah." One hand rubbed at a twitching eye, the other tapped on a thigh.

Jo wasn't buying it. "How about you come with me to the fairgrounds? You can watch me fall off a horse, clog my way to defeat, and then we can get drunk as my tits fall out of a saloon girl costume. What do you say?"

Kara stopped tapping. "You have another one of those costumes?"

JT came from around the horse trailer and ran smack into Addy—his momentum sending her careening backward before falling to the ground.

He knelt beside her. "Damn, Ad. You're as light as a feather. I nearly sent you into the air." He lost his smile when he noticed her tears. "Addy? You hurt?" He searched her body for signs of trauma. Besides a skinned elbow and palm, she appeared to be fine. But she kept crying. He scooped her into his arms, rubbing her back. "What's going on? Something happen?"

She pulled away and took a couple of deep breaths. Raising her chin, she looked him in the eye. "I'm pregnant."

The revelation sucker-punched him in the chest. "What? How?" *This had to be a joke. Please, God, let it be a joke.*

Addy narrowed her eyes. "The old-fashioned way, Jackson."

She never called him that unless she was angry.

He shook his head in confusion and denial. "No, you can't be. We used protection."

"You don't believe me?"

He latched on to any small scrap of hope. "Maybe the test was wrong. When did you take it?"

Addy stood and brushed herself off. "Just now. I went to the drugstore this morning. I was going to wait until tomorrow, or at least until after the festival. But it was right there in my car, and I had to know."

"You took it here? In the bathrooms?"

She nodded.

"Christ, Addy." He took hold of her arm and pulled her toward the parking lot.

"Where are we going?"

"To get another test, and do it in private."

Jo hurried through the crowd amid curious stares, wearing a flowing dress with a wreath of dead branches atop her long, wild curls. She spotted Levi as he popped up from behind the wooden bar.

"Thank God," she wheezed at the sight of him.

He smiled. "What's up, gorgeous?"

"I need you to walk Myrtle and me into the ceremony."

"Where's JT?"

"I don't know! I can't find him anywhere, and he's not answering his phone." Jo didn't have time to play guessing games—she had a horse to fall off of and evil to ingest.

"I'd like to help you out, but I can't leave the booth unattended."

As if on cue, Kara walked in dressed as a saloon girl. "Got you covered."

Levi's eyes wandered the length of her. "Kara?"

"No, the Ghost of Christmas Past."

"Ah, there you are. You worried me for a minute." He chuckled and came from behind the counter, slowing as he passed. "You're really rockin' that dress." He gave her a slow, sexy smile before moving on.

Jo dragged him out—but not before noticing Kara's broad smile.

There was no mistaking the results. Addy was going to have a baby.

JT sat on the couch in shock and disbelief. "Addy, I don't mean to offend you, but are you sure it's mine?" He expected her to be angry, to deny it. Instead, she glanced away.

"Addy? Is there a chance I'm not the father?"

She nodded but kept her eyes averted. "The last time I saw Tommy, right after we got together." Her red-rimmed eyes met his. "We were just supposed to talk. It could've happened then."

"Talk about what? And how...*Why*?" JT's mind swam with possibilities, but nothing made sense, unless..."Did he *force you*?"

She sat down and placed a hand on his clenched fist. "No. I let it happen, JT. I thought..." She swiped at her eyes and sat back. "Well, it doesn't much matter now, does it?"

Understanding dawned on him, and he turned to face her. "Oh, Addy. You did it for me—so he wouldn't take the farm."

He held her as sobs wracked her body.

Jo put a booted foot into Levi's interlocking fingers and pushed off, hauling herself onto Myrtle's back. She positioned her legs the way Jacks taught her and fixed her skirt.

"Normally I wouldn't get this close to the Winter Queen, but for you..." Levi said with a wink.

"Careful, or I'll put a hex on you," she joked before scanning the area. "I wonder where Jacks is?"

"I'm happy to take his place anytime you need help," he said, grinning up at her.

"Your talents are wasted on me, but I know someone who'd appreciate them. I saw how you looked at Kara earlier," she said, wagging a finger at him.

He laughed. "Yeah, well, it's the first time I've seen her wear something sexy. She's always hiding behind baggy clothes like she's ashamed of her body. And from what I could see, there ain't nothing wrong and a whole lotta right there."

Jo agreed and made a mental note to find out why. "It's obvious she wants you to see her that way, just...don't treat her like all the rest, okay?"

Levi lost his smile as he stroked Myrtle's neck. "I don't treat women badly, Jo. I've never had one go away unsatisfied or angry. They all know what they're signing up for."

"Pfft. They see you as a challenge—the ultimate *get*. I'm sure most hope to win your heart."

He shrugged, scratching behind the horse's ear. "Maybe so, but I've never lied to one."

Jo couldn't resist ruffling his dark hair. "Someday, Levi, you're going to give that heart of yours away."

Instead of bringing back his playful side, the comment had erased all signs of humor. He placed his hand on top of hers where it rested on the pummel. "Nothing's free, Jo. There's always a price to—"

He didn't get to finish the sentence before Jacks came out of nowhere and hauled him back.

JT was late getting to the fairgrounds.

He wanted to find Jo and have her take away the heaviness in his soul like she'd done so many times before. But the grip on his gut told him he was a fool. Once Jo found out about Addy and the baby, everything would change.

When he entered the barn, the scene before him made him see red. Levi was pressed up against Jo's leg as she gazed down, her hand in his hair. The intimate moment was the last thing he expected to see and the worst thing for his state of mind.

He wanted to explode like a spewing volcano and destroy everything in his path. Instead, he held his anger in check—barely. From Jo's reaction, he didn't do a good job, but she had no idea of what he held back, the rage he wanted to unleash.

"Step over the line again, Levi, and I'll lay you flat," he said, his lips curled in anger.

"He was helping me!" Jo cried out.

"To do what? Lift your skirt?" JT knew he'd gone too far but couldn't stop.

Jo's jaw dropped, and Myrtle became increasingly agitated. "What the hell's wrong with you?"

Levi came forward. "Fucking apologize to her."

Jacks looked from Levi to Jo, then back to his brother, his rage still in high gear. "You telling me you don't want her?"

"Hell, no. I'm saying you're being a *dick*."

Nothing I don't already know. He got in Levi's face. "Walk away now or crawl out. Your choice."

Levi stood his ground. "I'm not leaving until you calm the fuck down."

"You think I'd hurt her? I *love* her!" He was shouting now, and the sound of his own voice made him throw his hands in the air and take a step back. He needed to de-escalate the situation before he pounded Levi into the ground.

Jo's voice brought him back. "I'm fine, Levi. Please go."

Levi's jaw ticked, and he pinned JT with a cold stare. "You better get your shit together, brother." He gave Jo one final glance before walking out.

JT paced back and forth as he battled for control.

"Jacks, what happened after I left?"

He wiped sweat from his brow as the pain in his chest allowed for only shallow breaths.

"Jacks? Are you all right?"

No, Jo. I'm not. He strode over and grabbed Myrtle's reins. "We'll talk later," he said in a raspy whisper.

JT didn't know how he made it through the ceremony. The cameras, the people, the noise—it was all too much. He tried to focus on his breathing, but it was a lost cause. His fear and anger needed an outlet—a place to go—before he went crazy.

When they got to the bonfire, he pulled Jo off the horse, took the reins, and walked away without looking back.

The thing Jo had worried about most ended up being the last thing on her mind. Twenty minutes went by in a blur, and when it came time to dismount, Jacks didn't slide her body down his or whisper words of love. He didn't even glance her way before leaving with Myrtle.

She drifted through the rest of the ceremony in a trance, crowning the May Queen and taking the corn doll to start the bonfire. As everyone gathered around to celebrate, she made her way back to the distillery booth—a protective barrier around her heart.

"He just left you there?" Kara asked, pouring Jo another shot.

"Disappeared after I dismounted."

"Exactly what did he walk in on?" She glanced down the bar to make sure Levi wasn't within earshot.

Jo rolled her eyes. "Nothing."

Kara held up her hands. "I'm not judging, just trying to make sense of it."

"We were just talking."

She raised a questioning brow. "Just seems out of character for Jackson to go off half-cocked without a reason."

"Yeah, well, he did." Jo threw back the bourbon.

Kara eyeballed Jo's empty glass. "Better go easy on those shots. You've got the dance off coming up."

"Fuck it. I'm not doing it. I don't know why I'm doing any of this." She waved one arm around.

"Any of what?" Drew asked as he walked in, taking in the décor. "Ooh, I love a themed bar." He nodded his approval. "Wild West meets Cabaret." He looked over at Jo. "Why you dressed like Jessica Christ?"

She pulled the ring of thorns off her head. "Where's Deuce?"

"Fans. Gotta feed the need, honey." He motioned to the bottle of bourbon. "Got anything less wild? Say, a nice pinot grigio?"

Kara slapped down a napkin. "This isn't an actual bar. We're selling Fowler's Pond bourbon, vodka, and gin."

"Oh, well, then a G&T, please." He gave Kara the once over. "That color's good on you."

"Thanks." She poured his drink. "Got an opinion on my hair?"

He rested his chin on his palm. "Natural?"

"Yeah."

He waved her over, turned her head from side to side, then stepped back. "Turn around." When she finished, he shooed her back behind the bar. "You've got an edge to you. I'd go shorter, maybe an asymmetrical stacked bob in a golden toffee, with high and lowlights." He took a sip of his drink. "Go to Rolo in West Hollywood. Tell him I sent you."

The right side of Kara's mouth kicked up. "I appreciate it. Thanks."

"Have him do your eyebrows and mustache while he's at it."

"Drew!" Jo admonished. "She's a natural beauty." She turned to Kara. "Don't change for anyone."

Kara put her fingers to her upper lip. "No, he might be right."

Jo narrowed her eyes at Drew before grabbing her costume from behind the bar. As much as she wanted to go back to the inn and weep into her pillow, she had a business to market. "I'm going to change," she said and went in search of a restroom.

Since Kara had insisted on the ruby red dress, Jo was left with the royal blue. The costume consisted of a corset and a skirt which gathered in front with a tuft of tulle, leaving a whole lot of leg showing underneath. Fishnet stockings with garter belts and a feather hairpiece finished the ensemble.

As she stood at the mirror shoving her breasts into the bustier, the door swung open and Addison appeared, visibly upset.

"Addison? Are you okay?" Jo turned from her reflection and winced at the daggers shooting from the other woman's eyes. "What did *I* do?"

"Isn't Deuce enough? Or Levi? You could have your pick of men. Why JT?"

Gobsmacked, Jo stood like a saloon-girl-gone-wrong, with one stocking around her ankle and half her cleavage unstuffed.

Addison obviously agreed as she looked Jo up and down. "I don't understand what he sees in you."

Jo cracked her neck, releasing old Jo and sending Jo 2.0 to bed early. "It must be my golden pussy. Gets them every time."

Addison continued, undeterred. "He thinks he's in love with you. Even after I—" She stopped mid-sentence, bringing her lips into a tight line.

Realization dawned. "It was you, wasn't it? You told Jacks about the pictures."

"I told him you'd leave him, but he won't listen." She moved closer, and despite her bravado, Jo took a step back.

"I've loved JT my whole life; waited years to be with him. Sacrificed *everything*! Then you waltzed in, and just like that," she said, snapping her fingers, "he's yours."

New and improved Jo was sympathetic, but Philly Jo wanted to squash her like a bug. She needed to find the sweet spot between compassion and annihilation.

"Can't help who you love." *Score one for the new me.*

"You'll get tired of playing the country girl. Once the novelty wears off and he no longer holds your interest, you'll leave him. So why be cruel? Go now before you do more damage."

Her voice became a soft plea. "Jo, you don't belong here. You must know that. Think of what's best for JT."

Jo scoffed, and bent to attach the hanging fishnet to her garter belt. "And that would be you? Even if I left, what makes you think he'd take you back?"

Addison raised her quivering chin. "I'm pregnant."

Jo clutched the sink with one hand and pulled herself up. "Of course you are." Her voice remained steady, despite the cannonball in her belly.

This. The familiarity of it. Hello, old friend. Waited for the peak of ripeness before plucking my heart out, I see.

"You don't believe me? I took a test this afternoon in front of JT."

Jo's limbs felt heavy as the energy drained from her body, but she still had some fight left. "The fact you're pregnant doesn't surprise me. But needing to prove it to Jacks? Yeah, that makes me wonder who the father is."

Addison crossed her arms. "If the baby's his, you'll never get him to leave Kentucky."

The statement confirmed Jo's suspicion, but it also fed her deepest fear. *He won't leave, and I can't stay.*

As she pushed past Addison and walked into the night, Jo felt a strange sense of relief now that the who-what-where and whys were answered.

It had never been a matter of *if,* only *when* things would fall apart.

On her way back to the pop-up distillery, Jo passed the pie table and noticed they'd finally been judged. She took a closer look.

She'd lost.

To Addison.

It was almost more than she could bear.

There were many things Jo did well, but few she excelled in. Making pies and dancing were in this category, and she'd be damned if she lost both to Addison.

"Focus, Deuce!" Jo stood beside him and went through the steps again. "We only have to clog for the first part of the song, then we can free-form."

Thankfully, Jacks had taught her some steps when they played their favorite songs for each other. They'd danced for hours to all kinds of music—until Jo played 'Pony' by Ginuwine, and Jacks showed her some of his own *Magic Mike* moves.

She shook off the memory and cued up a hip-hop song that worked well for both styles. She didn't fool herself into thinking they could win without Deuce's celebrity. It was the only thing that gave them any chance at all.

"Jo, we got this." Deuce gave her a side-eye. "Is it the quilt? Is that what this is about?"

"No, it's not about the quilt."

"Because I want that quilt."

"If we win, it's yours. Now, let's go over the steps one more time."

Jo should never have doubted Deuce's ability to win over a crowd. And for a big man, he was light on his feet. He threw in a couple of moves that were both comical and technically awesome. When he did his final pop, lock, and drop, the crowd went wild. The man was pure magic.

The victory turned bittersweet when Jo realized Jacks and Addison had dropped out of the competition. Still, Deuce gave a brilliant yet humble speech, received the prized quilt, and said it would hold a place of honor in his home. After one last interview, they headed toward the exit.

Jo took a last-minute detour to the judges' table and grabbed her pie. She caught up with Deuce and wrapped an arm around his waist. "You're gonna love my pie."

"Not saving it for Jackson?"

Jo looked down at the pie in her hand. "No, I think he prefers a more traditional one."

40

Cryin' won't help you, prayin' won't do you no good.
When the levee breaks, mama, you got to move.
- Led Zeppelin

After years of therapy, Jo knew the stages of grief. She'd sailed past denial, slept through isolation, and woke up in anger. She needed to talk to Jacks before it wore off and she started the next phase—bargaining.

A large boulder settled in her stomach as she reached for her phone. Three missed calls, no texts. The last around 3 AM. Out of childishness, or because she wasn't strong enough to deal with the fallout, she had silenced it.

When she hit the callback button, it went straight to voicemail, so she threw on some clothes, grabbed her keys, and headed out.

Ten minutes later she pulled up behind the old homestead, where Jacks' bike lay on the ground. Her heart skipped a beat when she noted the open back door.

She raced up the steps and found him on the kitchen floor in a bloody heap.

"Jacks!" Jo rolled him over and felt for a pulse. It beat strongly against her fingertips.

Thank you, sweet baby Jesus.

She leaned down and kissed his swollen lips before her hands and eyes assessed the damage to the rest of his body. He had multiple cuts and bruises on his face and head, and when she lifted his shirt, found multiple contusions.

She grabbed her phone to call 911.

A hand shot out and clenched her wrist. "Don't."

She tried to brush back a piece of hair that had gotten stuck in dried blood.

Why didn't I answer his calls?

Pulling in a ragged breath, she stood and went to the sink to soak a dish towel in water. As she cleaned the gash on his forehead, the one eye not swollen shut fixed on her. She placed a comforting hand to his cheek. "Oh, Jacks."

"You should see the other guys," he joked.

Jo's hollow laugh caught in her throat. "I bet." She bit her lip to stop from crying. "Listen, Jacks. I'm going to run over to the big house. I'll be right back." She tried to get up.

"No." His voice was strong and brooked no argument.

"You need help. What if there's internal bleeding?"

Jacks' head listed to the side. "Call Powell."

"Samantha? You need a doctor."

He squeezed her wrist. "No doctors."

"Dammit, Jacks, don't put me in this position!" Her hand shook as she swiped through her contacts. Finding Sam's number, she hit send. *Please answer, please answer, please answer.*

"Hello?"

She pushed the speaker button. "Sam, it's Jo. Jacks was in a fight—a really bad one. He doesn't want to go to the hospital. Please, tell him to go."

"Okay, stay calm. I'll walk you through what to check."

"Wait, what? He could be dying!"

"Jo, this isn't his first rodeo. If he thinks he's fine, then he probably is."

"You're both insane."

"Now, listen to me. Is he conscious?"

Jack's head fell to the side. "He just passed out again."

"Any signs of vomit or diarrhea?"

Jo looked around. "No, not that I can see."

"That's good. Now we're going to check his vitals and look for signs of trauma."

Over the next ten minutes, Sam asked questions and Jo performed rudimentary tests.

"Okay, Jo. It's time to wake him up. We need to see if there's any brain injury."

Jo tapped lightly on his cheek. "Jacks? Can you hear me? You need to wake up."

"Check his pupils. Are they dilated?"

Jo tried to be as gentle as possible. "No, they seem normal."

"Taylor!" Sam bellowed.

Jacks opened his one good eye.

"Rank and serial number," she demanded.

Jacks rattled off the information.

"Stand him up."

Jo looked down at his massive body. "He's enormous!"

"Get ahold from behind and lift him into a seated position first."

Jo hooked her arms under his. "Jacks, you have to help me." He complied, and Jo leaned him against the island. She moved to the front and held out her hands. One corner of his mouth twitched up as he grabbed hold. Jo hauled him up, the momentum throwing her off balance. She would have fallen backward had he not caught her. He brought her to his side and placed a kiss on top of her head.

"Any ringing in your ears, dizziness, or blurred vision?" Sam asked.

Jacks swayed to one side. "Nope."

Jo pulled him back by the shirt. "He's dizzy, Sam."

"He's drunk. Give him some liquids and put him to bed. He'll be fine."

Jo's eyes widened. "That's it? Are you sure?"

"If anything changes, call me."

Jo kept vigil until early evening when Jacks awoke. She gave him some pain meds and a bottle of Gatorade, then went into the kitchen to whip up some dinner.

Some time later, she heard him enter the kitchen and take a seat at the island.

"Thank you," he said in a gravelly voice.

She picked up her glass of wine and turned. He still wore the clothes from the day before and looked both dreadful and heartbreakingly beautiful. "Welcome."

They stayed silent for a while. Neither wanting to shatter the delicate truce—that moment caught between the past and the future, where they could pretend nothing had changed.

She pulled in a shaky breath. "You really scared me, Jacks."

"I'm sorry. Sorry about last night. About this morning. Hell, I'm sorry about so many things." He rubbed his jaw and winced. "Jo, I've gotta tell you something—"

"I already know. Addison told me at the fairgrounds. I guess she couldn't wait to share the good news." The words fell like acid from her tongue.

He exhaled heavily. "You and me...we weren't together then." His head shook slightly. "I'm not even sure how it happened. We only made love a couple of times, and we used protection."

"Made love?" The words stabbed at her heart, unleashing anger and jealousy, which seeped from every pore. "I can't believe you just said that."

The thin glass shattered in her hand as she tightened her grip. "Mother fucker!" Mesmerized, Jo watched the river of blood cascade to the floor and felt the tension leave her body.

Jacks appeared out of nowhere and pulled her toward the sink. He picked shards of glass out of her palm and placed her hand under the faucet.

She watched in fascination, feeling no pain at all. She cocked her head in his direction. "Is that why you did it? Why you got the shit kicked out of you? To *stop* the pain?"

His eyes met hers briefly before grabbing some paper towels. "I'll be right back. I need to get something to wrap your hand."

Jo looked over at the empty bottle and spilled wine. The ruby color so like the blood that continued to pour out of her flesh.

I think I might be drunk.

Jacks came back, limping slightly, and bandaged her wounds. "The answer's yes. It's why I got my clock cleaned."

Jo couldn't explain the feeling that came over her. Dr. Fielding might have called it empathy, but it was more than just understanding how Jacks felt. She connected with him on a level so deep and profound it spoke to her soul.

She slipped her free arm around his waist, and he relaxed against her. When he began to wobble, she guided him to a stool. "You need something to eat. I made a casserole with what I could find in the kitchen—so don't judge."

He gave her a crooked smile and rested his forearms on the counter. "I'd eat roadkill if you put it in front of me."

"Good to know your standards are low." She took the dish out of the oven and placed a large portion on his plate. She served herself a smaller amount and sat down next to him.

"Jo—"

"Don't." She squeezed his hand. "I need a little more time." *To sober up, to get my head around you being a baby daddy, to pretend this won't change things.*

Jacks finished the entire dish, including what Jo left on her plate, and drank another Gatorade. "Can you help me upstairs? I won't make it on my own."

"Sure." Jo cleaned up the dishes and grabbed a couple of water bottles, handing him one. "Hydration is key."

When they got to the top, Jacks halted. "I need to use the bathroom, and I'd love a hot shower."

"Oh, of course. Here." She opened the door and helped him in. "If you need anything—"

"Stay with me."

She bit her top lip. *Bad idea, Jo.* "Okay."

She turned on the water as he started to undress. She peered over her shoulder. "Do you need me to—" The sight of his erection stopped her flat.

"Sorry, natural reaction when I'm around you." He grinned, and the cut on his lip began to bleed.

Jo grabbed a towel and put it under the running water. She felt the press of his naked body against her back—his voice rough against her ear. "Leave it. It'll just reopen."

Jo dropped the towel, but Jacks didn't back up. Instead, he ran his hands down the sides of her cotton dress and raised the hem above her breasts.

He twisted a finger around her thong and yanked, the thin lace giving way easily. One hand went between her legs, and the other kneaded her breasts as he kissed her neck.

"Jacks, I—"

"Don't tell me to stop, Josie, because I don't think I can."

"I won't," she whispered, turning her mouth to his. She tasted blood and sweat, and nothing had ever tasted sweeter.

He wheeled her around as he whipped off her dress, her bra falling to the floor as he backed her into the shower.

The man was power and strength as he pinned her against the tile wall. And he was full of need. There were no 'sugars' or sweet words. Nothing but sounds of passion mixed with pain.

They needed this communion of the flesh. It told a story of love and lust, of need and obsession.

What it didn't convey was a happily ever after.

JT woke before dawn. His eyes adjusted to the small amount of light filtering through the bedroom window as he shifted to his side. She'd stayed. He gathered air deep into his lungs, feeling the sting from his bruised ribs—a small distraction from the pain in his heart.

By this time tomorrow, she'd be gone.

He drank her in, trying to commit her to memory. She lay on her back, one arm above her head, the other resting across her bare midriff. Mahogany curls spread over the pillow, her breasts, and down her body. He picked one up and wrapped it around his finger, toying with the idea of cutting off a small piece. A souvenir of their time together.

She moaned and rolled away from him. Without thinking, he closed the gap and pulled her in tight. "I love you, Josie. So damn much."

The next time JT opened his eyes, the sun was high in the sky and Jo was gone. He sat up, his eyes darting around the room. When he saw her clothes lying in a pile on the floor, he fell back, releasing the breath he'd been holding.

How am I going to let her go?

JT didn't kid himself into thinking she'd take what he could offer. Not now, when he knew he'd never leave this town, or desert Addy. He'd claim the child as his own, regardless of its paternity. He couldn't live with himself if he didn't.

"Good morning." Jo appeared in the doorway wearing one of his T-shirts and carrying two cups of coffee. The bandage on her hand showing signs of fresh blood.

"Thanks." He took a sip from the mug, his eyes on the wound. "We need to change your dressing." He swung his legs off the bed and started to rise.

Jo held up a hand. "Don't, it's fine. Really. I'll have it looked at when I get back to town." She placed her cup on the nightstand and stood in front of him.

He stayed seated, placing his coffee next to hers. She ran a hand through his hair, and he leaned into her touch.

"Jacks, when Addison confronted me at the festival, she said something. Something that made me think there's a chance you're not the father of her baby."

He sighed and pulled back. "It's more complicated than that."

"So, she admitted there was someone else? That she cheated on you?"

"Yes, and no."

Her eyes brightened. "She'll have to take a paternity test. I did some research this morning, and you can get one after nine weeks. Considering what you told me last night, the odds are slim your DNA will match."

The hope in her voice almost broke him. "Jo, it won't matter."

"Of course it will." She bent down and gave him a quick kiss. "We've been together three weeks, which means in six we'll know for certain. But we need to start thinking about what comes next—the actual mechanics of being together after the show wraps. We need a plan..."

JT knew he should stop her, but he couldn't bring himself to do it.

"...And I think I've come up with the perfect solution. The nonprofit I started to help small farms." She crouched down in front of him and put her hands on his knees. "I want us to run it together. We'd make such a great team. Think about it, we could help families not only survive, but thrive. Of course, we'd be based out of Philly, but we'd come back here all the time. I already have a list of farms in Kentucky and—"

"Jo, stop. You need to listen to me." He couldn't let her go on.

She blinked up at him. "I'm sorry. I just..." The color drained from her face. "Why won't it matter?"

Steeling himself, he closed his eyes and took a deep breath. "I'm going to take responsibility for Addy's baby."

She stood, devastation written on her face. One of her hands went to her mouth, and she shook her head. "Oh, Jacks, no. Please. Don't do this. Don't choose her over me."

JT rubbed at the tightness in his chest. "This isn't about Addy, Jo. It's about the baby, about doing the right thing."

"By claiming a child that isn't yours? What about the father? Doesn't he get a say?"

"Tommy will never get his hands on that child."

"Tommy?" Her incredulous laughter sliced through the room. "She fucked her ex, and you're defending her?" She backed away, her eyes wide.

JT moved toward her. "You don't understand."

"Then make me understand! Did he rape her?"

He shook his head. "No."

"Then she should've kept her legs shut."

The tight control over his emotions snapped. "She did it for me. *All of it!*" He raked his hands through his hair. "Addy had no intention of going back to Tommy. She did it to save Fowler's Pond. And having sex with him? That was to buy us more time. She sacrificed herself for me and my family, and I won't repay her kindness and loyalty by deserting her."

"God, you're such a fucking martyr," she spat out. "Addison chose to do those things— you didn't ask her to. She's playing on your guilt, your *goodness!*"

Jo spun around and took a few steps before pivoting back. "And what makes you think Tommy won't be a good father?"

JT knew he had to make her understand. "His whole family is poison. *He's* poison. Not a good one in the bunch. Tommy will twist that child, take their innocence, and make them into another egocentric, selfish, morally bankrupt Beuchard. They don't care about anyone or anything but themselves."

Her mouth dropped open. "You just described me, Jacks." She thumped on her chest, her voice laced with anger and pain. "I'm that person! I've tried to be better, but a part of me will always be, well...me...*that*."

"You're nothing like Tommy. *Nothing.*"

She huffed out a bitter laugh. "Oh, but I am. Everything you despise is standing right in front of you. You're just too blind to see it." She yanked off his shirt and threw it to the floor, snatching up her wrinkled dress. "I know my limitations, Jacks, and I'm not willing to bend myself into a pretzel to be who you want me to be—I'm not Addison."

"I don't want you to change. I love you exactly the way you are." Out of desperation, he reached for her, trying to physically stop her from emotionally slipping away. "Please, Josie. You are everything to me. I want a life with you; we can make this work. Just give it a chance."

She shook her head and unlocked his hold on her. "You ask too much. You say I'm everything, but you offer nothing."

Her words cut him deep. "I'm offering my love, my home, my life. I wouldn't call that nothing."

Her arm sliced the air in front of him. "On your terms! There's no compromise, no discussion."

"We're discussing it now, but if you're asking me to abandon Addy and her child, I won't do that. Anything else you ask—"

"I'm asking you not to sacrifice our future for hers."

"I don't see them as mutually exclusive."

Jo bent down to pick up her sandals, her hair falling around her face. "No, I don't suppose you would."

He knew the minute the fight left her, she'd given up on them. He watched her gather her things and head to the door, feeling powerless to stop her. "Jo," he called out. She halted with one hand on the knob. "I'm sorry," he finally said.

She closed her eyes briefly and nodded, her grip on the handle tightening. "Me too, Jacks."

Without looking back, she opened the door and walked out of his life.

41

Don't be discouraged.
It's often the last key in the bunch that opens the lock.
- Unknown

The axe split the wood in half, embedding its blade into the stump. JT yanked it free and leaned down to gather the wood, tossing the pieces onto a large pile.

"You building a bonfire, or preparing for a long winter?"

He turned at the sound of his sister's voice. "Hey, Cricket." He put another piece on the chopping block and cleaved it in two.

Undeterred, Lou Lou walked in front of him and put her hands on her hips. "Where've you been?"

JT rested the head of the axe on the stump. "I've been right here."

"I know. You haven't left this house in over a week."

He grabbed the handle, and with a decisive WHACK, drove its bit into the marred stump. Without a word, he walked past her and toward the house.

"Where're you going?"

"To get us some tea."

Lou Lou followed him up the back porch steps and sat in one of the old rockers.

A minute later, JT returned and handed her a glass. He leaned against the rail and faced her. "Don't you have work to do?"

"If you bothered to answer your phone, you'd know Vaughn and the rest of the crew left days ago. They flew out to Ohio for another segment and won't be back for another month or so."

"Yeah, I know. I *can* read." He drank deep, the cold liquid soothing his parched throat. "Wish they weren't coming back at all, to be honest." He cocked his head. "Didn't Vaughn ask you to go with him?"

"Yup. But I've got my goats, and the job at the veterinary hospital starts in a couple weeks."

JT gave her a wry smile. "I'm sure he was heartbroken."

"Devastated." She grinned and with a shrug, said, "I'm happy here, JT. I don't want a life somewhere else." She opened her mouth, then pulled her lips in, rubbing them together thoughtfully. "But I think you do."

And there it was. The real reason Lou came sniffing around. He stayed silent, sipping his sweet tea.

His sister continued, "You don't have to stay here for us. Mom and Dad aren't worried about losing the farm anymore. The new lender gave them a six-month grace period, and with the distillery and goats, we'll do just fine."

"It was Josie." Just saying her name hurt.

"Pardon?"

"The lender is Jo. She started a nonprofit and bought the loan."

Lou stopped rocking, her eyes wide. "Shut the front door! Do Mom and Dad know?"

"No. She wanted to keep it a secret."

"Then why're you telling me?"

He shrugged. "Thought someone ought to know, I guess."

She sat back with a contemplative stare. After a tick, she said, "Do you remember the summer you worked at that cattle ranch in Wyoming?"

"Of course, but I'm surprised you do—you couldn't have been more than five."

"It was the first time you'd ever left me." A sad smile ghosted her lips. "Anyhow, you came back wanting to join the rodeo as a steer wrangler. Spent your whole summer's wages—and then some—on Clive."

"Still the quickest, smartest horse I've ever owned."

"Not in the beginning. You couldn't get him to work for you. He'd pace the paddock and whinny like crazy—wouldn't settle down for nothing."

The only reason JT could afford the four-year-old gelding was because no one else wanted him. "I'm sure you're going somewhere with this."

"Dad found out he was in a bonded pair. Tracked Nello down and bought her. Clive was right as rain after that."

JT scrubbed at his face. "Lou..."

"You're *Clive*."

JT laughed. "Yeah, I got where you were going. But Jo's not a horse. Dad can't throw a lead around her neck and haul her back here."

"No, and you're now a grown-ass man, not a boy of fifteen, but if you dangle the right treat...Tell me why she left, and I'll help you get her back."

"This can't be fixed, Lou." JT drew in a deep breath and let it out slowly, deciding to tell her the truth. "Addy's pregnant."

She stilled, her eyes going wide. "Wow, you really did screw up. So, you and Addy—?"

"Aren't back together, no. But I'm taking responsibility for the baby." JT couldn't risk telling her—or anyone—that Tommy was the likely father.

"Of course you are. And Jo won't stand by you? Maybe I was wrong about her."

"Don't judge her for not wanting to be tied to me and a child that's not hers." JT pushed off the rail and walked to the end of the porch. "We all make hard choices in life, Cricket."

"But if Jo truly loves you—"

You offer nothing.

Those words had eviscerated him. Like a broken record, he played them over and over in his head—the repetition reducing their power to nothing more than a dull ache. "She's not coming back, Lou."

"Not with that attitude." Lou stopped rocking and stood. "You've always said nothing's impossible, so stop this pity party, buck up, and give her a reason to return." She wrapped her arms around his waist. "You deserve to be happy, JT."

A tiny ember of hope lit up inside him.

Nothing's impossible.

42

I once spent a year in Philadelphia, I think it was on a Sunday.
- W. C. Fields

Five weeks later

The smell of late summer stood in sharp contrast to spring; its bright, clean fragrance boiled away by waves of heat and stench coming off the street.

Jo had a little extra time before heading to court, so she popped around the corner from City Hall to grab a salad.

She'd completed all the requirements of her sentence and needed only to appear before the judge to formally be released from further obligation. She needed this—the symbolic closure. Then she could finally move on with her life.

"Josette?"

Her head swung around at the familiar voice. *Still handsome as ever.* "Masi. Hi, how are you?"

"I'm well, thanks. You?"

"I'm good." She turned briefly as the line moved forward. "Great, actually. I get my freedom today."

"Ah," he said, pausing. "That terrible business with Claudia. I'm sorry."

"No need. It actually worked out for the best."

He nodded as they inched forward. "We've come full circle, it seems."

She looked back. "How's that?"

"This is the cafe where we first met." He moved to stand beside her. "Do you remember what you said to me?"

She gave a short laugh. "I asked who you were wearing."

"It was an odd question—"

"You said scrubs." She leaned in for a sniff. "You still wear it."

"The cologne? Yes, I suppose I do."

Jo ordered her food and moved to the side.

Masi followed suit and stood next to her at the counter. "I remember finding you utterly charming."

Jo raised a brow and smiled. "Did you?"

"Oh, yes. I'd been having a bad day, and you came from behind and *smelled* me." He shook his head and chuckled. "You were so full of life, and that day mine was…well, so full of death."

Jo thought back to what he'd said in the hospital after the ball. How he'd compared her to a carnival ride. "Too bad I also made you sick."

He winced. "I've wanted to apologize for saying that. I'm terrible at explaining myself, and you deserved better."

Jo shrugged, no longer feeling the sting of his words. "It's fine, really."

He contemplated her. "Would you consider having dinner with me sometime?"

Jo thought for a moment before answering. Not because she was considering it, but because she wasn't. "I don't think so. We're not really compatible, are we?" The words he'd used that morning slipped out, but they were as true now as they were then—she just hadn't realized it.

He gave a small laugh. "Maybe you're right. You were always so damn *unpredictable*. Upsetting the order and calm in my life." He reached over and placed a hand on top of hers. "But you also added color to my gray days."

The words healed any animosity that remained. She gave him a light kiss on the cheek, said her goodbye, and walked out of the café grinning.

That night marked the first night Jo stepped foot inside a bar in more than a month. She looked around Dirty Gerties and wondered how it had remained the same when her life had become unrecognizable. Her sight caught on the plasma screen above Rick's head. It seemed forever ago she'd sat in this very seat and watched the news about three captive American soldiers. Nine months had passed since then. An eternity and yet no time at all.

Her good mood from earlier had turned to melancholy. Since returning, she often vacillated between nihilism and optimism. It was a spectrum of emotions, and she never knew from one moment to the next how she'd feel.

Rick sauntered over with a smile. "Good to have you back, Jo. The usual?"

"Thanks, Rick. That'd be great."

The door opened, bringing warmth and light into the dimly lit place. Jo didn't have to turn to know Holly had arrived. Her energy always preceded, surrounded, and followed her. The sheer vibrancy of the woman made any room come alive.

Jo stood and enveloped her friend in a hug. Maybe Holly's spark could reanimate her, and like Frankenstein's monster, she'd walk among the living again.

Holly pulled back. "How's it going, gorgeous?"

Jo shrugged and sat down as Rick placed a vodka martini on her napkin.

"Hey, Rick. You got any pear nectar back there?" Holly asked.

He pursed his lips. "'Fraid not." He tossed a napkin in front of her.

"Hmm, let's see. How about fresh grapefruits?"

"This ain't the Four Seasons, doll."

Holly nodded thoughtfully. "Is your cranberry juice organic?"

Rick walked away with a flick of his wrist.

"God, I love fucking with him."

Jo felt a pang of nostalgia, and her mood lifted. "So, how was your weekend? Big step meeting Ben's parents."

Holly rolled her eyes. "The six-hour drive turned out to be the most enjoyable part."

"Ouch."

Rick came back with a martini glass and a shaker. "House special." He poured the contents and left.

She eyeballed the blue concoction suspiciously before lifting her glass. "To clean records and new beginnings!"

Jo was happy to toast to that. "Cheers."

Holly took a sip, gave Rick a thumbs up, and turned to Jo. "If Scope and Listerine had a baby, this would be it."

They laughed and spent the next half hour dissecting Holly's weekend—from Ben turning into his father, to his mother's love of all things Hummel—ending with the couple having erotic sex on his parents' living room couch.

"He put his hand over my mouth. It felt like a scene from *A Quiet Place*—except, you know, without the aliens." Holly sniffed her drink and put it back down.

"Why don't you ask for something else? It's no fun drinking alone."

"You're right." Holly waved Rick over, pushing her drink forward. "You know how to make a Flaming Gorilla?" When he crossed his arms, she tried again. "How about a Bend Over Shirley?"

Rick tossed the contents of her untouched drink behind the counter and placed a new glass on Holly's napkin. "I can make a Redheaded Slut. You know that one?"

Holly laughed. "Know it? I'm the inspiration!"

A few minutes later he returned with a shaker, filled the glass, and blew her a kiss.

"Well, that doesn't bode well." Holly took a sip and choked, putting a hand to her throat. "I think I just incinerated my larynx."

Jo knew Holly's antics were more about lightening her mood than agitating Rick, and her heart expanded with love. "Want some water?"

"Nah." Holly raised her drink—and her voice—in Rick's direction. "Challenge accepted!" Rick let out a belly laugh as she swung back in Jo's direction. "So, when are you leaving for Kentucky?"

Post-production had scheduled a week of confessionals to provide narration and commentary for the previous months of filming. "Friday morning."

"How are you feeling about seeing Jackson?"

"How much time do you have?" Jo drained her glass for fortification. "As an optimist *and* a masochist, I'm counting the days until I see him." Her mouth twisted in a sardonic smile. "Levi told me they announced the pregnancy."

"Oh, Jo. I'm sorry."

Holly's sympathy almost undid her. She bit her lip to staunch the tears. "I thought it would slap some sense into me. Get me to move on. But my heart won't budge." She lifted her empty glass, wishing it were bottomless. Sighing heavily, she pushed it away. "I'm still madly in love with him."

Holly placed her hand on top of Jo's. "Would it have been so bad, moving to Kentucky?"

Jo shook her head. "Actually, no. I knew being with Jacks meant we'd spend a lot of time there, and I was fine with that. I loved the farm. But this isn't about where we would live. Jacks made a unilateral decision to raise a child with his ex—one that most likely isn't his. He didn't consider my feelings or how it would affect our future."

Holly pursed her lips and drummed her fingers on the bar. "I'm gonna be straight with you, Jo. I think your pride's a big factor here."

Jo straightened. "Call it what you want. I won't be an afterthought or take second to anyone. He chose Addison over me—*again*. That's not something I can live with."

"Keeping a child safe isn't the same as choosing his ex over you. However, it's also not a crime to decide the stakes are too high. Taking on someone else's kid…that's a big ask. No shame in admitting you're not up for the challenge." She softened her tone and smiled. "Maybe what you need is to start dating again. Plenty of good men still out there. *Speaking* of, the new partner at my firm is single," she said with a wink.

Jo arched a brow. "You want me to date the guy that took your promotion?"

Holly waved it off. "He didn't take it—they gave it to him. Did I mention he's an Aussie *and* a solid eight? Bump that to a nine on account of the accent."

The thought of dating—of being with anyone other than Jacks—seemed light-years away, but she played along. "I *am* a fan of both Vegemite and the Bee Gees…"

Holly didn't miss a beat. "…*He's* from a former penal colony. *You've* recently been released from the penal system."

Jo laughed, and as they continued to find humor in the silliest of things, she realized not everyone in her life had put her second.

Jo covered her nose and mouth as she hurried past the trash on Spruce Street and turned onto Delancey's tree-lined lane. The elegant homes with their impeccable facades, flower boxes, and brick walkways were just steps away—yet worlds apart—from Center City.

The harmonic sound of chimes rang as Jo entered her parents' spacious foyer. "Hello?" She peeked her head into the formal living room, and seeing no one, headed out to the back garden where they sat with drinks.

"*Josette! T'es en avance.*"

"No, I'm not. You said six."

Nowhere But Up

Élaine motioned to the bar cart. "Pour yourself a glass of wine. I didn't expect you until seven. Dinner won't be ready for another hour."

Jo sighed. Expectations, like habits, were hard to break.

The night's dinner started with a vegetable pistou, followed by a Roquefort and caramelized onion tart, and ended with a spinach and apricot salad with spicy lentils. Not one piece of meat touched the table.

After dinner, they sat on the patio with cheese and port.

"I talked to George today," Gil began, "he said you've assembled a great team for your board. Your donor database is impressive, as well. With your expertise in social media, you'll be flooded with applications and advertisers in no time." He beamed at his daughter, his hand reaching for hers. "Your mom and I are proud of you."

Jo squeezed his fingers, keeping her eyes averted until the prickling sensation abated. When she turned back, she wore a smile of her own. "I learned from the best."

The conversation continued with a mutual respect she'd always yearned for. Her animosity slipping away like so much time—time she'd wasted blaming them for her own mistakes.

Eventually, the subject turned back to her work, and the legality of doing business outside Pennsylvania.

"There are plenty of farms in the state that need help. Perhaps you should start local?" her mother suggested.

Jo shook her head. "I've spent hundreds of hours researching hemp agriculture in Kentucky. I think it could be a game changer for small farms that can no longer stay competitive. I'll try to implement other sustainable methods and niche markets locally, but I'm fighting against subsidies and higher profit margins."

They continued discussing various topics until close to midnight when her mother suggested Jo stay the night in her old room. It was on the tip of Jo's tongue to say no, but she accepted instead.

Building on the progress they'd made, she asked, "I have to go out of town for a couple of days, but when I get back, why don't we treat ourselves to a spa day with some shopping and lunch?"

Élaine opened her mouth, then pulled her lips into a tight smile. Jo waited for her mother to decline or comment on the frivolity of the day, but instead, she said, "I heard Victoria Roggio's is the place to go."

Jo grinned. "I'll make the arrangements."

43

"It's impossible," said pride. "It's risky," said experience.
"It's pointless," said reason. "Give it a try," whispered the heart.
- Unknown

The sun was high in the sky when Jo touched down in Lexington. She drove to the Iron Bridge Inn, which felt like a different place, filled with random people who, for various reasons, wanted or needed to be in this part of the world. An older couple lounged in the sunroom where Gail had held court, her desk replaced by wicker and chintz.

"Hey, stranger."

Jo whirled around. "Kara! I didn't think you could make it."

"We wrapped early for the week, and since Kentucky's on the way to LA, I thought I'd swing by and say hello."

Jo laughed at the ridiculous statement and gave her a hug. "Anytime you want to stop in Philly on your way to LA, you let me know." She took in her friend's appearance. "You look great, by the way. Love the hair."

"Thanks." Kara ran a hand through it and smiled. "When a famous stylist gives you advice, you take it."

Jo nodded. "That reminds me, did you get my text about Deuce's premiere?"

"I thought it might've been a typo. You really want me to be your plus one?"

"Absolutely. Holly has a conference in Geneva, so there's an extra seat. It's going to be quite a night." She lowered her voice so they wouldn't be overheard. "Deuce is going to come out publicly."

Kara jerked her head back. "At the premiere?"

"He would've done it by now, but his PR team convinced him to wait. They made a deal with the studio. The news will create a huge amount of publicity for *Blackthorne*. In return, they promised him a supporting role in an upcoming rom-com."

Kara tapped lightly on her lips. "You know, I bet I can get them to release some film of Deuce at the festival. He was brilliant. Really showed off his comedic side."

"That's a great idea."

"Full disclosure—I'm going to use it to get a promotion. That footage will bring in viewers for *HomeTown Heroes*. I might even put feelers out for a new position."

"Want me to ask around? I'm sure Drew and Deuce—"

"No, thanks," Kara said, cutting her off. "I don't like to owe anyone."

Jo understood. Helping someone was a double-edged sword. It changed the dynamics in a relationship and often led to a sense of obligation and resentment. The phrase, 'No good deed goes unpunished,' was coined for a reason.

"Listen, Jo. There's another reason I flew in. I wanted to give you something. You got a minute?"

Jo glanced at her watch. "Sure. I'm not due at the farm for an hour."

Kara's suite was on the main floor past the dining room. It had a separate sitting room with French doors to a patio.

"How'd you get Gail's old suite? I booked weeks ago and was given the attic room." Jo suspected it had something to do with a missing gold plate. *Oh, the irony.*

Kara shrugged and took something out of her suitcase, handing it to Jo. "I believe this belongs to you."

Jo reached for the shirt—*Jacks'* shirt. The one she'd taken after their first night together. Her heart thumped in her chest. "Where'd you get this, and why are you giving it to me?"

"The innkeeper found it. You left it in your room."

"Why not give it back to Jacks?"

"Because it's yours. *He's* yours."

"Kar, we've been over this. He made his choice." Without thinking, Jo brought the Henley to her nose. There was still a hint of his scent.

"That's your ego talking. Would you rather be happy or right?"

Jo shook her head, still holding his shirt tight. "It's been *six weeks*. He hasn't contacted me once since I left."

Kara sat in the matching chair across from her. "Maybe he's giving you space or thinks you don't want to hear from him. There could be a million different reasons."

"Or maybe he doesn't want me back," Jo said.

"That's bullshit. He loves you. But if he thinks you'd be happier somewhere else…"

"I've been miserable somewhere else." Jo let her head fall back and closed her eyes. It might have been pride and ego that caused her to leave, but she now realized it was fear that had kept her away. "What if he really has moved on? Maybe love isn't enough, Kara."

"But what if it is? You gotta take the risk or lose the chance."

Jo thought about her past relationships. How she'd ended them after the first sign of disloyalty or perceived slights—she never gave second chances. Maybe if she had, she'd be with someone else—*and not Jacks.*

That's what truly scared her. Living the rest of her life without him.

Jo stood with the shirt against her heart. "Thanks for returning it to me."

"It's what I do, Jo. Now go forth and prosper."

Jacks wasn't at the farm.

Jo hid her disappointment and went off to do her segment. She answered questions to fill in the gaps and added exposition to previously filmed scenes.

On her way out, the Taylors invited her to stay for supper. She accepted, hoping Jacks would show up. Brenda and Charles were so kind and full of praise, she wondered if they knew of her involvement in saving Fowler's Pond. Even Lou Lou thanked her for the goats.

An hour later—after promising not to be a stranger—she left the Taylors to search for Jacks and end her misery.

As she traveled the path between the two houses, the familiar sights triggered memories and emotions so visceral her chest ached with them.

Hindsight was easy once the pieces fell into place, when events of the past led to a moment of clarity. Of *rightness*. She belonged here—with Jacks.

Jo practically skipped through the fields, her hand brushing against stalks of late summer...wheat? Barley? She didn't know, but she'd find out.

Her face split into a grin when she pictured their reunion. Jacks would run out the back door and wrap her in his arms, place a kiss on top of her head, and call her Josie.

He's probably not even home...But he must know I'm in town.

Jo pushed away her insecurity and fear and crested the small rise which brought the homestead into view.

She loved the quaint house but worried it might not be the best place to raise a kid. It sat too close to the road—a child could easily dart into traffic. And the inside wasn't ideal either. Jacks had turned one of the downstairs rooms into a bath, leaving only one bedroom down and one up. They could make it work for a few months, but they'd need a bigger home if they were going to share custody with Addison.

She envisioned something open and airy—maybe in a neighborhood with other kids. She'd need an office. And a walk-in closet.

Slow your roll, Jo.

But like a steaming locomotive, she chugged down the track, picturing Jacks as a father. She would be a stepmother. *A mother.* They'd have their own kids one day. Maybe a big family like the Rabinowitz's. Where love and laughter—

Jo stopped dead in her tracks. She was no longer getting ahead of herself.

A long wave of gold whipped in front of Jacks' face as he swung Addison around. He was laughing as he placed her down.

Like a spectator at the zoo, Jo observed them in their natural habitat. They hadn't noticed her, too engaged in their banter and shared smiles. Their touch.

Her stomach revolted; the dinner she'd eaten close to making a return appearance.

A photo of them flashed in her mind—the one she'd uncovered during her STAN phase. The look on Jacks' face—the one Jo had yearned for—was the same. And like an unwelcomed guest, his voice echoed in her head, *"We made love. Made love. Love."* Of course, it wasn't just sex. He'd never stopped loving Addison.

Jo could barely stand the weight of it as her knees began to buckle.

Everything was better, cleaner, brighter in memories, in imaginings. But the intrusive nature of reality refused to be held back. The truth pushed its way forward, waving its hands in front of her face. *Look at me, look at me!*

And here she was, caught with her pants down. Her humiliation on full display as someone approached.

"It ain't easy lettin' go of someone you love," Charles said softly from behind.

Jo didn't turn or speak.

"You could go down there, maybe change things."

Jo bit her top lip, her eyes briefly meeting his. "But you don't think I should."

"That's not for me to say."

She was the piece that didn't quite fit—an outsider. She realized that now. Kara had gotten it wrong. She wasn't Jacks' perfect match, Addison was.

Jo swiped the last tear she ever intended to shed for him and turned toward Charles, who held out a calloused hand. She took it and walked back the way she came.

44

It's not always the tears that measure the pain,
sometimes it's the smile we fake.
- Unknown

Jo wanted to drive straight to the airport and hop on the next flight out of town. She didn't care where it was going, as long as it took her far away from this place.

No matter where you go, Jo, there you are.

She told that little fucker to shut up and pulled into the inn's parking lot. Once her bags were packed, she headed out, only to be stopped by Kara on her way in.

"Hey. Where are you going?"

"Home."

"I thought after we talked—" Her eyes widened. "You saw Jackson."

"I did, but he didn't see me."

"Okay, you're gonna have to elaborate."

Jo drew in a shaky breath. "Look, Kara, I know you mean well, but I can't do this right now."

Kara grabbed Jo's suitcase and put it down, giving her a hug.

Jo allowed the moment of comfort, then pulled back before she crumbled. "I have to leave. You were wrong about me and Jacks."

Kara shook her head. "I'm not wrong. I don't know what you saw, but there must be an explanation. Tell me everything."

Jo recounted the events, ending with Charles walking her to the car.

"Charles thinks Jacks is the father?"

Jo nodded. "That's what everyone believes. And who knows? Maybe it's even true." Her phone went off and she quickly silenced *Little Big Town's* "Wine, Beer, and Whiskey." She moaned, letting her head fall back. "It's Levi. He's been calling all day."

"Then let's not keep him waiting." Kara linked arms with Jo's and pulled her out the door.

Jo knew she shouldn't step foot inside a bar, but the pull to numb, to *obliterate* her pain, was too strong.

A warm breeze blew as they walked, scenting the air with wet earth and macadam. Jo lifted her face to the velvety sky where a crescent moon bowed to the stars that took center stage. A stark contrast to the opaque grayness of the city where no stars survived.

They heard the deep bass of drums as they rounded the corner. Cars filled the parking lot and overflowed onto the shoulder and across the street. Jo felt the energy vibrate all around her and pictured the animated faces inside, excited to start the weekend. She wanted to absorb their happiness and pretend she was part of it.

They entered to a cacophony of sound which fell like a balm over Jo, soothing and softening the sharp edges of her mood. She closed her eyes and let the invisible force weave through her, offering its embrace. *Come,* it said. *Drink from my cup. Ease your pain.*

Creatures of habit, they gravitated toward the spot where they often sat and nudged between two occupied stools to get Levi's attention.

He spotted them and put down a half-filled pilsner glass, walking over with purpose. "Why haven't you answered my calls?"

Jo balked at his clipped tone. "Calm down, Charlie Brown. I've been busy. Nice to see you, too."

He released a frustrated breath. "Sorry, it's just...I've been trying to reach you all day."

"Well, I'm here now, but I'm gonna need a drink before you tell me whatever it is that has your tighty whities in a knot."

He grabbed a bottle and filled three shot glasses, glancing to Jo's left. "Oh, hey, Kar. How are you?"

"Still invisible, apparently." Kara wedged herself next to Jo, grabbed the shot, and threw it back.

"You forgot to tap the bar first." Jo looked askance at her friend, then tapped the bottom of her glass against the bar in unison with Levi.

The man next to Jo leaned sideways and held up an empty glass. "Could I get—?"

"No." Levi poured another round. He motioned with the bottle to the two people on either side of Jo and Kara. "And both of you are gonna have to move." Grumbling, the couple reluctantly got up and walked away.

"Not gonna lie, that was sexy as hell," Kara said, sliding into one of the seats.

The corner of Levi's mouth turned up as he lifted his shot.

Jo sighed as warmth spread out from her chest, loosening the muscles she hadn't known were tight. She pushed the glass away and steeled herself. "Okay. I'm in the sweet spot—sober enough to listen, not drunk enough to punch you."

Levi pressed his lips together, his dimples making a special appearance. "You might change your mind after you hear what I have to say."

Before he could say anything, a loud cheer went up, and locals heading to the dance floor yanked both Kara and Jo off their stools. Jo decided to go with the flow, thankful to escape Levi's words of impending doom. Levi raised his arms in exasperation as the two disappeared into the crush of people.

As the motion of the mob moved Jo forward, she greeted familiar faces, receiving a few hugs along the way. Once ensconced in the line dance, her body softened and swayed in sync with those around her. She'd grown to love the cadence and rhythm of country music. Of its lyrical prose. The communal nature and repetition was a pleasant distraction from the ache in her heart.

Music and dance had always been a way for Jo to express herself—words rarely conveyed emotion the way movement did. It was her outlet, her scream, her cry. Her joy.

A new song started, and someone tried to hand her a shot. She waved them away with a smile, lost in the upbeat tune. After a few more, the tempo slowed, and she headed off the dance floor.

A warm hand grabbed Jo's from behind and pulled her back onto the dance floor. Lifting her arm into the air, the stranger whirled her around and brought her in close.

He was tall and handsome, and wore the cocky smile of someone used to getting their way. "Don't believe I've had the pleasure," he said.

Jo didn't have the energy or inclination to pull away, and having a man's attention spoke to her bruised ego. "Well, you have it now," she said, as he drew her in tighter.

"Oh darlin', you have no idea." He laughed deeply, the rich timbre full of mischief and mystery as they moved around the floor. She recognized the type. She *was* the type. Flirtatious and fun with no strings attached.

He kept their bodies pressed together—an embrace too intimate for Jo's liking—and put his lips to her ear. "I know who you are, and I've gotta say, JT's a fool for letting you go."

Jo stiffened. She didn't like being caught off guard, and the tone in his voice had an edge that sent a tingle down her spine. She tried to push off. "I think we're done here."

He continued to rotate her around the floor. "We've got a lot in common, you and I."

Jo's eyes closed briefly. *Of course.* "You're Addison's ex."

"Thomas Beuchard the third, at your service," he said with smug satisfaction.

As the song came to an end, Jo felt a tap on her shoulder. Tommy still hadn't released her, so she twisted her head around to see Kara, standing behind her.

"Umm, Jo, you might wanna take a look at who just walked in."

45

*I know you think you understand what you thought I said,
but I'm not sure you realize that what you heard is not
what I really meant.*
- Unknown

JT entered Levi's with one thing on his mind—finding Jo. The band had just ended their set and people moved off the dance floor, giving him a clear view of the couple still locked in an embrace. His heart squeezed in his chest when he met Jo's gaze. Seeing her with another man was a punch to the gut, but seeing her with Tommy nearly broke him in two.

The crowd parted like the red sea as JT made his way over.

"Well, if it isn't our Hometown Hero. Evening, JT," Tommy said, with a wide grin.

JT ignored him. "What are you doing, Josie?"

"I *was* dancing." She tried to pull free, but Tommy held tight.

His eyes snapped to Tommy. "Let her go, or lose that arm."

Tommy laughed, releasing his hold. "My, my. Seems you're not over City Girl here. Well, that's just too bad, isn't it? Seeing as you're engaged to my ex-wife."

"Engaged?" Stunned, Jo took a step back.

"Well, that's a twist I didn't see coming," Kara said.

In all his years of soldiering, JT had never wanted to kill anyone before that moment. It took everything in him not to twist Tommy's head off his neck.

"Let me explain," he said, advancing toward Jo.

She shook her head. "Sorry, fresh out of fucks to give."

Tommy hooted. "Damn, I like this girl!"

"Just give me five minutes, Jo. Please."

Levi appeared and gave her hand a quick squeeze before addressing JT. "You can use my office, and...sorry about earlier."

Jo glared at Levi before storming off toward the office.

Tommy made a show of watching her leave. "*Mmm, mmm.* I'm gonna enjoy tapping that."

The first thing a soldier learns is how to remain calm under pressure. The second is stealth—never let them see you coming. The holy trinity—speed, accuracy, power—well, that's what gets the job done.

JT was halfway down the hall before anyone noticed Tommy lying on the floor, gasping for air.

Reaching above the door, he grabbed the key, unlocked the door, and pushed it open, stepping aside to let Jo enter.

She leaned against the desk and looked down at her watch. "Your five minutes starts now."

He drank her in, unable to take his eyes off her. "*God damn*, I've missed you, Josie."

She huffed out a humorless laugh and shook her head. "What is it you want from me, Jacks? Absolution? Understanding? You'll get neither."

He didn't really blame her. "I just want you to hear me out, is all."

Jo crossed her arms and raised one brow.

Where to start? He took a deep breath and decided on the beginning. "When you left, all I could think about was how to get you back. I'd made a plan..." *Wrong direction.*

He shook his head and tried again. "Tommy found out about the baby—something about a doctor bill going to the wrong address—and confronted Addy. She admitted to the pregnancy but said it was mine. We told everyone I was the father, hoping he would back off, but instead he demanded a paternity test."

JT hesitated, dreading the next part. "Under the law, he can't force her to take one, not until the baby's born. But if we got married, he'd have no legal rights to the child."

Jo pushed off the desk. "Congratulations. Are we done here?"

"No." His arm shot out and grabbed hold of her wrist. "I still have four and a half minutes left," he said, glancing down at her watch.

She yanked free and stalked to the other side of the room.

"Thank you." He cleared his throat and continued, "I was in a bad way after that. Couldn't figure out how to get myself out of the hole I'd dug myself into. I'd begun to think—had even found a way—well, at that point, it didn't matter. If I married Addy, you'd be lost to me." He rubbed his forehead and paced back and forth.

"I don't need a blow by blow on your engagement, Jacks."

"I'm trying to tell you—" He released a sound of frustration. "I've got limited time here, Jo, and a lot to cover."

She crossed her arms and waited.

"One night, I got piss drunk and passed out in the horse barn. My dad found me the next morning, still pie-eyed and covered in shit. He grabbed my boots and dragged me outside."

JT stopped in front of Levi's desk and picked up a spiked ball. He tightened his grip and globs of silicone oozed through his fingers. Putting it back, he absently rapped his knuckles on the wood.

Just spit it out.

He pivoted and met her gaze. "He pushed my head into the water trough."

Jo stilled.

"...Your body never gets used to the sensation of drowning. There are no training protocols to prepare you for that

combination of panic and pain. It's the perfect interrogation method because your body stays intact. But your mind... After a time, it breaks you. It breaks everyone."

She studied his face, reading his mood.

Reading him.

Without looking away, she dropped to the edge of the couch, the veil of indifference lifting from her heart.

"I was sucked back in time—a waking nightmare so intense I couldn't distinguish the past from the present." He rubbed at the center of his chest, his expression pained. "I attacked him. Sent my dad to the hospital."

"Oh, Jacks," she whispered, having no other words.

"Once he came to, he told the cops he'd been dragged by a horse. Refused to press charges." He looked up, anchoring her with his stare. "As soon as they released me, I checked myself into the VA hospital in Lexington. They have a thirty-day treatment program for PTSD. I've been there ever since."

Jo had been naïve to think her love would heal him—that listening was therapy and her body was enough to make him forget. "I knew you were struggling, I should have—"

"You helped more than you know. Never doubt that. This is all on me." He picked up the ball and absently tossed it back and forth. "I had counseling when I first got out, was taught some coping skills, but there's no silver bullet, no one-size-fits-all treatment. Every soldier's experience is different." He watched the silicone transform as he tightened his fist. "There are seven core values you live by in the Army: loyalty, duty, respect, selfless service, honor, integrity, and courage. You don't leave them on the battlefield when you go home. Like memories, they're ingrained in you." He set the ball back on the desk. "You learn to sacrifice your comfort for the welfare and safety of others—your happiness for theirs."

Jo had gotten used to Jacks' way of speaking, of going around, behind, and sideways. Weaving disjointed fragments together that take you on a journey. A slow float down a sleepy river on a summer's day. Or a heart-pounding creep through the dark woods. You never knew where it would end, but there was always a point, a purpose, or an allegory. But today, Jo desperately needed the abridged version.

"I get it, Jacks. I've always gotten it. It's who you are, and I'd never want to change that." Without a second thought, she went to him. He held her close, breathing her in, and placed a soft kiss on her head. The familiarity of the gesture made her eyes burn with unshed tears. *I will not cry.*

She pulled away—like a band-aid, she needed to quickly rip off the last vestiges of hope and let him go. She tried stepping back, but he wouldn't let her.

"I think I have another minute or two," he said with a faint smile.

Every second she spent with him, every look, every word, just prolonged her agony. "No need. I absolve you of all wrongdoing and release you from further obligations." She attempted a light tone but failed, sounding flat.

He lifted her chin. "What if I don't want to be released?"

She shook her head. "Don't do that. Don't make me believe the impossible."

He huffed out a laugh. "Oh, sugar, nothing's impossible."

Confusion and anger warred inside her. "Stop it, Jacks. You're engaged to Addison."

"No, Jo. I'm not."

Her mouth fell open. "Why didn't you lead with that?"

"Because I *was*." He reached for her hand. "You need to know all of it. Then you can decide if what I offer is still nothing, or something you can work with."

She flinched. "I'm sorry I said that."

They heard loud voices in the hall as people passed by on their way to the bathrooms.

"Can we finish this at my place? I've got something I'd like to show you."

Not engaged. Those words were like a lifeline. "Let me say goodbye to Kara and..." She tilted her head. "Levi's apology...I'm guessing it had something to do with why he wanted to talk to me earlier?"

Jacks drew a hand down his face. "I'm guessing, yeah."

"You want to tell me or should I ask him?"

"Nothing much to tell. I called him for a ride, is all."

"From the hospital?"

"Yeah."

Jo was pretty sure it hadn't been thirty days. "Is that allowed?"

"*Define* allowed."

Jo rolled her eyes. "Can they kick you out of the program for leaving early?"

He licked his bottom lip and glanced off to the side. "Probably."

"Why would you take that risk?"

He gave her a crooked smile. "I think that's pretty obvious."

"No Jacks, nothing's obvious!" She threw her hands up. "I *saw* you with Addison. You were laughing, and the way you looked, like that old picture, and your dad...I'm the square peg!"

He placed his hands on her shoulders. "I've got no idea what most of that meant. But my dad told me what happened—what you saw and what he said. I hadn't spoken to him since the day I left, and he wrongly interpreted the situation—you both did." He brought his hands to her face, holding her gently. "Levi couldn't pick me up, Jo, so I called Addy. She's the one who brought me home. *To you.*"

There were only two times in Jo's life when she ugly cried. The first was when her grandmother died.

The second, when she realized Jackson Taylor had put her first.

46

Life is a race, and what matters most isn't when a person crosses the finish line, but how strong they've grown along the way."
- Jen Stephens

After an awkward search for something to blow her nose with, they snuck out the back door and headed to where Jacks had parked his bike. He unlocked two helmets from his side bag and handed her one.

"Pretty sure of the outcome, were you?"

His answering smile did funny things to her insides. "Just optimistic." He gave her a soft kiss and fastened her chin strap.

Jo held on tight as they whipped through the streets. She'd forgotten how good it felt to wrap her arms around him, to feel every movement, to dissolve into him.

Ten minutes later, they pulled into the gravel drive.

Jo swung off the bike and turned toward the fireflies dancing in the dense darkness, where crickets chirped and bullfrogs rasped out a serenade more romantic than anything she'd ever heard.

"What are you thinking?" Jacks said, embracing her from behind.

She leaned against him. "That I love it here."

His hold on her tightened, and she breathed in deeply.

It smelled like home.

It was a stark contrast to the city, where shades of gray enveloped the sky and the sounds of sirens, people, and the occasional gunshot lulled you to sleep. The scent of ethnic food, asphalt, and rot became unnoticeable after a while, a backdrop to the vibrant colors of urban living.

"We're gonna get eaten alive out here, sugar." Jacks said, shaking her from her musings. He took her hand, and they walked up the porch steps. As he pulled open the wooden screen door, Jo smiled to herself. No more worrying about triple locks and alarm systems.

They entered the kitchen. "Would you like some water? Something to eat?"

"Just some water, thanks."

He filled a couple of glasses, and they drank in silence. Looking around, she noticed the table covered in papers and walked over. A computer sat on top of a large schematic, held down by various objects to keep it from rolling up.

"What's all this?" She took in the stack of notebooks, folders, and papers held together with clips. Her eyes caught on a familiar binder. She picked it up, pivoting around to Jacks. "Is this my research from the show?"

"It is." He came to stand beside her. "It's one of the things I wanted to show you." He pushed his laptop to one side. "This is a survey of the farm." He tapped a square on the map. "Here's the original homestead, and this," he said, indicating an irregular red border that surrounded it, "is the area to be subdivided." He glanced over, catching the look of surprise on her face.

"Your parents are selling part of the farm?"

"Yup. *To me*," he said with a gleam in his eye. "The acreage will include the pond, the fallow field with the airplane hangar, some wooded land down to the river, plus a little more. Most of it isn't used for anything, so the loss in land value won't be significant to them." He pointed to the pond and surrounding pasture. "Except for here. The animals use it for grazing. Since it's right in the middle of everything, it has to be included, but there'll be an easement allowing the farm unlimited access."

Jo tried to wrap her head around what he'd just said. "But how? Why?"

He huffed out a laugh. "How can I afford it, you mean?" He absently rubbed the back of his neck. "I've had nothing to spend my money on for over ten years, and I've made some good investments—not enough to settle the loan, but enough so my folks can pay off creditors and invest in some modernization. As for the *why*, well that's where you come in."

The implication smacked her in the chest, radiating warmth throughout her body. "You did it for me?"

He slid his hands down her arms and linked their fingers together. "*For us*," he corrected, placing a soft kiss on her lips.

She secretly pinched herself. Nope, not a dream. She wrapped her arm around his waist. "Tell me more."

For the next half hour, he told her of his vision. How he planned on growing industrial hemp using the airplane hangar to process and dry it. He showed her additional research on the different types of plants and their uses, explaining which would grow where, depending on the soil and sun exposure.

"I already have a grower's license, thanks to the show, and since I'm focusing on environmentally sustainable agriculture, I decided to sell the new plane to Reed. And here," he said, circling an area with his finger, "on the north west slope, I'm going to combine contour farming with cover crops—something you highlighted in your research. With any luck—"

Jo threw her arms around him, nearly knocking him off his feet, and began peppering him with kisses.

He chuckled, holding her tight. "So, I take it you like my plan?"

"Like it? I *love* it." Her face softened, and she lowered her mouth to his. "Almost as much as I love you." She tried to deepen the kiss but he stopped her. "What's wrong?"

"Not a thing." He gave her a reassuring smile and rested his forehead to hers. "I need to tell you the rest, is all. So we can move forward with nothing between us."

"Okay," she said carefully, taking a step back.

Jacks cupped her cheek. "Don't shut down on me now."

She closed her eyes, feeling the warmth of his hand, and took a deep breath.

"Look at me, Josie." When she raised her eyes to his, he continued, "Once I got my head out of my ass, I knew I couldn't marry Addy—even if you never came back to me—because I didn't love her, at least not the way I should. I also realized I had no right to claim the baby if it wasn't mine. So, when she came to visit me at the VA, I told her how I felt. It was the hardest, most honest conversation we'd ever had. But it was good, too." He glanced away, running the back of his hand along his jaw. "I'm still going to be there for her, Jo. I won't cut her out of my life."

Jo bit her top lip and nodded. She'd been willing to accept those terms before...Had anything really changed? The memory of their embrace pushed its way forward. "Jacks, what I saw earlier. The two of you—"

A slow smile transformed his face. "I can imagine what it looked like, but had you been there thirty seconds earlier, you would've seen Addy on the phone with her doctor." He grabbed her hands and held them between his larger ones. "What you *saw* was my reaction when she told me the results of the paternity test."

Jo lost all feeling in her extremities...*and* the ability to speak proper English. "Baby not yours?"

He flattened her palms against his heart and laughed. "No, Jo. Baby not mine."

She collapsed against him—like a triathlete at the end of a race—exhausted, but euphoric.

Jacks held her close, gently rubbing her back. When he tugged lightly on her hair, she tilted her head back and focused on his intense blue stare.

"I wanna take you upstairs, Josie," he said, placing soft kisses along her jaw and neck. He lifted her up as she wrapped her legs around his waist and carried her to his room.

He laid her on the bed and stretched out beside her. At first, they just stared at each other, grinning like a couple of teenagers. When their hands began to wander and the kisses became heated, Jo took the lead and pushed him onto his back, straddling him. She hooked her thumbs under the hem of his T-shirt and mimicked his Kentucky drawl. "Lift up, sugar."

He laughed and grabbed the shirt from behind. The muscles of his chest and abs tightening as he pulled it over his head.

She began a slow exploration, reminiscent of their first night together, when he took his time getting to know her body. Only this time, the roles were reversed. She started with his eyes, his nose, both cheeks. His mouth.

"You're everything to me," she whispered in his ear—her voice so full of emotion it caught in her throat. Jacks' grip on her hips tightened in response and she smiled down at him before lowering her mouth to his neck. She spent some time there while her hands gently caressed his shoulders, gliding over his pecs and down his arms. Her tongue worked its way along the planes of his chest and along the ridges of his six-pack.

He made a sound deep in his throat when she unfastened his jeans. "*Babe,*" he pleaded as she tugged them down, her mouth taking a leisurely stroll across the V-shaped groove of his hip.

She winked and mimicked him again, "Shh, don't worry, Jacks. I'll take care of you."

He huffed out a laugh as she scooched to the end of the bed and stood, pulling off his boots, jeans, and boxer briefs.

With heavy lids, he watched her undo the knot holding up her halter top. With one tug, the piece of silk slipped from her body and onto the floor. As she undressed, Jacks sat back against the headboard, his jaw clenched with restrained need.

Kneeling on the bed, she massaged her way up his well-defined legs, her tongue teasing its way higher.

The duvet beneath her tightened as Jacks fisted the material. "I've had six weeks of wanting you, Josie. If your mouth even touches it, I'm gonna go off."

She smiled wickedly, wanting very much to test his theory. Without taking her eyes off him, she lowered her mouth to the rock-hard flesh between his thighs. A deep, raspy sound escaped from his lips as his head fell back.

In less than a minute, the hypothesis had proven true, and Jo squealed with laughter as Jacks flipped her onto her back.

"If you steal the honey, beware the sting," he said in mock warning.

Then he showed her just how wonderful it was to be a thief.

Epilogue

Celebrate endings, for they precede new beginnings.
- Jonathan Lockwood Huie

For many, Memorial Day weekend signaled the start of summer and a time to open beach houses left dormant all winter. The Singer Estate in Margate was no different. This year, however, the seven-bedroom home was bursting at the seams with guests, because it was also the premiere of *HomeTown Heroes Special Edition*, featuring Jacks.

The previous fall, after he finished his treatment in Lexington, Fowler's Pond Distillery had its grand opening. Everyone flew in, including Jo's parents, Holly and Dreuce—a nickname the media had given the newly announced couple—and whose celebrity helped make the night a huge success.

It had also marked the official end of filming.

Jacks had insisted the show include the VA hospital and its need for more funding. He opened up about his PTSD, sharing the spotlight with other vets and their struggles.

It was a departure in tone for the feel-good show, but they agreed to remove any romanticized version of his service, his football career, and his relationship with Addison. They focused instead on the plight of the American small farmer, highlighting diversification and sustainability. In the end, Gail got her love story by adding previously chopped footage of Jacks and Jo, dubbing the pair 'the soldier and the socialite.'

Thomas Henry Beuchard the fourth, was born March 4 to Ms. Addison Jenkins and Mr. Thomas Beuchard the third. For Addison's concession in naming the child, Tommy agreed to give up primary custody, attend parenting classes, and allow Jacks and Jo to be the godparents to little Hank—a nickname everyone except Tommy thought was perfect, just like the little boy himself.

As the credits rolled on the two-hour special, they all clapped and cheered—except for Holly. She was too busy crying and blowing her nose.

Drew looked around in dismay. "It's like the time she cried over that sad little flower growing in a sidewalk crack."

"You're heartless, Drew!" Holly said between sobs. "How can you not to be moved by Jacks and Levi offering all those vets jobs?"

"Not moved enough to tears, honey. Although I almost cried when Jo wore that awful baby-blue seersucker dress. What were you thinking?" He turned a horrified face toward Jo.

Before she had a chance to respond, Jacks stood and offered his hand. "Wanna go for a walk on the beach?"

Their nightly walks had become a ritual and always ended with a trip to Jo's favorite ice cream shop.

She grinned and grabbed hold. "First one over the dune wins!" She squealed as he picked her up and placed her behind him.

"That's cheating!" With bare feet, she raced out the back door after him.

Once past the dune, he slowed and looked over his shoulder. She laughed and sped up, jumping on his back.

"We'll call it a draw," he said, turning his head to receive her kiss.

Jo squeezed him tight as they made their way to the water's edge, then slid down his body to walk beside him as he hunted for shells. Having never been to the beach, Jacks gathered shells like jewels, and it melted her heart. He stooped to pick another one up.

"What's this one called?"

Jo examined it, although outside the common clam or whelk, she was clueless. "Mollusk?"

He brushed it off and stuck it in his pocket with a half dozen others.

"So Levi and Kara," Jo started.

He shook his head while toeing something in the sand. "You'd think they'd be a little more discreet." He continued on, the chipped shell not making the cut.

Jo nudged him with her shoulder. "If you hadn't insisted on getting up at the crack of dawn to see the sunrise, we could have saved everyone a lot of embarrassment—and the cost of a new kitchen table. I'll never be able to eat on it again."

He smiled over at her. "You have to admit it *was* spectacular."

"Please tell me you're talking about the sunrise."

Jacks laughed and ran ahead.

"Hey!" she called. "You're going the wrong way. The Dairy Bar's back there."

"Later." He walked backwards, waiting for her to catch up. When she did, he grabbed her hand and pulled her toward the dunes.

"Where are we going?"

"You'll see."

A short while later, they stopped in front of Lucy the Elephant.

Jo raised a quizzical brow. "It's closed."

"Exactly. I wanted to see it without all the people."

"Yeah, but that's trespassing, and since I have a record..."

Jacks ignored her and jumped the fence. Jo climbed over and crouched down, which honestly, made little sense to her. A stooped figure seemed just as easy to spot as an upright one.

"It's going to be locked," she said smugly as they reached the elephant's leg, but to her surprise, it wasn't.

Jacks grinned and held the door open. They took the side stairs to the ornate howdah at the top.

Years of memories flooded back, making her pivot halfway up to say, "Fun fact—it's the oldest roadside attraction in America *and* the largest elephant in the world." Jo knew everything about Lucy.

"Is that right?"

Jo nodded knowingly. "She also survived hurricanes, floods, and a fire accidentally started by a bunch of drunk kids." She entered the howdah. "Did you know she used to be a tavern?"

"Nope."

Jo hadn't been inside Lucy since her Mami died. She'd been afraid the memories would splinter her heart into a thousand pieces. Instead, the tight hold of grief loosened.

They went to the railing where they could see the twinkling lights of Atlantic City. "I used to come here all the time when I was little, but never at night. It's beautiful."

Jacks wrapped his arms around her from behind. "Your father told me it used to be your favorite place in all the world."

"Did he?" Jo's inner child sighed. "I guess it was." She leaned against the solid warmth of his chest and peered out to sea. "Lucy and I had many adventures. I had *quite* the imagination."

Jacks lowered his chin to her shoulder, their cheeks touching. "Where is it now?"

"Hmm?"

"Your favorite place."

The wind blew a strand of hair across her face as she turned to him. "Anywhere you are."

He gently swept it away, his hand lingering against her cheek. "I love you so damn much, Josie."

A million tiny firecrackers went off inside her chest when he went down on one knee.

"Marry me, and I promise you a lifetime of adventures."

Jo barely noticed the ring as she tackled him backwards and kissed the word 'yes!' onto his lips.

The End

Note from the Author:

Thank you for reading *Nowhere but Up*. If you enjoyed it, please consider leaving a review on Amazon. If you would like to be notified when the next book in the series come out, please contact me at bobbiwhitewrites@gmail.com or visit my Facebook author page.

I'd like to thank my family and friends, critique partners, readers and editors. I'm eternally grateful for all your contributions.

Made in the USA
Middletown, DE
31 July 2022